A BLUSH OF MAIDENS, A
FOOLISHNESS OF OLD MEN

ALSO BY WILLIAM D. SKEES

Computer Software For Data Communications

Before You Invest In A Small Business Computer

Writing Handbook For Computer Professionals

(WITH PETER J. FELL, M. D.)

The Doctor's Computer Handbook

A Blush of Maidens, A Foolishness of Old Men

Stories, Essays and Poems

William D. Skees

Author of Body Abstracts-Pregnant Nudes and the Rayanne, Noor and Sandy Mysteries

All best wishes
Bill Skees

iUniverse, Inc.

New York Lincoln Shanghai

A Blush of Maidens, A Foolishness of Old Men

Stories, Essays and Poems

iUniverse books may be ordered through booksellers or by contacting:

iUniverse
2021 Pine Lake Road, Suite 100
Lincoln, NE 68512
www.iuniverse.com
1-800-Authors (1-800-288-4677)

This is a work of fiction. All of the characters, names, incidents, organizations, and dialogue in this novel are either the products of the author's imagination or are used fictitiously.

ISBN-13: 978-0-595-42137-4 (pbk)
ISBN-13: 978-0-595-86477-5 (ebk)
ISBN-10: 0-595-42137-7 (pbk)
ISBN-10: 0-595-86477-5 (ebk)

Printed in the United States of America

To my mother, Barbara Boyd Skees, a writer before me, my inspiration and my confidante, whose spirit enlivens these stories, essays and poems.

CONTENTS

A KILLING WAY

It was something about the way rats had of running. A rat runs low and silent, legs nearly hidden beneath its body, its naked obscene tail sliding cowardly behind. It was something about the arrogance of it, how they moved. Even in the daylight. Shouldering close along the wall, where the walls met the ground, where the falling rain drew up the gravel and kept the grass from growing, in the shade of clapboards and broken things.

As a boy he had killed a mouse, or so he remembered. His family were poor and, like many city poor, ignorant of tools. What tools they had, had many purposes. They kept their flour in a flour bin that fitted loosely into a broad lower compartment of the kitchen cupboard. Where it swung down to allow you to dip a cup. Where you didn't dare open it to look inside unless you were told to get some flour. The compartment was lined with tin, and the flour floated lazily up into the air if you so much as opened a crack. His mother found a mouse in there one day and slammed the door on its soft grey underbelly. Its head stuck out and thrashed about frantically. "Kill it," she had ordered him and handed him a broom.

He knocked at the tiny head with its two black eyes. Knocked again and again at the nose jerking up into the sky as if drowning. Knocked at it till finally blood ran out of the tiny nostrils, and the head went limp, and he could pick up the soft warm body with newspapers and put it out into the garbage. The garbage can was a hot, fetid thing in the summer air with swarms of startled, bloated white maggots writhing inside when the lid came up.

As a boy he had killed a mouse, at least he thought he had killed it. But he didn't think you could kill a rat.

*   *   *   *

A rat was a perverse, dirty thing that bit little children who slept on the floor. But a mouse could maybe be a good thing. His classmate's father had caught a whistling mouse once. Kept it in a cage till the newspaper came and wrote a story about it, and Roscoe said they could hear it whistling at night while they were all in bed. His classmates called Roscoe by the nickname Sonny, but the boy who killed the mouse didn't know that, and he got the names mixed up and thought for months that Roscoe was the name of Sonny's whistling mouse.

Sonny dropped out of school in the eighth grade, and the boy who killed the mouse had forgotten about him till he appeared one day outside the open high school window, hollering over the sound of the teacher's voice for a boy named Jerry to throw him the keys to the delivery truck. Sonny had gotten a job working for Jerry's father during the hours while Jerry was in school studying.

This Jerry was the class clown and, impossibly, the heartthrob of the school cellist, and went on to become a Doctor of medieval English literature. The cellist raised two sons and gave a reading of a feminist paper in favor of women priests when the Pope came to visit. The Pope thanked her and asked her to sit down.

Being poor they killed their own chickens. His mother could do it but his father was best at it. He'd take the bird by its head and spin it round and round in his hand, wringing its neck till the body flew off, bounced against the garage wall, and flopped to the ground. It would jump around bleeding through the stump between its feathers till at last the headless body fell over, legs kicking out at the grass. Sometimes there might be two chickens, especially on a Sunday, because his father, who was a big man, liked a big Sunday dinner. Usually they were Rhode Island Reds.

Having a backyard to kill chickens was actually a step up, because you got to go inside to the bathroom afterwards to wash up. Before that they had lived in a place that was not quite country and not quite town, a little place with a hydrant out in the front yard where you went for water. Its nozzle was turned upwards so you could drink out of it when you weren't filling a pail. You had to run the faucet a while before the water turned cold and good to drink.

The bathroom was a two-hole outhouse that you got to by walking through the chicken yard. If you were a little child you carried a stick, like a short beanpole, in case the rooster tried to flog you. The kinds of chickens his dad killed were Rhode Island Reds. He had never seen his father kill a Dominecker. Domineckers were more agreeable and they laid the most eggs. But the rooster was a Rhode Island Red. Rhode Island Reds make the best roosters.

Once a classmate's father gave the boy two pigeons. There was an epidemic of ringworm that year and the boy who killed the mouse felt deliciously daring to visit his classmate's house where the two boys of the family had to wear stockings over their shaved heads because of the ringworms. He was proud of the pigeons he came home with and his mother named them "Patrick" and "Patricia."

His father fastened a wire door to a ramshackle outbuilding with palings warped and rotted. The father built a shoebox sized wooden nest on a crossbeam and the boy filled it with straw. Through the wire mesh door the boy saw the female go to the box. The male flew close up beside her and turned circles cooing throatily in the way of pigeons. After a few days the boy saw that the female no longer bobbed her head nervously in the nest when he came to feed them. Surprised at his own boldness he reached up to her in the straw and found nothing but a backside and tail feathers. Rats had eaten away her entire underbody. There were no eggs in the nest.

The ringworm boy took chemical engineering and made himself into an oil company executive too busy to attend their class reunion. The executive's mother smoked always and died early of cancer in the lungs.

*   *   *   *

When the boy who killed the mouse ran away from home, he wanted very much to believe he had gotten chased off, but in fact his father would have been happy to keep him around for the fun of beating up on him. The truth was that he had feared more the humiliation of the beatings in front of his friends and had run away to avoid the shame. His sisters took the blows. The father died, the boy grew up. The boy's friends pitied him because his father died, and the boy who killed the mouse wondered how their minds had frozen like mastodons in ice without understanding what the father was to the son.

There was less killing but after he learned to drive and notice things he came to wonder what happened to the cats and dogs run over. Who picked up the carcasses or dragged them off to the trash? In later years he came to realize that crows and beetles came when your back was turned—small wonder that people believed in spirits and things that made no reflections in mirrors.

His mother kept a parakeet that in his senior high school year developed an affliction. Its appetite fell off. Its eyes got rimmed with white scales, one leg drew up, and a wing dragged. Eventually it could not keep itself upright and would flop jerkily about the floor of its cage, rustling spastically among the torn sheets of newspaper.

"I want you to kill it," his mother told him, and she went outdoors. Even in his high school years they were poor. There were no tools, and the boy who had killed the mouse took a paring knife to the neck of the parakeet among the blue-green feathers and heard the bones crackle as the knife bit through.

It was not a sharp knife. Poor people had to make do as much out of lack of knowledge as out of a surplus of want, and his one grandfather who had an emery wheel for sharpening knives was an hour's drive away and there was neither gas for the car nor permission to drive. Ultimately the bird died of the weight of the boy's body pushing the knife through its neckbones, more crushed than sliced.

The mother threw away the parakeet's cage. Later she raised a Pomeranian dog when her daughter went off to school and married. In its first year the dog lost an eye. Pomeranians have a popeyed look. Some call it bug-eyed. She kept the dog till it died, sweeping up its shed hairs, and bringing it in from the summer heat. It died right after she bought herself a room air conditioner.

*   *   *   *

In adulthood, between wives and alone in a subdivided ante-bellum apartment with wide plank floors and cracks so broad he could see between the joists, over a period of several nights he woke to a coarse wood-cutting sound, like a big-toothed saw drawn over dry kindling. Slow, steady, deliberate, it would persist for fifteen or twenty minutes then stop. Lying in bed he could not make out just where the cutting sound came from. One night, reading in his kitchen, he heard it again. From an unused cupboard, and just behind him. He rose on tiptoe and jerked open the cupboard door.

In the wall at the back of the cupboard, about eye level, he saw an irregular hole, about the size of a half dollar, just big enough for the triangular black shape inside it, the under side of the upper end of the head of a rat, long teeth showing, a pointed nose above, and a black eye peering sideways. A malevolent, unblinking eye. He slammed the door, and listened for it to panic and fall back down between the walls. But there was no sound. No movement. That night he slept poorly. Next day he nailed the top of a soup can over the opening in the wall. The cabinet had been bone-empty. Couldn't have smelled of food for all the desiccation of its years standing empty. It still bothered him, what the rat was after.

*   *   *   *

He told all of these things to the man beside him on the concrete stoop. The sun was hot coming after the morning's rain, and he could feel it on his knees. Soon someone would come from inside and move him back further into the shade, and out of the sun. If they didn't forget.

Lately he had begun to worry if they would remember. He was pleased today that his roommate felt like talking, he hoped it would last. He had done his best to entertain the old man, remembering to laugh out loud in all the funny parts, to speed up in the beginnings and to talk a little slower at the ends.

Now the boy who had killed the mouse turned, as best he could, to look at his companion. The old man was asleep, his head fallen against the cloth tied round the wings of his wheeled chair. Past the old man, in the narrow trench alongside the building where the raindrops still dripped from the roof, the boy who had killed the mouse saw a dark movement. A rat ran along in the slight hollow, deliberate and intent, its feet scarcely visible, trailing a thin naked tail.

YOU

I think you danced in glory
    The sun about you shone
I think you always were
    At birth I knew your song

I know and dream the feel of you
    In lonely, sacred times
Your hair and hips and breasts and grace
    And, still, how young you are

Beyond this candle's light
    Beyond that stand of trees
Beyond the turning of my path
    Across our brook from me

That you were there I firmly knew.
    For shards, reflections, scents of you
Though perfect, you must bear
    At least some of the blame

Forgive my doubt, forgive my fear
    Forgive my ever failing
Just see me go, an instant grieve
    Before my son is yours.

A KENTUCKY
WONDER

It was his turn to stay all night with the Goodakers.

Stay all night. In later years, miles distant and careers removed, his memory had come to rejoice in the sound of those words. His children, who grew up to be accountants, had no truck with romantic notions, and called it sleeping over. His grandchildren, innocent victims, joylessly "spent the night."

Strictly speaking it was really Jimmy Goodaker's turn to stay at his house, but no one ever came to stay at his house. Not because there wasn't room. There wasn't any more room at the Goodakers'. They would sleep on pallets, sharing a thin quilt on the cool wide-planked wood floors.

Too bad, his ponderous body had no memory of the light exhausted sleep of childhood, where you passed out any old where and woke up hungry, and there was no taste of stale things in your mouth and no oily puffiness about your face.

The day had been all about running and playing and finding ways to be where no one would have dared ask leave to be. In the woods, in the barn, especially in the barn and up in the hay, and especially to be, actually to be, in the hayloft with the girls, he didn't know why, but it savored wickedly in his thoughts, the sound of it resonant in his memory.

Maybe it was the smell of straw, dry and dusty, wet and warm on the nostrils. There was something about the stretching up and stretching down of climbing the ladder, close nailed to the planks where you could barely manage a toe on it, which you'd think came from climbing close ahead of, or close behind them, but it came just the same climbing by yourself. He didn't know.

But the night. The night. After the plates had been cleaned and the table cloth spread over the condiments and the covered dishes, and what was left of the ham wrapped and set in the pie safe, they watched impatiently while Datha dried and set away the plates and silverware her mother washed on the stove and Marguerite rinsed in a big steaming enamel pan she had to stand on a box to reach, standing on a box there between them. The Goodakers had electricity but their country habits were strong in them and the lights would go out as they moved out onto the porch, leaving the house black behind them, and the grownups to go whispering off to the front bedroom.

The Goodakers' was a back porch sitting kind of house. Some were front porch kinds of houses, where you'd sit, and the Goodakers did too, from time to time, of an afternoon, after your housework was done, and watch the occasional car or wagon go by. Wagon people always called out. Car people waved. No one passed without waving, chin jerking or nodding, even out-of-town people. But at night you wanted to sit on the back porch at the Goodakers'. That was where the morning glory vines grew and you could look through their black patterns and see cut outs of the sky and wonder where the flowers went when they closed up of a night, and see the moon pass over.

It was a strange thing, this moon, that you never told anyone about, but sometimes it would race through the clouds all by itself when you were sitting still like tonight. Sometimes it would just hang there, and sometimes, when you were walking home at night from watching the Holiness Church people jumping and tossing their babies in the air, peeping through the door left open so the heat and hollering could escape, sometimes like that the moon would just ride along beside you as you hurried home, passing behind the trees and sliding its arms from branch to branch. Your moon was flat. You thought everyone else's was too. You were disappointed to learn some saw it fat like an orange. Some things you wish you'd never heard.

Datha grabbed up a sackful of beans and a dishpan. Said she needed to do something with her hands while they sat. Maybe older girls were like that. He'd always been good with children. Babies, he'd learned early, when they were fretful you could pick them up and whisper in their ear and they'd get all quiet right away. Adults, he later learned, were the same way but they were too heavy to pick up and often wouldn't let you in close so the only way to calm them down was by talking real low. So, as he might have expected, tonight the littlest ones climbed up on him in the swing. One leaning on him. Bessie snuggled down on her side with her head on his lap, bare feet tucked up close to the back of her overalls.

As Datha talked he let his hands run idly over Bessie's head, and traced the outline of her ear with the tip of his finger. You did that sort of thing then. Later, when he was in his forties and she was in her thirties she had tried to seduce him, but he had not succumbed, not that he had fought it, just that being unskilled he had misunderstood the signals till way too late.

After that she had gotten a divorce, and he'd wondered if it had all started from that night.

They say infants start out autistic then grow out of it. He wondered if it were not really the other way around, because more and more as he grew older he could see where things, a lot of things, might have started off with what he did or might have done or didn't dare to do or try.

Datha was a great storyteller. They could count on her. You could tell she was thinking about some things, then she looked a long time at him. Clemmy Larry and Jimmy Goodaker sat quiet and eager. They knew what kind of startup her stories needed and wondered where it would lead. Bessie pretended to be asleep, but he could feel the restlessnesses of her, and tested by lightly lifting his hand only to have it fretfully restored, as a sleeper, tossing, might do. Marguerite sat sullen and alone. There was a sassiness about her at times, "an itch," her daddy would say, "and nowhere to scratch it."

"I'll tell you about your great-great-granddaddy. It's something you'd best know anyway, and it's true. He was a rotten no-gooder and your cousin Missy was his daughter. I wasn't there and I won't tell you how I know, but I'll tell you what the snake doctor saw."

His mind called up a picture of a bomber-shaped dragonfly and he wondered what a dragonfly could see. There was a hint of moon just to the left of the porch post. In the blue-black darkness a darker shadow of the barn stretched toward him. Datha's apron was a faintly checkered shaped of dark and darker squares close by, the beans a black nothingness in her lap.

*   *   *   *

On a day in early autumn, the leaves were mostly green. Only here and there in the woods far off you could see spots where there was some yellow and red. It had been hot in the kitchen with the morning cooking and, though it was warm days outside, it felt cool to her when Missy left the dinner table, picked up her wicker hamper with her good arm—not the withered arm—and, carrying the dirty clothes with a bar of lye soap resting on top, headed off for the pond. She had a way of walking with long rapid steps that took her quickly up over the rise behind the house and down through the brief woods that screened the pond from the barn and cribs standing where the hill crested.

No wagon tracks led down to this pond. Neither did the livestock ever water here. The horses used the pond over in the fenced pasture nearby and there were other ponds out where Tom White's milk cattle and a few head of beef cattle fed. The only path to this pond was kept worn by Melissa's bare feet and by the hounds that you could sometimes see roaming loose.

On the kind of steamy morning this had been, Missy once saw a paw print in the soft dirt where the path was bare and another time she had seen the flanks of a gray brown animal slide off through the trees as she carried her hamper down to the pond. Before she was born, Tom White's father had claimed to see a wildcat at the pond. If it were true, it was the only wildcat any of the families in Lester County had ever heard tell of.

This was the cleanest pond on the farm, and that was where Melissa did her wash. The fresh spring down the hill, the one in front of the house, was for their drinking water. Besides that, there was no level spot around the spring, nor water deep enough for her to work in.

Tom White's father, old Bill White, had died before Melissa was born. He had built a shed up by the pond near the woods. It was open on the side toward the pond like a half covered porch and, on the small raised floor inside, Melissa kept her two wash tubs and her scrub board. She also kept there a small bucket with a wire handle to fill the tubs.

In the drowsy noontime sun the water looked cool and pleasant to her. The small wood and the hill behind the pond broke whatever slight breeze the house had enjoyed through the morning and the noonday meal. Under her long print dress, Missy felt hot. She set the tubs where they would be at arm's length just at the edge of the pond. It relieved her to put her bare feet in the water as she stooped to fill her bucket. With no other way to catch up her skirt hem, she gathered it through her apron waist, and, enjoying the cool feel of the water on her ankles and calves, filled the tubs more slowly than usual.

She set down her bucket, placed the scrub board in the first tub so it leaned against the side, and sorted all the white clothes into the tub, mostly family underwear and her own cotton socks that she wore of a Sunday.

Maybe she felt something. Anyway she looked up at the shed and saw her father sitting on the edge of the raised floor, with his old shotgun across his legs. He was watching her. How long had he been there a' watching?

Now the Whites were not great talkers. She had nothing to say to him, he said nothing to her, but she tugged at the skirt bunched up in her apron and felt better when the length of it dropped around her legs. She took up one of the cotton stockings and draped it over the washboard, where she could rub the lye soap against the smooth fabric.

The first stocking yielded its dinginess quickly. She squeezed it in her hand and watched the soapy water run down over the washboard. She dropped it into the second tub, picked up its mate and began to scrub again. This one had a grass stain from last Sunday's baptizing. The stain helt out against her knuckles and she forgot about her father as she fought the discoloration with her good hand, squeezing and rubbing, squeezing and rubbing the sock against the wash board.

Suddenly she yelled and jerked upright. "Pappeee!" She grabbed at her exposed and bleeding neck, the sock falling from her hand. It stang and burned where he had hurt her.

Ever since she had entered her teens, he'd taken to sneaking up and trying to pinch at a pimple on her face or neck. Tom White had grown up mean. To torture a risin' on a poor helpless child like Missy with her withered arm, that was just the kind of thing he liked to do. It tickled him to see her cringe and try to duck away. He liked it best if he got blood or yellow pus on his fingers. But the rough hateful touch of his dirty, thick callused hands sickened her more than the pain. Afterwards she would feel the rising bruise and imagine it festering on her.

"Haw, haw! I got that one, didn't I? Didn't I get that one?" He danced back a step as she snapped her head away, the long black hair flipping behind her shoulder and catching there. He danced back toward her. She could see the dirt that was part of the skin and stubble of his face, and behind him the little shed with the shotgun lying again' it.

She staggered back, retreating into the deeper water, her toes sucking the brown mud, the hem of her dress swirling in the brown-green mix boiling up from the bottom.

"Let me alone, Pappy." She looked at his flat greasy hat, not at him. "I got washing to do. I ain't aiming to fool with you."

"I got washing to do-oo." He stretched his mouth wide and wagged his jaw, mimicking her words in falsetto. He ducked his head, and grinned sideways at her. Then, holding his arms like a boxer, the long sleeves flapping about his skinny wrists, he commenced to snatching around at the back of her neck, first one hand then the other, as she dodged from side to side, her long hair snapping before his hands.

He had another trick he'd do, even at home, where it aggravated her mother but she couldn't do nothing about it. If he couldn't get at her from the front he'd grab for the top buttons at the back of her dress. Everybody wore high collars then. He'd rattle his rheumy laugh and gloat at her struggling to fasten herself up again with her one good arm. Any fix where he could get her good arm caught up so she had to twist herself up or fling herself about to get free, he would gloat at the withered arm dangling and jerking, and laugh that ignorant laugh of his.

Well he could have got a holt of her and thrown her down in the water. Why he didn't I don't know. He bent over at her and snatched at her with little pinching gestures, but he couldn't catch her. Then he grabbed at her twice with the same hand. She misjudged her dodge and he caught her collar in his right hand. He grabbed the fabric and jammed his fingers in at the neck where he felt the sharp knobs of her backbone. She jerked back too late and the button broke off.

"Damn you, Pappy!"

"Damn you, Pappy!" he mimicked in a lower pitched, whinier voice, but he hung on to her collar. She stopped and caught her breath. She thought it was all over, but he hadn't had his fun yet. He giggled low like he was thinking. Then he suddenly jerked again at her neck collar like the reins of a saddle horse that he expected to move at his command.

"Damn you, Pappy!" he mocked again. He tugged at her collar like he was trying to pick up a game that had gotten interrupted. When she wouldn't move he looked at her half silly, the way a dog would look trying to get you to throw a stick.

She looked back up at him with scorn in her face. The gray head, the railroad handkerchief in his overalls pocket, the empty hammer loop, his blackened face, not dirty with the brown of the earth and fields hereabouts, but the gray black grime that grows over days from the smoke of a coal burning grate and the soot of kerosene lanterns. That and never bathing none.

"Go way, Pappy." Like speaking to a child. "Take your filthy hands off me and go wash." Her breath caught, her heart jumped. His look had changed from stupid to mean. She must have said too much too strong. Something that challenged his authority, something that offended his dignity, scraped at his pride, something that caused him to dig deep and nasty to get his game going again.

He reached down, still holding her collar. Reached into the warm mud at the water's edge, where the heavy silt had already begun to settle from her deep sucking tracks. He squeezed up a handful.

She sensed his mind and tried to back away, pulling against his hand holding at the collar.

"Don't do it, Pappy!" She tried to block him with her good arm, spreading her fingers as wide as she could. But he was quicker and smacked her left cheek with the rank dripping mud. Its slime oozed over the curve of her jaw, down the light brown skin of her neck and onto the collar flopping limply on her shoulder.

The fun was on again. He stooped for another handful, but this time she caught him off balance and jerked herself free. She stepped backward into water up to her knees. Her dress dragged heavy in the water, pulling at her.

Surprise showed briefly in his eyes. He straightened and stepped toward her. The water came in over the tops of his shoes. The feel of it roused him to move faster. He caught at the fabric of her dress and got hold of her breast. He pinched hard. Her eyes opened in horror and pain. He turned loose.

"Pappy!" An injured, accusing, high-pitched righteous scream. "You'll go to hayull for that." Shock and hurt filled her eyes. Blinded, she fought the hot swelling her face. She stumbled to one side, dragging her skirt, almost falling. Struggling to get away, stirring angry dark clouds of mud, she tried to gain the bank.

Oh, he was brave now. Taunted by her threat. Goaded by this new way to humiliate her, he raced her back to the drier crust of autumn mud around the pond, and got there first. On the dry bank now he danced along sideways in front of her, grabbing at her other breast, his thumb and forefinger still feeling the smooth print cloth and the soft firmness beneath it.

Humiliated, humiliated beyond her nightmares. The rage within her began to build up. She slowed her frantic thrashing. She would not let him see her brushing tears with her good hand. She blinked them out of her eyes and stopped. "I ain't comin' out, Pappy." She saw his grin of anticipation drop sideways on his face and his eyes go cold. "You can stand there till supper, but I ain't comin' out." She stood still, feeling the pond-warm water creeping up her skirt.

"Aww, are you a scared of your pappy?" he whined.

"I ain't a scared of you, and I ain't a comin' out neither. Just let me alone."

"Who's gonna hurt you? You got tender tits?" He grinned big, pleased with himself.

"Pappy! Talking like that ain't right!" Her words carried out over the still pond like an eight year old's, tattling home.

"Oh, *ho*, Pappy. That ain't right!" He mocked her, dragging out the words. He looked hard at her, eyes cold. A glowing red flush above his cheekbones accented the grime on his skin. He turned away from her, and walked back to the shed. He sat down on the raised floor, but he did not pick up his gun. Instead he nudged the butt of it with the toe of his shoe, just like a schoolboy would do, poking at his buddy to share a good joke.

Missy watched till her father was settled, then she came out of the water hard, her feet making sucking noises, her skirt dragging full, wet and heavy behind her.

When she felt the drier mud and grasses at the water's edge, she stooped and grabbed up the hem of her skirt. She squeezed the water out one-handed, keeping her body turned toward the shed. Her skirt weighed on her and the water ran in thick rivulets across the dampened mud, seeking the deeper water of the pond. Her experienced hand worked thoroughly around the skirt. The energy of her fist soon worked some of the frustration and anger out of her body, though the humiliation lingered in the flame of her cheeks. Resentfully, she picked up the white sock floating in the galvanized tub and attacked the stain again.

All at once' he was back. His thumb and forefinger pinched the bruise of her neck again. He pinched with all strength to show how well he knew it hurt. The pain brought the hot tears back to her eyes. Her teeth tightened against the pain, but she wouldn't cry out. Unable to lift her head against his rough knuckles, unable to pull away from the grip of his fingers, she forced herself to continue scrubbing the sock. She could not see the washboard, she could not see that she had convulsively wrenched all the moisture from the sock. It was a dry thing wadded up in her hand that she moved back and forth against the corrugated board.

"Haw, *haw!*" He took hold of her collar with his free hand and, releasing the throbbing bruise on her neck, grabbed her shoulder inches away from the angry red, swollen mark. "Here's another one, ain't it?" But he gripped only the fabric of her dress in his hand. The other held her shoulder. "I'll get it. I'll get it!" He jerked at the button which caught, then tore free. He jammed his hand down the back of her dress, to where he could feel her backbone, all the while holding her slender shoulder in his right hand.

"Pappy, don't. Stop!" Clutching that pitiful white stocking, she pushed on him with her good hand. But she was on lower ground than he was and could only get the side of her arm against his body. She couldn't muster the leverage to push herself free or push him away. Her stiffening up roused him on. Here was his kind of game.

"Don't stop. Don't stop!" He mocked her, quick and breathless this time. He pushed down at her shoulder with one hand, pinched at the skin of her back with the other.

She screamed out and grabbed for the washboard, but he kicked away the tub, its water made a tall wave as it flushed out into the pond. It sent out a half-ring that widened with increasing majesty till it reached the bobbing rushes at the far end, lifting a snake doctor where it rested with long wings flattened and sparkling in the autumn sun …

The snake doctor's tiny claws gripped the soft surface of the reed as it rocked gradually into stillness. No sound of the struggle or its frustration, or of its sweating attempts at escape, or of its conquest and shock in the hot autumn dust ruffled the insect's sensitive antenna. Nor did the brilliant prisms of its thousand glistening eyes register more than a distant confusion of colors from the gray jacket and dirty blue overalls superimposed on a print checkered, dust covered, muddy blue dress across the pond ...

*   *   *   *

In the silence there came a mighty tiredness on him, and an unsettledness in his spirit. Marguerite was grumbly. "But what happened to Missy?" she asked.

"She borne Tom White a baby that come out dead. Then she up and killed herself with his old shotgun. They put the both of them in the same coffin. It was made out of pine wood. Our great-grandma on Mama's side went to the burying. She could remember the wagon passing by a carrying the coffin, going slow. You could see where the blood come seeping through. They didn't keep a body long, not back then."

Now it's your bedtime."

He had to wake Bessie in his lap. Clemmy Larry and Jimmy Goodaker got up too fast together. "Let's go make us up a pallet," Jimmy Goodaker said.

ARMY LETTER

Princeton, Kentucky
December 5th, 1960

Dear Son,

Your father and I were awfully pleased hearing you'd decided to re-enlist in the army. "Uncle Sam needs you," as they say, what with keeping ahead of the Russians and all. You know it costs the government more to train a new man than to keep a veteran soldier, and that all comes out of our taxes. Son, you don't know what it's like having to pay taxes. Seems like we never have anything real nice. We always have to put it into tax money.

You're better off staying in the army, son. They's nothing for you to do here. Guess you heard after you'd been gone 8 months that nice Grace Pellen you used to go with married Dr. Fowler's son. They looked awful sweet at the wedding. Guess he won't have to go into service after all, him being a family man now and all.

It wasn't long after his father bought them that nice little house—doctors make good money, you know—she surprised them all with a family. The boy is darling. I saw them in the doctor's office last week.

There aren't any jobs here, either. Even with the Democrats in office now we can't expect a miracle. Most of the high school boys are enlisting now, right after graduation. They can't get work at the Arvel plant. Seems they'd rather hire women there.

Mr. Wheaton that runs the plant turned down Arvel's plan to switch to automation, too. Seems it's cheaper to hire women. Those poor girls, they all have to take what jobs they can get. Almost all of them are supporting a family and a husband that can't find work. Then, too some of them poor girls lost their husbands in the Korean misfortune. And some husbands just run out after trying to feed a big family got to be too much.

Son, you're so much better off in the service. Your dad and I would sure hate for you to come back home and find everything dull and no future. Just the way you left it. Keep writing us when you can.

You know we love you,

Mom

P. S. A tube blew out in the new color T.V. last night but we got it fixed this morning. We were glad of that. It's like the 1950's again, with people coming over here to watch like they used to when we got our first one, that big old black and white one. Remember that?

Joey sends his love and asks if they let soldiers send their kid brothers any allowance. He needs it for gas and dates and such. Ha. Ha.

P. P. S. I re-read your letter. We were just shocked about Grace's brother getting shot for a traitor. What would possess him to try to sneak over to East Germany? His family won't never live it down, I don't think.

COAL DUST

Watching him is like coming back to your seat at the end of the movie. You try your best to remember what you know and you can't help but wonder what you missed—and which was the best part.

He lies dying before you, under blankets and clean sheets, in the only bed in a three room house, the bed he shares with his wife of 50 years, and you try to imagine how the two of them managed to raise twelve children, almost all of whom are in this tiny house at this moment, some around this bed with you, some in the living room. The sons are accompanied by their wives which only makes the tiny house smaller. The daughters, those that are married, have left their husbands at home. It is because of these women that there is food to eat and Uncle Charlie's wife Lucy is glad to be able to offer you some. It is wrong to refuse.

Uncle Charlie was the youngest of four children. The oldest child, my grandfather, was put out to work when he was twelve years old. Their mother, my great-grandmother, was widowed by a work accident. She took a second husband. This man, Grandpa Hopper, told her, "I'll take that one yonder in the crib, but them other three will have to go some'ers else."

My grandfather and his sister went to neighbor farms to earn their keep. The girl married by the time she was fourteen, and she and her new husband took the remaining brother, who was too young to work. He was eight years old. Meanwhile, Uncle Charlie, now lying before me, slowly dying of black lung disease, was allowed to stay with their mother, my great grandmother, and she spoiled him. That's how it came to this, we think.

Uncle Charlie had the dark good looks he had inherited from my great grand-mother's children. Their skin was dark, their eyes like eagles' eyes, and they all had dark hair. The family still thinks it was Indian blood. All I know was that, of his twelve children, the ones that inherited that same dark skin and dark eyes were irresistible to women.

"The bloodiest, meanest knock-down drag-out fight I ever saw," another uncle told me, "was two women fightin' over Louard Boyd. One of 'em had him and the other one wanted him." Louard was one of the dark-looking sons of Uncle Charles and Aunt Lucy. Louard didn't have twelve children like his dad, but Louard married nine times, including twice to the same woman. In between everything else he did, Louard was a Baptist preacher with his own congregation. Now he pretty much doesn't do anything anymore.

Louard's daddy, this Uncle Charlie dying in front of me, was a gifted carpenter. "Charlie can do anything he takes a hand to," is what my grandfather said of Charlie, his brother. Charlie taught himself to play the piano. He never owned one of his own, but he could sit down at anybody's house where they had one and pretty much play anything they asked, mostly gospel. He could sing, and so could almost all his children. One of them was younger than me and I had a crush on her. That same dark eyes and skin. I have a tape of her country-and-western music performances that I hope to keep with me forever.

This girl, my cousin, married a musician who played nightclubs and juke joints and ran a music store. I had a letter from her not long ago. She is not in touch with all her brothers and sisters and doesn't know who all they married or all their children's names. But it's a large family.

This uncle of mine lying before me, really my great-uncle since he's my grandfather's brother, lost his thumb and his forefinger in a construction accident. Didn't slow him down. He lost them before I was born and I lived to hear him play the piano. What a voice!

When I would come home summers from college, I'd ask my grandfather about the family, the way you do. He'd say, "Billy, Charlie ain't drawed a sober breath since before Easter."

I worked one summer for an uncle in my mother's generation. Everytime Uncle Charlie came into this uncle's store he had a whiskey bottle in his hip pocket. Caldwell County was dry which meant he'd be out somewhere on the highway when he picked up his next bottle.

When he came to visit my grandfather, he'd pull up in the driveway, whiskey in the front seat between him and Lucy, the three youngest girls in the back. They were all three pretty girls, especially Jerry, the one I was struck on. Jerry was the youngest of them. Faye, the one next older than Jerry, married a man who also loved singing and they went to gospel competitions all over the south, taking their children, all good singers, with them. One teenage daughter was killed in an automobile accident before they stopped winning shows.

Wanda, the oldest of these three girls was cross eyed. They say she married a man who was a lot older than her. Anyway he paid to have her eyes fixed. I've not seen her since she grew up but I still hope I will someday.

My grandfather's oldest sons Rex and Russell were, of course, the closest in age to Uncle Charlie. When all of them were much younger, living in and around the little farming community of Lewistown, Uncle Charlie would come walking over through the fields and collect whichever one of them was handy, then they'd go fishing. That's probably where they learned to drink. They didn't learn it from their dad, my grandfather. He didn't believe in drinking in front of children.

Both those uncles, Rex and Russell, were navy men, stationed in the Pacific during World War II. Russell lost an arm in the battle of Midway. He taught himself to write with his left hand, steadying his paper with what was left of his right arm. I think he holds the record for the world's longest engagement. He met his girlfriend in a Navy hospital in Brooklyn, New York, in 1945. She still lives in the apartment she first rented when I worked in Manhattan in 1957. She looked after him till about 1999.

Uncle Charlie, the man dying in front of me now, had been a master carpenter but work was unsteady during the Depression. He went to work in the mines and that's where he contracted Black Lung Disease. Mine owners then were as smart as they are now. Any evidence you might be a problem down the road they got rid of you. The fact is the mines got rid of their workers every chance they had. Miners kept wanting to unionize and that always meant profits taking a hit.

My own grandfather, Uncle Charlie's older brother, was a railroad man. He job was called "hostler," which meant he got the locomotives ready for operation. He'd get the fires going and put the locomotive on line wherever they needed it. He could drive the big engine himself, I was surprised to learn years later. But the fact that he could turn that monster around didn't surprise me because I used to take his lunch down to him at the roundhouse and I knew how the big turnstile worked. Because of his dark skin the other men called him "Woo Fang." I guess that was some kind of a putdown in post-Depression Western Kentucky, but Pap-pa, which is what we called him, was easy going so it didn't cause any problems.

Probably Uncle Charlie could take care of himself; I never heard of anybody landing a nickname on him. My own father was a different story; during those same hard times he joined the CCC's to find work and he was sent to Oregon. My daddy's nickname was "Mule." There a fellow camper called him some name, maybe that one, maybe another one; my daddy broke a pool stick over the man's head and the CCC's sent him home, back to Princeton, Kentucky. When he married my mother he was working at a grocery store, earning ten dollars a week.

This man, my Uncle Charlie, lying in the bed with his children either around the bed or in the other room, had the nine children—five daughters and four sons. All of them had beautiful names, but I think the names were thought up by Aunt Lucy. I just don't want to give Uncle Charlie credit for that.

Besides Jerry Jacqueline, Faye and Wanda, there were Velma and Galena. Isn't Galena a pretty name? It wasn't till my own adult years that I learned that Galena was a kind of ore you mined out of the rocks. Galena was so beautiful, the kind of woman that would easily smite a worshipful second-cousin like me. She was run over and killed one night walking home drunk.

My grandmother, who was Pap-pa's wife and Galena's aunt by marriage, had no use for Galena. My grandmother was a woman given to strong feelings and instant judgment. She told me again and again that my sister's personality was more like her own. "Marilyn," she said, "is like me. She calls a spade a spade. You're wishy washy." She hurt me and she knew it. Truth to tell I really wished I could be like my grandmother, but she was right. I really did see things in shades of gray. I still do, and there's nothing I can do about it.

This man, my great-uncle Charlie, lying on the bed and dying in front of me used to come over on Sunday afternoons to play cards with my grandfather and their middle brother, Uncle Albert, the one that their sister, my great-Aunt Ollie, had taken to raise as an eight-year old. They played "Long Nine" which they told me was like "Sel-Pitch". I don't know, because I never learned to play either one. I know it involved a lot of hollering and laughing, and whiskey and smoking. All three men, even Uncle Charlie with two fingers missing, could roll their own cigarettes, but Uncle Albert and Pap-pa preferred pipes in those days. Later, in his eighties, Pap-pa took up cigars but I think that was because his fingers were arthritic and he didn't want to bother with loose tobacco. Uncle Charlie's good hand, with the full set of working fingers, had yellow stains where he held his cigarette.

Standing around the table watching two generations of uncles playing cards like we did—there were always some of Pap-pa's sons playing, too—it's a wonder all the smoke didn't make us kids sick. It would have been too bad if we did though, we would have been banished out of the house. Looking back to that before television time I wonder what was so fascinating to us about watching a bunch of older men playing cards.

This man lying on the bed in front of me now. What could be so fascinating then and what could be so precious now about an old and dying great-uncle? Why, when all of his children, some of them older than my mother, and some of their spouses fill this tiny house, does it feel like I have lived here, too? And why, when we get up to leave, and we go out to the yard and I feel this powerful urge to kiss his youngest daughter, my cousin Jerry—well and legally within even our strict church's allowable limits of consanguinity—do I not?

THE COLLECTOR

When the day came that Norris Trecladder was able to make a down payment on a house he was a happy man. It was a respectable sort of house, not large, built on the plan of a square with one room in each corner and a bathroom in a sort of add-on off the kitchen to the side. The two bedrooms were identical in size and the kitchen was smaller than the living room which together balanced the bedrooms. There were intercommunicating doors between the rooms, without any space wasted for a hallway which Norris considered a plus. Sadly there was no attic, but then the rafters would likely not have been strong enough to support the weight of what he might store there so it was probably just as well. All in all the house was quite promising and Norris looked forward to the realization of his dream.

He had determined in childhood that he would be a collector. There was a certain romance in the notion of being a collector, that selfless application to a cause greater than oneself, to the assembling, aggrandizing, accumulating, annotating, assorting and arranging of something special, something purposeful, something in which there would be great intrinsic value not necessarily because of the value of the objects themselves as much as because of the diligence, the energy and the organizational skills which were his greatest personal assets and with which he would imbue and invest his collection.

He walked proudly and energetically through the house and back through all the rooms again. He did this several times as he rejoiced in the growing realization of how really little furniture he would need for his meager needs and how very much more room that would need for his collection. He pictured in his mind how his collection would grow and how neatly it would fit into the space available. The prize items in his collection he decided would be displayed in the sunniest room, but he would install curtains so that he could regulate the amount of sunlight falling upon them, in case they were sensitive to sunlight. After a few minutes he decided that it might be better to rotate the choicest pieces of his collection just in case there was some hidden danger that had not yet occurred to him in leaving any one item too long in a place of prominence. There is, for example, he told himself, if nothing else the problem of dust. Whatever is on top of something must necessarily accumulate more dust than what is underneath.

He thought about this for awhile and then thought that he would dust every item in his collection every day, at least every day. But what if his collection doubled in size? Well then he would dust every item in two days. If it doubled again he would get to it every four days and everything would still be all right. It was just a matter of remembering his powers of twos tables, he thought, and Norris Trecladder had a very good memory, which boded well for his prospects because he planned on eventually having a very large, if not to say substantial, collection.

He took a last final tour of the house, picturing his collection fitting squarely into the corners of the rooms and being worked snugly and in a craftsmanlike way into every neat quarter inch of the wall space in every room, allowing necessarily but grudgingly for the odd angles of the few essential items of furniture that had to stand here and there. He resolved to look for furniture that was on the small side and that had right-angle corners and square-ish sides.

At last it was time to leave and return one more time, but only for the last time, to his one bedroom apartment where he would sleep tonight before moving in tomorrow. He lingered in the front doorway a long while, dreamily envisioning his collection ensconced in majestic array spread imposingly but accessibly throughout the house and he beamed with contentment. A momentary wrinkle clouded his broad brow, then flickered away.

There was the problem, a small problem, but one that had to be solved and soon. It was the same nagging problem that had niggled at him since first he had conceived the notion of this mighty venture. It had an annoying way of coming up whenever he was at his most buoyant with the fascinating prospects of his glorious lifetime pursuit, his Everest, treasure, his Holy Grail.

There was the pesky fact, minor compared to everything else, but true nonetheless and all the more irritating—a tedious, bothersome thing that he would like to swat away like a fly, but it always came back—the tiny nit of an annoying notion. He had not yet decided what to collect.

A COTTONWOOD
HIDING

"She's a girl, Mother!" said John Oberhausen. "She just can't be going with us." The sister he was talking about punched him between the shoulder blades.

"I'll go or you'll regret it," said Hollie. "You crash Becky's party, I want to be there and see it for myself. No fun hearing you brag about it later."

At the dining room window, John lifted a piece of brown lace so he could watch their sister drive off. Hollie could see perfectly well through the lace without pulling back the curtain. What she missed in detail she supplied from her imagination. Hollie was a sophomore and a critical witness of upper classmen's excesses, having accumulated several large notebooks of observations.

They saw their sister Becky slide over close to Tom McInerney as the car pulled away. Becky and Tom were a proper match. There were only fifty students in the Orion high school and Becky, being the only senior girl, was head cheerleader. Tom was captain of this year's football team. There were twelve particularly athletic boys in the school, enough to make up a football team in the fall, first and second string basketball teams in the winter and the spring baseball team. He had been captain of last year's basketball team and he would have been last year's baseball captain but he had sprained his ankle in practice.

"Your father won't like it," said Mrs. Oberhausen from the kitchen.

Her husband was the town barber, the town watchmaker, and the town postmaster of Orion, Kansas, population 257 by the highway sign. The businesses of Orion stood in a row along two blocks of the only fully paved street in town.

There were the McInerney's farm implement store, a grocery, a bank, three churches, the volunteer fire department, and the Oberhausen's combination barbershop, watch repair and post office. The homes of Orion sat irregularly along the streets off Main Street, backyards opening without fences onto cornfields that stretched way off to infinity.

The Oberhausens' youngest son, Spud, helping his mother at the sink, was still in grade school and, being much occupied with frogs and road kills, possessed of opinions that were pretty much ignored by everyone but himself.

"I don't care if she comes," said Richard Dunlap, looking up from Becky's yearbook at the dining room table. Richard was the outsider, come home with John from college for Thanksgiving break. Where the Oberhausens were sandy haired and tall, Rich was dark haired, with a touch of olive in his skin. He was less muscular than John, and more studious.

"Hollie, I think it best not," said Mrs. Oberhausen.

Richard was fond of his roommate's mother. He got up lazily to come over and lean against the kitchen door where he could watch Spud and her scraping pumpkins. She handed him two small ones. "That ought to be enough. I need the rest for pies and canning."

"Can we have some toothpaste, Mom?" asked John, "And some soap?" He crowded in beside his mother, and put his arm around her waist for a moment. Then he took a butcher knife and sliced Rich's pumpkins into rings. He was much taller than his mother, with crew cut hair and freckles. His hands were quick and sure with the knife. He was a pre-med student, going for a surgeon.

Mrs. Oberhausen spoke into the window above the sink, where Hollie could see her reflection from the dining room, "Johnnie, you boys won't do anything dangerous?"

"Mother!" said John.

Hollie came over beside Rich close enough to feel her side touching his. "We'll be careful," Rich said, and stepped out of Hollie's way.

Later, when it was dark and the town's lone streetlight was a distant thing reflected off the bank's facade, when Mrs. Oberhausen had taken her papers to grade on the dining room table, Mr. Oberhausen had sat down beside the living room piano with his newspaper and Spud had gone off to find dead critters, John and Rich went across the yard to the garage carrying two burlap bags loaded with pumpkins rings, soap, and toothpaste. They found Hollie sitting rigid in the back seat, arms crossed, chin up, wearing blue jeans and one of John's college sweatshirts, with Mr. Oberhausen's hunting cap on her head.

"Dad will be mad, Hollie," said John, frowning, but Rich laughed.

"He knows," said Hollie, "besides, Rich asked me to."

"Now, Hollie," said Rich. She clapped her hand over his mouth. She could feel his grin stretching under her palm. He bit the soft underside of a finger. She pulled her hand away, slowly.

It was a long ride, on straight roads that went for miles between the cornfields, each turn a perfect right angle, alikeness everywhere and darkness. An occasional descent into a cottonwood grove marked a creek, then up to the same flat cornfields again. At last John slowed, pulled off the pavement and guided his wheels into a pair of tractor ruts that led between fence posts. When the motor's sound died they could hear faint distant music, and, as their eyes grew smarter they could pick out a glow of window lights across the field.

"Hollie, stay here," said John, in a low voice.

"No," said Hollie.

John gave Rich one of the two burlap bags, long and limp, with pumpkin lumps in the bottom. "Keep it up off the ground."

Rich zipped up his jacket. Hollie liked Rich and she did not trust her brother not to hurt him.

"Keep low through the cornrows," John whispered. The beat of the music got louder, heavier as they slipped through the field, crouching, John was in the lead. He stopped.

"Fence ahead. Be careful." He got down on hands and knees and moved on.

Hollie took Rich's hand. Bent over, heads below the corn. The darkness pressed on them, immense from all sides.

John slowed and Rich reached out to him. Hollie felt his arm jerk. Something kicked inside her. It knocked her to the ground. As she fell she heard the burlap sacks dropping into the corn stalks around her.

"John?" called Rich.

"Damn … cattle fence! About killed me."

Silence.

A minute, maybe more. Then John spoke. A coarse whisper. "We'll have to crawl under."

"Can you see it?"

"Yeah, it's pretty high. You can get underneath if you do like me. Hollie, stay back."

"No," said Hollie.

They crawled on, dragging the bags, through corn stubble near the outbuildings. At the edge of the yard they halted.

"Get the antennas and the windshields. I'll do the tires." In the light from the house windows they could see his silhouette fumbling for a screwdriver blade that would fit inside the tire valves.

Rich and Hollie crawled to the cars silent and black in the yard. She fished out pumpkin rings and he hung them on each antenna, then they went around again and she soaped the side windows while he smeared toothpaste over the windshields. It was quick work and they hurried back to the edge of the yard as quickly as they could without making a fuss. John's was slower work. They could hear the hiss of escaping air as he went from car to car. Once they heard a door open. Rich put his arm around Hollie and pulled her up against an outbuilding She pushed her breast into his side. She had taken a bra from her bigger sister and felt the air space inside give way as the stiff material crushed against her.

*   *   *   *

Going home she sat between John and Rich, listened to them talking and laughing. She asked if she could lay her head on Rich's shoulder, because she was sleepy.

"No, Hollie," said John, but she had already set her face to look asleep.

They were home before midnight. Her father frowned when he kissed her good night.

"You're too young to be going out at night with boys," he said. "I want you to promise me you'll stay close to Johnnie or Spud when you get out of the house like this."

From upstairs she could hear Spud telling about frogs and starting the back-writing game he had invented for Rich. Tomorrow she would write on Rich's back. She was glad Spud had thought of it.

Next day, Thanksgiving Day, Becky got grounded bad. Grounded till after Christmas. She had not come home till three o'clock. Her dad was awake and waiting in his chair by the upright piano that carried her senior picture in its ivory frame. The party had broken up about midnight, but the talking and clasping had kept them almost an hour before they'd noticed the flat tires and they had told one another it was too late to call home.

Mr. Oberhausen was a stern man. He was shorter than John, scarcely taller than his wife or Hollie, and he stood possibly half an inch shorter than Becky in heels. He came from hard working immigrant parents who tolerated high spirits but had no patience for irresponsible behavior. Becky was confined to the house, except for church and school. Whoever had crashed the party was no worse than young women who didn't call their parents when something happened. When Becky came to the bed she shared with Hollie she told who she suspected.

But you don't know why, do you, Miss Stupid? Hollie thought.

Next day was Thanksgiving, which, to Rich, most of all, meant eating. Rich was barely out of his teens. His body was thin. He was big handed and big footed with a face that needed filling out to match his ears and nose. So Rich's Thanksgiving Day was a good family meal, and secretive college laughs with John, mixed with modest hopes for a greater share of Becky's attention, and deep disappointment that she spent her free hours on the dining room floor in the center of the house, commiserating with Tom by telephone.

After dinner Spud closed himself in the garage where he could take his time skinning a rabbit. John and Rich took a box of shells and John's .22 and tried a few target shots in the back yard. They borrowed the car and Hollie tagged along.

There was a cottonwood grove by a creek a few minutes' drive out of town. This time she rode in the back seat so that there would be room for the rifle up front. They left the car by the road and walked back into the trees. Hollie carried a coffee can and some paper scraps for targets.

"Can you shoot?" she asked Rich. He was city bred—from a town she'd never heard of, several states away from Orion.

"Used to could," he answered.

"Let's see can you hit that songbird," said John.

"Johnnie!" said Hollie.

"Hush, there's lots of them," he said.

She watched, biting her lower lip, as Rich raised the rifle, sighted quickly and squeezed before the gun had a chance to move on him. The bird popped off the branch and fell in a clump of feathers.

"Poor little thing," said Rich, as he picked up his bird. "Wish now I hadn't done it. What you want to do with him?" He handed his kill to Hollie. She took it solemnly.

"Throw him away. The foxes will get him," John said.

Hollie set up the can for them and later she stuck paper in the tree limbs, but Rich had about lost interest in shooting, and she wished she were alone with him in the cottonwoods, wished John had stayed behind to help Spud with his rabbit.

That night they got Becky to play the piano. Spud wrote messages to Rich and John by tracing large block letters on their backs with his finger. When they asked him to switch to longhand to make it harder he said he didn't want to do that. So Hollie took a turn and wrote long messages on their backs, making

Rich's messages so hard that she had to repeat them again and again till he guessed right.

Saturday night before John and Rich went back to college, with Becky still grounded, John drove Hollie and Rich and Spud into Horton for the movies. Hollie sat between Rich and John. Rich took her hand once. John saw it and whispered in her ear. She changed seats with John and stared resentfully at the screen till the movie was over, refusing his popcorn. She punched him once when he asked what was wrong and refused to speak.

Becky was up when they got home. Mr. and Mrs. Oberhausen had already gone to bed. Spud and John went upstairs to look at rabbit skins. Becky said she would show Rich her yearbooks if he wasn't too tired.

Hollie undressed in the girls' bedroom off the dining room. She opened the door a space and saw Rich and Becky kissing. It was a long kiss. She turned off the night stand light on her side and slid into a cold bed. For a long time she lay stiffly, staring at the ceiling in the dark, listening for sounds from the dining room.

*   *   *   *

John changed from med school to chemistry, took a doctorate and became a teacher, like his mother. His wife of twenty years left him unprepared and heartbroken. Becky took a professional degree, married, divorced and remarried. Raised three children. Spud married a Bolivian woman he met on a dig, took a degree in anthropology and became well known in FBI forensics.

Hollie kept a songbird's feather in her brother's college yearbook next to Rich's picture, where he is still young today, dark haired and thin. She married Tom, the football captain, when he came back home to manage his father's farm machinery business. After Mr. Oberhausen retired she took over the postoffice. When he died they nailed shut the doors of the barber shop-watchmaker's store and converted the two rooms for farm implement storage. After Mrs. Oberhausen's death the county abandoned the one room schoolhouse out in the country where she taught, but being brick it could not easily be torn down and it is available now to art students from Horton looking for atmosphere. Rich changed schools at mid-term and was lost to the Oberhausens. If he is still alive somewhere he will be surprised to hear about the yearbook and the feather.

THE GOOD LIFE

His name was Cumberland Pell. Cumberland it was written in the bible, and Cumberland on his marriage record, but by the time the census came around his mother had taken to calling him Comely. Comely Pell.

Try, and you can see her the day the census taker came by. It would have been a warm day. He would most likely have come on horseback. She would have been wearing a gray dress that came down to her ankles, with a bonnet made from feed sacks. You turned the feed sack inside out and there was a brand new pattern you'd never seen before, usually flowers, sometimes checks or polka dots. She was wife to the largest land owner around, known as Squire Pell because of his holdings. If she'd used that name she'd have said "Squahr Pell," because that's the way her people talked back then. But you wouldn't have to worry about how to say it in front of her because she always called him Mr. Pell.

She'd have met the census taker on the front porch on a warm day and one of the children hanging around watching would have been sent to fetch a dipperful of water. He'd have taken a deep drink and left enough in the bottom to swirl around its enameled bowl and flung it underhand into the flower bed. Her flowers would have been pansies and morning glories. She was partial to pansies and morning glories.

She'd have sat in a cane bottom rocker and he'd have sat on the steps. "Comely," she'd have said when she got to her son's place in the lineup. The record shows that she included the names of cousins staying there, being careful to add last names if they were different. The census taker, not knowing any better, would have put the last names down as middle names, like Annie Pete who was there. Unless she gave him three names, like Tom Lynn Franklin who was a hand on the place that year. "Comely," she had said and, later, when he came to be an old man with a beard down his chest, smelling of earth and of raw pine lumber, Uncle Comely was how he was known to all the people younger than him, which was pretty much everybody, related or not.

He had another name, too. It was a name he had earned on his own as a young man, "Fight." Yes, Fight. Uncle Fight Pell. But unless you had lived there you wouldn't know how to pronounce it. Fight. To someone who lived there long enough to hear the way people talked, the delicious vowel may still come to the ear, but it comes fainter and fainter with time. That's the way things go. If a memory is not precious what good is it? Besides, you wouldn't know how to reproduce the sound in your own throat if you had heard it. It's that particular flavor of the long "i" that sounds like a shorter version of the short "a" in "fat," only drawn out. So let it go. Comely he was to most people, so Uncle Comely'll be all right for this story. Uncle Comely he'll be.

Squire Pell died young and left Comely to look after his mother and the land.

Land does not tend itself. The most direct way to make money off of land is to sell it. When his mother needed medicine, or when the garden out back came up shy of what they needed Comely would sell off a few acres. "That much less to be a' seeing after," he told her, and there was always food. What with the canning she had put up and whatever here and there that the acreage brought.

Without your tending it about the only thing land will give you is trees, and Squire Pell had left Comely a sawmill. It stood beside a shallow stream under a long tin roof held up by pine poles that left it open on all sides so you didn't have to sweat too much in hot weather. When it was cold you covered up more.

With the sawmill's long leather belts, gears, flywheels and a good blade Comely cut many a board foot of yellow pine. It was a sunny site that made its own deep shade, and smelled of pine trees, black pitch, machine oil and wet dogs. Between milling a bit for others, logging some for himself and selling off what was logged Comely would buy his mother a new dress each year out of the catalog and she would hang it up to wear of a Sunday. She was fit to drive a team to Sunday school herself, pretty much up to the end.

She had Sunday-go-to-meeting hats to wear left over from the squire's days, but she made her own bonnets for every day. Dresses and aprons, too. Comely's "overhauls" they bought ready to wear out of the catalog. One pair would last him years, for he was of a mind to rotate every other month.

After his mother passed away Comely tried his hand at cooking but at first he had no talent and he was glad when Tellie Sawyers accepted his proposal and came home to the Pell place to cook and mend. She was a tall, horsy woman, square faced and tanned from field work, for her pappy took all his girls, of which he had a plenty, to be field hands. "Ain't got no boys," he told Uncle Comely. "I reckon a woman can earn her keep same as airy a man." Her mother must have taught her something about living indoors, too, because she was one to keep a pretty fair house. You'd go to visit and there'd always be something to eat, set out on the kitchen table under a cloth to keep the flies away.

There was a parlor to the house in those days, a room where you never went except after church meeting. In it was a pump organ that Uncle Comely's sister Dorothy Jane would come play of a Sunday afternoon when the preacher came by. Uncle Comely had a loud unashamed voice that came up from deep in his throat and when the four of them played and sang you could hear it way off down the road where you might be pitching knives or back in the woods a squirrel hunting. You never heard Uncle Comely singing during the week, not even when he was working, because his way of singing was for the Lord's day and the Lord's day only.

When the moving pictures came in and Aunt Tellie would have liked to have gone they didn't because the saw mill took up the week days and you wouldn't want the Lord to come for you on a Sunday and find you at the picture show. Maybe they would go of a Saturday. That was when farm people went to town and tied their mules at the hitch rack where the water troughs were handy. Maybe she did get to go on a Saturday or two, there for a spell, but it would not have lasted long. After Willy Louis came along there was never any time for such as that.

Willy Louis was simple minded. Uncle Comely would take him along to the sawmill sometimes but he always had to keep an eye on him around the saw blade. Willy loved to watch the big saw spinning and he liked to catch the saw dust in his hands. He always had saw dust way up his sleeves. Aunt Tellie kept him in long sleeves all summer long. In that respect she looked after him just like she did Uncle Comely. Same clothes every day of the week. The only difference was what was underneath, and it was long flannels from the first of October to the first of May. Hot or cold, that was her way.

They were well taken care of, Uncle Comely and Willy Lou. They made out, that way, and the land grew smaller each year. When the spring came around there would be less of it to worry about, and Uncle Comely was not much of a hand to take on about worries he needn't to mind about.

Only two things he mainly worried about. He wanted to live long enough to take care of Willy Louis and he wanted to live long enough to look after Aunt

Tellie. Willy who liked shiny things and Aunt Tellie who turned off puny in her later years.

Willy was crazy about marbles. Always one pocket of his overalls lumpy and heavy with marbles. "Marvels," he called them. Not because he couldn't say marble, maybe he could, but marvels was what Aunt Tellie called them, and that's where Willy Louis got it from. He would trade you any time you came by. There was a shade oak grew in the front yard, down close to the road. That's where he'd take a chair of an afternoon to sit and wave at whoever came by. They always stopped. "Trade marvels?" he'd ask. "Trade marvels wiff Willy?"

Willy Louis'd trade you any kind of a marble. Even his best taw he'd swap off if you wanted to swap him out of it. He was partial to the shinier marbles, especially the clear ones. Best of all he liked the ones you could see down deep into, the kind with a cat's eye in the middle.

He was afraid of knives, though, and if you'd slip one out of your pocket he'd go to hollering and here'd come Uncle Comely getting after you to let that boy alone and don't you come aroun' 'yere teasing Willy Louis no more. He had a good mind to tell yore daddy on you and if you can't do no better than that he'd take a notion to sic the dogs onto you before you knowed it. And things like that.

But Aunt Tellie was always proud to see you coming. She liked company, and if you behaved yourself she'd bring out tea. She made the best tea ever you drank. She put sugar in her tea while it was still hot then cooled it off in the well. Honeybee honey couldn't be sweeter. You could hardly keep the sweat bees off your face all the way home when you'd been drinking Aunt Tellie's tea.

Two of you come to visit together was what tickled Willy Lou the most. He liked to listen to people talk. He was really a good hand to listen, better at listening than at talking, since you couldn't make sense out of what he said most of the time. He'd listen really close and watch your mouth when you said something. He'd laugh and grin when you cut up and made jokes. If you brought something funny along with you, like an old hat, why he'd put it on and he'd commence to carrying on and laughing up a storm. He'd laugh about himself wearing it just as much as you'd laugh looking at him. You'd point at him and make fun of him, and he'd point at himself, too. He thought he was as funny as you did.

But Willy Louis was changeable. If you went too long without cutting up and just start talking in a regular way it seemed like it made him nervous. He didn't like it too quiet when company came, which was a funny thing when you think about it, seeing as he was by himself most of the time. You'd think he'd get used to it.

You never got to stay too long. When Aunt Tellie or Uncle Comely had had enough and run you off, there'd be Willy waving bye-bye to you, sitting there in long sleeves and bib overalls, never getting up from his chair in the shade. It's not there anymore, that shade oak down at the bottom of the yard where the road ran by. No road either. The interstate cut it off and it's grown up woods again.

Uncle Comely told all his living kin, who were nothing left then but cousins, him having had no nephews or nieces and no grandkids of his own, that he wanted more than anything else to live long enough to take care of Willy Lou, and he did.

Willy lived to be thirty-something, maybe forty at the most. Uncle Comely buried that boy himself. The little cemetery was right out back of the house, where the road didn't reach. Wrought iron fence all around, twenty feet or so each way. Maybe six or eight graves there all told. Planted with cedar trees for shelter. Cedar lives a long time and mostly doesn't wither up like other trees when tree blights are going around. Not like the elms or the dogwoods. Cedar lives on.

Uncle Comely's holdings grew smaller and smaller. There was left just him and Aunt Tellie. She turned poorly as she grew older but she kept up the house. She had more time to herself and when she grew tired of bare walls she had the parlor papered, but she did the kitchen walls herself. Them she covered with pages from the Sears and Roebuck catalog. If you were over at her house and you were a young woman she thought was putting on airs she'd take you over to the some picture with a girl in it that reminded her most of you. and, "Looky here," she'd say. "When you can be a lady like this, then you can carry on like that. Till then you're gonna behave around 'jere." And that would be the end of it. If you wanted to stay you behaved. Otherwise you'd worn your welcome out.

Toward the end of her life some of the girls came visiting in shorts one time. "Lordy me," she said, "you go right home and put something on! Mr. Pell ain't never seen my legs above the ankles and you get out of here right now before he catches sight of you!"

By that time Uncle Comely and Aunt Tellie were old and set in their ways. If you were a girl and wanted to go visiting the Pells then either you wore slacks, which they didn't seem to mind, or you wore a dress.

Some time in his middle years while Willy Louis was still alive Uncle Comely had taken up making pictures of people. He used a wooden camera that stood on three legs and he'd bury his head under a black cloth and you'd hear him growl, "Now smile Purley Sue," or "Look a here, John Earl." Your name wasn't Purley Sue or John Earl, but if you were a girl you were Purly Sue and if you were a boy you were John Earl. Quick as you'd look sharp he'd squeeze the bulb shutter and it was done with. Next day you'd come over and pay your dollar and he'd hand you your picture. Mostly it looked like you. But he would not tolerate a fidgety child and if you wouldn't hold still for him he'd hand you a picture where you could tell it was you by your clothes but he'd made your face all blurry. If your mother or father complained he'd say "You bring them childern," he called little kids childern, "back here when they've learnt to sit still."

When he was down to the last few acres that weren't so easy to sell he traded off his camera gear for more parts down at the sawmill and went back to cutting lumber. After Willy Louis died Uncle Comely wanted to live long enough to take care of Aunt Tellie, and that's probably what he thought about of a Sunday morning when he sat outside in the wagon waiting for services to end. He may even have prayed. If he had then his prayers were answered. She died in the church, right there in church during the hymn singing.

They carried her out and laid her in the wagon, everyone standing around. Some crying. He wore wire rim glasses, so dirty from the sawmill you wondered how he could see out of them. He took them off that day and rubbed the lenses with his railroad handkerchief. When he put them over his eyes they were wet on both sides and his whiskers were wet and dripping onto his beard.

Some said they'd go back up to the house with him. "I reckon I can manage," he said, and told the preacher to come along tomorrow and see about the burying. The warm red earth fresh turned spilled over and some of it rolled downhill. If your eyes were wandering and not paying attention to the service you might notice how the spilling grains of dirt came to rest against the lighter green where Willy Louis's grave was mounded up. His tombstone still looked brand new when they came out later to set hers up.

There was money needed to pay the preacher and some of the cousins thought Uncle Comely should buy Aunt Tellie a new dress which he never would have stood for on a good day but he gave in, and by the time it was all over and done with he'd sold off more acres and there was only the land that the house itself stood on, with the graveyard on one side and the garden and chicken house on the other.

That and the sawmill. You walked downhill and along a two rutted track through the woods to get to the mill. Most any day you'd find him puttering around in the shed there by the creek where he kept some tools. If there was any lumber cut you'd see it stacked up. There was less and less wood cut as the years went on. Maybe because it was a two man operation and it was hard to find a helper. Maybe it was easier to haul your logs off to where they had power mills.

Maybe there just came to be less milling around that part of the county. Anyway he'd be there if the weather was good. Fiddling with something. If you'd hang around long enough you'd hear "Well, I'm a goin' back to the house." Not too loud but you wouldn't miss it if you were listening. You'd feel like you could tag along. He wouldn't ask you to come and he wouldn't say no.

He walked pretty fast for an old man, going along the woods trail where it was all grown up and hard to see where to walk. But when it came to going uphill he'd really leave you behind if you didn't shake a leg.

If there was a grownup with you he would have told you not to ask for anything, and pretty much you wouldn't want to once you got to the Pell place. There was nothing left of the house but a narrow front porch with a sagging roof and two rooms. The front room had once been the parlor. Now it served as kitchen, bath and bedroom. The bed sagged too, and had bricks in it, perhaps to keep the newspapers under them from blowing off with the front door open. You would have liked to know what date the newspapers were but you daren't ask.

The only light of an evening would have been from the coal oil lamp in the middle of the kitchen table, but its chimney was so blackened you wondered if it made enough light to read. When you walked in, mouth open, eyes wide, you would let the screen door slam behind you. You'd look back and you'd see where the screen had pulled away from the slats and rolled up on itself, ragged around the edges. Before you could turn back around you'd get bumped in the thigh and it'd be the leathery horns of a nanny goat trying to get out the door.

"Set by that there organ," Uncle Comely'd say and in the shadows'd be Aunt Dorothy Jane's pump organ under all kinds of dust with magazines and things you didn't even know what they were all piled up on it. If you had a mind to, you could sit down, and put your feet on the pumping pedals. They made a big clumping sound, and if you went to pulling on the knobs you would hear a whishing noise and if you'd push a finger down on one of the keys, it would make a great thin whistle and you'd see Uncle Comely looking over at you with eyes you couldn't see because of the light reflecting off his glasses or the sawmill dust on them, you didn't know which, and you'd stop pumping and the sound would get all tired and peter out with a hopeless sigh.

There would be a part of a loaf of bread on the table, and some jars of something, but no smell of cooking in the house. What does an old man eat, you'd wonder.

There were stairs in one corner leading up to nothing because the upper floor and the other rooms had been torn down and hauled off, probably for stove wood. The only thing left to see indoors was the back room which had a dirt floor and was more or less a lean-to with one window and an outside door. Most of the back room was taken up by a cedar box coffin, warm red in the corner and set up on chest high cedar posts. Uncle Comely had built his own coffin to be buried in and you'd be invited to admire it. It was pretty. Very pretty. He would run his hand over it and you could see the whiskers twitching back toward his ears as he probably smiled at you.

On the way out, on the porch, you might notice a string hanging down from the roof. It led across the yard to the chicken house, drooping from pulley to pulley. "Of a rainy day," and you didn't know he was there beside you, nor yet that you had stopped to stare, "I pull on this end and the chickens comes out. See 'yere?" It was true. He would pull the string and you'd see a tiny door slide up in the plankboard building leaning to one side across the yard. You'd stand there watching, hardly daring to breathe. A cautious beaked head with a red comb and wattle and rust colored feathers would push out and twitch nervously from side to side. Then all of a sudden she'd bounce out the door in a huffiness of flaming bronze feathers.

"That there's a Rhode Island Red," he'd say. "They's good layers." In a few seconds a gray-checked, heavier bodied bird might follow, "That'n's my Dominecker. Only got me one a them."

You would leave, thinking this time might be it, the last time you'd ever see him. What was it he said, that last time, the real last time? Would he have waved to you? Probably not. You maybe don't remember, he'd have stood on the porch peering in your direction, eyes hidden behind the dust and the shine of his glasses. But what was it he had said that time? He'd said, "I got my goats to milk, I got my chickens for eggs. Don't everybody live this good. Do they, boy?"

A FELT BEAT

Matthew went into seventh grade that year and got straight A's which set our daddy to bragging around his drinking buddies, but it shamed the rest of us kids and our mama so bad that we could not look his teacher straight in the face.

That was the year I was in fifth grade. Chloe Anne was in third. Those were pretty near the right grades for us. Nobody knew it when school started but Chloe was on the brink of having visions, and that was the year Mama took Jebbie down and signed him up for first grade. Chloe Anne and Matthew and me all knew it was just asking for trouble but she said Jebbie was six year old and she didn't want no trouble with the law.

Being in first grade Jebbie got home before we did, even though Chloe and I ran all the way. Matthew tried not to look like he was running where his friends could see him but he was moving fast all the same. Matthew got through the door before Chloe and me and left it hanging open.

Mama hollered, "Last one in better shut that goddamn door." Chloe didn't even punch me when I shoved ahead of her, we were that worked up about Jeb.

There wasn't a scratch on him.

Jebbie was easy to scratch. He had real fair skin and a bony little body. A bee sting'd swell up on him as big as your fist. Airey a mosquito bite would get all red and angry, with a black top to it. It'd bleed and scab over where he scratched at it 'cause he just couldn't let it alone. We'd take him blackberry picking and weeks later he'd still have them big long crimson welts that made you hurt just to look at them. I know, because I was the one used to have to give him his bath.

You could count every rib under his skinny little hide. Them hips of his were as sharp as razors. When Chloe was littler I had to bathe her too. Lay a wash rag on her and it would just skid right off her little round bottom. Not Jeb. It was like trying to soap up a scrub board to get at the dirt on him, bones sticking out everywhere.

Well, they wasn't a mark on him anywheres that day. When we come into the kitchen he was just a settin' there drinking Kool-Aid with ice in it, easy as anything, Strawberry Kool-Aid was his favorite, everybody else liked grape. He was a drawing circles where the glass had sweated circles on the table.

"Nobody hit me, nobody hit me," he yelled out in that loud way of his. Sing-song like he was making fun of us.

"You better shut up or I'll make you think nobody hit you," was what Matt said, but I could tell he felt good about Jeb. Him all relaxed like that. Him all in one piece and drinking Kool-Aid that way.

"Mattie," Mama said. "Don't."

That was all she said about it, but I could tell she wasn't happy, the way she was a standing there at the kitchen sink, wringing out her drying towel and kind of studying the back of Jeb's head.

We learnt later from one of the other first grade boys that Jebbie had pretty much hung back all day long. He sat kindly quiet in his seat—that would have been something to see—and didn't say a word. By the end of the day his teacher had commenced to treating him like he was retarded. She up and called Mama a few minutes after we got home.

I tried to tell her something, but Mama acted like she was going to smack me. "Well, he's probably just shy. Yes. Probably so," she said into the phone.

After Mama hung up we all had a big laugh, even her. Jebbie acted like he was going to laugh, too, though he never had much of what I'd call a sense of humor.

Matt smacked the table right hard and busted out hooting. Chloe commenced to yelling in that high shrilly screech of hers and I don't know what I did but I remember I just about had tears running down my face. Jebbie shy? Boy, we'd love to see that.

After a while I saw Mama wasn't laughing anymore. The rest of us stopped laughing, too. We stood there in the kitchen, the afternoon sun hot on screen door, staring at Jeb, because somebody had to figure what to do. Mama went to looking thin, the way she done when things worked out to where she couldn't deal with them. She got real thin looking, and shorter. She was taller then than Matt was, but if things got to her she'd get all caved in looking and that would make Matt look big beside her. Then Matt would act like he had to do something. He leaned over Jeb with his hands on his hips. "All right, now, Mr. Smart ..."

Jeb got a wide-eyed panicky look on him. "I'll talk, Mama, I'll talk!"

"Not too much, Hon, not too much," was all Mama could manage, but she kind of straightened up a little.

Something got into me. I didn't want anybody to get off too easy. I knew it could end up bad if we just let it go with that. "Mama, once he opens his mouth he don't know when to shut up," I said.

"You just better let him be," Matt tod me, "or I'll shut you up for good." Mattie was a lot bigger than me but I didn't think he was all that smart, still don't. Mama acted like she was going to say something, but she let it go. She give a big sigh and hung up her drying towel beside the window. She pulled the stopper out of the sink, and wiped her fingertips on the checkered curtains where they draggled in the soap dish. She put an arm around me and told him, "Mattie, let's hear about your day."

The table wasn't set yet but we pulled out our chairs around the table, Jeb drawing in the water puddles again. Well, it seemed like Matt had brought home a bunch of quizzes that was supposed to show what he'd learned last summer. I don't have to tell you the only thing Matt hadn't forgot over the summer was mowing lawns, riding his bike, playing baseball and shooting baskets. He was in trouble and he knew it.

Jeb come out in that whiney voice, "Don't worry, Mattie, I'll help you. I'll help you." Matt looked relieved. If Jebbie give him the answers they'd all be right. Never was a book come into the house that Jeb hadn't read cover to cover as soon as he was big enough to turn the pages without eating 'em, coloring on 'em or tearing 'em. He never forgot a thing he read, including who wrote it and what was on page thirty-seven. I'd be first to tell you it didn't feel right lettin' him help us that a way. Something about it don't feel right about it till yet.

TRAIN TO PRAGUE

So it was agreed. It would be a kind of verbal strip poker. Neither of them could remember how it started. He had been seated first. The head waiter gave him a particularly nice table, reassuringly laid in hefty silver with monograms worn ragged into brassy smears, and bare, substantial flatware. There were no glasses on the table, a table firmly anchored to an unbroken view of the banded countryside that swung toward him and away, rushing swiftly where it ran closest to the window, somewhat more leisurely in the middle distance and nearly motionless at the horizon where an occasional tree or building swiped past, like a chalkboard eraser, to reappear almost immediately, serene and content, riding a straight, flat line between earth and sky.

The waiter, with a mechanical air, had deposited her opposite him, and he had wished to think the man a dedicated romantic, but couldn't make himself believe dining car waiters were like that. They said good morning in what each hoped was a European sort of way, discovered they were both Americans, hoped the other hadn't noticed, and tried to see how long they could make each other think they could sit knee to knee with a stranger and conduct their modest affairs as if they were alone.

She looked at the menu. He stared out the window. She looked out. To avoid her eyes in the window, he looked inside the car. They saw themselves avoiding one another and felt naive. She felt an urge to reassure and spoke into their personal circle of silence.

She was sorry about the way she looked. She had had a bad night. Was it the Polish border guards, he asked, that had grilled him in his sleeper at Catovice, with that brash bullying air they had, of the militarily inferior? Or was it the Czechs who, scant seconds later, when the train had lurched a few feet across the border, entered his sleeping compartment the same way, fully armed, also with submachine guns, bursting in with a sudden loud noise like a quick cut on the sound track of poorly edited movie, as if to catch him at something illegal?

"No, it was bad dreams, I think," she said.

"Yes, I know what you mean," he said. He wanted to sound objective, worldly. He hadn't slept much, himself, but he had dreamed a lot.

During breakfast they found themselves leaning forward, drinking too much coffee, hoping their bladders would hold and wishing the face they saw had been more ... something ... neither could have said what. Yes, he was getting off in Prague. No, she was going on to Vienna. Yes, it would be their first time in their respective cities. Each hoped the other would have a good time, and wished they had been there themselves so they could recommend a place to stay, something special to see. They had heard the museums were wonderful.

It was a safe bet, the business about the museums. Each thought himself too cosmopolitan to say what the other had said, and regretted the witless, unmemorable, tourists' words that lingered in the air between them.

Did she dream much, he wondered? Her dreams were usually scary, and she tried not to remember them, she told him. His were usually silly, mostly adventure stuff he said. He was putting himself down. It was a way he had. But this night she had remembered hers, she said. Could he remember his dream?

He was in a hotel room, a tiny hotel room, very European, but in America. He knew that. He knew his wife-to-be was in there, too. It was their room. It felt crowded. It looked, in fact, a lot like his sleeping compartment on the train, but viewed from slightly above. Her parents arrived. No, they didn't come in. He had no sense of them coming through a door. But there was a sense of their coming to be in the room. They hadn't been there when the dream first started. There was a sense of talking about the wedding tomorrow, but not of the actual words being spoken. He knew in his dream that he didn't want to marry this woman. It felt wrong. His fiancee was not at all right for him. She was wretched. A negative, whining, small person. But he loved her father and respected her mother profoundly. He remembered feeling the closeness of the room, how the four of them crowded up, knees and shins against the bed, too formal, too stiff in one another's presence to sit on the bed.

Now it was the woman's turn. He waited, looking at her. He relaxed his face so as not to stare.

She had gone into a building, an enormous building, she remembered. They hadn't wanted to let her in. But she had had to get to her boyfriend, she said. Boyfriend was the word she used, but it hung between them like a note played wrong. She meant lover. Both of them knew that. She couldn't remember seeing the people who wanted to keep her out, but she was aware of them and how strongly they were set against her. She frowned, thinking.

Yes, the feel of the building, the hotel building, had been strong in his dream, too, and it seemed to him that after the small room he had been out in a vast atrium from which he could see the many levels of the hotel, and a tall isolated elevator structure that stood like a rectangular column some distance from the many layered balcony effect of the different floors. Maybe it had been a glass enclosed elevator that passengers could see out of, maybe not. He hadn't been in it, but the structure of the elevator and the solitude of it had seemed important to him.

Freudian, she thought, settling unhurried now into the silence.

"I wonder," she said, "what all this about buildings means. I don't feel like an architect who would know about the place I got into, but I do know I got past the people who wanted me to stay out, and after that I somehow got into a hallway. It was a long hallway. I knew there were many, many rooms. Not offices, but rooms of some kind off to both sides of me. I don't remember any doors actually, I just had this feeling that there were lots and lots of rooms on the sides of the hallway. And there were lights, I distinctly remember the lights, in the ceiling, leading away into the distance."

She turned quickly to the window, letting the looming trees pull her eyes away, then swung back to him, waiting.

Why all the rooms, he wondered.

"Then I was in the hotel room next door," he said out loud. "I don't know how I got there. My aunt and uncle, did I tell you that's who the girl's parents were? They had gone down. There was some to-do about them going down to the front desk and arranging for the room. It's as if I knew they had gone down there after they went and came back, and as if, at the same time, I had really seen them down there making the arrangements. Like I had known it and heard about it all at the same time."

She looked at him as if she were having a hard time following that part.

"You see," he said, "I knew they wanted a larger room for the party, or the reception, whatever it was, with space for people and food, finger food in little dishes all over the room. They wanted the wedding to go off right. There was a low sort of coffee table in the main part, and an alcove with a bar, where a man dressed in white could stand and serve, I don't know whether I actually saw him or whether I imagined what he would look like if he were there behind the bar. My uncle and aunt were definitely in the room, but I think the guests had not actually arrived, but I was imagining what it would look like later with them standing around talking and snacking. And I know my cousin-and-my-bride-to-be was really standing there, because I could feel her negative presence, radiating all that pessimism. You know I never did actually see her in front of me like I could see them. She was always behind and to the side of me, but I was aware of her being there and of this dark feeling that flowed out of her."

"Your cousin? You were going to marry your cousin?" It was the first comment either of them had made out loud about the other's dream.

"She's adopted. It would have been O.K. At least I think so. But what bothered me most, was I kept saying to myself this is the worst possible bride you could have picked. And kept wondering how I could get out of it without hurting my aunt and uncle. And those alarm bells I always hear when I get in trouble in my dreams started ringing. It's something that tells me it's a dream. I can wake up if I want to, I can stay and see how it comes out, but I don't have to get stuck in it. Sometimes it says 'Get me out, get me out.' Sometimes it says 'I'll change this and that, then I'll stick around a little longer. See what happens.' What happened in yours?"

"I saw him coming. Way down at the end of the hall. He was tiny at first. Lights were on him, and he saw me. I started running. He smiled, real big, and kept coming to me."

"Did you get to him?"

She didn't want to tell this part. She faltered. "No. No, I was almost about to, but I woke up. I don't know why I woke up. The train was going fast about then. Maybe it threw me against the wall. I know that kept happening all night. Did you go ahead and get married?"

"No, I bailed out." His dodge was deliberate.

"In your dream?"

He would be honest. "No, I bailed out. I pulled myself out of my own dream."

"Why?"

"I don't know, I couldn't stand getting stuck in it. Besides," he tried a grin, "I'm already married." The grin didn't work. It felt foolish on his face.

"Oh," she said, quietly. He thought about her profile in the window. He felt abruptly, with one of those startling convictions that always brought release, how fun it would be to go sightseeing in Vienna with someone. Someone to see Belvedere with, and Maria Teresa's Palace, and sit in a coffee shop and share exquisite little cakes, and sip long, lingering teas and look out the windows at the streets.

How to bring it up? He would be direct. "I've been thinking," he tried to speak softly, "that maybe I'll go on to Vienna after all."

There was a long silence, into which gradually the talk at the nearby tables began to seep, rising slowly like the deep warm tides of the Carolinas. She turned and gathered herself from gazing at the distant, flowing rooftops. The tide receded.

After a long, long time she said something.

"Funny. I was thinking of getting off in Prague."

THE GLASS EYED BOY

His father told his mother that a boy's tenth birthday ought to be a special day, something he would always remember. It was. Shortly after he unwrapped his new BB gun, Bobby Lee Claypoole shot out his own left eye.

"You never seen the like a' blood," Bobby's father told the other truck drivers over at the feed mill next day. "Run right down his face. Ruin't his Sunday clothes. Who'd a thought they'd be so much blood come out of one little kid's eye?"

He said it with more than a little pride. "Damn kid brother come in a throwin' up. The way his sister taken on you'd a thought somebody'd done died."

It took a while before his glass eye came. The first few days Bobby Lee had a white bandage taped to his face. After that, till the new eye came, he wore a black patch like a pirate. The girls down at the school said "Oooh, don't it hurt?" The boys shrugged and said, "Guess you can't shoot no more." And Bobby Lee was afraid at first that his dad wouldn't let him, but as Mr. Claypoole told Mrs. Claypoole, "Hell, I figure the boy's done learnt his lesson, Hon."

Indeed Bobby Lee had learned his lesson. He did not shoot out his other eye. He tried some shooting a little bit each day. His father gave him change to buy bags of BB's till he got to be a pretty good shot. Not fast but pretty fair with a target. At least he could shoot. He'd been afraid he couldn't but it turned out he could. And that was okay. Besides, it was not what he feared the most.

In time the new eye came. The color didn't match his good eye as much as he'd hoped. The girls looked at him, running their eyes back and forth in that

- 47 -

searching way girls have of looking at your face. They asked him, "Can you take it out?" He showed how it came out and offered to let them hold it. They all said, "Eeyeeww wee!" And backed away.

None of them but Buckle Ann Dougherty ever took his glass eye in her hand. "Felt real funny," was all she told them afterwards. He didn't look too scary in the mirror was what he told himself, which didn't matter a whole lot. It was not, after all, what he feared the most.

Bobby Lee took up hunting when he turned twelve. His father gave him a Remington 22 rifle. He moved up from blue jays in the summer and chickadees in the winter to rabbits and squirrels year round. He tried his hand at baseball in hot weather and was a fair player but not a first pick. Turned out he was better at basketball, when cold weather sent everybody indoors. Short and on the stocky side but fast, not a high scorer but often as not in the starting five. Couple of times the refs blew time out while everybody searched for his eye but it didn't happen so much they had to kick him off the team and he was satisfied. Anyway it wasn't what he feared the most.

In his teens Bobby Lee dated a lot. Girls were fascinated by his eye. They looked at him in that scanning way and said things like, "Your eyes are different." Then when they found out about his glass eye, they'd say "Unhhhh, uh," and then they'd sigh and ask him all about it. The group dates started off with church outings and with picking up corn left by the harvesters, and there were unsanctioned outings like skinny dipping in the quarry. He was lucky the swimming parties were at night because he had to take his eye out to go underwater.

Buckle Ann was his first single date and, after he had fumbled and wrestled with a whole slew of other girls, the first to see no harm in going all the way. After that he might have gotten turned down just any number of times, but it didn't happen. If it had he would have gone on just the same, because it was not really what he feared the most.

In his senior year Bobby Lee worried that he might not make it into college, and his worries were justified. He wound up staying home. The summer after graduation Bobby Lee and his best friend Johnny Mack Huddleston got into a fight with a pint of Old Crow between them. They were down behind Goldnamer's Five-and-Dime over in Dawson. Bobby Lee cut Johnny Mack's left ear half off and was getting ready to slice him up with the broken off whiskey bottle when the sheriff came around the building with his pistol in his hand and hollered at Bobby Lee, "Best you let go a' him, Bobby Lee Claypoole. If you don't they'll be carrying you home in buckets, time I'm finished with you."

Hopkins County was dry and the town of Dawson had a reputation for being hard on drunks. But Mrs. Claypoole had relatives in Dawson and, come sentencing time, the judge commenced to talking about how a poor one-eyed boy's got a hard lot in life. He said how a kid like Bobby Lee ought not to be put in jail and sent him instead to a work release program over near home.

Two years later Bobby Lee's luck played out. There was no judge to argue his affliction when he got into it with two guys, a fancy pool player from Louisville and the big guy that traveled with him. Bobby Lee was never much good at pool. His close vision was bad, what with him only seeing by one eye. Still, he thought he was winning till the game got out of hand.

When the big guy's fist hit him in the stomach his glass eye popped out. He was on the floor half trying to feel around for his glass eye and half trying to pull the big man down when the other guy come up with the cue stick and slammed him in the Adam's apple. He died right there.

His father told his mother at the funeral, "Bobby Lee weren't a feared to die. He lived hard. I s'pect that glass eye's what done it. Makin' ever'thing hard on him that a way. Wish't I'd never laid eyes on the damn BB gun." She squeezed his arm and they comforted one another like that all the way to the cemetery. Later on they moved away and took the two younger children with them.

No one but the undertaker knew they buried Bobby Lee without his glass eye, only a wad of cotton under the eyelid. A couple of days later the pool hall owner found the eye back of the wood stove, scratched up and more grey looking than blue. He kept it in the back of the cash register till he sold the place. When the new owner saw the eye, by then it was scarred pretty bad all over. He thought at first it'd make a good china egg for his bantie hens. Then he decided it was too big and threw it in the trash. Besides, it was the wrong shape for an egg.

When she'd been a grandmother several years her husband asked Buckle Ann, who by then was going by Becky Anne, didn't she used to date a glass-eyed boy and what was his name. She looked at him in genuine surprise. "Why, I can't for the life of me remember!"

Neither, as it turned out, could any of her former classmates who now played bridge with her. "I can't believe I'd a forgot a thing like that. I can still see him. All that curly blonde hair." "No, it was a crewcut," someone else said. "That glass eye … you remember how it was the wrong shade of blue for his other eye?" Another said, "No, both his eyes was brown. He was a brown eyed boy." Truth to tell they'd all forgotten him, and it was too bad, because that was the thing he had feared the most.

GLASS LOCOMOTIVE

You can see clearly. She tells you it will break. She does not tell you it is too expensive—in this memory of your grandmother—but it must have been.

It is hot, so hot. Finally, magically she places the glass locomotive in your hand. It is a marvelous thing. It is so beautiful that sixty years later you can see it yet.

The floors of the train station are made of polished marble. There are lines painted and people walk inside or outside the lines and follow them here and there, dragging their suitcases behind them, carrying brown paper sacks of food.

After sixty years you do not know how long your sweating fingers admired the locomotive.

It did. It fell. It smashed. Candy everywhere, candy rolled under the oak benches. And glass. Tiny thick pieces of broken glass.

ROLL CALL

Miss Green was our first grade teacher. At least that's the way we would have spelled the honorific in those days, although we pronounced it Miz Green, like in the Uncle Remus books. If we could have spelled in first grade we would have written Miss Green, because that is what we thought our parents were saying, though they would probably have written Mrs. Green. From personal knowledge. Just the same, they would have pronounced it Miz Green, just the way we did.

This was at East Side Elementary School, in Princeton, Kentucky. The building stands derelict today. They've left it unrazed, intending no doubt to cast it in bronze someday as a memorial to us who went there.

Miss Green sat at the back of our class and we all faced forward so she could see the backs of our heads. On the second day of school I was allowed to take two shiny dimes and to go over to the creamery and buy a milkshake for lunch. It was a thrilling experience that never was to be repeated, because somehow the lunchroom opened at school and I began to eat there.

Once a friend shared a recess treat with me and I must have reported it at home because the next day I was sent to school with a brown paper sack containing apples cut into quarters with instructions to repay the kindness. The original treat must have been something store-bought, like a candy bar or something that came in a box, and I may have felt that what I had to offer would not measure up because at recess I could not find my benefactor. Fortunately there was a little blond haired girl who went to our church that helped me out of my predicament. We stood upon what we thought was the huge wooden platform from which the three metal runners of our slide protruded and consumed all the apple slices which I do not remember having turned brown. Maybe apples didn't in those days. Lots of things that wear the look of old and worn and run down now were bright and bold and wondrous then.

We were given a Scottie to color, with a plaid scrap of a blanket on his back. I colored mine purple with a green blanket, and thought it looked quite nice, not as nice, you understand, as the girls had done, with the curls and whiskers of the dog accented in dark brown, with light browns and blacks spread lightly and evenly in between, but nice just the same. Miss Green pointed out in a low voice so none of the other children would hear that dogs aren't purple. Well, I hadn't thought of that, and I knew she was right about dogs in general, and, I supposed, being a teacher she was right about Scotties too, but I felt I had to defend what I had done—I was less tractable in those early days. "But it's not a real dog," I whispered back. What she said next I don't remember, probably I was too embarrassed by my boldness to listen.

I believe the lunches were twelve cents then. We carried the coins in our pockets, and at lunch time lined up and followed Miss Green down to the basement where we flattened our small selves against the walls of an enormous hallway and watched the huge bold fourth graders and older children push past us.

There came a day when it was very important to me to acquire a paste pot. It must have taken some persuading to get my mother to buy it for me. I remember it came in a fat round jar and was all deliciously white and smelled heavenly, plus there was a broad flat wooden stick that came with it, officially, I suppose, and I carried it in a brown paper sack all by itself, the mile and a half or so we used to walk to school at that time. Distracted, probably, by the awesomeness of what I carried and likely daydreaming a little bit of the dashing impression I and my new paste pot would make on my first grade class, especially my friends a fat boy with black hair and freckles, a boy named Mike Boitnott who I thought had the world's most exotic last name, and the blond haired girl, I came in late, and was devastated. There was a girl, some strange girl, a girl I had never seen, sitting in my seat, sitting at my desk. I don't remember that I ever looked at her face, maybe not for the whole rest of the year. But it wasn't the girl I was thinking about. It was my paste pot, and I couldn't believe Miss Green had done this to me, had let this happen to me. Me the boy with the purple Scottie and now the fresh new paste pot.

I don't remember what happened about the desk and the paste pot. I just remember standing in the front of the class, so far from Miss Green's desk in the back of the room, helpless and paralyzed and wishing I were somewhere else or dead.

That was the first year we had photographs made. I wish now there had been a class picture with Miss Green whom I'm sure I loved, and all the other children. What there was, and I knew where it was for a few years but I don't now, was a single photograph of me. I believe it said East Side School and gave the year. I was leaning slightly to the side and there was a flaw in the image. The flaw took the shape of a white cloud with two tails, and my great aunt who was a saint, if Protestant churches had saints, told me that was my soul and what she said reconciled me to the strange composition.

*   *   *   *

In second grade our teacher was Miss Lester. I am told every little boy falls in love with his second grade teacher, and I suppose it was true of me also. I do know she treated me very well, and I'm sure I thought I was a pet of hers. I remember that one day when I was about in the fifth or sixth grade I had gone back to Princeton where my great aunt was a seamstress, and Miss Lester came in for a fitting. She didn't know me from Adam. I loved her too much to hold that against her, but it was not until my twenty-fifth class reunion that I learned from a priest, also a former teacher, who had known us in early pre-adulthood and who might have been presumed to recognize us in later years, that there are so many young faces going through so very many changes, that they can not reasonably be expected to recognize us. They have not, however, forgotten us. We must tell them our names and then they remember the child. I must stop now for I am tear-ing in a most unmanly fashion.

THE HUMILIATION
OF JOAQUIM
HEFFELSTADTER

I came into this world on the twenty-ninth of February, which was a great inconvenience to my two brothers and my sister who had hoped to be otherwise occupied on that particular night, in a year when Prohibition was winding down and the Great Depression was cranking up.

Brother Tom had expected to be in Brooklyn riding with a friend in a Model A. Jesse was supposed to meet two girls and a fellow named Mattie at a speakeasy. Florence had finally gotten the man of her dreams to promise to take her to a cinema and she was working on a campaign strategy to deal with the territorial scouting expeditions she expected from him.

They were all disappointed. Mother believed in neither hospitals nor midwives and, able general that she was, assigned them each such a uniquely disagreeable responsibility in connection with my arrival that they made it the keystone of their complaints about me all the rest of their lives. I am fortunate that I have outlived them all and no longer have to listen.

Tom wanted to be an auto mechanic or a race car driver or at least a chauffeur to some Manhattan Brahmin. He would have met a famous actress or singer and lived a life in the public eye. As it was he took up accounting, then banking, moved to the Midwest, rose to become a bank president and died husband to a farmer's daughter, father to five chubby blond storekeepers and silent partner in a chain of adult video stores. Tom often told me that if I hadn't ruined his big chance with cars he would have been a different man. His children were nearer my age than he was but he would never let me visit them. He said he didn't want them dragged down to my level.

Jesse, being the most congenial of my siblings and the family's practical joker, connected up with his Model A friends after all. He went on to marry both girls, one at a time, with a marriage to a third girl, whose name was Sofia, in between. Jesse was talented in marrying. He did it well and often. I was the only one of us who made it to his funeral.

There were six of his wives there and twenty-odd stepchildren. Jesse never claimed any children of his own. I think he had some children with women out of marriage but being married seemed to discourage his dynastic impulses. Jesse quit school in his senior year and took up bartending, for which he was particularly well suited. He eventually opened his own place out on Long Island. There was never a more popular bar in all of Hempstead. He added a restaurant which earned him more money than he could spend, put on a lot of weight and died of emphysema.

Except for nominal sums to his wives, all of whom survived him, he left everything he had to me. Hardly a day goes by that one of them doesn't call me with some new reason why they should have gotten more money or some new discovery about how unbelievably selfish and miserly I am. How can I be so unlike my brother? I am not surprised. Where he was of middle height, fair and good looking I am gaunt, knobby, dark haired where I have any hair, and oddly potbellied for a skinny guy. Worst of all I am stupid where he was bright, slow where he was witty, and no kind of fun to be with. What is worse in their eyes, I do not understand the terms of the estate trust that he set up. I cannot explain why I am not allowed to give any of the money to his spouses or their offspring.

Flo, the only girl, was undeniably Mother's favorite. Together they designed clothes, drawing color sketches of ensembles they thought would look especially enchanting on Florence's precocious frame. She was an exceptional woman, my sister, and always looked good. She was red headed and fair skinned, without freckles, a coloration more like Dad's cousin-by-marriage Blake's than either of my parents'. Dad had a Teutonic look with blond, tightly curled hair. Mother was classically Italian. Flo inherited her nose.

Mother and Florence despised me, Florence because she had the day-to-day feeding and changing of me, and Mother because I came at a time of great inconvenience to her, just when she should have been able to call her days her own. Tom, Jesse and Flo were all in high school when I was born and it was time for

Mother to hold teas and visit with her friends. Not that my needs caused her to stay home. She turned everything about me over to Flo. It was just that she could not stand other women criticizing her for being out when she should have been home. I stole her best years, her society years. I had no right to be born. I was inflicted upon her because I was the product of an immaculate conception. Mother told me so and I believe her to this day, because my one and only child was also immaculately conceived.

Editor's note: the alert reader more closely attuned to theology than Heffelstadter will realize he is talking not about immaculate conception here but about virgin birth. Joaquim was not especially church minded. His religious upbringing, given his family circumstances, was pretty much hit or miss.

That I was immaculately conceived was obvious to everyone. I look no more like my father than Florence did. If anything I look more like another of Dad's cousins by marriage, the one we called Uncle Victor. Victor was half Italian and half Irish. He was thin and cranky, his chin prominent and bristly, all traits I share. He never laughed but he had gray eyes like mine that were deep set and thoughtful, with scraggy eyebrows. Mother claimed he was poetical. If so I never saw anything he wrote. He came around from time to time looking rumpled and neglected. Mother had a way with people. She was kind to eccentrics, all but me, and he always looked cleaner and better pressed when he left.

Mother had a big family, counting in-laws. With Dad on the road so much she got awfully lonely. The sight of me hanging around depressed her so that I used to stay in the boys' attic room just to avoid giving her pain. She liked to have men folk around. They laughed loud and stayed long when they dropped by. I wanted to spend time with them because they made a big fuss over me and sometimes brought me presents but she would send me upstairs. After the uncles left my presents would already be in the trash bin when I came down.

Much as Mother disliked me, Flo hated me even more. There was no embarrassment she would spare me. She would make child size versions of the outfits she and Mother designed and dress me up in them for Tom and Jesse to make fun of. A willow tree grew down at the end of our yard. She would cut a limb from it to switch my legs if I dared to complain. She would switch harder if I cried. Mother said I brought it all on myself for trying Flo's patience, why couldn't I try to be agreeable?

I did not do well in school and several times I tried to run away. Mother never came to look for me. When I came back she'd say: "Don't carry on so, I knew you'd be back when you got hungry."

The times I was gone overnight it was Tom or Jesse who found me. I'd usually make it as far as the ash piles down by the railroad yards where I'd get soot and cinders all over me. At first I'd be happy. Then I'd get hungry and try to lie still till I died. Tom or Jesse would come and I'd dread being toted home again. Then Mother would leave the room and Flo would take up her willow switch and she'd light into me till the blood came.

The last time I ran away I got way yonder further and they never found me. I found them after I'd grown up and married, but none of them was pleased about it. I wished then I had just let it go. Probably the only good that came of it for me was Jesse's leaving me his money but by then I wasn't needing it.

I tried this and that to live on between when I was a runaway kid and when I was a grown man. Most of it was honest. The best I ever did was learn from a drugstore man how to make up a home remedy medicine and sell it. That's what I got by on. By accident I learned you could cure just about any skin condition with aloe. Aloe was easy to grow and you could re-pot it and grow more. I mixed the juice with water and a skinch of pepper vinegar for taste and sold it door to door. I was still doing that when I met my wife.

She was probably the best thing ever happened to me. She pushed me till I was making dozens of bottles at a time and she got them into stores near us, first through farmers' markets then through variety stores. We never went national, or even statewide, but we made enough to get out of the trailer after ten years and into a real brick house. We were living in the brick house when my beautiful baby boy was born, the most beautiful thing I'd ever seen. I still feel that way.

Like mine, his was an immaculate conception. How do I know? My wife and I were never intimate the way you'd be to have a child, that's how. Plus his coming brought us more happiness than we'd ever known up till then. Connie, who was never what you'd call a jolly woman, was all happy over it. She began to sing little songs and smiled a lot when my friend Seth was visiting. I met him when I was first a runaway and living on the road. I knew his visit would be good for us. Seth always had a way with women and, sure enough, in a few weeks Connie began to soften up. She laughed at his jokes. With me, where she'd never really been demonstrative before, she took to putting her arm around me sometimes and giving me a quick kiss on the cheek.

I admit she got a little solemn at first after Seth went away, but after we got a card from him saying he'd drop in on us when he was back this way Connie perked up again and started singing under her breath. A few months later along came little Adam. Seth never did come back.

Connie chose the name Adam because it was Seth's brother's name in the bible and she thought Adam reminded her of Seth. He does look a lot like Seth. Same blocky build, eyebrows meeting in the middle, no ear lobes, just like Seth. He was a darling child and he's grown up a fine man. It was because of him that I met Jennifer.

Fancy people are a cut above me. My customers were home people and stores where you didn't go in the front. With my customers I go to the back door. If I'm lucky they let me in. Jenny came out my customer's backdoor one day when I was making a delivery. Adam was with me. He was about ten years old and Jenny made a big fuss over him.

She had bright brown eyes like buttons, with perky black eyebrows and a sassy page boy haircut like a cover girl starlet. Her little girl was inside, she said, and would we wait because she wanted to bring her out to meet Adam? I couldn't think of any way to get out of it. I am not much for meeting people. I didn't know many friends of Adam's and certainly none of their parents. I was in a marginally respectable business and, since Adam had come along late, I was older than his friends' parents. So I came out from the alley into the sunshine, and stood holding Adam's hand, thinking about my next delivery.

Jenny's daughter was about two years old, skinny and shaky in shorts and a shirt, holding onto her mother's hand and walking shyly toward us with an open smile and only half a set of teeth. Long fat curls made her look top heavy. She squeaked when she yelled: "See ... Adam. See ... Adam."

"Isn't she darling?" Jenny asked.

In a way she was but, compared to her mother, a little pathetic, which I should not have noticed.

"Adam, this is Melanie," Jenny said. "Shake hands with Melanie." Adam's hand was short and stubby but it swallowed up Melanie's little fingers.

Jenny went on with a lot of mushy kid talk for a while, trying to raise up an interest between the two kids that neither of them would have felt naturally. Then she looked at me over Melanie's head. "Why don't we have a picnic where the children can visit? It's Melanie's lunch time."

"We got to get our deliveries out."

"Oh, don't rush these children," she pouted. "Adam's hungry, aren't you, Adam?"

I didn't think he was, but Adam said yes just to be polite.

"Now all we've got is apples and cheese crackers, but we've got plenty to share."

"Don't make a fuss over us," I said. I knew Adam was not crazy about apples and cheese crackers.

"Melanie really likes hamburgers and French fries, don't you sweetheart? But we're making do right now." She hovered over her daughter again, with a kind of sorrowful sound in her voice that cut me a little.

"If Melanie wants a hamburger, Adam and I can take you to the Little Castle," I heard myself saying. I wondered where that thought came from.

I'm going to skip the part about how Jenny said yes and we drove to the Little Castle, sitting three across in my truck, with Melanie in her mother's lap. We heard a lot about how tough it is to be a single mother while Melanie nibbled about half her hamburger. Jenny ate her own hamburger, the other half of her daughter's and both their French fries, plus a strawberry milkshake. Melanie sipped a little milk. The mostly full glass was still sitting there when we left.

I learned what it's like to be married twice before you're twenty-five years old and to have a daughter by another man who then wouldn't marry you. The worst part was hearing about being attacked by a father and an uncle as a teenager, things a man like me would rather not hear from the girl herself. It was more natural to hear that kind of stuff from my wife who would had heard it from a friend. We would have been scandalized together and glad it didn't happen to anyone we knew. Here I was hearing it close up and in the flesh. Everyone sitting around us probably heard it too. Then how hard it was to get by on babysitting jobs and looking after other people's children. Did we need someone to help with Adam?

When we finished our meal I paid the check. I asked would she let me give her fifty dollars. Not charity, which she was against, but for something that Melanie, such a beautiful child, might like to have.

Women have this way of asking personal questions just to be talking, even inexperienced young women like Jennifer with nothing to gain by it. Was remedies what I sold for a living? Was Adam my only child? Did we live in town? Whereabouts? What a coincidence, that was only around the corner from Melanie's babysitter! Did my wife work? Would it be any old trouble at all ... she knew it was out of our way, but we'd had such a good time and all ... if we gave her and Melanie a lift home? Wouldn't the children enjoy spending a little more time together?

I didn't see that Adam at his age would have much in common with a kid practically a toddler, but he said "I don't mind, Dad," and we gave them a lift home. Turned out they lived in a trailer park in a two-toned charcoal grey and pink trailer like a DeSoto with a living room at one end and a bedroom at the other—Adam and I didn't need to see the bedroom but Jenny would love to show us around—and a little bathroom opposite a shallow closet with bamboo sliding doors. The kitchen was part of the living room, the corner next to the bathroom. Couldn't she just fix me some coffee?

"We're already behind on our deliveries."

"But you have just been so nice. We'd love to show our appreciation. Really just anything I could do for you? Really, just anything.

I left with the funny sound of that word "anything" circling around my head. It sounded like a word that meant more than it was supposed to. I wondered, while we worked that afternoon and I couldn't shake it out of my head, what "anything" meant. After that I wondered about myself and why I was thinking about that word so much. Then it wasn't so much Jenny, her face or her build that I saw but orange and pink shapes without any recognizable form but lots of arms, and a hot, damp cuddly feeling. The sound of the word "anything" and the shape of her mouth as she said it were on my mind when we got home. The garage door opening made me think of the way her lips had thinned and stretched wide over her teeth as she stressed the word and drew it out.

I needed to forget about Jenny. I was glad when we got inside where my wife could holler about how late we were and how we never thought for a minute about her. Why weren't we ever the least bit considerate? People ought to be more considerate of other people, especially those who were always sacrificing for them. Just look at Adam. How was he going to grow up with no better example than a father like me that needed somebody after him all the time just so he would have enough get up and go to keep a roof over our heads and what precious little else we had to say grace over.

Connie had a way about her, when she had her piece to say, of pulling up her eyebrows like hinges holding a gate and making a face like a bad taste in her mouth. It was always better not to look straight at her at such times and neither Adam nor I could. We'd go ahead and clean up.

"Yes, ma'am," Adam said.

"I know," I said.

Supper was not ready. Didn't matter when we got home. Supper was never ready but my wife needed somebody to talk at and Adam and I had learned to sit and listen. There were things the paper boy had done wrong about where the paper had landed on the porch and slid off. Why did he have to fold it square and all boxy, when rolled up like the Courier-Journal boy's would be just fine? Why was it when the grocery boy came all he did was dump it on the table and run? Didn't anybody take the time to be civil anymore?

Just like you, Adam. You were raised to be polite, and what good did it do? Look at you.

I looked at Adam. He looked O.K. to me, maybe a little skinnier than he ought to be, but nothing else was wrong. He reminded me of Seth and I liked Seth.

Ours is a small town and my truck was brand new and came in a Chinese red that my wife had picked out because it would be good for business. We had white and yellow lettering on the side, so we must have been easy to spot. I should not have been surprised next day that somebody was agitated and waving from the sidewalk with a little sprite of a girl hopping up and down beside her. Jennifer.

Melanie were so tired. Would it be too, too much trouble for us to give them a ride home? They were in no hurry at all and they would just ride along quietly with us till we got over their way even if it was really late in the evening. They would be so quiet and no trouble at all. By that time Jennifer was in the truck. She sat by the window holding Melanie in her lap and, though she was on the other side of cab, she managed to touch me lightly on the arm as she leaned around Adam and widened her soft brown eyes at me.

When we got to her trailer couldn't we just stay long enough to have some Kool-Aid? It was all in the world that they had to give us what with the electric bills so high and Melanie just having to have air conditioning for her asthma. Couldn't Adam play outside with Melanie just for a few minutes while we visited? There was no time for visiting. Adam knew we didn't tarry when we made our rounds. That was my rule so I knew it too. I did find fifty dollars in my billfold that I could spare. "For little Melanie," I said. Jennifer brought up that "anything" business again, with the same way of working her lips and jaw. I came away remembering how her eyes had moved around my face and how small and vulnerable she seemed.

The first fifty dollars had disappeared from my billfold without causing a scene but now the total came to one hundred dollars which was a lot of money for us. We had to hold off on something, I forget what, maybe back-to-school clothes for Adam, I don't remember, but Connie noticed it and was not happy. If business was off—which was my excuse, I didn't know why I was holding back on her but I didn't want to bring up about Jennifer and Melanie—then why wasn't I out and doing something about it rather than sitting around with my feet up and the T.V. on?

She was right. I did my best sleeping in front of the TV. Connie and I had twin beds and often at night, rather than disturb her, I'd turn on the TV. I'd wake up with snow on the screen when the channel went off and the sound of static jumped out. Sometimes that's the way she'd find me in the mornings if I couldn't muster the energy to walk over and turn it off. I honestly tried to sleep in my own bed but sometimes her grinding on her teeth the way she did would addle me to where I couldn't stand to be in the same room.

I wondered why there was only one bed in Jennifer's trailer and where Melanie slept.

I found the answer to that before I knew I wanted to know. We were all in the truck again and somehow in the tangle of getting in from where we'd run into each other in a parking lot Jenny had wound up in the middle with Adam next to the window and Melanie riding in his lap. "It'll be just fine," Jenny said, "You won't get fresh with Melanie, will you Adam?" Adam was looking out the window and probably hadn't heard. I blushed for him.

I honestly don't remember what started it, but I became aware that Jenny was talking about how she kept Melanie with her everywhere she went, even sleeping in her bed, how Melanie kept her warm at night. She never enjoyed sleeping by herself anyway. It was especially bad after Melanie's dad left, before Melanie had been born. She'd been so alone in that big bed all by herself.

It didn't look all that big to me.

And here Melanie was, two years old, keeping her company. The only thing was, she hadn't really felt like a real woman again since Melanie was born. It hadn't mattered so much right at first, but now she wished she could feel that way again, did I know what she meant? At first I didn't but I said oh yes, anyway, the way you do to keep a conversation going. She looked at me with those move-around eyes, like we shared something that nobody else knew. Which was silly because the only other people around were Adam and Melanie, aged 10 and 2 respectively, who I hoped hadn't caught on because that was when I figured out what she meant and felt foolish for being so slow to catch on.

I told myself that, whoever she might be missing, it was not me. Afterwards the "anything" picture of her mouth and lips crowded it out.

I decided that Adam's helping me on my deliveries was taking away from his school work. The next time I gave Jennifer and Melanie a ride home Adam was working out arithmetic problems on the kitchen table at home, while his mother dusted or watched TV or whatever she did in the afternoons. This time Melanie needed a nap even though it was the same time as usual and she hadn't needed a nap before, but this time she did. She rooted around crankily on the couch a while, and Jennifer said why don't we talk in the other room, which I knew was the bedroom. The only place we could sit was on the bed and she was so tired from all the walking she could just stretch right out. And, despite how weary she must have been, it turned out she really had meant "anything."

A grumpy, tearful Melanie awoke and came whimpering to the door. I hoped there was something in my billfold that might help, something that I could do for Melanie. All I had was thirty-three dollars. Jenny said oh, I shouldn't feel like I had to do that. She felt better about it after I told her it was not in any way something for her, just something I wanted to do for Melanie's sake.

By the time the kids were out of school for Thanksgiving I was over a thousand dollars short. Connie took to going around the house red faced and puffy eyed. What were we going to do? Where was all our money going? What happened to all our customers? Now it wasn't so much the teeth grinding at night as the tossing in bed that drove me down to the TV.

Wednesday afternoon I came home early. I had run out of remedy and Jenny had not turned up in the Kresge's lot where I usually saw her. I was thinking of getting in some wood this evening, so I wouldn't have to get up Thanksgiving morning till late. I had been feeling unexpectedly good lately. Physically, I mean. My conscience was giving me fits, but I was used to things not going well for me anyway and I thought I could bear up. Jenny had said "anything" again last time I saw her and I guess I was wondering what there was left for the word to mean when I came in the kitchen door and saw Connie at the table, tipped back in her wooden chair, holding the phone in her lap.

I smiled at her, still feeling good. I got a welcoming frown.

"You remember Jennifer Wiskoff?" The way she sounded the last name it sounded like wish cup.

"Yeah." You shouldn't lie. Pretty soon you forget who you lied to and what you told them and then they find you out. "Adam and I gave her and her daughter a lift."

"Yeah, I know." Her mouth got long and I flinched, because I honestly didn't have any idea what to say.

"Adam told you?"

"Boy, you're lucky you're who you are. Not nobody else."

"Why?"

"That was Mary Grace Bumpers on the phone. The last two months …"

She was talking about my months, the best I'd ever had, my brief afternoons with the blinds drawn and a two year old little girl sleeping on the couch in the next room.

"… this Jennifer Wiskoff woman has been sleeping with two men at the same time."

"Two men?"

"Boy, that woman is something. Taken 'em for all they're worth. One of them a Baptist preacher. Seventh Street Baptist Tabernacle. Both of them married men. Don't know what they thought they were doing. You want to guess who the other one was?"

I could feel the hot blood rising up out of my neck. My ears started to ring.

"One of your customers! If you pulled something like that I'd have you arrested."

Now it was my knees. Fluttery, like bubbles in a Christmas light.

"Man that run the Kresge's store. Him it was, noontimes, in his office, with that little girl running wild all over the store. Baptist preacher of a night. Lord, that woman. It's a wonder she didn't take up with somebody else in the afternoons!"

THE COMMAND TO SEE

It's hard to resist a royal command. Most of us are not self starters. If we are going to succeed, the majority of us must set aside all this nonsense about self-motivation and personal challenge, because we haven't the drive nor the energy to succeed without someone cracking the whip over us. In short what most of us need if we are all to achieve what the rarest of us achieve, is a bully lurking behind us, a slave driver hovering over us—we need to be given a royal command.

It is certain, for example, that I—for one—would never have succeeded in my life's work if I had not been driven to it.

Oh? I thought you knew. I imagine all the places that don't exist. That's what I do for a living.

THE INDIAN
WOMAN'S PLACE

Four years after he left, Ormand Benninger returned to Rio. The same woman was sitting in his doorway. She sat on the same mat as before. Hers he assumed. Her knees were drawn up, her ankles tucked away and invisible under her skirt. This time instead of two children occupying the mat with her there were now three.

Her face had the look of the many displaced Indian tribes of the interior—prominent cheekbones, dark skin, deep brown eyes that could have been black. Her hair was black and unadorned. There was a smell about her, but it was not the smell of destitution, nor of filth. Nor was it yet a smell of small children, at least one of which should have been in diapers. He wondered idly what the homeless used for diapers.

Yet she was not homeless. His doorstep was her home. Even with her family of three there was some space unoccupied on the mat which was not a mat at all, nor yet a blanket, but something grey and cloth-like, spread over his doorstep. It almost covered his doorstep, but not all of it. There was room for him to pass by, a foot or so of exposed concrete step. Somehow, four years ago, the furniture movers had gone in and out by that doorway and somehow there had been room for them to pass and for the woman to remain, only then there had been just the two children. Would there be room now to move the furniture out and leave the family undisturbed?

The children were quiet, just as he remembered. The two that were old enough to move about independently crawled from one side of the mat to the other, or stood up and walked a few steps then sat down. But quietly, always quietly, as if talking, or singing, or whining or crying were all forbidden. No, not forbidden, because something that is forbidden can still be done. One could, for example commit murder. There were consequences, but even the forbidden was possible. Here he was dealing with a case of what was apparently impossible. It did not seem to be within their powers to make noise of any sort.

In the earlier months of his occupancy he had thought of this fatherless family as squatters. Were they not after all occupying his front doorstep? Was it not his home that was being invaded? Had they not taken something that was not theirs? Something that was his and was being taken away?

The landlord pointed out that they were not really in his house, not really. They were outside. They were really on the street. In fact they were street people. Well why, then, didn't they go back to the favellas? The favellas, Senor? But they do not live in the favellas. They live in the streets. People in the favellas have houses, Senor. True, some of their houses are nothing but cardboard boxes and there are no toilets, except the roads, but at least they have houses of their own.

He thought about the toilets and for almost a week he found himself obsessed by the toilet idea. Where did they go to do their … what people had to do? In those first few weeks he had more free time and he spent a great deal of it during the early days of his tenancy looking out the window hoping, well, not hoping exactly, but trying, yes, trying to catch them at it.

At first it was trying to catch them, like culprits, sneaking about to do something they shouldn't be doing. Then it was different. Then it was trying to make sure, for their sakes, for the sake of their health, that they were doing something that truly needed to be done. But it was not done, not that he saw. My god. they never defecated!

But maybe they never ate. He watched for signs of their eating. There were, he had observed early on, nothing that looked like the remains of a meal. No crumbs, for example. No streaks of grease from a chicken leg.

There was no evidence of food, yet the other signs of food were all abut them. After all, this was Brazil, the most cosmopolitan country in the whole world. Not cosmopolitan in the sense of worldliness and wittiness but in the sense of having everything from all cultures, and keeping them, alive, distinct, vigorous, in bold bright colors.

And smells. The street in front of his doorway was alive with smells, the smells of a thousand meals cooking, of restaurants of every possibility and ethnicity and all measures of seasonings. All this food and none consumed by the family on his doorstep, them and their dark grey mat on his doorstep.

But while it might be accurate to say that the family never appeared to eat, the family as a whole, he had once or twice seen the littlest ones eating, what he thought were ... Chiclets. Chiclets, little pillow shaped squares of sugar and, well, sugar. Chiclets sometimes appeared on the mats of other street people, but those Chiclets were for sale. You bought the Chiclets, you went away.

He made up his mind to confront the landlord once and for all. Why can't they go away like other people, he asked. But Senor, other people have places to live. This woman and her family are street people. The street people have no place to live except where they are. They are people of the streets. That is where they live.

But why my place? Why not the doorway next to mine? But Senor that is the doorway to a store. There are people going in and out all day long. It would be difficult. He tried that for a while. He tried going in and out all day long. The woman never looked at him. Sometimes the children did. But after a day, and maybe fifty trips in and out he gave it up. It seemed to inconvenience the family.

CREATIVITY

Creativity is a pot that we dip into.
Sometimes we dip deeper.
Sometimes we dip longer.
Sometimes we get it all over us.

KING OF A SMALL MOUNTAIN

It was a whole day before anybody realized my late husband was missing. And it took two full days for them to find him. He had been living in a trailer at the time. You want to know why, if Pete had the reputation he had, nobody was living there with him? Well, I'm not saying nobody was living with him, I'm just saying that nobody else was there at the time.

Everybody knows it was me he depended on and me he could always come back to but those were bad days for Peter McKinnon Tally. Even so, it'd be odd if nobody was living there with him when he disappeared. There were some he lived with that I knew by name and some I knew by face so I guess there was another bunch, too, a bunch nobody told me about. I'm old fashioned and I come from the South where respectable people don't talk about certain things.

But here's my point. He was my husband. My legal husband, if not my husband in the church, and I have the right to say what I am about to say.

I know about men. I was the only girl in a family of five brothers. My father came from the country and he believed that men were to be waited on. My mother believed that way too. I ironed shirts from the time I was old enough to see over the ironing board. My mother had supper on the table when my father came home from the boatyard where he was a welder, and I did the dishes. Those boys never lifted a finger to help. As far as I remember I didn't resent them not helping because it was natural, and you don't resent what's natural.

We were raised religious. Fact is my brother Donny went off to be a Christian Brother, you know, where they teach school and make wine? That's important, the part I mean about Donny, not the other, because I think it was because of Donny that I first learned something about Pete that's part of the reason they found his body in the woods, but I'm getting ahead of myself.

Our baby brother is named Jamie. He is the youngest of us Hendricks, and although I was second oldest and the first one to marry, he was the first of the brothers to get married after me. Are you following this? It's very important, as I'll explain to you in a minute.

I was out of high school and doing my running around, trying my best to imitate the wild life, when I met Pete. He was oily, but I was always attracted to oily men. There is something wicked about oily men, like you're doing something naughty letting them talk to you and get all over you.

Peter McKinnon Tally was not a handsome man, not like Cary Grant or Rock Hudson. He was stocky and crude, a kind of Edward G. Robinson looking guy. Fact is he looked real pretty lying there in his coffin, the prettiest I ever saw him, but he didn't look natural, the way they had to comb his hair down over his forehead. He had a nice forehead. After we had made love I would lie there and let my hand play over his head while I looked at him and I remember how I loved to brush my fingers over his forehead, side to side and up through his hair.

I know how it must have been with the other women because after I met Pete I could not get him out of my mind. Looking back I can see it was not an obsession. It was an addiction. You might think I don't know about addiction, not being an alcoholic or a smoker, but I know what addiction is. There was a time for I can't remember how long when I could not think of anything else except a pleasure I had found with myself, and I could not break myself of that no matter how much I tried.

Well it was the same way with Pete. I knew he had been married. He had three children, I found out soon enough. If I married Pete I would have to marry outside the Church. But nothing else would satisfy me. I had to have him, so we ran off and got married. Turns out that running off to get married was how he came by his first three children and running off was the only way he ever got married, but I'm getting ahead of myself again.

We had four children of our own, and I raised his three and my four and got them all through high school. Pete made good money but he couldn't keep it, and I worked part time to keep the children together till they were grown up. Pete being a salesman who was on the road a lot meant I raised them mostly on my own and I believe they got better upbringing under me than any other woman Peter McKinnon Tally ever went after.

When my four children were little my baby brother Jamie got married. Remember I mentioned him? The woman he married was named Wanda and she was almost old enough to be his mother. Now don't get upset, it's not all that unusual for the baby of a family to marry an older woman. That's the kind they've learned to love, because their love comes from older women. Don't argue with me about what I'm telling you. Do you want to hear this story or not?

This lady Wanda had a daughter named Nina. Being from the South we pronounced it to rhyme with that bird's name in the pet stores, the what-you-call-it, Mynah bird. Well, Nina was fourteen when my baby brother Jamie married her mother, and two years later, when she was about sixteen, our brother Donny came home from the Christian Brothers for good. It was at the time when a lot of religious were leaving their orders, not just brothers but priests and nuns, too.

One thing led to another, and before you knew it Donny and Nina were engaged and I took all seven of Pete's children to the wedding. Now I am about to make a sexist remark and you will just have to accept it, because it's true. Women want to know about relationships and how people are connected to one another. It's important to us.

So, now that I've said that, I will answer the question that all the women are thinking. Yes indeed the youngest brother married the older woman, and his older brother married her teen aged daughter. It's true. These were legal marriages, they are in the county records, and Donny's and Nina's was even in the Church.

It's not so unusual after all for brothers to marry a mother and daughter. I know some other people it happened to, only in their case it was the older brother married the mother, and that was the more natural way. They grew old together and they died close together and the younger ones, who are old now, are still in love. As far as I know all the problems they faced in life were problems that came to them, not problems they caused by going against nature, like Peter McKinnon Tally did.

I've had people come up to me and say "You must be very wise" or "You must be a saint, to put up with all you've been through." But it's not like that at all. It's just that if you live long enough you eventually see how everything that starts up comes to work itself out and that's what finally happened to Peter Tally.

There are some that say that Nina never would have settled down for long with Donny anyway. He bought her a trailer. They say everything that goes around comes around; it's funny, but that's the same trailer Pete was living in when they went looking for him. They found his body off in the woods, not too far from the trailer. Yes, I could have told them where to look, and, yes, it really was the same trailer where Donny and Nina set up housekeeping.

We all saw the way Pete cut up with Nina, but I was still pretty young at the time and didn't think much about it. But now that I know what I know I will warn you newlyweds that if they start having secret jokes that they are the only ones that laugh at, and if one of them has to take the children somewhere and the other one offers to help and things like that … well, then's the time to look out.

They ran off together. Pete hadn't been home that day, and I hadn't thought anything about it, when Donny called up and I could tell he was crying on his end of the phone. He said Nina had gone and had taken all her clothes and not even left him a note. Nina's mother Wanda wouldn't talk to me about it, like it was my fault somehow.

It's not so big a town that I didn't find out after awhile where they were living. I can't tell you how many times I called over there and how many times I called Pete at work. He wouldn't let me come see him at work, though. He said "Are you trying to make me lose my job?" And stupid me, I bought it, like somehow I was the one doing him wrong.

I even went over to their house a couple of times. However he managed it he had gotten them a nice little two bedroom place, with a driveway and a mailbox out by the highway, but that girl didn't know a thing and hadn't even put curtains up or anything. After a while, by the time Pete wasn't spending any more time at her house than he had been spending at mine, I felt sorry for her and I went over and helped her fix up a little. And I took the younger kids along with me. After all, she was my brother Jamie's stepdaughter, even if she wasn't anything to me by Pete.

With Pete gone from my house, for some reason I felt like going back to church again, where before I had only sent the children, and to this day I go regularly, and I have coffee every Sunday morning with my mother and the women I grew up with. At least I did till they found Pete's body. Now I don't know what I will do or what will happen to me.

I think the next thing was that Nina ran out on Pete. It may have been the other way around, but then I could be getting it mixed up with his other women, some of whom he married, and with other houses, some of which I've visited for one reason or another, or other trailers, like the last one. All the women and the girls run together in my head sometimes, and I don't know if anybody alive could tell it all the way it really happened. But I want to get on to them finding his body.

I said "girls" before and I also said I was stupid. Stupid is probably not the worst word I could have used. There are those who have been harder on me and said that I should have been looking out, knowing what I knew, and maybe they're right but my grandmother always said "Hindsight is one hundred per cent," and besides what satisfaction is it to them, knowing that what is done can't be made over?

Yes, there were girls. Girls by me, two of them, and girls by his first wife, also two, and some girls by other women. And it was girls led to them finding his body, in fact one of the younger ones was with the men who found him. All I knew was, after they grew up the girls I raised hated their daddy with a passion. Stupid me, I thought it was because I was acting unchristian about him, since he had run off and left me and all. And I couldn't help resenting it. Lord knows I tried to do my Christian best.

Even after he was living with Nina, and later when it was with other women, when I found out where he was I would invite him over to see his children because I knew he loved them and a father has a right to see his own children. I would try to get him to do things with them, to take them to Mallard Park or to the picture shows. I wanted them to have as normal a life as possible growing up. I wanted them to be with their daddy when they could, and each of them to have some time with him to themselves if they could. And that's what I tried to do as long as they were in my care, growing up.

And they did all grow up. My boys made fine looking young men, all taller than their daddy, getting their height from my side of the family, and the girls making beautiful young women. Being Hendricks, my girls had full shapes, nice shapes, a little early compared to a lot of the girls their age, but I was proud of them, proud of all of them, because Pete's girls by his first wife grew up good looking too.

Now the part about the gun. Pete loved to hunt. That was probably what he loved best, next to women—women and girls. Don't get me wrong. He loved his boys too. He took them hunting with him. That's how I happened to end up keeping a gun. It was his target pistol from when he lived in our house and used to take the boys out target practicing. That's how come I knew about the woods, but nobody called me till after they found the body. I guess nobody thought I would know where the body was.

If it hadn't been for that gun and the way things have changed, Peter McKinnon Tally would be alive today. Really it wasn't so much the gun. The way Pete was acting, some day sure as the Lord, somebody was going to kill Peter McKinnon Tally, only it wouldn't have been this soon, I'm convinced of it. So you see, it comes down to the fact that the world has changed.

I said Peter McKinnon Tally was an oily man and he was that, down to the very end. He was an oily salesman, a man who could sell anything. To a certain class of people that is. I don't know exactly what there was about him. He was not handsome, as I said. He was short and on the heavy side. But he could convince certain people, mostly ignorant people, ignorant like I was when I dated Pete, and like Nina was when she met him and all the other women were, the women and the girls.

And Peter Tally would never change. The Lord made Peter Tally a certain way, and that's how he was meant to be. Just like I am the way the Lord made me, and you are the way you were made. He would still be chasing a certain kind of ignorant woman today, if the world had let him alone the way it used to.

You see, when Nina ran off with Pete, her mother Wanda did what she was raised to do. She didn't talk about it. She just went on as if nothing had happened. But since we all knew about it we could look at her and know how she must be hurting inside, and she would know by the way we didn't bring it up that we were hurting for her. We would have kept on. That way nobody would have mentioned it in front of the children. After a few years, or in a generation or two, the grandchildren at least would be spared knowing about it. The scar would heal over and the hurt would disappear, and it would be as if it had never happened. Maybe Nina and whoever wound up in Pete's bed after her would wise up and straighten out and maybe move away and start life over somewhere. Or they could come back into our family and no one would say anything about it. Well, like my own daughters, for instance. They would just be a little wiser, that's all, and they would keep their girls away from him and we would get on with our life.

But that's not the way it is now. Now your children are taught in school to use words about their bodies and what happens between men and women and to talk about things like that to other people. And, here's the part that got to Pete, they're taught to tell an authority person if a man gets out of line. Then, the next thing you know, the police are involved and the lawyers, and there's a whole generation of young parents busybodying into what's going on in families they're not even kin to, and things start showing up in the paper. Of course it will print the man's name, but not the name of the child, or even of her parents. As if that were the fair thing to do. That's just not the way we were raised.

I think that's what hurt Pete the most. The way things had changed, and the way people couldn't take the things he did and go on about their life in a normal way. They had to get the law into it. That's where Pete drew the line. He had been a kind of a king. A free man, not like a king of the road, more like a king of the mountain. I don't think he could have lived with that.

I believe it was a daughter of one of his daughters, maybe one of ours. I think that's where the law got involved and I believe that's why he came by my house asking after the gun. At first I thought he wanted to use the gun on one or the other of them. I wouldn't tell him where it was, but I left the bedroom door open when I went to the bathroom and I haven't looked to see, but I imagine it's gone from where I kept it.

We talked for a while about the people he loved, especially his children. He ate some of my cold cornbread and drank some buttermilk. He looked so good. His hair was not as gray as mine. I got gray just raising his seven kids. I honestly don't believe he ever worried enough about anything to get gray hair, not until this, and I can't help holding that against them for what they did to him.

He did leave a note I heard, and I hope he told them off in what he wrote, for, as I said, we just weren't raised that way.

A PERFECT LITTLE
ROUND HEAD

"Look at these games!" said the midwife. "Can you believe it?" Dolores Montoya waved a tiny thin hand at the array on the dinette table. "Monopoly, Scrabble, Parcheesi, and Lord knows what." All in stacks of soft, mealy, swaybacked cardboard boxes.

Dolores was a petite woman in a loose print dress than came almost to her ankles. Dainty and graceful, with large sad eyes, she had waist length black hair, and moved her small frame with solemn economy. "When she calls me she says 'I'll have games you guys can play while you wait.' Then she tells me how close her pains are and I'm like 'No way we're gonna be playin' no games, you can forget about that.' And now look at her!"

There were three of them in the dining room. Besides Dolores the midwife, there were childbirth coaches Maurina Peake and her daughter Mandy Ann. Another woman, Jennifer O'Herlihie, was in the closet-like kitchenette out of sight.

Maurina wore blue jeans with a red plaid shirt. A heavy built, tall woman with short dark brown hair showing grey streaks and a broad, friendly face. Mandy Ann was even taller with long reddish hair and strong, well filled limbs. Freckled faced in a granny dress with a long apron at war with her knees, she might as well have worn a sign saying "First Time Birth Assistant."

In the next room Karla Untermeyer lay on her side facing the windows, her backside toward them, a frayed bathrobe vaguely draped over shoulders and hips.

Mostly she was bare and outside her robe, breasts heavy, legs skinny, stomach tight. Mostly she was too warm. Her feet were on top of the sheets in enormous moosehead house slippers. It was winter and she could see snow outside, but the apartment was heavy with too much heat.

The midwife opened a window. Welcome cold air billowed into the living room, a make-do room with a single frayed chair, stuffing showing through, a sofa missing its cushion, and a large screen television like a platoon sergeant at the head of a line of stereo components.

From the bedroom came Karla's suffering voice, a faint whimpering plea for more almond milk. Jennifer O'Herlihie called back to her from the kitchenette behind them, "Jus' sec."

Jennifer was pregnant also. Also late term. Also breech. And her first baby, too. She was here because she was curious. She was here because she was anxious. Anxious and aching. Aching to find out, to see and to be afraid, if it should come to that.

Jennifer's hair was pure black, and coarse, falling loose to her shoulders. She wore maternity jeans with an elastic pouch in front, with a light blue smock over the top. She sweated in the kitchen steam, and she also wished the apartment was cooler.

Against the living room wall each woman had deposited what she had brought along. As if by prior agreement each had carried in with her a soft, limp bag of essentials. There was the midwife's kit, with thin latex gloves, baby pads and stethoscope. There were the childbirth coaches' pouches, with books and herbal teas and more baby pads.

Then there was Jennifer's duffel, a more random affair. It contained a pillow, in case she had to stay overnight, synthetic against her allergies. Wool socks for if it got really cold, a condition she hadn't felt in months. A dress, her only other print maternity dress that fitted, in case there was blood. And a box of soy milk, because Jennifer and the two coaches were vegetarians. Karla, lately introduced to all of them, was a step ahead. She was living the vegan life. No animal nothing, not even butter or milk.

Dolores the midwife was comfortable in the vocal near-militant world of vegetarians. Homebirth advocates tend to be firmly committed in lifestyle. Their children are for the most part home schooled. For herself, in matters of diet, politics and childrearing, Dolores was "… flexible, just plain flexible."

What Karla wanted now was almond milk. You give a homebirth mother what she wants. Jennifer the-also-pregnant found it in Karla's refrigerator. She cleared a space on the kitchen counter by the sink, shoving aside mushroom bits, fragments of asparagus stalks, apple cores, paring knives, saucepans and mugs awash in puddles of cold teas. Between jars of herbs for steeping aromatic teas she set a jogger's water bottle, filled it from the limp plastic coated carton of almond milk, and screwed on a lid with a plastic straw.

"God, that tastes so good!" Karla moaned, rolling her eyes, and smiling weakly at Jennifer. She raised herself on one arm to get a better position and sucked noisily at the straw. "I thought my contractions would hurt. I knew they'd hurt. Just never dreamed they would hurt this much." She winced at the memory, then another pain caught her and she moaned for real, tossing the bottle dramatically onto the night stand, and dragging her wrist across the surface of it to half lift her weight off the bed.

Mandy Ann, the apprentice coach, had been listening for the contraction. She came barefoot from the dining alcove and climbed up onto the bed behind Karla. "Tell me where," she said.

"Here."

She began to knead Karla's thighs with her fists in the spot where Karla had said.

"Hey, Karla, now ... think about your baby ... I want you to think about how pretty she's going to be ... think about what a good mother you're going to be ... think about little Monty ... think about what a good mother you will be to her ... think about all the wonderful things you will do together ... Montana is such a beautiful name for a little girl."

Fist downstroke, fist downstroke, with every downstroke something new for Karla to think. Something new to distract her. Think about this, Karla, think about that.

Karla's one extravagance for this baby had been a sonogram. They all knew to expect a girl.

"... you and your darlin' Monty will have such a happy life together ... think of how she will look at you ... think of how she will want to be held by you ... think of ..." She massaged lightly and slowly, downstroke, downstroke, following the rhythm of Karla's pain ...

Mandy called out to the others, "She says she's double peaking."

"Won't be long now," said the midwife. I'll check her when she's resting. Less than an hour, I think. She's doing okay."

"She wants to go to the bathroom." Mandy leaned out of the bedroom.

"Sure. Whatever she feels like. I'll check her when she's back in bed."

A forlorn draped triangle on thin legs with moosehead slippers darkened the hallway. "You guys find everything you need?"

"Don't worry about us. We're fine," said coach Maurina. She waved a mug. "Good tea."

"Thanks," a quick wan pain of a grin, and Karla shuffled into the bathroom. She dropped the bathrobe and lowered herself onto the toilet. She tried to drink from the plastic straw. Mandy followed her in and tried to rub her neck and shoulders.

"No, God! Just let me be for a minute."

"Hey, okay. All right. No problem."

The phone rang.

"Can you talk to your mother?" Maurina called from the kitchen.

"Yeah, tell her to hold on." Karla dragged her mooseheads back into the bedroom, no clothes on, breasts tight and full, hanging heavy on her swollen stomach. Mandy followed with the bathrobe, and helped prop her up on pillows. Karla took the time to get comfortable.

"Yeah, Mama? ... I'm fine.... Not long.... No, not long now. Yeah, he was here.... Said he'd call later.... He will, Mama.... Yeah, Mama.... No, I know he will.... Yeah, he will, Mama. He said he would.... He didn't know how much.... I will, Mama. Yeah.... O.K. ... You, too.... Bye."

She lay back on the pillows and handed the phone to midwife Dolores. All four women had followed her into the bedroom. "Can you believe that? My mother. She's worryin' about child support. She says 'Make him pay that child support, Honey'." This last she said in a mocking, whining voice, twisting her mouth and rolling her eyes.

She rocked her shoulders heavily toward the wall and rolled her hips away from them. "He said he's going to pay. What can I do about it now? I'm having a baby for God's sake. My own mother! Lot of help she is."

"He will love this baby," she turned her head to look at them, then dropped back dramatically onto the pillows. "He will love my little Monty. I know he will. He will love his little girl." She closed her eyes, thrusting out her jaw against another the pain.

Maurina helped Mandy Ann to massage Karla, sitting on the side of the bed so that her own shadow blocked the light from the window, working on Karla's back. From where she had crawled full length onto the bed Mandy drew up her legs and, in a half reclining position, worked on Karla's thighs. After a while Karla raised a hand for them to stop.

"I'm double peaking now," she said. She had closed her eyes in memory of the pain, she was speaking to no one in particular.

"Yeah, I know," said the midwife. "If you're ready now, I'll check you." She drew on thin rubber gloves, and inserted the fingers of one hand into the soft dampness between Karla's legs, in her other hand she held a sterile cloth. Karla's knees were up, feet apart. She tipped her head back and grimaced.

"Good God! What the hell are you doing?"

"Just looking at things. You're dilating just fine. Won't be long now. You can sit in the tub if it will feel better."

"Yeah, anything." She leaned, this time, on Mandy's arm, going into the bathroom. Maurina balanced the faucets to "good-and-hot but not hot-hot," as directed. It was crowded in the small bathroom, the three of them plus Karla's big stomach. Mandy helped her into the tub. In less than a minute the next pain came. Mandy laid a towel over the soap tray so Karla could lean against the wall, and gently rubbed Karla's shoulders again, making small circles near her lower neck. In the rising steam Karla's blonde hair curled and pasted itself brown against her bare neck.

Another pain. Karla leaned away from Mandy and hunched down till it passed. The phone rang again. Maurina left them to answer it.

Without raising her head, staring down at the water, Karla said "It's him. I know it is."

It was.

"Yeah, tell him to hold on," to Maurina's question from the bedroom. "I'll be there."

Mandy helped dry off her legs and hips, and all that had gotten wet. She left her frayed robe in the bedroom. Mandy followed along behind her, dabbing at wet spots she had missed.

"Yeah, I'm glad you called.... No, I'm fine.... Yeah, Dolores's here.... You know, my midwife.... That's right, you met her.... Yeah, and Maurina and Mandy. No, you know my childbirth coaches.... Yeah, coaches.... Yeah, from the Bradley childbirth class. I told you about them.... Yeah, that's the ones. And Jennifer O'Herlihie.... Yeah, well she's just another client of Dolores's. You know, like me.... Well, honey, she's breech, too, and Dolores asked if she could come and see what it was like—no, that's all.... No, it's not a circus. I promise you, it's not a circus. Because they want to help me, that's all. No, I didn't mean it that way.... Honey, I love you. You know I love you.... O.K. ... Well, I don't know when. Dolores says 'soon.' ... No, I'm naming her Montana, you know, I told you.... You know why.... Sure, when you get off.... Well, call me.... I love you.... Yeah, 'bye."

She had squeezed out the last words through clenched teeth. There had been another contraction. After it passed she said, "He forgot. Can you believe that? We met in Montana, and he forgot.... I can't believe it. He forgot. What an asshole."

She said it to all of them, standing around the bed, a forlorn look on her face. A little girl forgotten, once again. There was silence.

Then Dolores took a quick, loud breath, "Hey, I want to listen to the heartbeat."

She pressed the black stethoscope against the lower end of Karla's bulging stomach. "Okay ... yeah, okay." It was a cold instrument with the usual ear pieces and a black rod about ten inches long ending in a cup that she pressed against her own forehead while she held the pickup end on Karla's skin. "Okay."

"Now let me check you." She had set aside the stethoscope and was probing with her fingers. "Yeah, she's coming down. I can see an arm. Let me just check. Here."

"Okay. Let me see about the cord. Okay. We're okay here. I'll just move that arm. Just clear that arm."

"God!" said Karla, "Watch it!.."

"You're doing fine," said Mandy. She was massaging Karla's upper thigh on the side closest to her. "Can I get you something?"

"More almond milk," said Karla. "No, wait. Stay here." She suddenly grabbed at Mandy's sturdy arm. "Oh-h-h. Whoops! ... ah-h-h, yeah-h-h-h!. "After a long couple of minutes, a weak smile, a very weak smile. "Oohboy, that was a mean one."

"She's coming now," said Dolores. "I want you to slide down to the edge of the bed. You'll be more comfortable there. Yeah, that's right. Try to brace your feet on the floor if you can. That'll make it easier for the baby to drop." Karla pulled herself awkwardly with Mandy's help toward the foot of the bed, where Dolores had arranged an old sheet, worn but clean.

"Maurina?" said Dolores, "How about you getting up here on the bed behind Karla? Yeah, like that. Yeah, legs on either side. That's right. Now slide up close where she can lean back on you. Yeah, Mandy? Yeah, that's right. Put some more pillows behind your mom. That'll give her something to prop up on. It's not long now."

With quick, busy movements she started spreading plastic backed baby changing pads on the floor. Jennifer pulled out some more pads to help.

"Hey, no, Jennifer, I want you to monitor the heart rate."

"Right," Jennifer's voice was tight and faint.

Dolores nodded as Jennifer switched on the fist sized black box and. pressed it against Karla's lower stomach. Jennifer read the LED numbers out loud. "Yeah, that's good."

Then, peering in where her fingers were holding Karla open. "Hey, good. I can see her. Mandy get me that mirror. Yeah, in my bag." Without looking up.

Mandy came back with the mirror, a wooden framed mirror about six inches square with thick rounded edges. Karla reached desperately for the mirror, hand flailing. Mandy caught her hand and closed the fingers around the mirror. She pushed it down between her knees. Her movements were jerky now and anxious. "Yeah, I see. I guess. Here, take it back." Mandy grabbed for the mirror as Karla let it go.

"Okay. Now, when I tell you to push, I want you to push," said Dolores. "Really push." Karla nodded grimly. Mandy had wet a towel and touched Karla's forehead. Karla leaned into the damp, hot towel as if for comfort. She tensed. Her lips wide with pain. Maurina was still behind her, supporting her weight. She clenched at Maurina's knees on either side of her hips. She had kicked off her houseshoes and was naked on the edge of the bed leaning against Maurina, hot and sweating.

"This next one's it," said Dolores. "When it comes you got to push. You got to push hard."

Karla braced. On command she pushed. She tried to look down at her crotch but her head had to stretch back, had to. Her head rammed up and back onto Maurina's ample breast. Karla hurt. Too much pain to look and push at the same time. After the contraction she looked. She burned. It was a fire between her legs. Like a bright razor stinging cut and a bonfire all at the same time. She snatched at Mandy's mirror. What she saw was large and grey and wet with matted black flecks. She saw Dolores's fingers underneath. The fingers were inside of her, too, supporting the lump of the baby, guiding it. The whole damn world was crammed into her crotch.

"O.K. The next one's the big one. Get ready." Dolores braced her body, hands tight.

The next one came. The burning was volcanic. Karla twisted her head to the side in agony. She opened her eyes and looked down. About ten inches of new baby was squeezing out butt first, between her legs, its weight supported in Dolores's hands. Another contraction. She pushed again. More burning, maybe not so hot as before. How could she tell?

Montana was out.

"See? Perfect little round head!" said Dolores. All triumphant she handed Montana up to Karla. "Perfect little round head. I told you. That's what you get with breech babies. A perfect little round head!"

Karla sucked in a quick hard breath. Her eyes wildly, hungrily swung to her baby, this baby that had come butt, feet and hands first into the world. The body had come out still as death. Now it started to squirm and twist and make little snuffling noises.

Karla caught at her own breath, spastic, like it would never come back. Quick gasps, rounded sucking lips. Still breathing jerkily she took the baby between her breasts, and laid her skin to skin. "She's beautiful!"

They were still connected. The long, kinked grey-purple cord dangled from Monty's tummy to Karla's vagina, where her legs hung open, feet on the floor, her back resting against Maurina's chest. With one hand propping little Monty secure between her breasts, resting atop her stomach big with the placenta still inside, she grabbed at Dolores with the other hand and grinned a sweaty grin up at all of them. Then she nodded down at Monty. "You were right," she said to all of them as she looked at the child on her stomach, "a perfect little round head."

LOVE AMONG THE SWISS

Desertion is perhaps the most serious offense a soldier can commit. The punishment is death. In love, desertion is the cruelest act one person can commit. The punishment is not inflicted upon the deserter. It is suffered by the ones left behind. This thought was on the mind of David S. as the car worked its way along the banks of Lake Geneva, the lake that the French-speaking Swiss call Lac Leman. He had deserted his lover and he had deserted his country. There is a name for those who desert their own country. They are called ex-patriots. There is no name for those who desert their lovers. There is not a word low enough in any language.

LOVIN DON'T

"Lovin' don't last—Cookin' do" his tee-shirt read.

He made his milk from dry powder because afterwards he could drink it warm, with foam on top, and it reminded him of drinking milk from the cow, just after it had been separated.

MACUMBA

The lone pointing finger of the Eiffel Tower trails through the low, black clouds of November that remind Parisians that snow can happen even in the City of Light. A sculpture in steel, M. Eiffel's Exposition monument boasts no function save to embody a Gallic arrogance and the peculiarly French mixture of the masculine in its phallic outline and the feminine in its delicate tracery. A fitting symbol for a civilization that traces its lineage from the Romans and their wild Frankish subjects.

But M. Eiffel felt steel had other uses and erected a tower in Lisbon, equally ornate in steel embroidery, but more utilitarian, as befits an older civilization that goes all the way back to the Moors, gaunt astronomers and visionary architects who begat short dark offspring of sheepherders and fishermen who in turn built monuments of wood that floated on the ocean, seaborne chariots that found secret ways to the Indies, and later claimed the dampest, hottest, richest bulk of South America for their own, the Mother of all countries, the better part of all the Amazon, and pampas like the Argentines and gold and silver, and riches of kinds yet to be imagined—Brazil, to which they bequeathed their language and a free spirited willingness to marry whomever they met and begin new races.

The use of the wondrous steel tower of M. Eiffel in Portugal is to lift pedestrians from a busy downtown Lisbon shopping street to another street directly above it on the steepest of the many hills over which Lisbon lies, its coral roofs awash in the sun, its shoe shiners industrious in the streets and the smell of wine and cooking squid strong on the air from the Al Fama district with its face to the River Tagus and the slow, dark big-bellied sails of its workboats.

To its giant offspring Brazil, a country so large that her distant motherland could be tossed and forgotten among its anthills and hidden beneath its mountains, Lisbon willed a broader vision of itself, and, north of Rio, along a beach that goes forever in both directions in the state lovingly called Bahia, called into existence the city of Salvadore, and, because this beach stretched her naked limbs below a fertile hill, caused both an upper city and a lower city to be constructed, the two to be joined by a modern version of M. Eiffel's Lisbon pedestrian tower, built of cement as appropriate in a land where the termites mean death to wooden structures and the water and salt bring diseases of the skin to things made of metal.

Here, in Salvadore, in Bahia, in the upper city on a warm spring day in September, a witch leaned back against a stone wall overlooking the ocean harbor, stretched out her arms to either side, threw back her head and waited for the tourist to take her photograph.

She was short, not running to muscle and thickness, like the bystanders with Portuguese blood, but skinny with the Indians' copper brown skin, thin nose and high cheeks. She wore a loose blue cotton dress with a necklace of colorful ornaments. Her bracelets were simple slender bands. Her feet were sandaled, with no white showing underneath. Her hair was black and loose, her skin soft and shining. She composed herself and waited, with a predator's patience and the eyes of an animal, for the flurry of metering, focusing and composing to cease.

A man whose skin showed more brown than hers, a man in working clothes, with the thick broad hands of the Portuguese ran up.

"No!" he said to the tourist, in English, "No pictures. Witch. Macumba witch."

She frowned at the workman. He backed away, eyes on the tourist, not looking at her. She stretched her arms further along the wall behind her so that her small chest lifted slightly with the arch of her back and turned her face again to the camera, eyelids lowered in arrogance. She was young.

The tourist had stopped adjusting his camera's controls when the man ran up. He looked stupidly at the man for a moment, then shrugged, turned back to the woman and clicked his shutter. The woman pushed herself awkwardly off the wall with one hand, and extended her other to the man, who placed a dollar in it and said "Thank you." She nodded once, in the solemn imperious way of Indians, and watched him walk away.

She turned her animal eyes on the worker who had spoken out. He said some words to himself and quickly left the terrace. She was alone. She turned to look down at the lower city and out over the water. To the north, between sheltering peninsulas lay sailing yachts at anchor. In front of her an ocean tug was entering the harbor and, below, several large freighters were docked and stowing cargo.

Closer to her on the dock there were small boats off-loading produce and closely packed about were stalls of sellers of things from the farms. Her fingers lightly touched the crinkled dollar through the fabric of her pocket. She tossed her head and walked down to the pedestrian tower. Inside the sliding metal doors she backed sideways into a far corner and looked darkly at the attendant. He was a young man in a grey uniform, short like her, and dark, but with more brown and less red in his skin. He asked no money from her, he avoided her eyes and collected five centavos apiece from three other people, closed the door and took them to the lower level. She was the last to leave. He looked away as she passed.

MAM-MA AND REX

We called our grandmother Mam-ma. She had a way of fidgeting, nervously curling the smaller fingers of her hand, gripping a handkerchief or a dust cloth by the back fingers.

Her son, whom we call Uncle Rex, makes the same gesture when he talks, holding his hand almost vertically, jerkily curling those smaller fingers toward the heel of his hand.

MICHAEL'S DAUGHTER, CLYDE

Chapter 1

"Because I have something to give!" That too familiar look in her eyes, where no one could reach her, perched beyond reason, a feather's puff from hysteria.

The dog Mollie raised her head briefly at the sharp change in the rhythm of human voices, tugging long ears through her paws. The other skiers had left the two women, the fire needed tending. The oak floor beneath them was hard and cold. From outside, into the hollow that swelled out behind her daughter's voice, Michael heard the thick wind heaving and twisting and felt the branches outside brushing back and forth against the shingles where the eaves of the lodge reached out to wrestle the trees.

More snow had fallen today. More snow this week than in all the preceding winter months. The last of their tracks were erased hours before in the steady accumulation of whiteness. Black pines stood near the lodge. Near enough that the sudden release of a branch's snow load exploded audibly inside. The moon was out, showing the lodge too small crowded by pines tall and close, an isolated woodlet surrounded on three sides by open fields of snow, and tucked snugly up against the mountain's bare flanks behind them.

Michael eased out of moon boots and socks, and stretched her feet toward the fire. She considered them critically. Browned by overmuch lying about on beaches, deep mahogany on top, fading to paper bag brown on the undersides, the arches crinkled and shiny, like nylons in need of washing, fish belly white underneath. Her toes were tipped in deep red, chipped like dime store china, their joints perpetually bent into miniature elbows, knobby and cramped. She rested her heels on the stone, feet tilted toward the warmth.

She looked across the circular fireplace at Clyde's feet. Also bare, also perched on the hearth ring, but lower, so that the sharp edge of the stone creased their bottoms. Small and smooth. Even bent over the way they were, crimped toward the fire scarcely a line showed on the soles of her feet. Her daughter had pretty feet, Michael thought, with the kind of thinking where pride and envy contended jealously. Soft, smooth and lightly tanned they were, where even the sharp lines of ankles were softened by a leavening of that slow miraculous evolution of young girl into young woman that lingers long and changes what is rounded and soft into what is graceful and lithe. Her toes were unpainted. Straight and firm with the relaxed assurance of the habitually unshod.

Michael considered the gradual graceful sweep of Clyde's long johns, from the back of her ankles to the underside of her knees and up into the elegant curve of her hips and decided that she and her husband had wrought well. Perhaps Clyde was less tall than some women, less commanding than others. She might have been out of place on a fashion runway but she was full medium in height and there were the touches of her mother in her that charged a room when she entered and there was the glow from her father that lingered when she left.

In all it was a wonderful work they had wrought, a work fashioned carefully and thoughtfully over time, tensely guarded against the diseases, injuries and malefactions that might have done damage to other, less precious children. A work of near perfection, lovely face, full lips, tidy figure, elegant hands, glorious waistline, a complexion for the ages. And now this moment.

Michael thought of their room. Bare floor, oval braided rug between two beds. Thought of the long night ahead lying there feeling the sullenness of her daughter turned away from her in the stillness, unable to comfort her child.

Soon it would be time to face the night. Here she and Clyde had come because she had insisted, because for her it had begun here, a personal pilgrimage. A pilgrimage not for truth but for closure, to make things come out right, to make things make sense, to make Clyde love her again, to find the soul of David so that they could start again. Because this is where she had found him, because his strength had come from these hills and from these pines, from the old, low profiles of the Laurentiens with their distant European peaks just far enough from Montreal to be a separate world. A road, and a long, tiring drive away.

They had come for the skiing. A place to come with friends, or as a couple. No place, really, to come alone. They had come with friends, both of them, and that, she thought, was the fate part. Because her friends had wandered off, leaving her toasting her feet at this same big round open fireplace, on this stone ring just the right height for stretching out from deep chairs. There had been a woman playing the piano off in a corner, Brahms she thought, another stray from another group. It must have been a night for straying. He had come, sat down not too close, talked about the fire and cold feet and asked her name. "Michael," she'd said with the laugh that came on the good days when she liked her name, and he'd fallen in love with her then. Because of her name.

Maybe that's not a good reason to fall in love, because of your name. But it could be. It could be like a test the king would give a knight to go out and kill a dragon to prove he was worthy. But knights didn't do that really. There weren't any dragons. They just spent a night in the chapel, dressed in armor, trying not to fall asleep or lose their balance without their squire to set them upright again. Humpty Dumpty was a knight, imagine all that armor all over the ground. Yard sale! Come back. Pernoctation, or something like that they called it. Lovely word, pernoctation. See, it's all in the word, all in the naming of something. Give a pretty word to an unlovely thing and it improves the thing at once. Give an unusual name to something and it lives forever. He should have lived forever. When I get to heaven I mean to ask him why he left me so early.

It had been a night like tonight, fresh snow piling up, promising great skiing tomorrow, the kind of deep powder that reminds you to lean back just a little, to keep your tails free in the turns, and, most importantly, to be the first one down whatever trail you took so yours would be the first tracks. It was the kind of night that was all about promises, promises that—in place of the heavy clouds that brought the snow—there would be clear sunny skies so the snow would glisten and glimmer in mounds and hillocks, like frosting on rooftops, and tall mountainettes rising up to reach eaves and branches.

A long time that night they had talked. Not so much what they'd had in common as what each had found in the other's adventures and opinions, a fascination beyond expectation. He had been to Russia. She had been to Japan. He had taken up skiing in his thirties. She had always skied. He taught. She consulted. She had flown. He had come by train.

Why would anyone take the train today, she had asked, more a joke than a question. But he had taken her seriously and told her about the marvels of travel by train. There was room to walk around. You could stand up straight and walk comfortably. You could go from one car to the next, see how different the people were in each car. Between the cars was the best part. The metallic smell of raw iron rose up, mingled with steam. You watched the car ahead wrestling your car beneath the armored plates and wondered what would happen to you if they ripped apart and your car went sliding backward down the dark tracks.

Maybe she had fallen in love with him for that, but not at that moment, like it had been for him. She was hard to touch, but gradually, by little bits over time, she had come to love the way he had of finding small pleasures in everyday things, the things that frustrated her ambition, that constrained her pace, blocked her view, resisted her threats, clustered about her, insisted on being themselves, refused to change for her sake.

Those things that she hated—and there was a muchness of them in her life— he accommodated and cherished for themselves, and absorbed them. He thought of them in settings like jewels, in frames like paintings, in poems floating in space. And for that, over hours and days and weeks of learning about him she had come to love him.

It was unlike her to love, and she found herself to be a new person because of him. Now, because of him, Michael had a daughter to love, she who never should have loved anyone. She was grieved to find her daughter living somewhere in her mind that Michael could never reach because her daughter, like her husband, possessed that lonely, exalted access to those innermost keeps of blackest dungeons and loftiest parapets that other, worldlier mortals, like Michael, could only sense and shudder at.

The dog Mollie dropped her head, a sudden movement that caused her ears to flop outward like dancers' arms and settle gracefully over her paws. Michael looked at Clyde, seeing the same defiant eyes as before and thought again how this child at her worst was the worst of both her parents, the profanest possible blend of her mother's quick, intense propensity to hate and her father's ability to lose himself in his own ideas and dreams.

"And what is it that you have to give?" she asked Clyde. Not so as to learn, but to fling an offering into the silence between them. There was nothing to learn. She felt she knew what mothers had known, since the crusades and before. When the allure of self sacrifice is stronger than a young woman can resist, in the exalted delusion of her inner strength, she tells herself that whatever comes she can always give her body. An instinct for the harem, Michael thought it, and the thought disgusted her, for mesmerizing as it was to see in operation, she had never experienced the harem instinct. She wondered sometimes if nature had left something out in molding her woman's form.

"Yes, what?" she repeated.

Chapter 2

"I am a teacher, Mother." Clyde had prepared herself for this question. Michael wished she had asked something harder. "A trained teacher. I can teach."

Yes, thought Michael, and what is it you know, you who's never been away from home? What can you possibly teach some wild Indian child?

"The New Mexico desert, for God's sake!" Michael said aloud, her taut voice ringing high in the half darkness.

"It's not a desert, Mother, it's sheep and cattle country. They live in real houses and they drive real trucks."

"Where will you stay, Clyde? Where will you sleep?"

"There's a dorm where they let you stay till you find your own place. Families have rooms to rent, and there are houses too that you can get. The Navajo nation said so, and the Bureau of Indian Affairs said so. O.K.?"

Her daughter's words drifted through Michael like snowflakes through the frozen trees outside. Inside her was an image of Clyde far off in a tar paper shack yielding zealously to a long line of sullen Indian boys in greasy ponytails and headbands, each differentiable from the rest only by some minutia of his particular grievance against some authority somewhere. Her daughter, Miss Heartfelt Sympathy personified, Idealism Unlimited, the world's biggest pushover.

"Why you? Why does it have to be you?"

"Mother, that's a chicken crossing the road question. The formula answer is 'why not me?'. Really that's the way I honestly feel about it. There's no reason I can't report to New Mexico and start teaching. I can always find a room. People have to rent rooms."

Michael's eyebrows tightened, raptor's wings arched and poised to launch.

Clyde flinched. "No, don't say it. My mind's made up. You'd go with me. You'd move me in. You'd get me started. No way, Mother, no way."

The eyebrows collapsed.

"Mother?"

Michael's eyes had taken on a distant look, unfocused and empty.

"I was just thinking," Michael said, from where she had gone. "Those who can, do. Those who can't, teach. Did you ever hear that?"

"Yes. From you. All the time."

"But don't you think it's true? What can you really do? And what do you really know? You've been with me all your life. I've looked after you. You lived with me even while you were going to college. You've never even been away. You've never been on your own."

"I've been to Europe."

"You chased after Charlie Woodruff to Europe. He left you in Lausanne. You called me from Geneva to wire money. I sent you a ticket home."

"I found my way to the U.N."

"Do you think there'll be a U.N. in the Navajo nation? Who's going to look after you? Who will you run to?"

"There are hospitals. There are police."

"Right. Indian police. What do they care about Anglo women or Gringos or whatever they call you?"

"I'll be their teacher. They'll respect me."

"They'd respect a Navajo teacher a lot more. And a Navajo rapist a lot more than some white woman immature little girl without the sense to stay with her own people."

"I'm a grownup. I'm capable of making my own way."

"And paying your own way?"

"I will be when I start earning my teacher's pay."

"And what enormous sums will you be hauling in?"

"Enough to live on out there. Things are cheaper."

"Sure, if all you eat is rabbit and corn. You don't remember our Indian vacation? You don't remember the trading posts?"

Everything had cost more. Soap. Socks. Cans of chili. Potato chips. Cokes. Everything that came from somewhere else. Everything that was sold in small lots. Dirty children buying a single soft drink. Nothing in quantity. No large size, no giant size, no economy size of anything. Only small size bottles and cans. Local tomatoes twisted, lumpy, mottled. Oranges small and few, and dry. No apples. Candy in small sizes and only a few kinds. Flat, squarish, bleached pine shelves, too much of the wood showing, big empty spaces between the cans and plastic wrappers.

How had it looked through Clyde's eyes, she wondered. The good part would have been outside. A boy flicking a long brown bull whip sinuous in the twilight dust. Two girls, watching with quiet brown eyes, standing with shoulders touching, an island of little people in the gravel, arms hanging woodenly beside them.

Inside, the storekeeper stern, lined and sun browned, his wife silent, unsmiling, watchful. Knowing something kept to themselves. Yes, Clyde would have liked being brown. Enigmatic. Knowing. Secretive. Close.

Clyde would have liked being like that.

Chapter 3

How easily her longjohns slide off, Michael thought, watching Clyde as they undressed. Like straightening hose, she just runs her hands along the curves of her, and off they slide.

She thought of her own hips, wide, deep. It took a scissoring, seesawing, up and down motion of hips and knees to climb in and out of anything snug. A woman's dance, in a woman's body, of deep valleys and steep rounded hillocks. But it was Clyde's body she would have chosen if you could find bodies on display when you walked by with a shopping cart. The same tight young body that would serve as her daughter's emergency fund among the heathen, carnal aborigines. God, it takes a lot to change the mind of a child.

How easy they sleep. Clyde had slipped beneath the covers, scarcely lifting them above the sheets, turned halfway to the wall, and immediately begun to breath deeply, slowly, evenly. Michael had lost her again.

For Michael it would be harder. She lay on her back, looking at the ceiling. Rough beams and plaster. Cracks wide enough to show dimly in the reflected moonlight. No window shades, no blinds. Just curtains. Curtains make a room too dark, too close. Better to turn off the room lights and undress by feel and by memory.

Unhappily, hers was a good memory, and Clyde's words and her own resonated through her mind. A competition, a tournament of tests and trials, of feints and thrusts, of openings and advantages, of gambits and misses. All her mistakes, all the times she should have steered her daughter, the times she should have erected traffic signs to point the way. Signs that would have allowed Clyde to see without being told to see. That always worked best. Clyde liked most the ideas she thought were her own. That's the trouble, right there. I let her know too early how I felt.

She turned on her side, toward the wall and away from Clyde. It was lonely in this bed. Twin beds, separated by a night stand and a braided rug. She missed David. She wondered if a young woman Clyde's age could miss a man. Told herself she missed, not any man, but David. Michael had grown up with sisters. Never slept alone till David died. Out of her sisters' bed and into David's. Never been alone, now she was about to be.

For Clyde it would be the other way around. An only child. Watched over by her parents, twin-minded about safeguarding her. Playground. Playroom. Bedroom. School. She may not know what sharing a bed is like, long term sharing. For her the thrill would be in the change. The thrill of a new adventure.

Me, I've had the adventure. This is it. I don't like it. Without David I have only Clyde. I'll not give her up. Not yet. She turned over, toward Clyde, slowly bringing herself to focus on her daughter six feet away. Clyde breathing softly, backside toward her mother, silver in the darkness, with grayish shadows of billowed triangles and mangled lines marking the Indian pattern of her blanket.

Teacher? Why did she want to be a teacher? That was a long time ago, when a teacher, or a nurse, was what a girl wanted to be. Now she could be anybody. Business, science, medicine, computers, for God's sake. Teacher? Better than a nun.

Thank God she had gotten Clyde away from the nuns early, as soon as the signs appeared. Weekly confession. Reconciliation they called it now. Prayer books. Little pictures. Extra homework, staying after for extra credit. She had put a stop to that. After all, private school was private school, wasn't it? Private schools cost the same whether the money went to the pope or to some other foundation. What difference did it make whose pocket it went into? The only difference, really, was the clothes. Uniforms, after all, were cheaper than dresses. Maybe too much thinking about boys. Who knows, the nuns might have suppressed that a little. Now this. The whole state of New Mexico, the whole Navajo Nation, filthy old Indian men, Indian boys raunchy and greasy. My innocent head-in-the-clouds little girl.

Michael heard Clyde turn over. A light sound. The bed barely whispered the sound. Michael rolled over to face her daughter. In the reflection of the moon's light Michael thought she could see the ridges around her daughter's eyes, formed by her ski mask, worn tightly to keep out the snow and the cold. She could make out the contours of forehead, eyebrows, nose, lips and chin, the hollows of her eyes. Michael had often traced the face of the child with her fingers and later tried to commit the face of the young adult to memory, like a poem you exercise over and over till it comes effortlessly and at will. What if I go blind? How else can I make sure I've got this picture with me? People don't realize how easily you could lose your daughter's face. And I'd be left with nothing. All alone in the dark, without the most precious thing I ever had.

She had carried Clyde like a crystal figurine she thought might break. All nine months, but only seven she had known about. Thirty-nine weeks. Exercise, how she hated exercise. Exercised because the doctor had told David she should, and David had wanted her to. Clyde had come hard. A painful birth, extraordinarily painful. They never told you how hideously painful it could be. Bad enough you would never want another one. She will never know how I suffered for her.

Michael rolled over again, face to the wall. Behind her Clyde stirred, groaned a word. Michael held her breath. The sound came again, deep, like a phonograph record at slow speed. Like a name, like Cal-something-Burr. A man's name? It came again. "Cal-ee-burr."

Chapter 4

It was good, waking up with an appetite. It came from skiing all day the day before, but it also came from a tossing night of restless worry. Still it was good to be walking out into the bracing air, to see your breath clouding, to feel the cold on your face and at your neck, with the recent warmth of the bed still cozy inside your thermals and jacket, toes warm in your moon boots.

Once again Michael had admired the ease and grace of her daughter's dressing. Across the braided oval rug, secure in the wholesome good looks of her youth, Clyde had slept till the last minute. Michael had risen early and agonized over her makeup, so difficult for day wear, and then had gone through the drawers of her rough-finish bureau three or four times before settling on combinations of materials, fabrics, zippers, velcros and stays that no one but herself was likely to see the whole day.

Michael was almost completely assembled when she managed to persuade her daughter to get up. For Clyde it was merely a matter of brushing her teeth then slipping into something clean. For Clyde it was a matter of sliding something smoothly over the top and pulling something else smoothly up over her legs and she was done.

Michael had never been able to dress easily. Her body had always been skinny. Angular and knobby as a child, all elbows, knees and hips in her early teens. Thin and top heavy in her late teens, with broad shoulders and a low chest. Nothing went on or off easily, no fabric but what caught somewhere, or bunched up somewhere, or pulled too tightly in one place and needed smoothing somewhere else. No jewelry went with any outfit on the first try. Everything needed holding up, comparing, turning this way and that to catch the light, cast the wrong color and be flung aside only to be rooted through and tested again, till some compromise trinket, some inferior combination, some lowest common denominator could be arrived at and tolerated till time to undress.

Everything looked good on Clyde. The most garish, obscene, asymmetric, angular, clash-colored brooch, necklace or earring transported from her body to Clyde's took on new life, became quaint, charming, antique, precious. God, if she didn't love her so desperately, she'd hate that girl!

Chapter 5

Breakfast was in the big building, through the woods and a short walk down the hill. Four stories and a couple of underground floors, it was massive and gray, with walls of stone, and solid, with a high pitched roof to protect it against the snow. Inside was warm and the smells of breakfast billowed into the lobby. At the half-door to the right Michael unbuttoned and unzipped her complex outer gear while Clyde slipped eel-like from her parka and got coat check tickets for both of them.

The maitre d' had been looking for them and walked quickly across the carpet to stop them. Many apologies, a large party had arrived last night and he'd needed their table to seat them together. Could he put them with another group? Just for a short while? Michael gathered herself to complain, to demand the manager, but Clyde said "Sure," quietly, happily, and it was done. They were on their way to a table of strangers.

Two men, younger than Michael by many years, but only a few years older than Clyde, sat facing each other over glasses of ice water, salt and pepper shakers, and silverware, napkins in their laps, menus gone, waiting for their coffee, empty place settings on either side of them. They sat back surprised, then rose grudgingly when the waiter introduced Michael and Clyde. Their names were Jeff something and Bob something. Michael wasn't sure, and hoped she wouldn't have to remember.

Jeff sat on Michael's left and wore a white turtleneck under a white knitted sweater with raised and braided rope work. He had reddish yellow hair and a reddish gold tan and freckles showing through. Bob had thick black rumpled black Italian hair, a squarish face, a bold mustache with the thick neck and crowded shoulders of a weight lifter. He had the dark look that goes with a permanent tan in a rugged, high cheekboned setting, but skin too smooth for an outdoorsman. Clyde was very happy to meet them. Puppy-like. If she had a tail she would have wagged it, thought Michael.

Clyde and her mother had been here almost two whole days and hadn't met anyone. How long had these guys been here? Michael's eyebrows arched, and her makeup hardened into the crinkled, oily look of coated brown paper.

Bob did the talking, mostly. They were up from The City, New York City. What a coincidence, so were Clyde and her mother! Michael stretched her lower lip over her teeth and nodded for the waiter's coffee in its thick silver pot. Cream? Shook her head no.

Clyde was oblivious to coffee. Yes, Michael grudged, why would her daughter need caffeine when she had hormones?

Jeff Something was in accounting. Bob Something was in construction. They had gone to school together and Bob's business used Jeff's firm. How small town, Michael's first contribution to the conversation was deliberately ambiguous and provocative.

"Well, it is a close neighborhood. A community, like a small town really." Bob had warmed to Clyde. Didn't everyone? Jeff, who had been moving a piece of bacon around in the dregs of yolk on his plate, nodded agreement to Bob's opinion of where they grew up.

And where was Clyde headed, now that she was out of college? New Mexico? To teach Native Americans? Sounded romantic. Thanks, thought Michael, waving her menu at the waiter. She would have bran, some kind of bran cereal, and wished that Clyde, too, would pay attention to her health. But no, Clyde would have bacon and eggs, with orange juice and hot chocolate and toast. Foolishness. Couldn't she see what this kind of eating was going to do to her in the long run? No, there are no long runs with young people.

"Did you say your name was Clyde?" Bob had begun to take an interest. Great, two ski bums. "I never heard of a woman named Clyde."

"My mother's name is Michael." Thanks, Clyde. Michael felt her lips tightening, tried to manage a conspiratorial grin.

"How about that? I never heard of a woman named Michael, either. Did you?" Bob turned to look at Jeff. Jeff shook his head. "How did that happen? How did you come to be named Clyde?" He had lost interest in the mother-name, but the daughter-name was fascinating.

"No big deal. I'll tell you later." Clyde was distracted by the enormous tray from which the waiter was carefully handing out her various dishes, steaming under silverine covers, revealing thick white dishes with royal blue crests, ringed in red. All her dishes steamed except her chocolate, whose steam was sealed under a mound of melted marshmallow cream, from which a cloud escaped and coated her forehead as she tipped her lips into the foam. She emerged from her cup with a wet face and white mustache, a darling imp, curls a-tangle, eyes fresh and clear, cheeks high and flushed as she realized everyone was looking at her.

"Delicious," she said, with a sigh. "I love it here." And so, immediately, did everyone else, because of the little girl in her.

Chapter 6

The chair-lift deposited them fifty feet or so from the jump off. Everything was white up here. The pines were covered with a soft marshmallowy icing from the snowmaking guns, and the windward sides of the ski patrol shelter was coated with horizontal streaks of ice laced with bands of snow.

Luckily she had neither disgraced herself nor embarrassed her daughter getting off the lift in the scramble at the top ("keep your tips up"). Sliding to a stop as they formed up their group at the precipice, she would have liked to lean coquettishly on Bob or Jeff and squeal something vulnerable and girlish like "Oh, catch me!" but it wasn't in her.

Clyde had bounced lightly off the chair as it reached the ridge of snow built up by the attendant for their disembarking, and glided effortlessly over to where Bob and Jeff waited, leaning on their ski poles. Clyde re-engaged the straps of her poles in a single graceful motion as she came out of the chair and was fully strapped and ready when she weight-shifted and spun around to back into position waiting for her mother.

Michael slid awkwardly down from the chair, weight precariously centered over her skis, and after a few slow seconds came to a halt, then pushed herself heavily, grunting, over to the group to stand leaning backward against the stiffness of her boots while she struggled into her pole straps. "Where to?" she tried to shout gaily, but it came out more a hysterical squeal.

"Let's do Monkey Business again," called Clyde.

"We haven't done Maiden's Folly," said Bob, laughing.

"Or Hero's Run," suggested Jeff, quietly.

"Yes, Hero's Run, let's do Hero's Run," said Clyde.

"But that's a black diamond," protested Michael, in a voice too high.

"Yeah, maybe we ought to stay away from the black diamonds, today," Bob said.

"Why?" asked Clyde. "Mom can do the blacks, can't you Mom?"

Why does this have to be an us versus you thing? thought Michael, but she answered, "All right, we'll do it."

"If you don't want to ..." said Bob.

"It's O.K. Don't worry. We'll do Hero-whatever. Let's not just stand around. Which way is it?"

Chapter 7

At last she was free. On her own and driving down to The Big Res. It may have been a mistake to fly to Denver instead of Albuquerque. Certainly it was the longer way to get to the Navajo reservation but goddammit it was her life and she was going to live it. Two-door, brand new car. Long term lease. Wish they'd had red. White would do, more practical in desert country anyway, with dust and rocks and everything. Wish they'd had a convertible. Love to feel that wind in her hair. Well, same thing. Too much dust, anyway. Still, it would have been nice. She was more the convertible type, anyway that's how she felt she would have been if Michael had ever let her have one. Forget Michael. She was on her own and headed for Navajo country by way of Durango.

Durango. A magic word that sang out of her memories and beckoned to her from cowboy movies and western novels she didn't even remember. She hoped it didn't turn out like El Dorado, Illinois. God what a bust of a town. A dried up, forgotten, used-car-and-diner kind of place that no one but Trailways Bus Line ever heard of. There ought to be a law against giving beautiful names to stupid places. Didn't anybody understand how important a name was, she asked herself, a young woman with an old man's name.

Looking forward to seeing the town. Motels north and south of town, no problem getting a room. A nice tourist information center just south of town. Easy to get around. Everyone had told her that, all along the way. Michael said don't tell strangers where you were going. What did Michael know? How can you enjoy life if you don't meet people? Did Michael enjoy life? Clearly not. That explained the answer to the question. You have to take chances. Takes a big risk to make a big win. That's why Michael never won. Forget Michael. She was going to enjoy herself or die trying. Hope it won't come to that.

She deliberately bypassed the downtown. She would save that till she had consulted with the tourist information people. Get all the brochures first then she'd know what to look for and what to appreciate. She found tourist information just south of town beside what they call in the West a river. Thought they'd know better in the West. It was nothing more than a swift running stream, maybe thirty feet wide in places. She thought of real rivers in the East—the Hudson, the Mississippi, the Ohio—decided what the heck, in Rome she would do as the Romans did. If this was their idea of a river, she'd call it a river, too.

She parked her car in the only spot of shade in the whole parking lot. A lonely cottonwood, that looked as if it would have been happier down by the river. She thought about locking up, took a look at the sun and decided to roll the windows down instead. Took her purse and walked over to the river just in time to see a rubber raft—loaded with tourists in bright red life jackets that flashed bold in the sun—come careening and bobbing around the pilings of a low bridge and go bouncing past, occupants all scared into silence. Seconds later another raft came up, surprising her how quickly it swished past. This raft was blue, an old worn blue, with dark blue life jackets.

After they had gone she stood looking at the river. Admiring how the sunlight glinted off the swirls and crests of the busy water as it darted and divided over rocks and between snags and logs and over sand. Something about the clearness of the air here, maybe the light. What could it be? She looked closely at some Black-Eyed Susans leaning out of the river's banks. Amazingly rich golden yellows. Luxurious deep rich brown rounded centers, like freshly mixed chocolate in a rough crusted mound. She looked up and around at the mountains, close enough to be touched and the brightly piled towers of white clouds. It all had a fresh scrubbed, painted look as if the dingy patina of reality somehow failed to settle here. She would have to think what it all meant. Later.

Now for tourist information.

The entrance was in the back, she would have to think about the significance of that, through an entranceway consisting of a wooden deck and stairs appended to an otherwise brick building. Someone's idea, she guessed, of how to give a western look to a functionary's workplace. Inside the lady behind the counter held a job that consisted of handing out brochures and assuring patrons "you won't have any trouble finding it, it's all in there."

"In there" it told her, was a train she could take that went up into the mountains and back. Well, she was already up in the mountains and she had ridden trains before. She would skip that. There were shops offering all kinds of western artifacts, from old authentic handmade to new authentic handmade, and some galleries that seemed to specialize, one in Remington cowboy-and-snow-bound-cattle themes, one in Indian faces rugged and west-facing, and one specializing—unaccountably—in clowns and circus performer faces. She would have to check out all three.

Wait a minute. Here's a brochure in bold red and yellow, crisply folded into three parts—rodeo! And it's tonight. Every Wednesday this month, but particularly tonight. She shouted a quick "bye-bye" to the brochure-and-reassurance lady and hurried out the door, stopped on the deck long enough to buy a Coke from the big red and white machine placed right where the sunlight would make it most noticeable and remind her of thirst, whether she had one or not, then out to her car. Even with the windows down, in no more than the spotty shade provided by the young cottonwood, her car had already grown warm and stuffy inside. Odd how in the crisp mountain air you were cool at this time of day walking around, but the sunlight was so brilliant it warmed right through the glass, raising your car interior to the boiling point. Now that she had her evening planned she would need a motel room, didn't want to be looking around tonight after the show.

It was easy enough to find a motel. Prices were all about the same. Only issue really was how far back from the highway they sat. The further back the less road noise, but the smaller the grounds because of the steep fall off down the mountainsides. Also whether you wanted a room facing the mountains in front, across the road, or facing the mountains in back, across the river. Small as it was that river was everywhere, twisting and coming back on itself. Either that or there were several branches, each way the canyons went, out of Durango. In any event there must have been a fortune made in this little town out of bridge construction. Every road must have crossed a river—she would call it a creek dozens of times in the privacy of her motel room—and who knew how many roads there were in Durango?

Her bags safely stored out of sight behind the folding doors to the closet, she lay back for a minute on the bed. It felt good to straighten out her back and ease the tension of her legs. Her crotch felt tight, it was stinging a little where her underpants drew up. She eased a finger between hem and flesh, it felt like a more soothing stroking was in order. It felt good, nicely relaxing.

Suddenly, the door flew open. A dark, heavy set man sprang in, something flashing silver in his hand. She jerked upright in horror. He stopped and stood awkwardly for a moment, as if registering what he had just seen.

"What the hell are you doing in here?" she screamed at him, backing up against the headboard to where she could feel the cushioned vinyl behind her.

"Room check, young lady." He spoke hurriedly, in a gruff voice as if reciting a rehearsed line, to cover his own embarrassment.

She looked at him numbly. He stood still, and dropped his arms to his side. "I'm the house detective," it was a leather bound badge he held in his hand, "young woman checks in alone, might be trying to sneak a whole car load of kids in here ... to ... for ... no telling what."

He looked at her like he was trying to keep his eyes on her face and away from where he had seen her and what he had seen her doing.

"Ah ... sorry," he said, slowly, as if trying to think his way out of a tangled problem. "Every thing's O.K. Go back to what you were ... Uh, forget it. Sorry."

"I'm going straight to the manager!" she told him, her voice level and deep, as anger began to drown her fear. "I'm going to ask him what you're doing here, what kind of a place this is. I'll get you fired!" Now she was really mad.

"O.K. O.K. My mistake," he said, backing out into the hallway. "look, here's free drinks." He held out a card in his hand, standing out in hall, reaching in. When she didn't move from the bed, he stooped and laid it on the carpet, said "sorry" again, in a soft voice, and pulled the door closed.

She sat there awhile, at the head of the bed, listening for his footsteps, but could hear nothing on the carpet outside through the thickness of the closed door.

She thought about what had just happened. Go to the manager? Well she still might do that. Mostly she was just mad and embarrassed about what she was doing when the man burst in. He had no right. He was probably telling the manager right now and they were both having a good laugh. She ought to just leave right now. But they had her credit card number. She'd still have to pay. Maybe not, she'd report it to the credit card company. Goddamn hassle. Or tell the police. Maybe later. Meanwhile ...

She slid off the bed and locked the night chain on the door. At least she could relax now. She'd turn off all the lights. He couldn't get back in. But she didn't want to stroke herself now. The moment was gone. Besides there were the galleries to see, dinner somewhere, and the rodeo. Damn, what a way to start sightseeing.

Chapter 8

She found both kinds of shops. The kind that sell new made-for-the-West artifacts, wearable or collectible. And the kind that sell old, unearthed and reclaimed
artifacts, from guns to chaps to saddles and broken farm and ranch implements
that have had no cosmetic or restorative attention beyond elementary removable
of mud. Complete with authentic rust. And this was the kind of store she liked
the best.

There were places that served more than you wanted to eat for more than you
wanted to pay, and there were the fast food places. She opted for fast food, figuring the cowboys would have done the same.

Main Street was not long, but there were nameless stores between the interesting ones, the galleries and the collectibles emporia. Sometimes so many of the
characterless, the drugstores, the dime stores, the locals-only bars and hardware
stores, that she frequently crisscrossed the street to get to what seemed a nearer
attraction than the one out of sight further down her side of the street. And sure
enough, after a few hours of this she could use a rest, a sit down somewhere. She
had just noticed an upstairs gallery of shops and a sign that said—she could
scarcely believe it—cappuccino! Surely not, not in Durango, Colorado.

What anticipation. A chance to sit back, draw her legs up deliciously out of
her shoes and stretch out at a sidewalk table, sip cappuccino and watch the world
go by. She climbed the airy wooden steps that led up from the sidewalk and, from
a whole new collection of shops, found the cappuccino place. Inside it looked
more like an ice cream parlor which it turned out to be. Operated, she was dismayed to see, by two teenage girls, one of whom may actually have been pre-teen.
Where was the dark-haired Italian gangsterish waiter that should have been hovering about the tables? He was absent. So, for that matter, were the tables. It was
stand up service only. And no fat Italian with stained apron behind the counter,
but then neither was there the gleaming steel monster of the tubing and the spig-
ots and the steam that marked an espresso machine. She asked the girls.

"Oh, I know how to make that. I have the recipe here. Hold on." The older
girl was cheerful and eager for the adventure. Her younger companion looked
equally eager to assist. "Yep, here it is. Got it. Wait just a minute."

There came the sound of the pouring of hot water. What? No steam? There
was the opening of a refrigerator. What, no hot milk? And there it was. The older
girl proudly handed out over the counter … a styrofoam cup? I am going to sip
cappuccino from a styrofoam cup? A cup that tastes and smells of plastic? How
will I be know what I'm drinking? I have to be able to let all my five senses swim

in cappuccino to enjoy it. I have to taste it, to smell it, to see it, to feel it. Hell, I can't even feel the heat through this stupid foam cup. Damn.

She paid for it anyway, figuring her feet could stand the rest, and she would find an outdoor table, and she would sit out there and watch the people go by, legs tucked up under her, and she would let the tiredness slowly drain out of her, and she would feel the sensuousness of being curled up out in the sun, but she wished it had been real cappuccino.

Chapter 9

She sat down across the work bench from him. There was laughter in her wide set eyes, her high cheeks were flushed and both sides of her perfectly bowed mouth quivered, threatening to lose all restraint. He was an artist. He noticed those signs in her, and they frightened him.

"I have something to tell you!" She was like an archer's bow, pulled tight.

"Yes, I can tell." He ached to share the deliciousness of her anticipation, but a coldness inside him forewarned him this was to be her joy, not his.

"Doug and I are engaged." She had come breathlessly to a cliff, ready to hurl herself into flight, if only he had the right response.

"Well now. Well, well, well. That's wonderful news! I had hoped for that." He had come back perhaps too quickly, like a commander waiting in the field for exactly that message. "That makes me happier than you can imagine."

Her eyes narrowed into a puzzlement.

"I'm happy because now I can relax. I can relax around you. I can relax with myself. I have peace of mind."

Even more puzzlement, hands beginning to trace nervously about the table.

"I'll tell you why. For two reasons. First. Doug is perfect for you. He's what my kids would call a keeper. I liked him even before I met him, because you said he liked to be silly with you when you wanted to be silly. I knew you were thinking seriously about him, when you said you wondered if it was all right, him being two years younger than you. And then I really liked him when you introduced us. I could tell that you were the most important person in the room to him, even though he talked to all of us, and circulated around. There was a certain way he had of admiring you in what he said and in the way he looked at you. Comfortable without being sappy."

She began to relax in front of him. The expectation went out of her shoulders. Her body weight began to come down on her hands, lying on the workbench they had been worrying a few seconds before.

"Is that it? Both reasons?"

"No. The second reason has been a secret. I've had to keep it from you. Because I couldn't afford to tell you. But now, thank God, I can tell you. And it won't still mean anything to you. No, not yet. But when I am gone and you are older it will mean something to you then, and so I'm giving it to you as a gift."

She registered the blank look that young people reserve for old people in that moment of choosing between toleration and tuning out.

"This reason is …"

She looked at him. At least he had her this few seconds more.

"You see, I've fallen in love with you several times." Now it was he who could not look at her. "The way, the foolish way, that an a middle aged man falls in love with a young woman." Now he could look at her. She had reddened with embarrassment. The happy news she had brought to share was sullied. It would never be as pure, as good again. He saw that she wanted to be somewhere else, anywhere else. It was hard to take, realizing he had had no sexual identity to her. He would have to hurry if he hoped to make this gift worthy of her time.

"But I couldn't say anything. I couldn't have stood it, doing something stupid. I couldn't have stood knowing I might be harassing you. Or stood your rejecting me. Or laughing at me."

Her cheeks reddened and puffed below her eyes. He could feel the burning. "So what difference does it make now? Why can you tell me this now?" About her was now an air of circling the wagons, of defending something critical. Her future with her man?

"Well, see, now you belong to somebody." He caught the stiffening. "Oh, I don't mean belong in any subordinate sense that would offend the equality of a young feminist today. I mean belong in the sense of a matching pair, the way bookends belong to one another, the way Sunday belongs to the week."

Another blank look. Losing her again. Hard to give a gift that a person will have to get older in order to appreciate.

"What I mean is, now you know who your love really is. If it had been possible for anything I said to confuse you or to threaten your composure, you might have felt bad about yourself, thinking some way that you were contributing to my delinquency and the ruin of my marriage. If you were alone and vulnerable. If you felt your biological clock ticking. Any of that might have made you a victim, somehow. Well, I don't mean victim exactly, but I might have embarrassed you."

She projected restlessness, really wanted to be somewhere else. Hurry.

"But it's worse than that. I wasn't just thinking of you. I'm older now, and, if we'd ever … if it had happened that we had gotten together and I couldn't or we couldn't find a way to …"

At last a look came into focus. A look he thought he recognized. You're disgusting. He felt himself shrinking into himself. The workbench between them, all twenty four inches in width, seemed a vast football field, and her a tiny spectator. A spectator but not a fan, about to head for the exits.

"Funny thing," she said. "I fell in love with you one summer … and I was ashamed to tell you. I thought you might laugh at me."

That, now, he understood. The part about falling in love. He had been close enough to her that he could ask questions without getting intrusive. He had asked her what it meant to be in love.

It had come about when she was talking about a friend ...

"A boyfriend?"

"No," she had said, "just a friend. We hang out together."

"You don't date?"

"No, we hang out."

"So, he's a friend who happens to be a boy."

"Right."

"What's the difference between a friend that's a boy, and a boyfriend?"

"Well, I guess you sleep with your boyfriend."

"Like a lover?"

"Well, probably you love him."

He had gotten quiet. It took a while to translate it all into terms he understood, and she had asked what was the matter. Then he told her it all seemed too loose and amorphous to him. You didn't seem to have clear signals about what stage you were in, how when he had been single you first went out in mixed groups, maybe not actually the same number of boys as girls. Then you dated, doubles or triples. He could tell she was astonished. By the time you were dating—to her—you were sleeping together. Then you single dated. Then you went steady. She had no concept of going steady—to her after sleeping together came living together. Then you got engaged. More amazement—to her getting engaged was a compliment paid to a sleeping partner if living together seemed to work. Then you got married. She lost interest here—the idea of commitment seemed to spoil the whole scenario, getting engaged was the climax of the entire cinematic production.

"You left out being lovers," she chided, rousing herself, making a point.

"No, it's the same as I said, except lovers is what you are if one of you is already married and you can't do the engagement and marriage part.

"Well, you left out the sleeping together part. When do you start sleeping together?

"After you get married."

"You're kidding!"

"It didn't always work out that way but everybody acted like it did."

"Then it sure took your crowd a long time to get to the important part."

Now, today, he understood. At last he understood.

"You mean there was a time once when you were thinking about sleeping with me?"

"Sure!" She gave him a big grin. "Bummer, huh?"

Chapter 10

Tonight, thought Clyde as pulled her sweater over her head, and slid her blunted fingers through her hair, fluffing out the loops and knots, tonight she will try again. Tonight I must be ready. Tonight I cannot fall asleep. If I must lie awake all night, I will endure this night. I will live tomorrow.

"Clyde?" Her mother's voice high and wretched across the darkened room. No moon left to show the rug between them, the bare wood floors, the rough log walls around them. The open, curtained doorway to the bath with its painted metal shower stall leaning askew out over the sink, fastened only by its shower head and faucets. The single door, the door to freedom, made of planks, with planks crossed on the inside to hold it together. Held closed by a hook, a hook between her and liberation. No light shining through the cracks. No hall light. No one to help her. Alone. And her mother starting again.

"Clyde? Clyde, did I ever tell you why we named you Clyde?"

"Yes, Mother, you did."

"But did I ever tell you where the name came from?"

"Yes, you've told me."

"I'll bet you think we named you after somebody we knew, didn't you?"

"No, Mother. I didn't think that. I know you didn't know anybody named Clyde."

"Would you like to know the real reason. Would you like to hear it now?"

"Mother, I know the reason. All the reasons. Let's leave it, now. O.K.?"

"You know, if you don't like your name, you can change it."

"I know that."

"You could have whatever name you wanted."

"Yes, I know."

"You could even have 'Michael'." A giggle.

"I wouldn't want that."

"Why not? It's a pretty name."

"No, it's not."

"Well, it's a strong name."

"No, it's not. It's a weak name." Clyde turned her head in the direction of the door and the way to freedom.

"Why do you say that?"

"Because it's true, Mother. It's a nothing name. A compromise. From a man and a woman who wanted a boy. All it says is that they wanted you to be a boy. It says that the only way they could love you was to give you a boy's name."

"Clyde! Is that what you think? I was the youngest child. How could I not be loved?"

"Yeah, they would love you. Once they made you over. Once they made you into something else."

"How can you say that about your own grandparents? You make them out to be monsters."

"Well, they were monsters. They had to be, to do that to you."

"You can't lie there and say that. They were good people. My mother and father. Your grandparents!"

"I don't know. I never met them."

"They were good people. They would have loved you."

"I'll take your word for it."

"Why are you using that tone of voice with me? All the love I've given you, and this is how you treat your own mother."

There was a silence. A blessed silence under which the challenge lay, the challenge to comfort, a corporeal thing between them. A thing that would grow, ugly and bloated, a hurt, wide and bruised, that Michael would nurse and feed till she suffocated herself or until Clyde dispatched it with the formula, the only formula that would work.

Hating herself for giving in, hating her mother for the challenge, "All right, Mother, let me hear it. Tell me how you came to name me Clyde."

PROLOGUE TO THE MOSH PIT

It was enough that he was a black man, playing a game with an Indian's name. It was enough that she was white and a sort of blonde married to a child-man earning three million a year. And spending more. It was enough that she got pregnant in high school and they married in college and he turned pro and walked away, no, ran away from school and never looked back till the end. It was enough that by the time it was over they had eight cars and a truck, they had three kids and one on the way that she didn't know whose it was. It was enough, or should have been, but in the end it was not.

THE MOSH PIT OF OZYMANDIAS

Being married to a pro football player is like being married to a navy man. Sailors and football players are gone for weeks at a time. When they come home they want life to go on just like it was before they left. They think they're going to be in charge again just like they were before. Forget that you have been taking care of three children and running the house all by yourself.

Yeah, you had a live-in maid and, yes, you had a sitter when you went to the mall but ... You were the one that called the furnace people. You were the one that got the driveway paved. You were the one that fed the kids and carted them around. The goddamn kids. You get the biggest van they make, all nice and clean smelling, and one month later it looks like a latrine and smells worse. And the seatbelts. You know how long it takes to get three kids into seatbelts? It takes all goddamn day.

Sure you take your sitter with you. Big help. She's supposed to be watching the kids. She's watching the guys instead. Any guy you know looking at a woman with three kids? No, they're looking the other way or checking out your sitter. Can't a woman have a life?

As I said it's like being married to a navy man. The first rule is don't ask what they did while they were gone and the second rule is don't tell what you did. Whoever thought of that was right and that's where I should have left it.

Not likely I'd have found out about Little Miss No-hips if I'd let it slide, but I was onto him and onto him about where he'd been and didn't they ever let you out of training and what did you do at night. Come on really and hey I won't get mad. Even then he probably never would have told me but I wouldn't let up on him after he threw the oldest kid up against the wall and I saw I'd really, really gotten under his skin. So I kept after him and I could see he was getting madder and madder.

I used to think he was cute when he got mad. His skin would get a deep ruby look under that fudge brown and I'd know, like, when to stop. He never laid a hand on me though he beat up on the kids now and then. Nothing big time like you take them to the emergency room or anything, but it tore me up to see him do it and I flat out told him if he wanted to throw somebody around why didn't he pick on me. But he wouldn't.

I could scare him, I don't know how I could scare him. He weighed three times what I weighed, maybe more. He could trash me anytime he felt like it. I don't know why he never hit me. Came near it though. Never did.

I was riding him and riding him and it got to where he couldn't take it. Then he drank a beer like he wasn't supposed to, what with him in training and all, and he yelled it out at me all at once. Well it was Little Miss Nohips. That wasn't her real name. Her real name is Sueann Teagarden. Can you believe that? Sue-fuckin'-ann Teagarden! What kind of a wussy ass name is Sueann Teagarden?

I knew who she was. Always hanging around. What kind of woman hangs around when it's a hundred and twenty in the shade watching men pushing a bunch of big old dirty old smelly old bags around in the dirt? Thought she was some kind of a reporter. Always watching. Maybe a sportswriter. Always thought I ought to see a camera and Channel Five News sign or something.

So I pitched a fit. Well, it was my turn. Started throwing things around. He hates it when I break up stuff, especially glass. Claims the kids'll get cut. Really paranoid about that, you know? As if it's o.k. when he backhands one of the kids, yeah and knocks the kid right up against the wall. Makes a whole lot of sense, right?

Well he's gone again for a week. Team's out of town. Only this time he doesn't come home. Great. We've got a place out west. Does he go there? Not so they tell me. Next thing I know I'm seeing credit card bills from Trinidad. Then I see Miss Nohips is in a convertible now. And guess where her tee shirt has a picture of on it?

Am I making this up? Next thing he knows his stuff is out of the house, UPS, FedEx, on the street, whatever. Two strikes and you're out with me. Shoulda been one.

That's all. I'm going back to college. I'm getting my degree. I'm getting a job, high school phys-ed teacher. What do I need him for? Bastard takes the keys to all eight cars. How am I going to get around I ask him? He writes me a check. I buy this little red Miyata. Keep it a week and take it back and get me a pick up truck. That's more me, you know?

*   *   *   *

By the second or third class we had all found out who she was. Maybe she was a couple of years older than most of us, but not so much older that anybody would have noticed. It would have gone on like that if she hadn't said anything. But it was not like her to hold back.

She was always up front with everything. Whatever we were doing, lecture, workshop, it didn't matter. She'd take notes, she'd do the drills, answer the questions, take the tests. Didn't matter. She was all business.

And she was up front with her life, you know? Something would come up, she'd say like yeah he dumps me and goes off to Trinidad with some bimbo with no hips, me with his three kids at home. Used to break me up when she'd come out with stuff like that.

I don't know. We hung out in the cafeteria a couple of times. Like she'd be there before class or I'd see her after. Couple of times we went out for beers. Sometimes she'd pay. Hell, most of the time she'd pay, like why not? Always something like he's got to pay for this, might as well let him do it. Like he doesn't owe it to me? She'd say that.

She gave you a fun time. Eyes always laughing. She didn't have to laugh right out loud. Her eyes were always laughing in her face. It was her way. I think it was kind of grinning like hey is this a dumb thing to do or what? She had this girl she'd hang out with. They were always doing stuff together.

There was a bar out past Leesburg. I don't know what it was about that bar. Maybe guys there got to know them, maybe it's where they met. I don't know but that's where she'd always be telling me she'd gone. No, when I went there nobody was hitting on nobody. Maybe because it was me there with her? You got me. I don't know. But she was fun to be with. Always laughing or looking like she was laughing inside. I already said that? O.K. so I'm coming to the part about the steel marbles. Just hold on a minute.

I was living by myself then and we started going to my place. Now and then, not as much as I wanted to. She claimed she couldn't get away except on class nights because of her roommate. I don't know why that was, because I'd hear later how she'd gone to that Leesburg bar with her stripper girl friend. Didn't I say she was a stripper? O.K. well this girl friend was a stripper. Anyway the first night at my place was good. You might say it was the best. It was like, hey, I've forgotten how to do this. Let's do that again. You know what I mean?

After that night she was real strange for a while, like hey do I know you? Then it was like when are you going to invite me over to your place again. The first night after she comes on that way was like it was never going to end. It was o.k., I mean the best, for a couple, maybe three times after that, then she's off me and it's hey do I know you all over again.

Like man, I'm beginning to wonder if it's worth it, then this stripper, I'd met her by now, invites us to go to this party, it's really a sitdown dinner at this artist friend's of hers.

It's a Saturday night. We'd never done Saturday nights before. She picks me up where I'm living at, but she won't come in. She's wearing this long black coat and she's got this dancing look in her eye. She's all smiles and laughing inside like what turned me on about her from the beginning but I don't know the half of it yet. We get to this dude's place and she drops off her coat, it's more like a rain-coat than a coatcoat, you know? And what she's wearing underneath is kind of like a cowgirl dress. It's short skirted and has fringe stuff along the bottom. There's a kind of a vest on the top with a kind of see-through blouse and the vest has fringes on it, too.

And all the time there's this laughing look in her eyes. Her friend the stripper says something to her and she kinds of jiggles her butt, my girl does, and the two of them bust out laughing. That's with us all standing there in the den. I couldn't figure it out. What's the joke?

So then we all sit down to eat, it's a chicken something with a pasta something else. I'd eaten better, it's not like I've never been anywhere, and she starts telling everybody about her and this chat room guy. Turns out she's been online to him just about every day and they started out right off going into a private room.

He's from New York, telling her how he's a big talent scout, and she sends him some pictures and next thing she flies up there. I don't know how she got away from those kids. They do lunch. She says New York people don't eat, they do lunch. Then they go out for dinner and he looks at some more pictures she's got. What did you do between lunch and dinner I ask her? She doesn't look at me she looks at her stripper friend and she lifts up a little bit on the chair and sits down again. The stripper laughs out loud. Then she scrunches up her face tight and she makes her eyes do that laughing thing and her stripper friend starts hooting.

All this time the stripper's husband has been sitting there looking like he's going to bust, and now he's had all he can stand and he starts laughing and he laughs so hard he starts pounding on the table. So there's the three of them having this big laugh, and this artist dude and his wife, one's sitting at one end of the table the other at the other, and me we don't know what the hell's going on. So this artist guy he makes this big deal about what's the secret and all, so they laugh some more and the stripper she whispers kind of out loud so we can all hear but like pretending it's just for the artist wife, "Steel marbles."

So the artist's wife she looks at my girl and she laughs out loud, "Steel marbles!" Then this artist guy he points at her, sitting there in her fringe jacket and see-through blouse, and he's "Steel marbles! What a hoot!"

What-a-hoot. I hadn't heard anybody talk like that in ten years. And she's the one now that's laughing the hardest. Eyes, lips, mouth, everything. Then she kind of lifts up off her seat and kind of shakes her butt from side to side, rolls her eyes and laughs like crazy. I am dense, I admit, but I am now catching on.

Like this girl couldn't go through an airport metal detector bare naked. I think, now that I look back on it, that we were out of there in probably half an hour or less, but at the time I think it felt more like twenty years. Did I say our first night together was the best? Well, I don't know, this one was better, well if not better, at least wilder. Yeah, wilder, but I'm not going to tell you about it. You don't need to know.

That was it. The last time. I never saw her again. She didn't even come back to school. I looked up her stripper friend where she worked, did I tell you they once tried out for a rock band together? Anyway that's another story. This stripper says she and the kids got back together with her husband. He's still playing football. I don't know what she's doing. I'll miss her eyes. Go figure.

ALCESTIS BY DAY

Prologue—Prince Henry

"God," said Cass, "this is the stupidest thing I ever let you talk me into. I hate it."

Small, dark and thin, shorts, sneakers, hands on her hips, she stood on the bricked esplanade and, without looking at the taller, heavier blonde beside her, spoke in the direction of a short, muscular taxi driver in soiled grey shortsleeved unionalls who was tying her bicycle onto Wyn's that was already lashed to the roof of his cab, its wheels dangling improbably over the sides. Other taxi operators were about, some leaning on their cars smoking, others gesturing to hesitant tourists and hurried businessmen in suits.

The driver, now aided by two other men, one wearing a fisherman's cap, tried to steady the bicycles and balance them, scraping the poor metal frames together, making Wyn wince at the sound.

There was no rescuing the bikes. The driver had slammed down the trunk lid locking away their panniers first off, making the rear of the tiny vehicle sag piteously.

She turned away from the torturing of her gear and looked off down the road. The Lisbon airport had the feel of being on a hill, and the bricks where they were standing formed a great flat circle that opened across from them onto a straight road through interminable rows of eucalyptus trees. The sun was warm and welcome after a wretched overnight flight beside a restless Cassandra. There was a Mediterranean feel to the morning. Breakfast had been scant and rushed, she could feel her socks damp and sagging. Cass had been in a foul mood, the only good thing about the morning had been the hot wet towels from the stewardesses. To hell with Cass and her moods. Cass, she decided, was not going to be a morning person.

She swung her backpack off her shoulder onto the bricks and pulled out their guidebook. Cass's copy had lost itself before boarding.

"Short ride into town, it says. Shouldn't take long, Cass."

"Better not," said Cass, and looked down at her feet. Small feet in small shoes, one without strings. Wyn shrugged and looked up to see the three drivers had tied thick white rope from the protruding bicycle parts to the car's side mirrors and there was their driver throwing his weight against the door to hold it open against the strings so they could get in. The other two drivers were looking at Cass. They nudged each other and laughed.

The hotel's registration desk occupied the entire width of a stall exactly the same size as the tobacconer's next door. They had to step over the woman on hands and knees with a bucket washing off the stone step and the front pavement. Their room would be in a building across the street. Cass followed the boy with the key who carried her pack. The taxi driver came up behind them, carrying one bike, while Wyn bumped the other one up the stairs, leaning forward against the weight of her backpack.

"God," said Cass, and dropped face down on the closer of the twin beds, arms outstretched, before the man and boy had left the room. Wyn held out a handful of change from which they each claimed a few escudos, and closed the door behind them. She dropped her pack in the narrow space between the two beds and looked at the room.

It was a corner room, with soft light from windows on two walls. Tall windows below high ceilings, windows set deep in a thick wall with shutters on the inside. Just like in the song, she thought.

The corner of the street turned just below them and already there was traffic and there were flower sellers to watch and newsstands, but she would leave that for later. She turned from the windowsill to look back into the room. The beds stood on either side of the door, sagging in the middle as if their mattresses were no more than cloth stretchers. In fact, though Cass lay on her stomach, her hips were sunk into the bed below the height of her shoulders and feet. Her laceless shoe had fallen back from her foot and leaned to one side exposing the bare heel and giving her foot a wedged shaped effect from this angle.

Wyn reached about under her own bed and confirmed that there was indeed no mattress. Some kind of roping and canvas spanned the bed frame. She could live with that. The bikes leaned together against the wall at the foot of Cass's bed. Below the window on the other wall was a broad ceramic basin resting in a wooden ring supported by four slender legs. In the middle of the basin was a bronze stopper with a small raised knobbed handle, and underneath was a grey shapeless bucket with a spout like a watering can. Two small towels as thin and brittle as paper were draped on bars attached to the washstand. Against the wall to the left of the window was a tall, narrow mirror. And in the small space between her bed and the wall, and out of the view of the window, on a shorter legged version of the wash stand, was the most beautifully shaped ceramic basin she had ever seen. White, with its own drain plug and a broad pan underneath. Graceful, with soft inviting curves to rest your knees, a marvelous, delightfully, naively simple and prideful bidet. She thought of waking Cass to tell her. The door knocked.

"… you," mumbled Cass into her pillow.

Wyn opened the door. A woman in a loose gray dress with a gray blue apron that wrapped all around her and a scarf beckoned her out into the hall. Wyn went out and closed the door behind her. She tried her key in the lock and fastened Cass inside, then went down the hall behind the woman. There was a narrow door halfway down the corridor on the left which the woman pulled open dramatically. Inside on a raised floor, in queenly dignity, and lit by a skylight, was a thin pedestal of a toilet with a pull chain hanging scepter like beside it, depending from an immense height and a box-like water chamber affixed just beneath the skylight. The woman mimed a question at Wyn and said something in Portuguese. Wyn nodded. The woman pointed to a roll of parchment-like paper on a box near the door then stepped out into the hall and closed the door.

At the end of the hall was another room lit by a skylight, a room with an immense claw footed tub, also on a raised platform. There was a metal hose and a small shower head-like fixture attached to the faucet, and on the wall a tangled contraption of loops and valves, that required a lighted match, as the woman illustrated with props from her apron.

Across from the bath she showed Wyn her own room, with a narrow cot, even more primitive than Wyn's, with no door but a curtain, and this she made Wyn to understand by signs and questioning looks was where Wyn was to find her when she wanted hot water.

Outside, rested and fed, and sporting a new shoelace from Wyn's duffel, Cass was a new woman. They had started with a table in the square on the blind side of their hotel. They had had roasted chicken pieces, potatoes and a Coke for breakfast, and had laughed and talked and watched the flower girl in front of the fountain, and Cass had taken off her shoe with the new lace in it and put one foot into the fountain while all the men watched.

They walked around the square and laughed about the shoeshine boxes. There were men getting their shoes shined on every corner and even in the restaurants while they ate and while they sat on the benches and talked to their friends. Every man had shiny shoes, even, as Wyn now remembered, the taxi drivers.

They walked the streets and laughed at the swans in the boulevard pools and challenged one another to imagine the wealth behind the soaring white homes built against steep hills, with black iron fretwork, and chauffeurs washing cars in lush, closed, walled gardens they could scarcely jump high enough to see into.

They met a small crowd of holidaying university students who knew some English and took them up to see the monument to Prince Henry the Navigator, and over to the castle that overlooked the Tagus river and the black boats with slack, dark sails that ran freight across the harbor.

By the time they had visited the ancient Moorish quarter of Al Fama, and ridden the streetcar that goes up the second steepest hill while remaining perfectly horizontal, and gone up the steepest hill in the outdoor elevator designed by the same M. Eiffel that built the tower in Paris, by the time all that had happened and darkness was setting in, there was a particular small, dark young man, of the many small dark young men who were with her and leading and laughing and pointing, who had begun to be mostly with Cass. And there was a taller, stockier, quieter young man whose smile was wide and showed very good teeth, and who drew particularly charmingly on cafe napkins, who had begun to be mostly with Wyn. The day passed breathlessly, and their good byes at the hotel's street door were rich with promises for tomorrow, and going to Escorial and Estoril, and to the Fado, which sounded like fun.

Brightly laughing and shoving, arm in arm they ran up the stairs to halt breathless and bouncing in front of the old woman's curtain and called boldly for their bath daring one another to be first. The old lady moaned and came out stiffly and bent over, one arm pushing off her knee at first. Gradually she limbered up and dutifully she lighted their fire for them, and though a scrub brush stood in a bucket on a tall stool at hand she refused to let either of them clean out her tub afterwards.

Next morning Wyn woke happy and looked briefly at the sleeping Cass face down on the blankets of the other bed, shapeless in her loose shirt and baggy shorts, one foot still half in a shoe. Wyn poured water into the waist high basin, slipped off her sleeveless, wet her face, dried and looked in the mirror. She liked her short blonde hair this morning, and she flipped it back from her forehead with one finger. She thought her blue eyes looked remarkably clear today. She considered her breasts carefully, turning first to one side then to the other. She thought of the tall young man with the wide smile, and considered her shape again, moving close up to see her hips better, and decided the Portuguese girls last night had gone to hips too early, probably from being too short and developing too soon, she thought. She caught the soft morning sun on her breasts and decided pink was the perfect color for nipples. Cass's she thought were too brown.

Across the narrow street a heavy set man suddenly leaned out the window and waved. She threw up her hands and dodged into the dark corner shadow between the windows.

Later in the square, sitting in the mottled sunlight of a wire chair beneath the palm trees around the flower seller's, she had a coffee with hot milk, and wondered how long Cass might sleep. After an hour of watching the going and coming in the square, and the men in black getting shoe shines, and the women in dark clothes, and the children in school uniforms, after an hour of watching the policemen with their grey uniforms and their white gloves and watching the grey pigeons, and the white fountain, and the white swans flashing brilliant in the sunlight, all the watching and the being ignored, and with still an hour to go till rendezvous with the students she went back to their room. Cass lay face down, nose in her pillow, lone shoe still precariously balanced under her toe, unchanged so far as Wyn could see.

There was a wide space on Cass's back where the skin showed between crumpled shirt and rumpled shorts. Wyn dipped her fingers in the basin and fluttered them over Cass's bare skin. No movement. Wyn lowered her whole hand into the water and felt the wet soft morning rising slowly up her wrist. Holding her other hand below to catch the drips she stepped over and slipped her wet hand up inside the back of Cass's shirt. Cass rolled over slowly.

"morning," she said, grinning slowly and opening her eyes with great deliberation, first one and then the other.

It is so good to see her smiling in the morning, thought Wyn. She came very close to crying.

Their university friends were on time. They all crowded noisily onto an electric train for the hour long ride to Estoril and discovered a fishing town with yellow beaches and boats hauled up with nets drying. There were young people on blankets, some in the severe black of streetwear and some in single piece bathing suits. There were older parents with little children who ran naked in and out of the water, and they found a motorboat to rent and a young man in black pants and a white suit to drive them around the harbor in it.

They ate and had wine, which the students said was good for digestion. They sang songs from American movies and chased one another in the sand, and got their clothes wet and had a wonderful time. In a rare quiet moment Wyn saw Cass sharing a cigarette with the same young man she had been with last night.

Wyn allowed the tall young man with the white teeth walk her away from the group and kiss her. It was good to be held and to feel his eager kisses.

They were loud and lively on the train going back to Lisbon. Their clothes had dried and everyone went to Fado which they found meant a darkened tavern and sad, solemn solo singing, mostly by a heavy Portuguese lady dressed in a vaguely Spanish way suggestive of a bull fight party, and which required lots of red wine to appreciate.

Later their two friends' roommates made a great fuss with arrangements to spend the night away so that the young men could invite Wyn and Cass up to their rooms at the university. Wyn tried to get Cass to answer her whispers. Could she find the hotel by herself? Cass was too busy kissing and snuggling with her young man, slipping her hands in and out of his pockets while he danced about and tried to pull her away from Wyn and her man, and finally he and Cass left.

In his room, which had only one window and was lighted well enough by a street light nearby, Wyn would have liked to comment on the sparseness, the neatness, the lack of books and papers. There was a bullfight poster on one wall, with dark colors hard to see. But she did try hard, through the flurry of undressing, to pronounce clear words about careful and about baby. But the young man pulled at her anxiously and kissed her and grew impatient. She rode him hard because he wanted her to, and felt the reality of him and wanted to let herself go and to reach for the highest she could reach. But she worried if he had understood his promise and bent down to his mouth to ask again and when he pulled outside it was too late for her and she had him between her legs and felt the patter of his moment in the small of her back and tried to hold him with her legs, and work him lower to get a better grip and help with his feeling, and now she was awake enough to think about Cass and whether she would be careful, and how she could hold her man, Cass whose legs were thin and scarcely met.

In the intimacy of later on she sought her moment of fondness, hoping he would ask if she had had complete pleasure, so she could leave out the part about the worrying and tell him yes and caress him gratefully, but he told her instead that he felt bad, because he believed in God and should not have gone outside, but that she was wonderful anyway and the sin was his to bear and he would be happy for her sake.

At breakfast in the university cafeteria, Cass came in fully awake and shared a cigarette with her friend while Wyn's student held her hand and looked at her deeply, and Wyn studied the reflections of the bright mural patterns of the gold and tan university buildings in his eyes.

In their hotel room Cass and Wyn talked about their men as they dragged their panniers up onto the beds and packed. Cass told Wyn all about her night. Wyn, for her part, told how her young man looked undressed. She did not tell Cass about holding the hardness of him with her thighs or about his disappointment. She said instead how he had had a cigarette later on, and how sour and nauseous his lips and the insides of his mouth had tasted afterwards. And she asked Cass how she could stand it.

Cass was pulling up the loose baggy shorts she would wear on the bike. Her shirt lay in front of her on the bed. She looked up at Wyn, in a slow, teasing grin. Her eyes were brown and big. She rolled her tongue around her lips.

"Tastes good in here," she said. "Want to see?"

"Cassie!" said Wyn. "God, no."

They looked at each other for a moment. Cassie's eyes were laughing. Wyn felt the hot blush rising, and turned away. She walked over to the window she had meant to look out of and stared off at nothing. Cass strode casually to the other window, the one from which Wyn had seen the fat man waving, and leaned over and rested her elbows on the sill, her shirt neglected on the bed behind her, and grinned out the window at Lisbon in the sunlight.

SUR LE PONT

Chapter One

Inches above her head the canopy had begun to brighten. A diffuse glow surrounded her. It would be misty outside. Wynona untangled her legs from the damp knots of her sleeping bag and turned to look at her companion. God, she thought for the thousandth time, how can she sleep like that?

Cassandra lay face down on top of her sleeping bag like something discarded in the night. Her arms were crimped above her head, enmeshed in her wild black hair. She wore an enormous tee-shirt, soft and translucent from too many washings. Her tan showed through the shreds of the shirt. It was so large on her that one arm came through the neck hole, the unused sleeve somewhere beneath her light body. Tiny bottom and boyish hips were loosely covered by a borrowed pair of Wynona's shorts, a lightweight, indifferent garment they used for swimming, walking, biking and sleeping—every thing but dress up. Except for a faint valley between her buttocks, it might have been a dishcloth for all the shape it lent her. Out of great limp holes two small legs stretched, lighter on the backsides, and grown muscular with the pedaling. The soles of her feet were wrinkled, heels apart, toes together like puppies needing love.

She is such a snot, Wynona said to herself.

With the growing warmth of the day, she felt she was afloat in the fertile smell of the two of them, a smell thick with body sweat, sandals, road grit, river sand, exhaust fumes, unwashed clothes, heat, rain, pheromones and urine.

She could go down to the showers now. This early the building might be empty. There might be hot water. The luxury of a solitary shower. An advance on her allowance of clean underpants. It was almost too good to pass up. But then there would be the loamy greenhouse smell of their tent to return to, and the ordeal of nursing Cass into wakefulness.

Wyn stretched a leg toward Cassie's knee, vaguely aware of the flecks of polish still clinging to her toes, dimly resentful of a distant Spaniard who'd turned out older than he looked. She pushed at Cassie.

"It's morning, Cass. Time to hit the showers."

No response. She kicked at Cass's leg, harder this time. "Get up."

Cass pulled away from her, trying to wedge herself under the tent wall. Wynona pushed again.

Cass pulled her arms down close, lumping up the raincoat she used as a pillow. She drew up her knees froglike toward her stomach.

"Wake up, Cass." Wyn swung her hips around, placed both feet on Cass's rump and drummed with her heels. Cass scrunched her pillow and turned her head away grumbling

"God," said Wynona. She got up on her knees, ducked her head to avoid the inside clotheslines, straddled Cass's backside and tickled at the ribs in the hollows of her underarms, wiggling her fingers in the sweat and heat of the short, black tufts of hair.

Cassie exploded into life. She yanked her arms underneath her, pulled up her knees and bucked. The knobbed ridge of her backbone jarred against Wyn's pelvis. Wyn's head snapped against the tent canopy and caught the clotheslines as she fell, jostling the tent, ripping the tent pegs.

Cassie rolled upright and backed into her corner of the tent. She wrapped her arms around her knees, her one bare shoulder pressed against the tent wall, her hair falling over her face, the leg holes of the borrowed shorts hanging wide and limp at her ankles.

"Don't you ever do that again!"

"God, Cass," said Wynona, "that's what you say every time." Her pelvis hurt and she thought of the Spanish man, she thought of the smell of olive oil and garlic and red wine, and felt the dust of Spanish roads. "Why don't you get up when I call you?"

"Why don't you leave me alone?"

Wynona turned away and studied the tent flap, listening for the sounds of other people going ahead of them to the showers, and thinking of the Spanish man. He'd had a nice car and a nice country house and servants. She would have liked having servants.

"Well, why don't you?" Cass said again.

"God," Wyn said to the tent flap.

There was silence till she turned back to Cass and said, as if to a child, "It's Avignon, Cass. We're going to see the bridge."

"Screw you," said Cass.

Chapter Two

They crawled out of the tent. The sun began to stretch tentative fingers through the Eucalyptus trees where the mist lingered in the shadows. Cass stood silently, head down, while Wyn made sure that both bicycles were still secured to the thorn tree by her bike lock. Cass's lock had lost itself somewhere in Portugal during their first week.

They walked along the road of crushed mussels, Cass's head down, eyes half closed. Wyn looked at the tents on either side. She wondered what kinds of people picked the big army tents and which had the little round ones. She wondered if there were any people traveling alone, if the men traveling together were gay, if the women next door were gay, if the mixed couples had made love in the night or would in the heat of the day, and if the couples with little children were married.

She no longer wondered which people spoke English. French campers spoke only to people they knew. She had told Cass it kept their privacy in a crowded country. Cass had said "Europeans are jerks."

Outside the concrete shower building two groups of smokers stood, talking quietly. Both groups turned silent as they passed between them. Wyn nodded "'tag" to the one and "'jour" to the other, getting soft "Bon jour's" in return.

"Do you have to do that?" Cass said inside. Wyn ignored her.

The first room was large. Along the outer wall were sinks and mirrors, each with a shelf for toiletries. A man with an enormous belly tilted daintily over one of them, tipping back his head to scrape beneath his nose with a safety razor. Two walls were lined with tiled sinks, shallow sinks for washing dishes, deeper ones for clothes. Each sink had a single faucet. In one of the sinks dishes floated in a miniature reddish sea with islands of suds scattered about its surface.

Dark hallways opened ahead and to the right. The right hand hallway was marked with a silhouetted figure in a skirt.

In the women's hall Wyn opened a toilet door. She was glad there was no sign of recent use. Even Cass had laughed at their first experience with a "Turkish" French toilet. Nothing but a hole in the floor and two raised foot-shaped slabs to stand on, with channels cut out of the floor for the water to run in and keep your feet dry when you flushed. The water chest was way up at the ceiling and the flushing action was so violent that Wyn would stepped outside and reach in to pull at the chain rather than chance a splash. There was usually a peg on the door for a person's bag, a necessity since you had to carry your own tissue. They used Baby Wipes.

After the first day squatting felt natural. Gravity was a good friend in the Franco-Turkish toilets, they had reminded each other. Wyn had thought about men. With both hands needed to keep their balance how could they aim? They would have to urinate and defecate by turns. "Piss and shit," said Cass had said.

Wyn suspected the men's side had urinals.

She looked for a shower a few doors down. Cass was grumbling next door. She found a peg for her bag and was grateful for the curtain that closed off the shower stall. She stepped out of her sandals onto the concrete, still damp from whoever had been there before. Wyn hoped her predecessors had healthy feet. Surely she was too optimistic, she thought. She mouthed a quick mantra to her personal god of cleanliness, slipped out of her shorts and shirt and slid back the curtain.

It was a single, push button control. She hated push button showers. She shoved on the button and stepped aside as the water gushed out—bitter cold. She held her hand in the spray till it turned at last to tepid and stepped in just as the water ran out. She set her teeth and forced herself to stand while the water gushed again, not quite so cold this time. She lathered up quickly covering her whole body in shampoo, then continued to spread the foam over her skin after the spray had stopped. The nascent roughness under her arms fretted her for a moment. It reminded her about Cass's stubbornness. Cass hadn't shaved her underarms since Portugal. At least Cassie shaved her legs. Cass would look like an ape, she thought, if she didn't shave her legs. The thought pleased Wyn.

Two more squirts and she was out rubbing off with the only towel she had brought, a hand towel. Next time she would bring two towels and leave one pair of shorts at home. If there was a next time

They brushed their hair and their teeth in the common room. Wyn took longer, though her hair was shorter.

There were more smokers outside the showers when they left. Wyn felt she smelled better and said her "Bon jour's" this time with more confidence, and was pleased to hear more voices answering this time.

"You are such a shit head," Cass whispered.

"Shut up," Wyn said.

Chapter Three

Walking into Avignon took less time than they had expected. It was rush hour and hundreds of little French cars and motor scooters crowded the bridge that led from the Campground Bagatelle across the Rhone to the gate of the walled city. "This is not the bridge," Wyn told Cass as they climbed up the staggered steps leading to the pedestrian walkway.

"I know that," said Cass.

"Have you ever heard of the Bridge of Avignon?" Wyn asked. They were at mid bridge now, walking fast, the only pedestrians, their voices raised over the traffic that revved up to the hump and down toward the wall of the town. Wyn could feel the warmth of the engines' heat and imagine the shower of dustules from the hundreds of exhausts. Her skin itched with the memory of the road, pedaling behind unmuffled cars up the hills of scorching highways. Off to their left a series of ancient broken stone arches extended halfway into the river.

"Well, have you?" she asked again.

"Of course I've heard of it," Cass muttered crossly, eyes on the square sand colored bricks beneath her feet.

"Good," Wyn said. Feeling pronounced relief she looked off to the left, up river toward the sun, and began to hum. Then she sang, in a light, high girlish voice. "Sur le pont d'Avignon ..."

"Oh, that bridge," Cass said.

"God!" said Wyn.

They walked the rest of the way over the bridge in silence, crossed the traffic circle, and entered through the gate under the sign showing a silhouetted car with a line slashed through it.

Inside the wall, which Wyn guessed must have been twenty feet thick, they emerged into a cocoon of quiet. No traffic sounds penetrated. They passed a teller window under a Tourist Change sign, and crossed a courtyard where a young man about their age was sweeping beneath a few tables and chairs. He saw them and gestured questioningly at his tables. They shook their heads.

Ahead of them a young woman in a dress turned a quick corner into a narrow alley and they followed. The alley had two or three shops and opened into a narrow street with dozens of shops, mostly clothing. The narrow street led into a larger street that might have allowed two cars to pass. Cars were pulled up on sidewalks, and they had to step out into the street from time to time to get around them. This street led up a hill past a church, and into a broad avenue, that opened into trees, flowers and outdoor cafes.

"How's this?" Wyn lifted a fleeting hand hip high, palm up, fingers toward the nearest table associated vaguely with chairs randomly shared by adjacent tables.

"Fine," said Cass. She dropped her limp pack in a chair, dropped back in another, propped up her feet in a third and ran her hand through her long black hair. "Fine."

Wyn set her pack carefully on the table, pulled up a chair, placed it precisely so she could see her pack, follow the line of cafes up the incline of the boulevard and keep Cass in her periphery.

"What do you suppose that is?" she nodded toward the fortress-like structure at the top of the hill.

"Who knows?" said Cass.

A waiter came up and wiped off the small circle of the table top. He spoke a question in French without smiling.

Wyn said she would have a croissant and a tea. She spoke in English but tried to gargle the "r" of croissant in the back of her throat, and used "un tay" for the tea, trying to clip the noun. The waiter raised his eyes, but said nothing. He waited for Cass. Into the silence Cass muttered "Coffee." The waiter quickly recited "one croissant, one tea, one coffee" in English, smiled and said "Right away."

"He likes you," Wyn said, looking away from the slump that was Cass.

"Why not?" said Cass. She scooted up in the chair to where she could hang her head over the back and ran her hand through her hair so that it hung down in wild strands over the chair.

"You look French."

"So?"

"Gallic."

"Garlic!" said Cass, with a noise like a stifled sneeze.

"It's good to hear you laugh," said Wyn.

"Bullshit," said Cass.

The waiter brought their breakfast on a tray and set out the dishes elaborately. Two lovely thin-flaked crab-shaped croissants, not like the thick doughy monstrosities from the train stations, a large empty cup with a spoon and a tea bag on a saucer, a small steaming metal pot, a half size cup filled with a nearly black liquid topped with minuscule bubbles curved into a half moon, with its own tiny spoon, and a bowl of sugar cubes. Cass took her legs off the chair and pulled up to the table, where she leaned over till her hair fell forward and almost hid her cup and saucer as she spooned sugar cubes one after another into the cup.

"God, I can't believe you do that," said Wyn as Cass at last began to stir the sugar cubes, lifting them now and again to watch them dissolve.

"Shut up," said Cass.

Wynona ate her first croissant in silence. She had made her tea right away while the water was still hot, removing the tea bag quickly before the bitterness set in. Now she leaned back and sipped.

"I know. It's the Palais des Papes."

"So what?"

"It's where the Popes lived during the Babylonian Captivity in Avignon."

"Babylon is out in the Middle East somewhere, not in goddamn southern France," said Cass, looking up, "and, besides, you only have one Pope at a time, not goddamn Popes."

"They didn't all live here at the same time, and you can have more than one."

"Why?"

"It's in the books."

"It's stupid, and I never hear of it." She reached over and took Wyn's second croissant.

"Cass!"

"Did you want it?" Cass held up what was left.

"You could have asked."

"I thought you were finished."

They counted out their money. Wyn added a tip. Cass snatched it off the table and handed it back to her.

"Service compris."

"I forgot," said Wyn.

They walked past a table of men. The men looked up, and their eyes settled on Cass.

"They always look at you," Wyn said after a few steps.

"So?"

"So, nothing."

They found the tourist entrance at the base of the fortress. Elderly Germans and young French children with their parents sat on the steps outside till their tours were called. The only English speaking tour of the morning would not begin for another hour.

They sat in the sun on the steps for a while. Wyn ran her fingers over the seam where the new concrete had run into the fissures and depressions of the ancient stones and wondered what a few hundred years of weather and feet felt like to a slice of rock.

Cass went exploring, then came back to stand on the step above so that Wyn had to look up past the billowing of Cass's shorts to see her.

"There's a museum with an art show. We can get in."

"O.K."

Cass shrugged her shoulders. As Wyn stood and adjusted her pack, Cass ran her hand through her hair and threw back her head to look around the square that fronted the fortress-palace, with its scattered groups of tourists, tables of coffee and newspapers, pigeons, uniformed soldiers, and pots of miniature cedar trees.

"Not bad for an old place," she said.

"God, Cass."

Cass nodded toward a small door set into the fortress wall. There was a poster in a thin frame on a stand outside. "Botero," it read, with some French words about contemporary something and important something.

In the momentary darkness of the inside Wyn located the money-taker sitting at a small table and they paid, each receiving a slip of paper in return. The art gallery turned out to be a series of medium sized rooms stacked one above the other as if part of a large tower. Botero's paintings looked more like graphic art than paintings. Stiff fat people with tiny features set deep in huge round heads, often with hats or helmets or, in the religious stuff, halos or a crown of thorns. Even the children were fat. The stylizing was so compulsive that the painting of the red cheeked prostitute and her businessman client could have been the Madonna and crucified Christ except for the background and headgear.

By the time they reached the top landings, out of breath, the sound of her breathing in the quiet hall and the bloated figures had made Wyn feel fat. She looked at her reflection in a document cabinet. She saw an athletic blonde with short hair and freckles, a tight stomach, decent hips, and the same breasts, no bigger and no smaller, that had embarrassed her so much in high school. She was trim but not slender, certainly not skinny. If anything she ran more to muscle these days, probably because of the biking. She was slightly taller than the dark haired girl beside her, the one with small hard breasts over a loose tee-shirt and wide clapper hiking shorts, the one that was laughing at her, white teeth flashing in the half darkness of the room.

"You're always looking at yourself, Wyn."

"Well, I care how I look."

"I don't?"

"Who knows?"

A door out of the top room led outside where they followed a boardwalk laid over a slate rooftop and rain spouts decorated with animal busts. They found a level battlement where they could look out between high thick walls and see down to the square in front of them where some ceremony involving men in suits and military uniforms was taking place. There was a band of half a dozen instruments and a man standing alone in front of the crowd, his back to the palace, speaking in solemn tones to people seated on a small platform. Before long the band began to play surprisingly loudly. The people who had been sitting on the platform stood up. When the song ended there was scattered clapping and the ceremony broke up into little groups of people shaking hands and introducing one another. Throughout the proceedings tourists in groups of three or four had strolled back and forth across the open square behind the speaker, chattering and laughing, some stopping to back up and almost bump into the man at the microphone, while they tried to get the whole palace into their camera frames.

Wyn looked at her watch. Still half an hour to go. They saw a sign that said "Terrace" and a narrow flight of steps almost hidden between high thick walls. The steps went up to a still higher part of the tower with a tiny bar, scarcely larger than a kiosk, just room enough for a young woman inside and a couple of empty tables with chairs out front. Cass sat down.

"We just ate," said Wyn.

"So?" said Cass.

They ordered Cokes, which came with glasses without ice. They tipped up, curling their tongues tight into the throats of the bottles. Cass belched, and grinned at her bottle. "I didn't know they were still making Mae West bottles."

Wyn frowned at her.

"You are English?" said a man. He was dark skinned and broad faced, about her height, Wyn imagined, in neat khaki shorts with a matching shirt and a small brown purse slung on a long thin strap over his shoulder. She looked away.

"American," she said to the far wall.

"Wanna sit down?" asked Cass.

"Cass!" Wyn frowned a quick warning at Cass. Cass mouthed the words, screw you. Then she flashed the man a big smile, and wiped back her hair with one hand, raising her Coke in the other.

"My friend, Ali," said the man, pointing to his companion, a slenderer, darker man with shiny black hair.

"I am Indian," said Ali, the sounds coming with a rhythmic underbeat, the consonants rolling around the back of his mouth. He smiled and sat down quickly.

"I am Asa," said the first man, "but I am Egyptian, not so favored as my cultured friend." This seemed to be a private joke between them. Wyn smiled faintly. Cass's grin broadened.

"Hi, guys," Cass said. "We're Cass and Wyn. I'm Cass. Cassandra actually, but I prefer Cassiopeia."

"Like the star," said Asa.

"Yes, like the star," said Cass, and stuck out the tip of her pink tongue at Wyn. Wyn rolled her eyes. Both men laughed.

"You are taking the English tour?" asked Asa. The girls looked at one another.

"It is all right. He is married." Ali said, pointing at Asa's round belly, which now that he was seated, hung slightly over his neat belt. Ali wore a sleeveless loose shirt and long loose trousers. There was a trace of sweat under his arms.

Up close Asa's face glistened in clusters of tiny sweat bubbles. Wyn imagined the two men had come straight up the stairs without stopping to look at the Boteros.

"Much married," laughed Asa, "that is why I love all women. All women."

"He does," said Ali, "it is true."

"But my friend, Ali, he is not married," said Asa.

"Why not?" asked Cass. She leaned down to the table with both elbows, chin in her hands, and looked up at him, letting her hair fall every which way about her face and shoulders. Wyn tried to catch Cass's attention by frowning and shaking her head. Cass ignored her.

"No one has asked me!" said Ali, and Asa laughed uproariously.

"Time for the tour, Cass," said Wyn, standing up.

"We are on the English tour also," said Asa. Both men held out their tickets as proof.

"Hmmm," said Wyn.

"Great," said Cass.

Downstairs, as they emerged into the square, Wyn asked "Why the English tour?"

"My friend does not speak French," said Asa. "But he speaks English, and Hindi, and he refuses to admit that he speaks German …"

"I prefer to speak English," said Ali, in a liquid rhythmic way.

"And so we take the English tour!" said Ali expansively, and loud enough for people to turn and look at them. God, thought Wyn. She led them up the steps to the English speaking tour.

Chapter Four

Cass stepped angrily onto the bridge. She hitched up her backpack so violently that the weight almost threw her off balance.

"You shit," she said to Wynona, hurrying to catch up behind her, "why did you have to drag us out of there? I was just starting to have a good time."

"You were getting loud."

"I was not."

"And silly."

"I was not." Cass was walking fast, head down, yelling the words.

"You always get loud when you're drinking," Wyn called to her. The wind had picked up. Some stars were visible above the trees on the shore ahead of them ahead of them. Behind them the city walls were floodlit. The glow reflected on the bridge stones about them.

"Wine's not drinking. And, besides, this was the first dance this whole stupid trip."

"You want to get us in trouble?"

Cass's elbows made chopping motions, her legs jerked stiffly in the wide cuffs of her cuffs. "They were married men."

"Asa wasn't."

"… and besides," Cass stopped and turned, "what was that shit about body hair?"

"Nothing," Wyn was surprised. "Nothing. You mean that stuff about French women not shaving?"

"Yeah, that."

"I was just going on with those guys. An Egyptian and an Arab. They never see women undressed back home. That's why they come to Europe. They love to talk about stuff like that."

"Indian. You told them I smelled."

"I did not."

"You said I didn't shave and it made our tent smell bad."

"I didn't. We were talking about French women and I said they didn't shave and I thought they smelled. It was another time that I said the tent smelled bad. I just thought they were trying to horn in on us."

"Wyn, you are so stupid. You actually thought they were going to follow us back to our tent? You thought they would crawl inside that stupid little rag with us? And which one did you think I was going to screw? The fat greasy Egyptian or that skinny little Ay-rab?"

"Well, I didn't know."

"Boy, Wyn. You are really some kind a' friend. You drag me all over Europe ..."

"Three countries."

"I get sore on the bike. I can't sleep on the train. We finally get to go out for dinner and you say I smell bad. You walk my legs off all over this stupid city till I'm too tired to dance, then you tell everybody we have to leave. And you know what?" Cass took a deep breath, her lips thin, squared and twisted in the reflected glow of the city.

"What, Cass?"

"I never even got to see that stupid bridge!"

"Cass," said Wyn, gently, "that's it, right there."

"Where?"

"There," said Wyn. She jerked her chin toward the old stone structure jutting half way out from the city into the river.

"The Bridge of Avignon?"

"Yes."

"That's it?"

"That's it."

"That's stupid it. That's it all right." Cass pushed herself away from the rail of their bridge and stomped off toward the campground. "I can't believe it. All of this stupid jerking me around. All of this stupid bicycle riding. I can't believe I put up with this shit." She was walking so fast now that Wyn had to run to catch her, and then she had to trot just to stay close behind. They crossed to the shore and stumbled down the darkened stairwell that dropped from the pedestrian walkway to ground level where the campground. Cass kept fussing, loudly at first then more and more softly, till as they passed through the campground gates she was muttering to herself. Wyn glanced back for a last look at the fortress castle across the Rhone and the deserted ruins of the Bridge of Avignon, now silhouetted against the yellow-white floodlit walls of the city.

In the tent Cass stormed through her bag and threw clothes and toiletries all over the tent flour.

"Cass," Wyn pleaded.

"Shut up!" Cass said. "I want to borrow your compact mirror. Where is it?"

"I'll get it."

"And your razor."

"You're kidding ..."

"No, I'm not kidding."

"... In the middle of the night?"

She followed Cass down to the showers. It was past midnight. She was surprised to find the lights in the concrete building were lit at this hour. Outside Cass's shower stall she listened to the water running. She heard Cass curse each time the shower stopped. She could tell by the sound that Cass was standing in the outer area and that she must be holding the mirror with one hand while she shaved with the other. The blade would have been fairly dull with long use. She could hear Cass grunt now and again with pain. Cass's head sounded as if it were coming from lower down the shower door than she expected. And it was taking longer than she expected.

"Cass?"

"What?" An angry, hurt voice behind the shower door.

"Cass, what's the matter?"

"Nothing's the matter." She grunted. The sound seemed to come now more than ever from lower than Wyn expected.

Wyn felt thick headed. Maybe the wine, she thought, and leaned back against the opposite door for a moment. She realized she was leaning on a toilet door and straightened up again. A Turkish toilet.

"I'm done. Do you want to see?"

"No, that's O.K. Look, you didn't have to do this for me. I'm sorry about what I said. Maybe I have a thing about body hair." She could hear Cass getting dressed inside. "It's just something about underarms ..."

"Underarms?"

"Yes, underarms ... Cass? Oh, come on ... you didn't?"

"What do you mean, underarms?"

"Cass, you will die on the bicycle! It will take you weeks! I can't believe you did that ..."

In the tent Wyn lay for hours, eyes open, staring at the underside of the tent canopy. She kept thinking of Cass in the cramped wet shower cubicle balancing the mirror, shaving between her legs. She thought of the stubble and the raw skin, and she thought of Cass lying there beside her, flat on top of her sleeping bag, one arm out of her tee shirt, face flat into the dirty clothes of her pillow, legs like small clappers in the larger, open bells of her shorts, maybe the raw chafe visible, exposed to the night air, the close, warm, fecund greenhouse air of the tent, close ...

Chapter Five

El Gee

It was in that moment, after interminable hours of hot, throat-dusted pedaling out of Madrid, and long, sore minutes after pulling to the top of the central Spanish plain, and limping into the only shade on the edge of the overlook, with the whole rust-and-lime plain spread opposite them across the crevasse, and the walls of the city cupping the map of its medieval treasure before them, in that moment, seeing Cass staring at the city of Toledo wrapped within its walls like a Spanish matron in her shawl, it was in that moment that Wyn remembered the impulse that had driven her to invite Cass to go biking through Europe.

Cass's eyes were up, not reading the ground as mostly she did when walking. Her eyes were open wide, not puffed and slitted like in the early morning. She was engaged, not indifferent as most times; she was intrigued, not cynical and not the cruel tempered, vicious vengeful vixen she could so readily become.

"Wyn," said Cass, lost to herself, afloat in this vision of Toledo, her small voice coarse in a whisper, "it's just like in the picture ... just like the painting ... you know that guy that did the long fingers."

"Yeah," said Wyn. "Wonder who that was?" It was unlike her to tease Cass, to tease anybody, but somehow she wanted to hold on to this moment and, if matching Cass meanness for meanness would do it, she'd try. God, how that little woman could make her cry.

"You know. You know," said Cass, impatiently. "I know you know. God, Wyn!"

It was gone now, but Wyn remembered That Look. Cass like a pixie. Short black hair turned under, dark eyes winking. They had been college seniors, different majors, but in extra curriculars together. And their float had won, and Cass had done, it seemed like, half the work, climbing all over the truck bed, nails, hammer, stapler, in sneakers, cut offs and tee-shirt, sweating, smudged, hair falling over an eye, pushed back each time leaving black streaks ... and freckles beginning to show across her nose. And later, tired and happy when the announcement came over the loud speakers, all the girls had come alive and jumped and laughed and hugged each other. And Cass had hugged everyone. And some of the girls had kissed cheeks. And Cass had kissed Wyn right on the mouth. Kissed her as they hugged. It was a long hug and it was over, and Cass's eyes were dancing, and she was back to jumping up and down and in and out the crowd of jumping and hugging sorority girls, and the kiss was over. And Wyn had one day thought of this biking trip through Europe, and thought who would she ask, and thought she would ask Cass, though she could not have said why. She hadn't thought of the float parade till now, she told herself.

And here they were, the whole of the seaward-looking country of Portugal and parts of agricultural and imperial and Moorish Spain behind them, browned and chapped and smelly, and Wyn tiptoeing around Cass's black moods, and the whole Iberian peninsula sunny and hospitable, and Cass most of the time a horse's ass.

"Dammit, Wyn. Who was it? You know, gave everybody long bodies and thin heads. Made all the men have women's hands, like. Who was it?"

Wen made a show of pushing her bicycle upright and spinning the pedals back to just forward of the vertical, and of balancing her weight against the heaviness of the panniers and the stuff bags. She pushed off.

"Let's find out how we get across. We'll need to see where we can camp before it gets too late."

The road fell down to cross the bridge, a graceful arched and empty delicate work in stone that carried across the deep cut between the hills. She could not hear Cass for the wind in her ears. Being heavier as well as starting first she'd been well ahead getting to the bridge, but Cass was fitter and tougher and she caught up crossing over the level part.

"That really pisses me off," said Cass, wrenching her words to the stroke as they pulled up hill again toward the city walls of Toledo now rising above them. "Just tell me the guy's fucking name, for Christ's sake."

"Book said something about a tourist office somewhere near the gate. Yeah, there it is."

"Wyn! Weeh-yun! God!"

They leaned their bikes against what might have been an olive tree—Wyn resolved to look it up, being compulsive about trees and other things that grow, and road signs, and museums, and artists' names and battle grounds and national boundaries and blisters.

There was a campground, the man said. He was reddish brown, as a Spaniard ought to be who lived outdoors, and balding. His grey shirt was sweated through and his ankles were swollen. He had the kind of paper house slippers on his feet that they gave you to wear over your shoes in museums, and he told them there were gypsies in the campground.

Cass could see that the notion of gypsies felt good to Cass. Cass shrugged her shoulders and wiggled her hips. It was all one motion and it was quick, like a shudder. There were men in the plaza in front of the tourists office and as men always did about Cass they picked up on her little jerk. She hiked up her biking shorts and stirred the crowd again, Wyn could feel it. Even the shoe shine man faltered. He hit two beats with one brush, and stopped with the other one high in the air.

Wyn turned away. "Let's get a drink, then check out the camp."

"Yeah."

They both ordered tea from the waiter who had come up immediately and asked Cass what she'd have. He was back soon with steaming cups and a broken toothed smile and the kind of fast and solicitous Portuguese-and-Spanish service Wyn feared would spoil them for the colder European countries ahead.

"So, what's his name?"

Wyn looked hard at Cass. Cass had pushed back her short black hair, holding her head down over the cup, eyes hidden from Wyn. The hair had fallen back immediately, like a tent flap, over the curling vapor of her tea. Something about the gesture caused a couple of chairs nearby to scrape against the courtyard stones.

Wyn had to hold this advantage. It was a physical thing with her.

"Gypsies," she said. "That doesn't sound good."

"You're always so fucking worried about stuff," said Cass. She had raised her eyes, and was looking up at Wyn through strands of her hair. "What are they going to do? Fucking carry us off? Maybe they'll steal our dirty clothes and wash 'em before we catch 'em."

Wyn laughed. She tried not to, but it came out. Cass threw back her head and grinned, a little girl pixie grin at her. For a moment it was magic. Like it was. Somewhere voices stopped, and men looked at Cass again. It was like it had been before. For a moment it was like it was then.

Chapter Six

"I got one," said Cass. "He's coming over after. How'd you do?"

"Good God, Cass. I don't just come on to guys. Come on.... Naw, did you really? Really, no kidding?"

It was just the two of them, Cass's eyes alight in that way she had of turning Wyn upside down and making her breath come short. Cass, black hair bouncing, imp's grin crackling, fire in the air.

Their tent was set up. Wyn's underwear was washed and hanging inside, out of sight. God knows what Cass had done with hers, or more likely Wyn's, because it seemed she was missing some panties and a jogging bra.

Cass hadn't answered. She looked up at the slightly taller girl, grinned bigger and dropped lightly onto the gravel. She settled back against a tree, eyed Wyn again, then slowly circled the tip of her tongue all around her lips, pulled her tongue slowly back inside, mouth still wide open, and very, very deliberately moved her lower jaw from side to side, mouth open. Then with a laugh she snapped shut her jaws, lunged forward, and flattened herself on the ground. She grunted and propped up her chin with forearms on elbows and raised her eyes to Wyn, letting her grin slowly spread over her pixie face.

Wyn dropped onto the ground opposite Cass and sat cross legged, sandalled feet on either side of her knees, and grabbed a fistful of her own toes in each hand and leaned over till she was almost eye level with Cass.

"Sometimes, Cass," she said, "I just don't understand you at all."

Cass, using her tongue, pushed out first one cheek then the other, and looked straight at Wyn, eyes laughing.

"God, Cass. What are you trying to say?"

Silence.

"What are you carrying on about?"

Cass rolled over on her back and looked up at Wyn upside down. "Weh-yuhl. There's one of him, right?"

"Yes."

"There's two of us, right?"

"So?"

Cass continued to grin up at her, face upside down.

"I said 'So?'"

"Yeah, so?"

"So? Goddamn it. So? So what?"

Cass flipped over, sat back and drew her knees up.

"Wyn, I swear. Sometimes you have no imagination at all!"

Wyn looked back dumbly at Cass, then slowly began to feel the flush building up behind her eyes and the hot flame beginning to spread across her cheeks.

"God, Cass! Are you saying you and me ... This guy ... I don't believe this ..."

Her throat tightened up hard. Like crying but without the tears. She was all dry inside. She reached for her water bottle. Her heart started doing silly things.

Across from Wyn, Cass pulled herself up a little straighter, slackened her jaw a bit and started making little spit bubbles on her lips.

Wyn got up on her feet, and stared down at her own personal pixie. "Cass, I honestly can't believe this. You just ... You always ... God-*damn* it, Cass!"

She turned and walked blindly away, tears coming down, now that she was out of Cass's sight.

The ground was uneven here. They had found a level place for their tent, level but gravelly. A few feet from their tent the sand and gravel had accumulated some tough grass that brushed coarsely at her toes and ankles and shins, but she scarcely noticed. Despite the hot tears she could see brilliantly, if not clearly, as if through glycerin, and she kept climbing up the bank till she came to the top and could look out on the plain and a view of the browns, tans, ochres and greens of Toledo from the back.

She thought of Cass and Cass's ways of making herself small and dependent. How she had fallen asleep on the plane with her head on Wyn's shoulder. How in the tent she would scrunch up and wriggle over beside Wyn, especially on colder nights. How she would walk head down, staring at her tiny feet, even on the most gorgeous of days, and how Wyn had to constantly call out to her to look up. Look at the Cathedral, Cass. For God's sake, didn't you see that? Look out the window, Cass, before we pass ...

God. Where did that woman live inside? Where did her thoughts go? For crying out loud, I haven't the faintest idea what goes through her mind!

She thought of the little black-haired woman-girl that made her buy the tickets and made her make all the decisions about where they were going, how they were going to get there and what they were going to cook, then most of the time let her do the cooking and generally left the dishes when it was her time to wash up. The girl-woman who left it to Wyn to figure out the rate of exchange and whether the water was safe to drink, who when she had to pay simply held out a fistful of whatever she had and let the vendors help themselves. Sometimes it wasn't even the right currency for the country they were in.

So why did the shopkeepers and the street vendors always seem so happy to sell stuff to Cass? Wyn they would bitch at and holler at when she messed up the change. Cass they would fall all over themselves for. Life was not fair. This little bitch. Her with her freckles and her dark brown eyes, or were they black?

Wyn thought about Cass's eyes for a long moment. Cass's eyes were like a thermostat. She'd look at you one way and you'd get all hot and flustered. Look at you another way and you'd feel like a refrigerator door opened. You'd go all day, her walking along, or pedaling along, eyes on the ground till it was like she wasn't there at all. Next thing you knew she'd look at you and it was like spring-time come all at once.

God, Cass. What's the matter with you? Can't you see this trip is supposed to be fun? Why do you keep screwing up everything? Everything.

In the evening the gypsies did invite them over to eat.

The girls brought fruit they had purchased in the market, and the gypsy women thanked them and set the fruit aside, but dinner instead was something spicy and juicy from a big pot that was actually cooked on a real outdoor fire. And there was wine and a wide, fat Spanish bread they had already learned to like because it smelled of alcohol and earthiness, and somebody had a mandolin and everybody sang songs the girls didn't understand, and they mouthed and hummed along in the choruses, and afterwards, a little melancholy but full and warm, Wyn went back to her tent and fell asleep.

Hours later Cass came in smelling of sex and sweat. She swore at her sleeping bag that Wyn had not rolled out for her, swung her hips and knees frantically from side to side pulling off her shorts, went outside to pee, came back in and fell flat asleep on top of her sleeping bag, face down, wearing Wyn's panties too large for her.

Cass's breathing settled into a deep rhythm almost immediately, and Wyn got up on her knees and pulled her sleeping bag out of the tent behind her, took it up to the top of the hill and sat there alone and hating, till the sun broke up the low clouds beyond the old, old walls of the city. She tried to think of Don Quixote and Sancho, but all she could see was Aldonza in a loose bodiced blouse with big white sleeves and a torn black skirt and no shoes.

She couldn't see St. Ignatius of Loyola, St. John of the Cross, St. Teresa of Avila or any of the other Spanish saints. All she could see was a stupid Spanish servant girl with black hair, bare feet, loose breasts and bottomless eyes that stuck in your heart.

Chapter Seven

Galadriel

The most beautiful lake in the world is Lake Geneva we call it, Lac Leman to the Swiss, but no one will tell you. Either the Swiss don't want anyone to know, or more likely they are used to living in full view of true beauty, a long, wide expanse of rising morning mist and snowy mountains painted around the sky. So Wyn told herself, gliding off from Geneva this morning, the faint snickety snick of her tires on the pavement, naked of cars this morning, and somewhere behind her, glum and oblivious Cass with her choppier cadence, muttering faintly over the swishing whine of her wheels.

They were pulling hard, rising steadily away from The City of International Peace with its immense fountains playing fantastic morning streams back and forth over the quiet broad waters. Further up the lake, with the peaks of France with their promise of early fall skiing well off to her right, Wyn could see what looked like dots of ghosting white that minutes later formed the billowing geometry of sails. Maybe a race, or at least a leisuring flotilla of Swiss good-lifers. She liked this country already, with their competence and affluence and propensity for hiring Italians, Spaniards and Slavs to sweep their streets, clear their tables and make their beds.

The Swiss were for making watches and chocolates and money, for running hotels and attending patrons, but not for cleaning up after them. No, that was for non-nationals and that was a forthrightness that Wyn could respond to. She would think of living among these vineyard husbanders, cheesemakers and bankers, who welcomed her modest budget every bit as warmly as they had fifty years of Charlie Chaplin's and the Aga Khan's and all the sheiks of Araby without conferring or even offering the benefits of citizenship to any of them. Yeah, she could relate to this kind of people. Piss on Cass!

Now the sun was higher, the vineyards were turning golden below and above them as they pumped along the hillsides. This would be the time of year, they had been told, for visiting some of the vintners for tastes of the harvests and finding the Swiss at their most bending, but Wyn was thinking of something more personal she wanted to do, something more directly a part of her life and Cass's. She twisted round quickly to check on Cass, complaining softly and indiscriminately to road below, lake alongside, and rounded soft clouds above them.

Now was as good a time as any.

She slowed up and drifted over to the side of the road. The shoulder was broad here and the sun was light and warm. She could feel the dampness rising from the lake as she came to stop and skidded the toes of her feet along the concrete edge of the highway. Cass came up beside her and hopped off. No cars were in sight.

"I want to have this out right now," she said without prologue, trying hard to catch Cass's eyes, but Cass had turned away from her and was looking out over the lake.

"So where's the monster?" said Cass, looking slowly off to the left, then shielding her eyes from the sun, turned back toward the right, and the direction from which they'd come.

"What monster?"

"You know the one. Like in the picture of the thing sticking up."

"What thing sticking up?"

"You know, like a guy's …"

"Come off it, Cass. You are such a shithead! Don't you ever think of anything else?"

"Yeah, but you won't listen." Cass turned and looked at her full in the face.

"That's what I want to talk to you about."

"Right. But first, where's the stupid monster? Where are the guys with boats and cameras and all?"

"That's Loch Ness, Cass."

"You said Loch Lomond, this morning."

"No, I said Lac Leman. This is Lac Leman, La-ahk Lehh-mahn. Loch Lomond and Loch Ness are both in Scotland. This is Switzerland, Cass. We haven't even been to Scotland, Cass. For God's sake."

Cass looked at her for a long moment. She was standing between Wyn and the sun, which painted broad glowing streaks of amber around the thickness of her hair. "Why do you always try to make me out so stupid?"

Cass turned away and lifted her chin for a second so that it tremble in the warm, moist air. A little later her shoulders began to quiver and she hunched them together in that little girl way, "Always. Always. Always."

Wyn took her by the shoulders and turned her around. Little girl hunching, the way Cass was doing, chin tucked down, meant all Wyn could see was the top of Cass's head.

Wyn leaned down. "Hey, Cass, listen."

Cass gradually, grudgingly raised her head. Wyn leaned closer, trying to read her eyes, to see through the tears, to see where Cass was in there. Cass raised up.

And kissed Wyn on the mouth.

A moment's hesitation. Her arms were still on Cass's shoulders. Wyn pulled away.

"God, Cass! Why do you do that?"

"I like you." The grin was back on Cass's little girl face. She wiped the tears off each cheek with her hand, leaving a faint smear from the bike glove, and ran her fingers through her hair. She tilted back her head and looked hard on Wyn. "Come on, Wyn. Are you such an ice ass you don't know?"

"God, Cass," was all Wyn could say.

"You kissed me back."

"You're crazy."

"You did."

"I did not, you fuckin' bitch!"

A long silence between them. Seagulls swirled up in gust of wings from the lake below them and circled around the two of them with their bikes and bags.

"Cass, we been biking too long. This is not working. I'm splitting."

Cass was slightly further off the pavement, just a little further down the hillside than Wyn, a tiny difference in elevation that only emphasized how small she was, and, over the top bar of her bicycle she raised her black eyes to Wyn and new tears went sliding down her cheeks, new freckles stood out in the wet and Wyn, standing tall and righteous on the far side of her own bike with the weight of the pedal pressing her calf, and beginning to recite the careful explanation she had been rehearsing afresh with each revolution of her wheels and each click of her odometer coming out of Geneva this morning, would have given her life at that moment to brush away those streaks and kissed those gritty cheeks.

She may have imagined it, but with the gulls way overhead and no sound close in but her own voice saying all the reasons why biking with Cass had become one long scourge to her otherwise serene, serious and happy life, she could surely hear the splash of each tear that dripped so forlornly and irresistibly off Cass's chin. The more Wyn went on, reciting her festered litany of Cass's shirkings of her compacted chores, and betrayals of Wyn's trust, and pilferings of Wyn's possessions, and her humiliations of Wyn in front of their acquaintances, and Cass's insensitivities, and cultural and artistic distortions and perversions and closed mindedness, the more she seemed to notice Cass's chin. At first it was wet, then adorably drenched, then trembling, then agitated, then wet and agitated and trembling and streaked, and so very, very, very Cass.

She stopped talking. She heard the sounds of her lecture dying away over the lake. Seagulls swept around them, and dived about her as she slowly laid her bike down, straightened up and walked around Cass's bike. Cass held her own bike rigidly with both hands, and turned her face, wet and defensive but brave, up to Wyn. Wyn put out both arms and took Cass by the shoulders. Cass looked up at Wyn, red rims beginning to glimmer deep watered from this close, in the salt of her tears, looked up hurting and brave.

Wyn forgot the next things to say, and circled her arms around Cass, and squeezed Cass's shoulders and Cass tipped her head back so she could look right into Wyn's face, and Wyn kissed her. Kissed Cass. It was a full kiss, lips on lips, mouth holding mouth, and a long kiss, with the taste of salt in both of them. And in the end of their kiss a truck roared by, close by, and the driver hit a loud diesel horn, right on top of them. And Wyn almost winced, and thought of pulling away and being embarrassed in front of laughing and pointing and shouting men, but inside of her her heart shouted "yes" to Cass's heart, and when she pulled away all she said out loud was "Tonight?"

Her face was burning.

And Cass answered, "Tonight."

Chapter Eight

A Few Good Saints

When she was in grade school Wyn had "gone to the nuns." The result of eight years of care and example-setting under the good Sisters of Mercy had left her neither passionately pious nor passionately cynical. Which was not to say she had been indifferent to what she was taught. She emerged after eight years with relatively good grades and a very active conscience, which with a particularly heavy load of guilt caused her to be one of the hangers-back in high school mixed socials for the first couple of years.

By the time high school ended she had wrestled her guilt feelings into some sort of an unresolved state of submission in the course of practicing wrestling in the back seats of automobiles belonging to the parents of some of the most attractive young men in the senior class.

Harder to shake, however, had been her rather solidly developed conscience and a personal, folksy, conversational relationship with certain saints she had come to know and become fond of back in grade school. And even at her most daring, when her comportment with young men near her age could easily have crowned some of her most memorable physical achievements with premature motherhood, she thought of her personal saints and depended, perhaps too naively, on their ability to keep her safe from the more catastrophic effects of her follies.

In a way she may have been right to pick the saints she chose. All of the saints that she prayed to or thought about were scamps of one sort or another. She tended to like the fallen saints who had come belatedly to God, rather than directly. St. Augustine, for example, was said by some to have had so much fun fornicating that he had prayed fervently that God would convert him, but not right away. She liked St. Augustine and thought often of his bastard son Dona Dei, planning when Mr. Right came along to argue strongly for Donna, if she had a girl, or Donald, if she had a boy. She tended to be especially fond of boys, having seen very little of them in grade school during her years of all-girl classes.

She had felt honored, nearly to swooning, at the first erection she had witnessed. In her mind she had made such a powerful impression on the young man on their second date that he had been overcome and unable to control himself emotionally for love of her, and the special person that she was. Later on she came to be less awed by her prowess with men to the point that she began to suspect them of being more interested in committing sex than in bestowing it. Nevertheless the road to that particular realization had been exciting and in later years she was unable to recall any physical adventure with a young man that hadn't left her with at least a little something to dwell on pleasurably when she found herself alone with her thoughts.

Not that she was totally unaware of the saints, like Teresa of Avila, John of the Cross, and Thomas Aquinas, who seemed to have been totally devoted to God from the cradle, but she had never taken an interest in St. Therese of Liseux, whom she had assumed to have been God's from birth onward, till the day she saw a movie where one of Therese's fellow postulants asked Therese if she masturbated. From that day Wyn included Therese of Liseux in her bevy of saints she could relax with.

After college a kind of change came in Wyn's saintly hookups. Having arrived at her twenties she began to experience vague misgivings about the mortal side of her life, and she began to depend more regularly on the kindnesses of her personal saints and to lay the burden on them of getting her prepared, at least a little bit, for the journey after death. This growing dependence on them had become particularly acute at one time in the first few weeks after school when she attended a funeral for one of her classmates, a suicide from asphyxiation by hanging. She had known the young man well, gone on dates with him, and more than once shared a bed with him. The death had touched her sharply not just because it caused the notion of her own mortality to resonate within her, but because she remembered he had been good to sleep with and the circumstances of his death reported to her suggested he had begun to look within himself for the orgasmic diversions that she felt she and any of several of their mutual friends would have happily shared with him.

Nonetheless there he was, dead, and here she was, alive, and thinking more and more frequently of her saints. They were good friends who could be expected to overlook her weaknesses and help her up when she was down. She felt it had been largely their influence, certainly not her own discretions, that had so far prevented her pregnancies and she had looked forward to the trip to Europe, confident that she might continue, albeit modestly, to meet new young men and to try various beds without serious or harmful effect. As an extra precaution she had already decided to travel with a woman companion, rather than a man, because she felt her saints could be depended upon to absolve her of the responsibility for occasional dalliances, but nightly cohabitation for endless weeks and months might stretch even their limits of the minor faults they would be willing to risk for her.

So it was that when she was sexually active she began to rely on saints like Augustine and the worldly elevated Elizabeth of Hungary, and when she experienced sexual frustration or simple loneliness, as she did when Cass would go off careless and predatory, she turned to the contemplatives and the mystics, like John of the Cross and company.

Chapter Nine

Raclette

"What you do is, you pick somebody who likes to drink."

There had been long shadows stretching away from the trees that surrounded the platform where they had at last alighted from the cograil tram. After many turns rising up the mountain's shoulder Wyn had eventually lost sight of Lac Leman behind them, but they had not yet reached the top at Rochez de Nays. They must have been somewhere near the top she had thought because what she had at first taken to be wisps of fog about their feet were actually cloud tops, her new friends admitted, blushing and red nosed in the cold wind urging them away from the platform and into the shelter of the trees.

'Rente,' said a single sign painted in black on a weathered board nailed to a slender post that appeared to be a straight trunk of a pine tree about 4 inches in diameter. Out of place, Wyn thought, in a country of German efficiency coupled with French self satisfaction such as Switzerland was. The signpost should have been of heavy gray metal and the sign itself should have been set in a stainless or aluminum frame with a clear plastic over machined lettering.

Unlike the other stops they had made this one had no paved road leading up to it. There were double dirt tracks that looked more accommodated to farm equipment than to automobiles which, instead of passing the platform and leaving it by the way on route to somewhere else, simply terminated there.

The four guides led off with their packs, walking single file down one of the tracks which dropped slightly away from the height of the platform, back down the mountain but off to their left. Ilsa followed them confidently, so Wyn and Cass fell in, carrying only the handbags they had brought.

The toe game Cass had been playing with Felipe had ended when at one point he had grinned at her and reached across between their seats and pushed the flat of his thumb lightly against the tip of her nose and they had exchanged broad smiles. Wyn had experienced a cheated feeling which had stayed with her even after Cass had remembered her and turned and said some things about looking forward to this evening, which on later reflection might have been meant differently than Wyn had chosen to think at the time. The feeling of having been cheated had lasted until Yves had gone up and spoken to the conductor/operator and gotten him to slow down and eventually stop at this mountain byway.

"Irreguliere," was what Wyn thought she heard the operator say, and it sounded close enough to an English word that might fit the situation. With a huge, exaggerated Gallic shrug the operator had pulled back on the throttle control just enough to ease them to a stop right even with the platform, and the tram had already started clicking softly forward by the time the last of them, Wyn, had stepped off onto the wide unpainted boards of the platform's surface. The tram was gone before they reached the trees.

Before them the tracks led through a narrowing, darkening tunnel of trees, some still yellowed, others denuded of leaves, and a few unhappy looking pines, scattered unnaturally among the maples and oaks. Their leaders had begun chattering away lightly and cheerfully in French even under the weight of their packs, while Cass and Wyn, more accustomed to biking and less comfortable in the thinner air, tried hard to keep up.

Across a fast running brook which they were glad to pass on a small clattering wooden trestle bridge the road began to lead uphill, toward the crest of the mountain again and soon even the Swiss fell silent from the exertion of the climb. At last Yves yelped "Voila!" and pointed to a smaller, fainter set of tracks leading away from the main roadway. This path was even steeper and its tracks were almost completely overgrown with grass. Felipe showed them a couple of gouges in a tree trunk that might have held fasteners for a sign and said "The name is Enchanted!" Or something like that, it sounded to Wyn's ear. Maybe he said "Chanté." It didn't matter. She had begun to regret more and more tying up with this crowd. It was late and what was going to happen to her evening with Cass?

She looked ahead at Cass as they climbed. Cass's head was as usual tucked down, concentrating on the ground before her feet. Consequently it was Wyn who saw the chalet first.

It could have been built from a postcard model. The trees had broken away, opening onto a meadow-like clearing with wildflowers, brown grasses and a few rock outcroppings, and right in the middle a russet two story building, with a steep, nearly vertical roof, and trim that was painted in swirls of reds, oranges and greens, a massive stone chimney at the side and a front door that was actually in two parts—an upper and a lower—and might have been used in the original fairy tale books. Reaching the harsher surface of the meadow seemed to have caused the twin tracks of the path to exhaust themselves and they walked the last few yards to the door through untrampled open meadow.

Yves signaled them to wait while he groped around behind the shutters of the right hand window and with a grin produced a large brass key, about eight inches long, which he held up and waved around in the air. Felipe took the key and turned in the lock and the door opened into a wide room that seemed to take up most of the first floor. There was a sort of pantry-like room and a sort of a bathroom in the lean-to part of the first floor that served as a kind of adjunct to the main room, but otherwise the big room was the entire first floor. Not even closets. There were pegs for coats, but they were all dressed lightly for warmer days and as it was chilly in the room they had nothing to hang up except Cass's and Wyn's handbags and the men's purses.

The backpacks were dumped on the floor and the girls, Candace and Martina, started rummaging through them while Felipe called the others to help bring in the wood. There was a large woodpile behind the chalet, out of sight of the entrance and the path. It was quite a large pile and, though each carried two loads into the chalet, their efforts left the pile virtually unchanged.

Felipe found long matches on the mantelpiece and with the help of some magazines and newspapers from beside one of the several couches soon had lighted the first of the smaller logs and then the others were in flames. Outside, through the windows, Wyn could see darkness coming on. She looked down the hill below them. Either there was no habitation or the woods hid the lights for all was blackness. She crossed the room and looked out the window on the uphill side. This window looked straight at the mountain's side, the chalet's own rock studded meadow. Only by twisting her head to look way up could she see above the meadow and nearby trees. There was a single light, very faint, reddish like a tiny distant beacon to warn off aircraft. She was stuck here for the night. Her night and Cass's night.

The Swiss had brought potatoes, already baked, which they set out on the table in the room and began to break up onto heavy china plates from the cupboard. They had also brought plastic bags of salad greens which they shook out onto the plates, leaving the rest to fluff up into large bowls. There were bottles of white wine which they uncorked, and wine glasses set out on t he table with forks from the cupboard. Watching the Swiss youngsters in action Wyn guessed that the two girls had not been here before. They opened first one cupboard door then another to find what they needed and always exclaimed excitedly in French when they happened upon something they could use. They turned up napkins and napkin rings and made an elaborate show of setting out exactly seven around the table.

But the girls had saved their most violent enthusiasm for the cheese that Felipe had carried in his pack. They both threw their arms around him and kissed him alternatively on both cheeks. "Raclette!" they shouted.

It was a creamy white sort of cheese, half a wheel, about six inches in radius. With a great deliberate show Felipe produced a large flat stone that had been leaning up against the fireplace and rubbed it clean with a towel. This stone he laid carefully on the hearth, close up to the flames where it would get hot.

By now it was getting dark in the corners of the room not close to the fire and Candace found a light switch that illuminated two tiny night light sort of sconces set into the back wall opposite the fireplace, and a loud rattle that eventually died away told Yves, as he explained to the others, that the pump had just started up and they would have indoor plumbing tonight, a pronouncement that caused the girls to blush, and set Yves and Felipe to laughing and poking at each other.

"What you do is, you pick somebody who likes to drink," Candace repeated herself. She lifted up the half wheel of cheese with both hands and placed it onto the flat rock so that the flat face of the cut side of the Raclette cheese was exposed to the fire. "Then that person scrapes off the cheese when it melts," she demonstrated with a knife, dropping the melted drabs of cheese over a spread of broken potato pieces on her place. "Then you give the person a glass of wine." And she demonstrated again, this time draining her own glass in front of the company.

Ilsa volunteered to be the one to collect the drinks of wine and to scrape the melted cheese onto people's potatoes when they came up to her. This turned out to be an idea of questionable merit.

Ilsa tried to imitate Candace's grand flourish but she was not a wine drinker and, after draining her glass completely for each of the six others as they came up in turn, she had begun to get loud and aggressive by the time the first one came up for seconds. It happened to be Yves, and as he bent over her she closed her hand over his lower leg, sliding her fingers up and down his calf, then she tilted back her head, fluttered her eyes and invited him to kiss her. When he did she slipped her arms up around his neck and as he straightened up she came upright with him and stood against him, kissing him and rubbing her hands up and down the back of his neck.

Felipe watched the two, half smiling. Candace and Martina looked at each other and laughed loudly. Cass nudged Felipe and grinned her pixie grin. Wyn, who was still working on her first glass of wine and was only part way through her Raclette and salad, looked curiously from one to another of the four still at table with her, then turned again to Yves and Ilsa as they lurched toward the door, Ilsa still clinging to Yves's neck. They were gone.

The door let in unexpectedly cold mountain air, and hung open, abandoned. Wyn shivered and waited for someone who spoke French to go close the door. No one got up so she pulled herself up and said, in English, "I'll get it." She looked out the doorway and saw Yves and Ilsa off to her left, slightly uphill from them. In the near darkness it seemed that Ilsa was reaching into Yves's pants pockets. She stepped back inside and shoved the door to.

"Ilsa has had too much to drink, perhaps?" Felipe called out from the group on the floor. Candace had taken Ilsa's place at the fire and Martina was getting up to be her first customer, plate in one hand, wine bottle in the other. Martina poured while Candace scraped, and before coming back to the group she talked awhile and joked with Candace. The two girls looked about the same. Both were medium in height, about five feet, five inches tall, and both wore their hair cut short. Both were blond but Candace's hair had a noticeably reddish cast, and she had brilliant blue eyes. Martina had heavy dark eyebrows and deep brown eyes; her skin was fair, almost as fair as Candace's where it was not browned by the sun. Martina's legs were stocky and muscular, where Candace was lighter built altogether, with thin legs without noticeable muscles.

As Martina lingered by Candace at the fireplace their talking grew louder and, though it was in French, Wyn could tell they had a lot to say about Yves. His name kept coming up and they broke into fits.

Cass had passed the bottle over her plate, Wyn's and Felipe's, and refilled all their glasses. At first, when Cass began to talk more toward Felipe, Wyn expected that Cass was filling an awkward social moment, so warm was the residue of her feeling for Cass this evening, but after a few minutes she saw Cass has targeted Felipe in Yves's absence and a left out feeling began to grow in her. She got Candace to scrape some more cheese onto the drier parts of her crumbled potato to which Candace merrily obliged, without Martina's leaving her, then went back to where Felipe and Candace were sitting cross legged on the floor, and sat down on the other side of Felipe, and, by way of butting in, asked him to repeat what he had just said.

"I said," he said, "or ... I think I said ..." His face turned a little red—Wyn noticed the bottle was almost empty—and his words sounded thick and slow. "... that American girls ..." Here he nodded toward Cass. "... have ... are ... very good ... fun. American girls ... are ... funny ... too." He giggled self-consciously. Cass, who had been watching him benevolently, her mouth stretched widely in a proud grin, leaned close and butted him lightly on the upper arm with the top of her head. She pulled back and looked up at him, her head tilted back in a way that reminded Wyn of Ilsa's at the fireplace with Yves a few minutes earlier. He reached out a finger and pushed down on her pert little nose. She grinned again, lifted her chin and kissed his finger. Wyn saw, and felt like something had fallen out of her.

Chapter Ten

Tonight

Wyn's hiking shoes, deep black in the moonlit snow, scrunched across the open wooden deck. She had had enough of being alone, of listening to the tossing pines, of guessing which flecks of moving shadows off by the woods were deer feeding, of watching moon shadows gliding silently and strobe like over sharp pointed big shouldered mountain silhouettes brightening momentarily into patches of rickrack forests of black and white, and grey valleys. It was quiet inside, the big lights were out now. She would go inside. She would drag Cass away from the others and she would talk to her.

They had swept in front of the door and the sudden change from extended crunching into silent footfalls took her breath away. She eased the door open and closed it behind her with a tiny click that echoed about the big two storied room and off the stone hearth like distant elf laughter.

In the faint light of the smoldering hearth there were dark squarish lumps of sleeping bags straggled before the dying fire, three. There could have been, should have been not counting hers, six.

She leaned back against the door and looked about her, sighing a faint cloud of mist into the last of the cold air that had come in with her. That would mean the guys were in somebodies' sleeping bags, somebody else's. Well, that would make Cass's easier to find. Hers would be the smallest and she would be flattened out on her stomach. There was no small bag, no little dark flat lump, on the floor. How dumb of me. She set her jaw and kicked her heel back hard against the wood paneled wall behind her. How really, really, really dumb of me.

A cold, heavy weight grew up within her and tugged at the walls of her stomach, sucking her insides toward itself. She pushed herself off the door frame and out into the room. Breathing jerkily, the lower rims of her eyes hot with stinging salt, she tiptoed clumsily between the sleeping bags.

Cass's hair was a black cloth that might have been wadded up into a tight black ball and wedged against a corner of the sleeping bag where it almost fell out of the bag she was sharing. Nothing but the top of her head was visible. She was face down.

Her companion's head was turned away from Cass, lying on an elbow, a stretched and twisted camisole gathered up under the arms, and underneath, light red in the faltering hearth light, the rise of one swollen breast and a crest of the dark chocolate circle ringing the Chillon woman's nipple.

Wyn collapsed onto her heels at Cass's head, furious at herself for not kicking Cass in the head, frightened of herself that she might. Cass's arms were doubled up under her head. Wyn took hold of Cass's hands and pulled her arms straight out of the bag, and bumped Cass's chin on the floor. The thump was muffled by the bag but Wyn could feel the impact through the floor.

"'the hell you doin'?" Cass woodenly turned her head away from the firelight. Her eyes remained closed.

Wyn put her mouth down to Cass's ear, whispering through the rank, tangled hair. "You promised me ..." Wyn's lips brushed at individual soft damp warm hairs and some stuck to her mouth, but she fought against pulling away, and bent over like she was she couldn't spare a hand from holding herself to keep from falling. "You said tonight was our night ...," dragging the hairs up and down against her mouth as she whispered. "C'mon Cass, for God's sake, what about that?"

"Hunh?"

"You stupid ..." Wyn caught up more hairs. "... asshole ..." She almost gagged. "... little bitch!" She blew out at her lips, trying to disentangle the hairs, without pulling away. The hairs were wet with sweat and oily. Some held fast against her mouth, tugging into the corners and slipping tiny threaded ends inside her lips and pulling at her own saliva.

THE MULE OF JACOPO VELLINI

A Boccaccian Tale

Not far from Palermo, in a small village better known for its grapes than for its scant inhabitants, there lived a poor vine dresser named Jacopo Vellini. His service to the wine makers and vineyard keepers of the town providing him scarcely enough to live on, he was able to number among his possessions nothing more than an old mule. Though she was much wasted, and somewhat forlorn to look upon, she was willing and nimble, and, as she bore him back and forth to his labors ungrudgingly, Jacopo loved her very much and gave her the name of Rosalina.

It happened that there lived across town a wealthy owner of many vineyards who had but one daughter, tall with black hair and eyes, to whom he also had given the name of Rosalina. Because of her position in the town this Rosalina was famous for being haughty, scornful and rude, and her reputation was well deserved. She was, however, favored by the gods with great beauty and, despite her reputation and her manner, she was zealously sought after by many of the young men of the village, especially those so well placed that a union of their families would increase the holdings of both, and who thus had reason to believe their expectations might be favorably realized.

It was a reflection of his manner of living and working and not of any slowness on his part that Jacopo was unaware of the woman Rosalina, for indeed he was quick witted and noticed all who came and went about him. To his credit, for he was sensitive and generous, he blushed mightily to learn from his companions that his beloved mule had a namesake so unlike her in every respect. Seeing his discomfort, his friends chided him roughly about the object of his affections, and frequently thereafter, with many winks and suggestive looks, teased him about the vine grower's daughter.

"And did you ride your fair Rosalina this morning?"

"Where did you spend your Sunday, Jacopo, toiling in the vineyards again with Rosalina?"

"Tell us, Jacopo, about Rosalina's hair," and "What is it like to throw a saddle upon your Rosalina, my friend?"

Though much grieved by their taunting, Jacopo was of a kindly disposition and kept his temper, though his curiosity about the other Rosalina began to grow, and he watched for an opportunity to see her for himself and to learn whether indeed her actions justified her reputation.

Greatly pleased was he therefore when he learned by chance that the very priest who taught him his lessons was also the confessor of the girl Rosalina. Being a laborer who went where he was summoned and who toiled till he was released, Jacopo was unable to go often to the priest, but at his first opportunity he hurried to the church. There he found the cleric, who was a great gossip, all too willing to discuss the wealthy vineyard owner who gave frequent sums to the church and his daughter whose charms were not entirely wasted on pious eyes.

The priest, though celibate in his old age, was not entirely ignorant of the ways of the world. Furthermore he had heard what the wags of the town had to say about Jacopo and the two Rosalinas. He had lately been grieved to learn of a bitter dispute between Rosalina's father and a neighbor of his who was also a vine grower, and who often hired Jacopo to work in his fields. Through reading the scriptures he had come to believe that all creatures should live in harmony, that discord should be confounded, and that those who caused distress to their fellow men should be put to shame. He further believed that kind deeds, at least those performed with a full heart, should be encouraged. Thus inspired by his philosophies he undertook to devise some means of dealing with several problems at once: the distress of Jacopo, the pride of Rosalina, and the bad feelings between the two vineyard owners.

He bade Jacopo tarry with him until the time of Rosalina's daily confession when he was able to point her out to the young man as she approached. The priest was pleased to see that Jacopo was much impressed by her comeliness. Quickly, before Rosalina arrived in his rooms, he sent Jacopo off to the vineyard of Rosalina's father's neighbor and bade him work closely beside the rock wall that divided the two vineyards and above all to speak loudly and earnestly to his mule all the while he was at his labors. Then he received the young woman and heard her confession. He found it necessary to pretend to be dismayed at her modest transgressions, for indeed she was aware of her own haughtiness and strove against it in her heart but alas she was unable to overcome the manner of her upbringing in her demeanor.

"Daughter," he said with much apparent anguish, "your offenses bespeak an unyielding nature upon which your prayers have had little effect. Therefore I am sending you out to a remote part of your father's vineyard where you may find favor with God by seeking Him in the natural world." He then bade her to go to a certain place and there to walk about praying silently and by no means to speak to anyone.

When she arrived at the appointed place she was astonished to hear someone calling her name, and thought it might be a voice from heaven. She was gratified at first to find the voice of God so youthful and lusty. As she drew near the wall separating her father's land from her neighbor's she heard God, as she thought, numbering her sins and crying them aloud to the fields.

"Ah, Rosalina, you have stumbled again. Do you never watch what you are about? Here, you want to go left, when you should be going right. Not so fast, you will soon wear yourself out, then what shall I do, my beloved?" Peering over the stonewall she saw God in the shape of a handsome young man following a mule. "What a wonder is this!" she thought. "To think that God would take such a form."

Then, forgetting that she was supposed to be walking about she crept along the wall and watched fascinated as the young man labored. She listened filled with wonder as he talked loudly about her and all her many faults, each of which she sadly acknowledged to be true. Her sorrow turned to joy, however, as she came to realize through his many protestations that God loved her beyond all measure. Her joy was further increased, when as the day drew warmer, Jacopo shed his shirt and his fine body shone in the sunlight, enrapturing her.

As the hours passed certain other signs she beheld from her concealment caused her to wonder whether this vision in man's form might have some traits of mortality about him. At last she became convinced that her young man was not a god, but a messenger of the gods, and as her passion rose she determined that, indeed, this handsome person who seemed to know her character so well and whose manly features so attracted her must be a personal gift to her from the gods. Whereupon, she attempted to leap over the fence and make herself known to this vision in man's form. In her haste, and encumbered by her many skirts, she managed instead to tumble, apron over wimple, onto the ground, suffering a great blow to her ample dignities that made her cry out in pain.

Meanwhile Jacopo had carried before him all during his work the face of the young woman he had earlier observed at the church, and had been cultivating a growing passion among the grapevines. His amazement was great therefore when Heaven apparently dumped this very creature directly in front of him with her many dignities delightfully displayed.

In the course of helping to sort out her garments, a matter in which he was quite active and well intentioned if somewhat unskilled, Jacopo became rather more rapidly acquainted with Rosalina's dignities than is usually the case, and finding the young woman favorably inclined to his attentions, Jacopo soon found himself making rapid advancement in her affections. Meanwhile the mule Rosalina found herself unengaged and took advantage of the opportunity to go to sleep.

Indeed, as evening fell they all three found themselves upside down in their day, for at that hour instead of falling asleep they were waking up. As it was now too late to return Rosalina discreetly to her father, they mounted the mule Rosalina and rode to the priest's house where they confessed certain features of their experience and expressed their great fear that Rosalina's father might take some action against them.

The practical priest hurried them off to the church where he married them quietly, with his cook and sacristan as the only witnesses. He then sent off a messenger to the owner of the vineyard where Jacopo had labored, taking the man into his confidence and assuring him that if he would only his cooperate his dispute with Rosalina's father would soon be settled. Upon the messenger's return he was sent out again, this time to Rosalina's father. The obliging mule carried him on both errands and was turned loose in the neighbor's vineyard without halter, reins or saddle.

At the house of Rosalina's father the messenger announced that he had just come from the neighbor's vineyard where Rosalina had been observed wandering about untethered and uncovered. Rosalina's father was distraught and cried out to the heavens, "This is surely the worst blow of all. I feared I could not marry her off well on account of her haughtiness, and now she has gone mad. I will never find a husband for her. What shall I do?"

He called his servants and instructed them that their mistress through no fault of her own had suffered some violent alteration, and that they were to follow the messenger who would show them where she was. They were to take her gently without frightening her, dress her in her nightclothes and lead her sweetly, no matter how much she might resist, up to her room where they were to stand guard and see that she spend a quiet night.

He instructed them that, being much distressed, he himself was going to bed and was under no circumstances to be disturbed. Then, providing himself with several bottles of wine by means of consolation for this latest calamity his daughter had caused him, he went up and locked himself in his room.

Some time later his slumbers were disturbed by a thunderous racket upon the stairs which he thought would surely bring down the house upon him, but he forced himself to turn a deaf ear, fearing this might be the last night of rest his daughter would ever allow him.

Next morning his worst fears were confirmed for, when his servants were assembled, he found them sullen and bruised. Several bore signs of being bitten and a few were scratched and bore great lumps and swellings about their persons. Meanwhile, overhead he could hear Rosalina tramping about making a great noise that filled him with terror. Finally, when he began to hear furniture being overturned and smashed he could stand it no longer and rushed off to the priest tearing his hair and calling to the gods for mercy.

The priest listened with feigned astonishment to the father's tale and then told him with a great show of sternness that surely he was being punished for his arrogance in mistreating his neighbor and for allowing his daughter to grow up so headstrong and careless. "I will send for the neighbor, that you may apologize to him and bring to a close this matter between you. Your daughter is a more difficult case however. Who would marry such a poor creature? Only someone accustomed to the worst of sufferings. Perhaps some ignorant laborer. But if I find such a person and am able to marry your daughter off to him, would you then take him into your home, treat him well, and make him your heir?" The father assured him that all would be done as he asked if only a suitably ignorant husband might be found who would assume the care of his Rosalina.

"Go you into the chapel, then, and prostrate yourself, considering what penances you must do. Remain there praying until I return. Pray with all your strength for you have set me many impossible tasks." Then the priest left him on his knees without even the comfort of a bottle and there the priest allowed him to remain for many long, dry, painful hours so that his workings would be considered suitably miraculous, for in this life little is appreciated that is not achieved at great cost. The priest then arranged for the couple to come out of hiding and the mule to be released from her prison and tenderly stabled.

At long last, when the priest felt the poor man could hold out no longer he brought in the neighbor, and Jacopo with his new wife Rosalina, where they were received with tears and kisses. As the happy procession bade their farewells to the priest and prepared to leave the chapel, the priest whispered in Jacopo's ear that in it would be in the young man's interest to change the name of his mule as quickly as possible.

"Considering all the good luck she has brought you I would suggest 'Fortuna'," he said.

SYMPHONY IN
BLOOD

I have no recollection of yesterday. I cannot even recall what happened a few moments ago. Nonetheless, since I fear I am about to die I will reconstruct as much as I can for you while I still have breath in my body.

I hurt and there is blood on me. There is a mirror in this room and I can see myself. I am apparently Asiatic, probably Japanese or Chinese, I think. My hair is black. My cheekbones are high, but my face is narrow. Japanese, I must be. Yes, Asiatic and Japanese, with small breasts, small hands and feet, what I can see.

The room is silent. The entire house, or building, sounds empty to me. I believe I have been abandoned. I have been left a tape recorder, why I don't know except for leaving this message to you, whoever you are. If you have done this thing to me I hope your conscience will not rest until you have found my next of kin and given them this recording, because I cannot believe you would turn yourself over to the police, not after what you have done.

I hurt and I am unable to move my legs, so I know I will not be able to reach the door before I expire. The door, as if you would have left it unlocked, after what you have done. I hurt but I must go on, because I hope surely someone must have loved me and must have cared about me.

NORMAN'S CAY

The Exumas, affectionately called among Bahamians The Family Islands, lie low and scant, nearly invisible till you are upon on them, some thirty to sixty miles east to southeast of New Providence. They are as exceptional for what they lack as for the wild inhospitable beauty they possess. Most of the island chain have no fresh water. Most offer no vegetation tall enough to give shade to creatures larger than the last few dozen surviving iguanas on Allen's Cay at the northernmost end of the chain. The soil is made of coral that slashes apart the unprotected foot. What plant life grows is thick of leaf and leathery, armed more often than not with spikes and hooks and husks. What thrives in animate form are insects of the biting and stinging variety and two kinds of bird life, the kind that twitters nervously and secretly in and out of brittle branches, and the kind that soars magnificently and philosophically too near the sun to see clearly.

In the summer these islands are cooked unceasingly by the most merciless of suns. In the winter fast moving cold fronts lash The Family Islands relentlessly, as if to tear down with flood and rain all the surface so many countless generations of coral creatures have given their bones to build up. Yet despite the hostility visited upon them by the forces of nature and for all the fierceness of their defenses these islands have been blessed beyond measure, consecrated and ennobled by an irrepressible obsession of the sea. The aim of the sea is to consume and reclaim these razor edged edifices that generations of coral animals have accreted through all the ancient ages of life on this earth. But against this powerful element the family of corals continue to hold out. Unable to prevail, like a stage door suitor continually frustrated by an unyielding diva, the sea has settled for bringing gifts of great value and beauty and leaving them garlanded about the Exumas.

Here, of all the world, the water flows most clearly. In its twice daily haste to sweep the banks the ocean scours every nettle, combs every waving frond and polishes every conch. With each tide it scours the walls and floors of each path it has carved into the shallow banks upon which these coral islands are built. Like a blind woodworker it fondly traces the hefts of the curves and hollows it remembers, and in doing so renders them yet more sculpted and polished. The result of this loving interplay between island and sea, between sand and spray, is a novel thing, a unique language that is made up of light and color and speaks boldly and honestly to the traveler.

White water, for example, means water too shallow to be safe, over white sand. Green water is of moderate depth over grass. Brown water, especially mottled brown, where the spots and striations are pronounced on the flanks of the swells, signals the presence of coral heads—stay away! And most blessed of all are the broad paths of cobalt blue that proclaim deep water channels, free of all obstructions. So clear and so well known are these words in this language that, except for the shipping lanes, the waterways of the entire panoply of the Bahamian chain are completely unbuoyed.

Ashore, more from the absence of society than from the presence of shelter, there is every opportunity for privacy. For what, you ask. Why, to explore, of course. If your feet are encased by shoes, preferably wretched castoffs, well worn, slashed and torn; if your arms are covered by long sleeves, preferably threadbare to admit air; and if your head is shaded, preferably by the broadest brimmed hat you can find in the straw market at Nassau; why then you can explore any island you choose. You will wear out before the novelty of discovery dies within you.

All about is coral rock, dark gray and vicious. Yet everywhere in tiny cracks and in broader areas where sediment has collected have sprouted the woody, barbed and ant infested flowering shrubs, casuarina trees and palms of the Exumas. A hungry iguana, lone representative of a once plentiful race, may come rustling up for a handout, making a ferocious rattling in the dry underbrush and sand, a queer combination of serpentine deadliness and bold foolishness, then rush away, making another comically fearsome commotion among the dry leaves.

Nameless, and innumerable, tiny finchlike birds busy themselves about the scrub. The open skies overhead are home to the frigatebird. Seagulls bob brilliant white in the harsh glare of sunlight reflected off the waves.

These islands, though low silhouetted lie close enough together that from each island the next island south or north is almost always visible, all along the island chain, from the inbred white descendants of Tory sympathizers from the American Revolution hiding indoors at Spanish Wells in the north, through the plush sports fishing port of Highburn Cay midway at the waist of the chain, to the Bahamians themselves, humble, broad featured and friendly, on the larger islands near Elizabethtown in the south.

But most of these islands are unpeopled. Most are little more than rock, stalk and bird, exposed to the sun. About the time you begin to think yourself alone in the universe you may come upon the abandoned foundations of what might have been a house, or what equally likely might never have been a house but only a foundation destined to be abandoned once laid, for these islands are mostly inhospitable to anyone who would seek to live on them for any purpose but to fish. They are of the sea and they turn to the sea, these islands. They have no patience and extend no comfort to those who would fasten, amphora-like, onto their coral backbones and bleached sandy flesh. If you come, prepare to live off the sea, and do not come to stay, for nothing endures here but sun and rock and wave.

OKLAHOMA
SWARMING

"Hell of a place to put a navy base," said Henry Bakersfield Chambliss, "smack in the middle of the desert."

"Elk City's not a desert, Hank," said his companion at the bar. "There's a war going on and we're in the supply business. Why not put all the navy supplies smack in the middle of the country? Keep the blankets and the ammunition safe from the Germans and the Japs."

Henry took a long hard drink and extricated his tongue from the narrow necked, sweating bottle. He was tall and thin, dressed in navy blues, with grey eyes and a young face with a receding hairline. "Hell, Tony, it's all politics, anyway. Probably some Oklahoma congressman with a friend in the War Department."

"Don't worry about it. You won't be here long enough to notice. You've been here what? Two weeks?" Antonio DiGracio was medium height, with dark eyebrows that met in a thick line over his nose, and black hair on the backs of the hands holding his beer. Like all the other men in the USO club he was wearing navy blues.

"Four weeks, almost a month. Teach this class then I'm gone from here. Get back to where there's ships … and water to float 'em in."

"Aw-w, you get used to it. This is cowboy country. And Indian country. You seen any Indians yet?"

"Saw one this morning. Thought it was a squaw wearing a blanket. Hard to tell. We're up on the third floor of the hotel. Saw her from our window, standing on the corner across the street. Showed her to my little boy." He pointed his bottle across to where a child and his mother were working a jigsaw puzzle, their faces bright in the reflection of the lamp hanging down over their table. He could tell the boy was getting sleepy by the way he leaned into his mother's side and aimlessly moved pieces about with his free hand.

Little Charlie had been excited and lively walking over from the hotel. Curious about everything in this new state. He had come from hills and farms and woods, two days on the train. Two days of dirt and the smell of iron punctuated by bouts of motion sickness and throwing up on the seats they'd had to sleep on and the floors the porter had had to mop up, out to this empty plain where there might or might not be cattle, or cowboys, or Indians.

Their hotel room was just big enough for a double bed and their two suitcases, one made of cardboard and one made out of tin. The hotel hadn't had any beds for kids. They couldn't afford a room with two beds, so they'd pulled out one of the dresser drawers and put a folded blanket in it and the child had slept in there.

If they didn't leave the USO before long he would have to carry the kid back to the hotel. His wife was big on catering to the boy and his younger sister. But at least she had had the good sense to leave the girl with her mother.

"You'll see a lot more Indians. They're in town for the rodeo. Camped in the park. Out Sutton Street, where the bridge in."

"I know where that is. Walked past there today. Me and the wife signed up for a tourist cabin."

"So you found a place to stay. Gonna be enough for you?"

"Not real big. Kitchen and bedroom all in one. Got a bath room. And a garage. Ain't got no car, so he gimme a break on the price. Anyway, it'll take my whole living allowance to pay for it."

"Just the same you're lucky, Hank," said Tony, "at least you've got your woman here."

"Yeah, maybe I am." Henry took another sip, letting the bite of the drink burn his tongue, and leaned back on the bar watching his wife and son. The kid was nodding. Comical how his little body jerked each time his head fell. Didn't seem like Betty Gail noticed. She was absorbed in the puzzle. Henry wished she had left the little boy home, too. It was war time. She ought to be with her man, wherever he was. You had to go where the Navy sent you.

She could have left the boy with Henry's parents. The grandparents weren't going anywhere, not with gasoline rationed. They would be happy to keep the kids. It's like she's keeping the boy between us, he thought. Well, he'd walk the kid's legs off tomorrow, moving their stuff to the tourist cabin. Then he could make time with Betty Gail. He liked the look of her hair, long curls hanging down over the puzzle, combed back off the front like Loretta Young. Liked the look of her skinny back and the shoulder pads and puffed sleeves. Good looking woman.

He would see if she had a nickel left, play a Hank Williams, or a Bob Wills and the Texas Troubadours and then they'd go.

The USO was getting busier as the sailors came off duty. He thought about the kid, gone to sleep now, leaning against his mother, head back, mouth open. The boy had been fascinated watching the jukebox pick up a record and flip it over. The kid loved the way bubbles floated up and down the lighted columns of the big rounded red and gold glowing jukebox. Not a bad kid.

On their walk into town tonight Hank had held the boy up so he could see the miniature castle in a jewelry store window. It had a king and a queen that went in and out of doors that opened and shut, and horses and a carriage that bobbed up and down in front. For the next several blocks Charlie had talked about nothing else—what moved the king and queen and how they kept from running into the doors, what made the horses go up and down, and how the castle could keep running after the jewelry man went home at night.

"Be sure to see the rodeo, if you can," Tony called to him as Henry picked up his beer and started toward his family.

"Yeah, maybe I'll take the kid."

✳   ✳   ✳   ✳

When the government issue timepiece on the wall opposite the windows showed four o'clock Henry Bakersfield Chambliss summed up his lecture notes. He tried his best to catch each pair of eyes, and asked for questions. As usual he got no response. He thanked his class for their attention and for a good week. He told them to tell their buddies that any of them he hadn't seen would be sure enough assigned to the final section starting on Monday, and stepped back to watch them crowd up and push their way out into the corridor.

The last man in line stopped to speak to him. He was young, and good looking with sharp features, dark eyes, a dark tan and cheekbones with pink highlights.

"Good class," he said. "I didn't know there was that much to Navy store keeping and supply."

Henry nodded, expecting the sailor to go on out the door.

"I've been noticing you looking at me all week," the sailor said.

"Huh?" said Henry.

"You were looking at me in particular. I'm Delosantos—Jimmy Delosantos."

Henry remembered the name from the roster.

"You knew right off I was a half breed, didn't you?"

"No."

"You knew, I could tell. But you couldn't figure out my name, could you?"

"I never noticed ..." Henry tried to think of some way to say he hadn't particularly been aware of him without hurting the younger man's feelings.

"Yeah, you knew. I can always tell. Well, my father was Mexican—Spanish really, and my mother was a Sioux. They're both still living." He waited.

Henry tried to think of something to say. Nothing came.

"It just makes me sick," Jimmy went on. "You guys think you're so much better than everyone else, just because your mother and your father came from the same country.

"Aw, not really," said Henry. He thought he was catching on now. "My mother's people were a mixture, I think. English and Scottish, and I believe my daddy's were Irish and Welsh."

"See, that's what I mean. "People like you think you're something special, don't you?"

Henry wondered what he had said that week to set off Delosantos. Where was the prejudice in warehousing and store keeping?

"Well, I'll tell you something," James went on, "you're no different from anybody else. There's no such thing as pure anything. It doesn't matter who my mother's people were. You go back in your family far enough and you'll find some of everything. You'll find Indian blood."

Henry tried to laugh. "Well, my grandfather did used to tell us he was part Cherokee,"

"Don't patronize me," said Jimmy Delosantos. "You'll find Negro blood. Hell, you'll probably find Jap blood."

Henry felt the blood glowing in his neck. He was getting warm in his navy wool, around his collar and upper chest. He looked away from Jimmy's angry eyes and out over the distant Oklahoma plains. Jimmy said something Henry missed, his voice rising and thin.

"Hey," he said, to interrupt Jimmy. The young man stopped, cheeks flushed a deep red. "Whatever I said, I didn't mean nothing by it. Look, I ..." He tried to think of something to add. He felt his eyes rolling. He couldn't help himself.

"That's all I wanted to say," said Jimmy. "You're no more pure bred than me or anybody else." He turned and walked stiffly out into the corridor.

"Damn," said Henry.

✳   ✳   ✳   ✳

Little Charlie fell asleep before the rodeo was half way over. Henry and Charlie had left Betty Gail at the tourist cabin, worn out from running after Charlie all day at the playground. She was going to wash her hair and roll it up. She'd be sleeping in curlers when he got home. Well, he and Charlie would have a big time, he had told the boy. They would go to the rodeo and see the calf roping and the Brahma bulls and the wild broncos.

The boy had been excited at first. He enjoyed the clowns, and the Indian dances, and the bull riding. He stayed awake long enough to see the calf roping start, but there just wasn't enough excitement in it to keep him up for the main event, the bronco busting. Henry had saved coins for two hot dogs, but he had had to eat his own and most of Charlie's. The boy had fallen asleep with a bite in his mouth. Henry had fished it out so the boy wouldn't choke on it.

He held the sleeping child throughout the bronco busting till his arms felt they would pull out of their sockets, then he hoisted the boy onto his shoulder and walked the couple of miles along the flat empty streets to the tourist cabins. As he had imagined Betty Gail was sound asleep. Unlikely to be in a good mood if waked up.

So he had put the boy to bed on his foldaway cot and gone out for a walk. Now it was early morning. The eastern sky was lightening with low bands of pink edged black and blue clouds.

God, this is an empty country, he thought to himself. About like the ocean, the way it goes out straight to the horizon in every direction. Worse than the ocean. He thought how, after his run-in with the half Indian, he had come home and taken Charlie and Betty Gail to the playground and how they watched little Charlie playing in the dust, sitting on the ground, and how Charlie had suddenly screamed and Betty Gail had run to him and had started slapping at his clothing.

"Ants!" she had yelled. "We got to get his clothes off."

And how they had run back to their cabin carrying Charlie and how he had grabbed the coal oil to wipe off the ants off his skin while she stripped him. There had been ants in all his clothes, ants in the pockets and in the folds, ants inside and out. When they got him naked they found ants in the creases of his skin, and in his hair, and—the image kept coming back to him—an ant crawling out from under the boy's foreskin.

You think crazy things at times like that. He had thought she should have let him have Charlie circumcised like he had wanted to in the hospital, and he had felt angry with her. Then she had taken up the naked boy—in coal oil on his body, coal oil in his hair—and she had loved him and sung to him and the child had felt better.

When the boy calmed down and when they checked him over one more time they saw that there were no new bites, no new stings on his body. Now they could relax, at least till the boy went out to play tomorrow.

These had been black ants. Big thick bodied black ants, that made holes in the hard ground the size of nickels and quarters. Around their cabin and the play-grounds there were also a race of tiny red ants and another race of large red ants. The big red ants were biters that left welts on the skin, The tiny red ants had a nasty sting like a bee. The black ants neither bit nor stung but they were every-where. Sometimes you would be looking at the ground and it would be like the ground was in motion around you, and it would be those damned black ants.

Hell of a damn country, anyway. Give it back to the goddamn Indians, he thought.

He crossed the bridge and walked up into the trees of the park. In the grey morning light he could see people quietly passing back and forth among the trees. He moved deeper into the woods so he could see better. It was the Sioux tribe. He had caught flashes of their teepees through the trees last week.

Now they were breaking camp. Hides and blankets were being rolled up and stored in wagons, with pots and tools. Horses were brought up and saddled. Some were hitched to the wagons, others tied on behind. He heard a couple of trucks starting up. There came a more urgent sense of movement, a brisker scat-tering of scurryings and carryings. There was the sound of trucks, then the woods went quiet.

He stood for a long time, looking where the Indians had been, at the earth brushed clean, the campfires covered over and spread level with the ground. He remembered what he had been thinking before he'd seen the Indians packing up, and he looked around the vacant woods. Even the goddamn Indians don't want this country, he told himself.

In the growing light he became aware of a new movement in the trees. Across the abandoned campsite, he saw a man step out from the woods. There was a familiar look about him. At first he didn't recognize the young man, not in the boots, and denims and the plaid shirt. Then he saw it was the half-breed. Jimmy

Delosantos walked slowly out into the center of the clearing, hesitated for a moment, then threw himself flat down onto the ground with his arms stretched out ahead of him. Henry choked back a shout of warning. Under the dry dust and sand scattered about there would be hot coals and cinders, dying now but dangerous still.

Jimmy lay where he had fallen, face down in the dirt, for a few brief seconds. Then he started rolling over and over in the dust. He kicked his legs and threw his body about in circles, scrunching his back across the ground like a sidewinder rattlesnake. His frantic writhing covered his body with dust, the same kind of dust that had covered Charlie with ants just a few hours ago.

At last the thrashing stopped, and Jimmy Delosantos gathered his legs and arms under him and shoved himself up. He picked up his hat where it had fallen, and brushed absently at his clothes, staring down at the ground around him where the teepees had stood—the teepees of his mother's people—and where her people had cooked their meals throughout this rodeo week. Then he straightened his back and walked off stiffly into the woods.

A long time after Jimmy was out of hearing, Henry Bakersfield Chambliss turned away from the clearing and walked through the screen of trees, out of the wooded park. From the bridge he could see the dry creek bed below and look out over the plain, past the rodeo grounds, to the distant government warehouses long and low in their early morning shadows. He could see off to the distant horizon. The early clouds were gone. It would be a clear sky all day and a hot sun the only thing in it. And below the sun, below the empty sky, on the hot hard ground today, they would all be crawling—the rodeo cowboys, the sailors in dress blues, the Indians, the half-breeds and the ants—the big red ants that bit, the little red ants that stung, and the big black ants that neither bit nor stung but crawled all over everything, and crawled all over you.

"Stupid place to put a navy base," he said to himself, "right in the middle of the goddamn desert."

ON VACATIONING
OVERMUCH

A week's vacation is a wonderful thing. It gives you a change of pace, a fresh look at a new world of activities, and rekindles your zest for tackling your workaday world when you get back to it.

A two weeks' vacation is even better. After the initial frenzy of holidaying there is time to gather your inner resources, go for long walks and take modest pleasures in the solitary moments you cannot avoid, those moments when family and friends have gone off on their own.

Four weeks, on the other hand, is too much time for relaxing, too much time for thinking. Four weeks is too much time to spend looking for distractions and too little time for tackling projects of consequence. So you are left to think about the things that need attention back home, about the things that have been left undone and, of those, which ones need to be at the top of the list, which ones matter.

Ultimately, by the time of the final week of a four week vacation, having prioritized all the various and mammoth projects that have come to mind, you find yourself thinking of the many ways your life is lacking, begin to look critically at the cocoon of your daily existence, even to your sartorial and habitual accoutrements, and begin to consider how you might at last make measurable improvements. You begin to make resolutions.

Resolved—To listen more to live music, and less to recorded music. There is a freshness about a live performance, especially if you are able to watch the musicians while listening. To experience the absorption of the cellist in her bowing, to feel the dance of the guitarist's fingers over and among the strings, and especially to become a partner in something that is real and unpredictable—those are the things the mind longs for, and the things it misses in recorded performances where what is there is always there. You realize that recorded music is what we use as we use a sedative, to relax us with its sameness, so that we arrive home from the office soothed rather than jangled but aesthetically unchallenged, mentally at ease rather than intellectually gratified. The pleasures of recorded pieces are in the lulling of their balm that quiets the nerve endings, not in the startling of imagination that thunders like flushed quail into the dark morning air of our thoughts.

Resolved—To listen less and read less of news, especially news of reported fact, and to read more and listen more to opinion. The problems with the reporting of fact are several and they are problems that only become evident when one is able to look through the reverse telescope of a long vacation. Some reports are irrelevant, such as how many dollars were actually embezzled and how many years before eligibility for parole, and by how many percentage points the public supports the athlete of the moment or by how many points the president's popularity has declined between elections. Many facts, including facts about nature and nutrition, are not worth remembering and if not are certainly a waste of time to read. The important facts to remember are those that will remain in the collective unconscious anyway and if you forget them you can always ask your spouse or your colleagues.

Opinion, on the other hand, is always fresh and always important. It is something original, the handiwork of another person's creativity, and the child of his needs, his interests and his fears. For nothing, it seems, after four weeks of reflection is more important to us than what moves and hurts and frustrates those whom we love and those whom we respect and those in whom we take an interest. Unlike feats of engineering and warfare for example, opinion does not predict, it does not allow us to extrapolate along the line of the predictable and the calculable. Instead opinion presents us with something like the early masses of a painter's canvas with something in shapes, a foreshadowing rather than a foretelling of what is to come. A feeling rather than a depiction of what the future is to be like. Opinion is something within which to dwell and to reach around and feel about as in a darkened room, rather than something to be boldly trod and closely measured.

Resolved—To spend more time in the company of children, especially infants. This should be self evident, but it is not. Watching adults, you tend to become preoccupied with the concerns of adults which are how you look and whether you are planning and executing all the steps that will someday take you from where you are, with all its deficiencies, to where you want to be, where things will be exactly as you want them to be and where you will surely be content. Watching children allows you to become aware again of what truly matters, namely that which is curious and fascinating within your immediate surroundings and whether you and your companions are happy and, if not, then why not and what you can do about it.

Resolved—To eat outdoors in good weather, without benefit of newspaper or radio, to eat and drink slowly and listen to the company about, including, if you are alone, the company of the grass, the squirrels or the honeybees, and, when eating, to eat more of fruits and less of meats, when drinking, to drink less of stimulants and more of juices and waters, to taste the water wherever you go and to try and remember the last time you sat with these companions and how they looked and what they talked about or what you heard, in the case of grasses, squirrels and honeybees.

PAP-PA

When Pap-pa Campbell fell and broke his hip, his second oldest son William R. whom they called Russ was the one that took a notion to fix it so Pap could get in and out of his platform rocker without falling. He called their cousin Charles who was a tradesman and a right handy carpenter and had him build a box they could shove under Pap's chair that would raise it up about a foot off the floor. All Pap, who was then in his upper eighties, would have to do was to back up to the chair and tilt himself backwards. Getting up he would have to do no more than to lean forward on his cane, slide out a bit, and be on his way. Later they set beside his chair a walker, a kind of portable light weight frame with four legs on rubber pads, and he used that to get about once he was out of his seat.

Pap-pa had little use for old people. His children had offered to take him to see his own sister, Ollie, who kept house for her granddaughter and a yard full of great-grandchildren. Much as he enjoyed being around the young people he was uncomfortable in Ollie's company. When he looked at her he saw someone who was not his sister, someone who was elderly and, if not frail, then at least brittle.

His sister, his real sister, was a tall, long haired, thin, dark skinned girl who went barefoot in the summers, who went haying in overalls with her brothers, who spoke up in a loud and laughing voice in company. She was a prayer meeting girl with a strong clear voice, rode the plow horses and knew how to milk a cow. Many a bucket of foaming warm milk she had carried in when her mother had sent her off to live with neighbors. Their mother had been a young widow. She had too many children to feed and the only man who would have her said he would take the baby but those older children would have to go.

Go they did.

Pap-pa was fourteen and big for his age, with strong brown arms and deep set eyes and a stern, serious look about him that came from his mother who had strong features with a prominent nose. Some people claimed she had Indian blood. He had been welcome on the farms close about. He was a willing worker and six years of school was all he ever needed. He had worked the fields from as early as he could remember. He knew horses, mules and plows. He knew threshing machinery and later he would know tractors. In adulthood he worked as a hostler in a railroad roundhouse, tending steam locomotives, cleaning out the boilers and starting up the massive cold machinery for each day's run.

He had ridden horses, ridden hard and won races, but he never owned a horse, never had a horse of his own. He had owned mules from time to time. Mules were good value. They worked hard, they worked steady, they had good health, robust health, and they were dependable. They lived a long time and worked willingly every day. He was a lot like a mule himself. Except for one thing. He had fathered eight children, which a mule could not. He had loved his wife. And he remembered the women.

He was not one to go to picnics out at the country church or reunions with his old bible class. That was what women folk did. Nor did he want to be reintroduced to people he had last seen forty or fifty years ago. On the outside he was an old man whose skin was too dark now ever to pale, though it had a laundered look to it now, an old man with thick black hair sprouting out of his earlobes, and bristles inside the folds of skin on his cheeks where he could not reach with the razor. An old man whose once black hair even now showed some dark grey strands among the thinning white, and whose right hip gave way if he tried to stand too long.

He was a man who after fifty years of railroading had gone back to farming; renting land for gardening, grazing and tobacco growing from friends and widow women all over the county, carrying a jug of ice water behind his seat in the cab of the best used pickup truck he could find, that he could pay for on time. He farmed like that for another fifteen years and then gave it all up as he slid helplessly and unexpectedly into his eighties.

For a few years after farming he mowed till the mower got too heavy and stiff to guide around the yard. He had been glad at first of the easy work, but finally the mower got too heavy for him to move.

For a while then he vacuumed inside. His wife told the grandchildren and the great-grandchildren that it was the sound of the vacuum cleaner that he liked. He liked that roaring, whooshing noise, she told them, but that wasn't it. It was the operating of machinery that he liked, and when his hip started to give way, he would go sit in his chair and leave the vacuum out where he could watch it and think about it, till at last the day came when he hadn't the strength left to take it out of the closet or put it away.

Then he sat. Hours and days he sat. The great-great-grandchildren came and he was introduced to them and he enjoyed holding the little ones. From about six months old, up to a year old, they were fun to hold. Up to about two or three years old they would come and climb up onto his lap and hunt around in his pockets till their mothers came and took them away. He could not remember their names nor who they belonged to. Some of these mothers were supposed to be his grandchildren and great-grandchildren they told him, but he didn't recognize the grown women as any kin of his.

His hands would get to trembling sometimes, and he would stare at them and wonder whose hands they were. Then he would wonder whose body he was in. He would look at the people around him in the living room where they all came to talk to one another in loud voices and call his name and try to get him to laugh. He would look into their faces one by one and wonder who they were.

Then he would remember the other faces, the faces of women, and men too, but mostly women that they had wanted to take him back to visit and he had not wanted to see after all these years, because it was the faces in his memories that mattered to him and they could not show him those faces, only old faces with eyes clouded and peering, and those were not the faces he wanted to see.

PEPPERMINT TWIST

"'s your name?" the old guy asked me.

"Berylinda." I don't usually do that. Give guys my real name.

"One word or two?"

"One."

"Pretty name."

"Yeah … You lonesome?"

"Me?"

"Right. You lonesome?"

"Nope, I'm fine, thanks."

Well, that's about it. I usually get up and move on when it plays out that way. Give it another shot. What the heck.

"Want a good time?"

"Who, me?"

Jeez. This guy was dense. No, the guy down the street, Charlie. "Yeah," I gave him an ol' buddy laugh. "You and me."

This one had start off strange. 'n I sat down on his bench, he moved over like giving me room. Hell, he could a made four a me. How much room'd he think I need? Look over me like I's a leaf blown down and me in my yellow low riders and matching belly jool, I'm talking the very best of my love-conquers-all coordinates. Minimal top, I'm not real big there anyway. It's usually the belly button gets 'em. This guy hadn't even noticed. If he did he didn't care. He hadn't said anything.

"Hey!" Maybe a little too loud.

"Huh?" Told you this one was dense.

"Yeah, I'm asking do you want to have a good time.

"Oh, oh yeah. Well, no. I wasn't thinking. No. I'm fine. Here ..." He took out some cash, pulled a ten and passed it over. I took it.

"Sorry," he said, and he smiled, "I'm not the droid you're looking for."

That done it. I felt my jaw go down, like I'd just stopped chewing gum. Used to make my mother so mad when I did that. Like I 'sposed to know what it meant. O.K. I seen Luke Skywalker, I seen it. Not like I never been anywhere, nor did nothin'. I laughed a little like I caught on. That's when he asked what my name was.

"Berylinda," like I said. Prob'ly shouldn't a tole him. Reason I picked him in the first place, old guys is easy money, usually. Don't take much time. Don't ask for much and don't hurt you none. This guy had the right amount of white hair, really thin on top. Not a lot of wrinkles though. Next time I'll be lookin' for more wrinkles.

He must a 'thought I'd be leaving 'cause he turned away and stared off the way he'd been doing when I found him.

"Hey," I said again. He looked around at me kind of surprised, more like people do when you think they're drowning and they bring their head up out of the water like one minute they're not there then the next minute they are.

He looked at me for a second embarrassed then he looked down at my feet. I was wearing those high heel sandals with the thin yellow straps that show my toes. I have long toes. Guys notice. He looked back up at me, more embarrassed yet.

"Something else? Berylinda?" Damn, he said my name. Never shoulda tole him. Never shoulda. Damn.

"Yeah, another ten." I was totally cool.

"No, I think that was enough. You need to get on with your work." Hell, what'd he think I was, a hooker? I mean, a cheap hooker? Well, one more shot. Maybe this one was a talker.

"'s your name?" I asked him. Like he asked me.

"Buck."

"Buck?"

"Like the singer?"

"THUH singer?" Like what singer?

"You know, Buck Owens."

Like I'd know some guy named Buck Owens. Maybe he was in the history books. I'd never stayed awake for a whole history class in my life. "Friend of Elvis, right?" I did my us-old-buddies laugh.

He looked at me like he was seeing me for the first time and let out this really loud laugh. Damn, last thing you need in my kind of work is guys laughing at you. I could see my reputation sliding. That'd do it for any guys in earshot. Damn, damn, damn.

"What?" I said, "what?"

He laughed again, but easier this time. "How old are you?"

There he goes with the questions again.

"Twenty," I lied.

"I'm guessing sixteen," he looked at me again, "or nearly."

I could feel my face getting red.

"How tall?"

"Five-five."

"More like five-even, or five-one, I'd say, without the heels."

See, what'd I tell you? Guys notice.

"Can you remember being a kid?"

Yep, I's right. I had me a talker here. I just might work this one if I stayed with him. My daddy'd been a fisherman. Maybe I'd learned something from him. Doubt it, though. Him nor Mother neither.

"Yeah, I's a kid once."

"I don't mean yesterday. I mean a real kid. Like first grade."

"Yeah, I can remember that." My eyes were scrunching. Mother hated that. I thought about Billy Hepwhistle. It'd been funny, him having a funny name and us kidding him all the time. Too bad he didn't stay funny. "So?"

"If you could remember ten times that far back you'd be where I was just now."

This was a weird one. I knew it. I knew it.

"You hear this music?" Yeah, I hear it. It's old guy music. Sixties stuff. That's what they play around this part of town. There's no parking. There's little stores. Old people walking around, buying stuff. Expensive stuff. That's why I work here. I said yeah.

"When they played this music I listened to it with a girl your age and about your size. She was a good listener. What they did I didn't find out till tonight. They made those records in a press and they stamped them in vinyl. What they did was they stamped us like we were right into those records. They were 45's then. And they stamped us right into the grooves. When the sound comes out we come out just like we were then. That girl I told you about? She's be your grandmother's age, but she doesn't have a face like your grandmother's.

What does he know? I never met my grandmother. Either side of the family.

"She has a face in the record that's just like the face she had then. I've never seen her other face. Probably I never will. It'd be better any way. She'd be the wrong person. This way she will always be the right person."

Good, he was getting mushy. Time for step two of the ten-step program. I moved closer. "It's okay," I said, in my mother's voice.

"No," he grunted. "You don't have to do that. Just get back over there. Shut up and listen."

"Ten dollars." I said firmly.

He closed his eyes. I think he closed his eyes. He was a long time answering.

"O.K." He dug out another ten.

Great, hope I can stay awake. I'm not doing bad, though. Ten bucks every five minutes. That's about a hundred twenty an hour. Better'n a lot of days.

A BLUSH OF
MAIDENS, A
FOOLISHNESS OF
OLD MEN

Returning to Krakow in the time of the apex of Soviet domination was like finding the fires banked and the family gone to bed after a hard day of working in the fields. He had taken the train from Warsaw, looking forward to savoring the mist-softened squares of apple orchards and wheat stands, and been disappointed by the silver screen of rain. He had hoped to be greeted by hearty, hefty, towering Poles in fur caps and babushkas, but had experienced only the backs of fellow passengers scurrying off down the narrow, cobbled streets glistening under the spotty street lights and slippery in the downpour, their heavy suitcases slamming knees and thighs. No one greeted Janusz Oblynsczi, the words he heard about him fell on cottoned ears, like a convalescent's, making him feel he was walking inside a glass cage with dead acoustics, with everyone else close by, but outside his bell, and Polish, where he was American.

PROJECT WOMAN

DATE: 8th day

MEMO TO: Adam, (Former) Archangel Lucifer

FROM: Archangel Gabriel

SUBJECT: Design Review Board—Design Objectives for Project WOMAN

Please be advised of your appointment to the above-referenced Design Review Board, the first general meeting of which will take place at an as-of-now undetermined date. Please consider the enclosed design objectives and return your comments at your earliest convenience.

DATE: 9th day

MEMO TO: Archangel Gabrield

FROM: Adam

SUBJECT: Design Review Board for Project WOMAN

In reading the Design Objectives I take exception to the following points:

1. "Our market review indicates that man should have a mate."—This is a popular trend among mammals and the resulting increase in the number of mammals seems to guarantee a steadily increasing market population. However, there is precedent among some life forms for species maintenance with-

out a pairing process. It could be that one member of this species will be enough. Introducing a new model into the currently well-ordered scheme would amount to taking unnecessary chances with the present balance.

2. "For economic and logistic considerations such as wearing apparel, consistency of nourishment requirements and interchangeability of parts, the prototype should be similar in every respect to Man."—This seems inconsistent, heretofore we have aimed for uniqueness in each new model, whereas the present model is acknowledgely perfect. Surely we cannot have it both ways.

3. "For improvement of his intellectual equivalent and stimulation of his creative ability, by way of maintaining his interest, the product should have a sharp mind and a tongue to match; physical appearance is of secondary importance."—I disagree here only with regard to physical appearance. Intellectually and creatively I have all I need and all I can use in my daily activities. It's the nights I'm worried about, and from the point of view of meeting the recreational requirements, I strongly recommend promoting physical appearance to first place.

THE SAN JUAN
TAKEOVER

Eventually a European arrives at that stage when he fantasizes about ruling a tropical country. This feeling probably comes over him upon emerging from a particularly cold and monotonously bleak winter, especially if he has spent it alone. There is something fecund and violable about a tropical country, a sensuous virgin longing for him and only him to waken in her the wanton and the feline, the jungle creature, the perfect mate. Rarely does the fantasy become reality, but it happened in *Lord Jim*, it happened in *The Viceroy of Ouidah*, and it happened to me. It was heady. It was exhilarating. But it was not fun.

RIO DULCE STORY

As an old man he remembered the light bulb, how it looked, and how it changed his life.

He remembered, too, an earlier bulb, one that was not a light bulb at all but a fluorescent tube that twisted in a half circle and was mounted high in the center of a dark grey ceiling. Its pale evanescence gave his schoolroom walls a weak gray look that in later life he associated with prison cells. Its light was barely a light at all, too dim to read by in the windowless concrete building where the school children gathered in his village.

When the rains came and the world was dark outside it was even darker inside the classroom. Then the students could no more read by the fluorescent tube that loomed small and distant above their young heads than they could read by the scant green light that oozed toward their benches from the jungle's breathy glow just outside the schoolroom door.

Later there was another light bulb, one that his father cupped delicately in one massive hand while the other hand carefully held a porcelain receptor hung with hemp twine from the gray ceiling. His father and some friends had spent days stringing heavy black wires that emerged from the jungle. The boy had looked into the denseness wondering where the wires came from. In some places they hung from branches, in other places they lay along the damp earth, snaking as far back into the trees as he ever dared explore.

He and his boyhood friends, dark brown from the sun, some wearing shorts, some wearing only shirts, some wearing nothing at all, stood in silence and watched as his father with great reverence slowly turned the bulb in the porcelain socket at the place where the thick black wire ended and where the twine strained to hold it in place a few inches below the ceiling. As a young man he had wondered how the wires and the porcelain fixture came to be in his village but he was too much in awe of his aging father to ask.

His father was one of the poorer farmers of the village. Some of his neighbors, in addition to their plots of yams and corn, possessed chickens or a pig, but his father had nothing besides what he planted and tilled. The boy did not know where his father acquired seeds and cuttings for planting, but he saw his father make the tools for working the ground. They were little more than sticks sharpened and shaped to the task.

His father's house, like that of most of the villagers, was a palappa, an open sided hut supported on sticks, with a thatch of palm leaves thickly laid, a house that his father built for a young wife pregnant with their first child. The palappa stood next to a structure with four concrete walls, one of which contained an opening that served as both window and door. This building had a roof of corrugated tin that made a loud noise in the rain and smelled inside of people, and of things that moulded and rusted and had dampness around them. There was a coolness about the building. It was sheltered from the afternoon sun by the canopy of the rain forest. A thin wedge of corrugated tin extended over the doorway making a tiny dry area for squatting in the evenings, the way their neighbor and his wife sometimes did.

One evening the police came, the policia nacional, and took the man away with them. Some said his wife turned him in. The policemen walked the man off through the jungle, one on either side, and one man in front armed with a pistol in a holster. The other men carried large weapons like rifles or shotguns. Later that evening the wife went away, carrying a small bundle wrapped in a cloth and balanced on her head.

That night his father went into the man's house and stayed a long time. The next morning, when the boy and his brothers and sisters awoke, their mother also was gone, taking with her a blanket and straw pallet. The children found their parents sitting under the tin overhang. The villagers walking by looked stiffly at the children's parents but said nothing.

For almost a week the boy and the other children remained in their house, in the palappa, but took their meals with their parents. Eventually the oldest brother, and the brother who shared his pallet, took their bedding into the concrete house. Gradually all the brothers and sisters moved there, but the concrete smell remained.

Only the palappa was clean and smelled softly of the forest. There he would sometimes go to sit alone and watch the rain splashing on leaves and running down in silver ropes onto the forest floor. When the palm fronds began to loosen in the thatch roof and fall out his father did not replace them. Eventually there were fewer and fewer dry places to sit when it rained and by the time of this light bulb and the black wires there was no place left beneath the thatch where the boy could sit and be dry when the heavy rains came up.

Of all the children he was the most intelligent and the only one for whom the printed words on paper became transparent, which they did from the very first days of his schooling.

Away from the concrete and windowless school house in the next village, where it was too dark to read and they did their reading out of doors, except for him who had memorized what was to be read—away from his own village and the palappa where he sat when it was not raining to read what he had been loaned by his teachers—away from these things he was taken by the nuns to the regional directorate and put into formal classrooms to learn. His father had plenty of other children to help with the planting, and did not suffer from the loss.

In the new school there were also no lights except for a dim thing that glowed indifferently from the ceiling, but there were windows, real windows made of real glass louvers which the nuns trimmed like the sails of a boat to admit the best balance of light and breeze. One could read all day in such classrooms. These walls also were made of concrete, but money from Los Estados Unidos paid for yellow paint and all but the chameleon lizards showed stark and bold against them.

He was gifted in language and in mathematics, the nuns decided, and must become an engineer. The nuns sent him to the capital where the university in turn decided that he must study electrical engineering and go to the States for a doctorate.

His father and mother were unable to come to the capital and see his plane take off. They were not among the many cheering relatives who sent their loved ones off with bundles and cardboard boxes for their new lives in the States. Like others from his country he sent letters home every month, but his parents could neither read nor write so he did not know that his mother kept every letter in its original envelope after looking for money, and he did not know it even after he returned from the states ... but all of that was later. Before that came the moment of his glory, the moment that even in his old age he remembered.

It was his genius, his giftedness that set him apart in the minds of the nuns and made him the focus of all their love of learning. Perhaps they needed a notable success, a poster child of their work, to justify and expand their mission, perhaps it was not that at all but a naïve and genuine pride in their discovery of a child with a quick and unexpected intellect. In any case it was their supreme joy to display him one day to the bishop in those first few years when he was studying in the provincial school, the one with the windows that let in the light and allowed a gifted child to read real books while the slower children caught up on their exercises.

He was to be presented to the bishop, the mother superior decided, in the company of his family. In her mind he was an exquisite jewel of rare clarity that would be revealed all the more lustrous for the rustic simplicity of its setting.

A borrowed jeep with an armed guard for protection was sent into the forest to extract his family. The family had no warning and his father had to be dragged from the field. His mother came also in the jeep, with great reluctance, her eyes wide with fear. They left several of the children behind to insure their peace of mind. Having lost one child, not perhaps the most useful but nonetheless one of their own, they were reluctant to lose any more children than would fit sweating into the open spaces of the jeep between their knees, their hips and the bodies of the soldiers. The children looked anxiously at the guns, the pistols, the rough textured khakis, the shiny black belts, the heavy boots, and the sunglasses of their guards, and they were afraid.

The boy's family stood silently in a row behind him when they were presented to the bishop. He answered for them in a loud distinct voice as he had been taught in the textbook Spanish of which his teachers were so proud. The parents' Mayan tongue would have been incomprehensible to the bishop and they in turn would have been embarrassed to use their limited Spanish in front of the bishop. He did not translate for his parents. That also would have been humiliating. Neither did his parents have any questions for the bishop, nor any other thoughts that they wanted communicated to His Eminence.

The boy knew that his family wanted more than any thing else to be released to return to their village and that they worried about finding their way home. He knew also that they had long since considered him lost to them. They were always surprised when he was sent home for school holidays, as if wondering how he appeared and disappeared, like a conscripted soldier forced to fight in the guerilla wars. Sometimes it seemed better to remain in the school during breaks and read what interested him than to assault his mother and father with his lack of consideration.

In his mind this audience with the bishop was a matter of payment. He was buying for his parents a great surprise, one that had been forming in his mind as the entire reason for this most unusual event, and one for which he must carefully be on his guard lest it slip away or lest he fail to make the full and correct payment. His answers were most carefully thought out and, when the bishop asked some textbook questions to test him, he dissected each answer most assiduously in his mind to see whether there was some hidden entrapment, some elusive twist of meaning that might escape him and prevent his making this special payment and erasing his debt.

To the bishop, of course, his hesitation before answering what were actually very simple questions—primarily of church teaching, Spanish colonial history and geography, the only areas in which the bishop himself felt comfortable—showed exactly the right amount of respect for the occasion. It was the dutiful rote recall of a bright but unremarkable child, the kind that one expected to bring out of the jungle from time to time to show that one's mission was not just to the upper class of the provincial capital but to all the region. The bishop was pleased with the boy's responses and directed the nuns to feed the child's family and allow them to spend the night in the empty caretaker's house. It was this miracle upon which the boy had focussed his hopes and for which he had composed, rearranged, diagrammed, weighed and reassembled his answers so carefully for the bishop.

In the boy's eyes the caretaker's hut was a marvelous place. It sat within the walls of the garden where the nuns walked after vespers, in a far corner down at one end, with thick-bottomed palm trees and a single broadleafed teak tree with bromeliads all around it. There was a tiny porch and, within, a single room with two cots. There was a chair and there were two windows with shutters that swung in and out with the breeze. An outhouse stood nearby. Indeed it was a marvelous place.

That evening after the nuns had fed them—there were several dishes which his parents and brothers and sisters had to refuse for their strangeness—they were escorted to the caretaker's house. Enough extra mats had been piled up by the front door so that, by sharing, none of them would have to sleep on the bare floor. This was an honor for which the boy felt particularly grateful and would thank the sisters most reverently next day.

His father looked carefully over the room. In the evening dimness he could see a single bulb in the precise center of the ceiling. It was nestled tightly in a porcelain socket exactly like the one in their own concrete house but there were no visible black wires. The child stood quivering near the front door, his shoulder inches from a wall switch like those in his classrooms. His father looked at him expressionlessly for a time. Then his father walked over to the wall switch and frowned at it. The man pointed a thumb at the boy. The boy closed his eyes and prayed. He pushed up the switch.

Even as an old man he could remember that moment. There was a click, then a light so bright he saw it through closed eyelids. He opened his eyes to a glorious radiance consuming the whole room. They all looked at the brilliant bulb until they had to blink against its glare. The afterimage lingered on the insides of their closed eyelids, a blue-green reverse icon of the light bulb in all its power. There was light in every corner of the room. He saw his brothers and his sisters in their orange, red, purple and green wraps. He saw his own parents and the colors of their eyes, the deep browns in which lighter browns and golds flickered. He saw the wrinkles in his mother's face and the big knuckles and black hairs of his father's hands. He saw feet all around him, some in sandals, and the bones and nails of their toes.

It was the greatest moment of his life. As an old man he saw that moment in his mind, and all the children who were there, and he remembered the names of the brothers and sisters who had been left behind at home for safety's sake, for insurance against the theft of himself, his own small self and his quick mind, too quick as old man for the body he came to inhabit in that later time.

His father directed that they bring in the bedding from the porch and the children settled around their father and their mother. The man said to the boy in a low voice, but one that all could hear, "It is a bright light. It is a very bright light. One could read with such a light if one were a teacher, or if one had a book." He looked at the boy, "Do you have a book?"

There was a book in the pocket of the short pants the nuns had found for him in the charity houses, a New Testament. The nuns had given it to their best pupil, the boy who represented their proudest accomplishment in this hot and humid country of the Third World, but the book was in Spanish and his brothers and sisters understood only their own dialect of the Mayan world, a world more ancient than the world of the New Testament, but not the world of the Spanish.

He opened the book and began to recite for them, in their tongue, what he had memorized from his geography class and his studies of the New World. He told them, in his teachers' measured pace, of the conquest of the New World, the battles of the great Spanish armies, the subjugation of his people, and their eventual elevation to the status of servants, miners and farm workers in this new country of the Spaniards' devising. All the magnificence of the Spanish lust for gold and land was in the words he gave them and he spoke without faltering.

Later he switched off the light and they lay quietly as at home, inside the close, damp concrete walls. Some of them thought of the Spanish deeds and how fine it must have been to be Spanish. One by one they fell asleep. In the morning the jeep and the soldiers took his father and mother and the other children back into the distant jungle and away from their gifted son.

*   *   *   *

As an old man he gave little thought to those days when he was stolen for his giftedness from the village of his birth. In the United States he studied first at the University of Miami where, without money, he had no distractions and graduated easily at the age of sixteen. He was too immature, both emotionally and physically, to have many interests in common with his classmates but he made friends, because of his Spanish, with some of the Cuban expatriates, including the older brother of the woman he was to marry.

She was a girl only twelve years old when he graduated. He scarcely noticed her then. But she, in the way of women, treasured memories of his soft voice, his straight black hair, and his proud nose and lightning eyes. She sought him out when she was sixteen and he was in graduate school.

Her family had been wealthy in Cuba and brought their entrepreneurial skills and profit-making instincts with them to Miami. Fidel chose not to interfere with their flight from his newly liberated island. Fidel did, however, generously bestow upon them vivid memories of their mother country by confiscating their lands and all of their property, and by taking over all of the money that he could find in any of the Cuban banks under their names. This thoughtful act of Fidel's was a considerable incentive to them to throw themselves fervently at every business opportunity they encountered in Miami and to teach a deep and ineradicable hatred of Fidel to their offspring.

From her sixteenth year she pursued him, first through letters of encouragement each exam season, then monthly letters, then weekly. Her letters initially were teasing in nature and light hearted, as befitted a woman in her teens. Soon the letters began to contain pictures, pictures at first of the family, the dog, the beaches and a new car, but eventually pictures only of herself—pictures of her in the uniform of the school band, in volleyball dress, on the swim team, in her prom dress and at her senior graduation. This last picture was delivered to him only days before she herself arrived for his coronation, the doctorate in electrical engineering.

At first he did not know what to do with her letters. He read each one and sent notes in reply to some, then in the last two years of his doctoral studies and during his thesis work he began to answer every one and to put even more earnestness into what had always been serious replies, as was his nature. In those last years he visited Little Havana, the American capital of the Cuban expatriates, and was invited to the homes of the wealthy expatriates who had established themselves there and elsewhere around the immense city of Miami. When it was learned that he traveled about on city buses, a car and driver were put at his disposal. Relatives of the young lady took his hand firmly and looked into his eyes as if verifying his worthiness and promised him opportunity if he would write to them when he finished his studies.

As it turned out any letters to her relatives would have been superfluous. Almost every member of her family came to attend their wedding, which took place in Miami one week after he received his doctorate. There it was decided, as if he were a commodity at their disposal, that such an outstanding doctor of electrical engineering graduate should be established in the research facilities of the giant IBM corporation just then expanding its Boca Raton operations. He was sure to be put in charge of something important and he would advance immediately.

It all happened. He and his new wife settled into the days and nights of Miami. There were parties by the pools of wealthier Cubans, with margaritas and piña coladas. He took his tie to work in his briefcase each day and wore it inside the air conditioned buildings, often replacing his suit jacket with a white lab coat. He attended meetings where he spoke with great seriousness and was supportive of the younger people who came to join his department, some indeed from his old country but none of whom spoke the particular Mayan dialect of his village.

Once he took his wife with him to visit his country. He showed her the place where the nuns had first taken him to learn. They rented a jeep and driver and with some difficulty found his village. Some of the people remembered his family but none of them knew where they were. There was an outbreak of fever with lesions and boils, and some of his brothers and sisters may have died. If the children had been buried no one knew where.

The lovely cool palappa with its thatch of palm leaves had been replaced with another palappa, somewhat further from the concrete house. The old concrete house still stood, though its roof was heavily rusted and had a few holes in it, not very big. There was trash inside, but no one lived there. The big black wires still stretched to the receptacle but one was broken and there was no bulb in the socket. Later he would try to forget this memory.

There was no evidence of the letters he had sent home over the years and he wondered how his family had spent the money he had enclosed, money that had increased as his own earnings increased.

They walked to where his father once planted. There was a strong young field there, tended by a strong young man, with large brown hands and good steady eyes, who had never heard the name of the family that once planted here. The only old name that this young man knew was the name of the man who sold him this field. The seller was now deceased and anyway the man who was now in middle age did not recognize the seller's name. At least this youngster tilling his father's field spoke his language and it gave him joy to rediscover within himself what he feared the nuns had stolen from him.

He asked for the man who brought mail to the village but was told that mail did not come these days to the village. At the district postal center he asked where his letters had been taken but was told there was no record of such letters. The man he questioned seemed uncomfortable. There was no more to be done.

They visited the capital to see the cathedral and the parks, then they boarded their scheduled flight and went back to what was now his home in Miami. He did not send any more letters to his family, or any more money.

There was born to him and his wife only one child, a son. Upon this child the mother lavished all the histrionic affection that was inescapable in her Latin heritage, and in the heritage of the privileged and the waited upon—the parents who had time on their hands, time to indulge the unspoken whims of their offspring, and overmuch money. The father, who had known genuine need, was more reserved with his giving and more restrained with his affection, but he loved his child with a warmth that the child recognized and returned unreservedly.

This child, too, was gifted. His mind was inspired and challenged by all things mechanical and electrical. He was not given away, however, to zealous nuns but was closely guarded by his parents and the many members and minions of his mother's family, so that he grew tall and strong in the soccer fields and the classrooms of Miami's private schools and eventually, like his father, attended the University of Miami and studied electrical engineering. There was a wonderful party, attended by hundreds of his mother's people and his father's business associates and their families, when he graduated. He went from Florida to the cold, clear-headed environs of Boston, Massachusetts, for his doctoral studies which he completed with distinction.

Although this son had been amply financed throughout his school career, his spending habits were more like his father's than his mother's. He had been a particularly serious and sober student, and when he received his doctorate the only extravagance he allowed himself was the acceptance from his maternal grandfather of a two-seated sports car which he prayed would not be red and indeed turned out to be a deep jade green. With this and the material good wishes of his mother's many family and friends he set off for a university in north central Kentucky where he had been asked, by colleagues of his professors, to direct a computing center and, subsequently, to found and staff a department of computer science.

He chose this career despite many offers from his mother's family to enter into business with them because he was more strong willed than his father and more assertive. To this boy his education and his fine mind were tools to employ in pursuit of his personal ambitions which, though modest, were his own, rather than servants of an unfulfilled need as was the case with his father. There at the university he prospered.

Living so far from him was hard for his parents. Eventually his father transferred his own consulting practice to north central Kentucky. His mother was persuaded more by her own desires than those of her family to give up all but two servants, a man and wife, and take up life in this middle-sized town where it was cold, but not bitter cold, in the winter and where the summers were soft and somewhat less humid than Miami's and where the trees were all different from what she had known before.

She filled her house with flowers and, with the assistance of her servants, kept them growing year round and in bloom as much as possible. She took an interest in the care and feeding of flowers. Eventually she joined a north central Kentucky garden club and subscribed to gardening magazines.

The son rose to prominence quickly in the university. He was handsome and had a slight Cuban accent. He frequently said "on" when he meant "in" and was fascinating to his female students, one of whom he found reciprocally attractive and chose to marry. She was of modest local tobacco farming stock and a social disappointment to his mother, but his father, now facing advanced middle age, looked forward to grandchildren who would become the central joy of his old age and was content.

There was a wedding of lavish proportions by the girl's family's standards but smaller than his mother had wanted. Still it was a social success and was acclaimed by a full page of photographs and text in the local newspaper. The photographer and his assistant were flown out from Miami at the grandparents' expense.

In advanced middle age, the man, now the father of a successful university department head, remembered the miracle of the light bulb and thought about how he might pass along the memory to his grandchildren. After all, that miracle had made their lives possible. He wondered if they would have his Mayan nose, almost unnoticeably sloped forehead and slight figure or if they would have the more robust characteristics of his wife and the taller, intent look of his son.

There were to be no grandchildren. His son and four other young, promising department heads were selected to represent the future promise of the university at a symposium in Denver. It was an occasion of national importance to the academic community. The assembly was expected to feature speakers from the federal government as well as a guest appearance by the governor of California. The governor was already in the news for leading a particularly public and expensive crusade to improve California's university system extending the opportunities of higher education to all California citizens and, controversially, to that state's many alien residents as well.

The man who was to have no grandchildren and his wife were among the families at the small regional airport to send off their proudest sons, these rising and dynamic leaders of these promising young departments with their brand new, modern and impressive department titles. A newspaper photographer, in jeans and long hair, made several flash pictures of the five young department heads and all their luggage with its heavy emphasis on briefcases and bound reports.

A private plane had been chartered to carry them from the university town to Louisville's commercial airport where they would begin their cross-country flight to Denver. The man in advanced middle age, and his wife who always cried at such times, watched the plane taxi smartly down the runway and take off toward the west, in the direction of Louisville. Their son's wife was standing with them. The runway ended just short of a divided highway and the plane rose above trees bordering a farm that stabled race horses across the road.

Suddenly the plane, which had been rising steadily, seemed to stall. They heard the engines' rattling power grow frantically louder but the nose of the plane tipped down and it fell straight toward the ground, head first behind the trees. Smoke was already erupting before the sounds of the crash reached them, faint over the highway, like the collapse of a distant ladder.

They were not allowed to see the remains, on the advice of their closest friends, some of whom were from the university's department of medicine. However, several of the bystanders, less closely tied to the victims, were requested to view the remains and help with identification. The bodies, taken in ambulances and hearses to the mortuary, were burned black and partially consumed by the flames. Teeth and jewelry, mostly watches, and, in the case of their son, a St. Christopher medal, aided in identification.

That night the mother's family flew in from Miami. There were twenty of them and it was necessary to come in two separate flights because they had decided to use commercial carriers and fly into Louisville. The man, now in advanced middle age and cushioned by an insulating sort of numbness, drove one of the cars that went to fetch them. His wife stayed behind to console, and be consoled by, the family of their son's young wife, all of whom lived nearby.

His carload of four women were sisters and cousins of his wife. Their anguish seemed mostly for themselves. They accused their parents and the older generation from Havana of failing to prepare them for such things as this. As children, they protested, they had not been allowed to attend funerals and wakes which might distress their young minds.

"We were led away," they cried, "when the body was laid out. We were not even allowed to look upon their faces."

"It would be bad luck," said one.

"No," said another, "they were afraid that it would give us nightmares."

"Even so," said still another, "they did not prepare us."

"No," they all agreed, "we were not prepared."

He delivered his passengers and then he spoke for a while with some of the funeral home's representatives. All that was needed had been done. In his absence his wife had agreed to what seemed to him inappropriately garish and expensive burial accoutrements but he felt the effect would be satisfying to her relatives from Miami. He and his wife would probably move back to Miami soon enough. He doubted that he could persuade her to stay in this place that was centered around her son's interests, not theirs.

The man in advanced middle age was an adaptable person. Miami was a warm place. He would manage well enough. His wife would have her friends and family. They would grow old together and be comfortable. This large sad hole that had opened in their lives would accompany them back to his wife's people and the wide sunny streets of Miami and would always be with them.

$$* \qquad * \qquad * \qquad *$$

There is sometimes too much sun in Miami. At such times it is impossible to read outdoors without sunglasses. Sometimes one seeks an inner room, the simpler the better, where there are few windows, and the walls, if not concrete, may be of stucco that is in some ways like concrete. In such a dark room one may turn on a light. It may be a single bare bulb that lights an entire room. As an old man he could remember how a bulb had once looked, and how that bulb had changed his life. That memory was not always welcome.

SISTER ROSE

Sister Rose Victor was the only person I ever met who had perfect pitch. She was a music teacher at St. Mary's Academy where I spent the last three years of an unexceptional high school career. You ask her for C above middle C and, bang, she sings it out, "Ah-h-h-h."

It's pretty, too, the way she sings it out. She taught you all, music students and just plain kids in the choir alike, to make an O with your lips when you sing "Oh-h-h-h," and when she sang an "Ah" note her lips made that same pretty rounded shape even though it was the Oh sound and not the Ah sound that came out.

She was short. Black gown, wimple, cap and all. A five foot ten kid could look right over the top of her. Except when she lost her temper, then she swelled up and turned dark red in the face and you feared something exotic was going to happen. She talked English just like you and me, with a Kentucky accent, but there was a cultured tone underneath her words and you were sure there was something foreign, maybe French, about her and whatever kind of eruption there might be it was sure to be exotic. You didn't necessarily want to be around to experience it but you sure looked forward to hearing about it afterwards.

SOMETHING OF MY OWN

Something of my own

So precious I would not yield it up to God, please?

Something of my own that perhaps only I knew

Whose joy was as much in the coming of it and the remembering of it as in the happening.

THE ST. THOMAS
HILTON

"Look at him," said Dave Spaulding. He pointed his glass toward the bamboo guardrail and the solitary man at the small table with a view of Charlotte Amalie's harbor. "You can tell he gets it whenever he wants it.

Dave's companion, Franklin Contalesi, looked and agreed.

Billy Bones McChesney, if that was indeed the man they were considering, was the beneficiary of a reputation powerful enough to breech all the known barriers of the Caribbean sailing community.

All the traditional geographic and cultural barriers. People talked about Billy Bones McChesney from the northwest end of the Lesser Antilles, where the Virgin Islands huddled up close beside Puerto Rico with its growling guard dog Viegas, to the southeast end where the Grenadines skipped lightly down to Trinidad and the glowering bulk of Venezuela.

They chanted the name of Billy Bones McChesney in the broad hearty East African English of Tortola and in the wild galloping Spanish of the far Dominican Republic. They swooned to his doings in the dry repressions of incestuous Dutch Saba, and beat out his name in the barefoot Carnival rhythms of French Martinique. The graves of the dead of the Swedes of St. Barth's rang with his name in the wind. Mighty was his echo in the sugar cane fields beneath the sullen volcano of St. Kitt's, and the Trades bore his legend from Dominica's Arawak Reservation to the scattered, feeble remnants of the once powerful Mayans downwind on the Yucatan.

His reputation had broken down the walls of class that divided the "Charties" from the "Yachties"—the boat renters who sail by the week from the boat owners who sail by the stars. Only the sailboat racers who flew in for a day or a month, who stayed forever young and blonde and brown, who partied long and drank hard, who bought the rounds and knew no lack of money and who loved everyone, they alone had nothing to say about Billy Bones McChesney.

And here in the flesh was Billy Bones McChesney, within talking distance, drinking his beer and looking back at them. Billy Bones wore flip flop sandals and khaki shorts with a tee shirt decorated in faded ship's flags that spelled out some nautical word. His hands were broad, his fingers were short with broad nails cut straight across. He wore a lump of a school ring, and a necklace of a single gold strand. His hair was thick on the sides and thin to balding on top and he showed at least a two days' growth of beard. He looked straight at Frank and Dave, neither critically nor defensively, but honestly with perhaps a tint of curiosity as if considering whether they had met before.

"See, Frank," said Dave. "What did I tell you? Not a care in the world." Billy Bones McChesney tipped his glass toward the two men.

"Let's go talk to him," said Dave. "Naw," said Frank. "He's famous."

But David Spaulding was already moving, and Franklin Contalesi followed him over to the small man with the big ring. Billy Bones waved his drink in a half circle encompassing two chairs from nearby tables. They dragged up the chairs and sat down. This close to the water a breeze reached up from under the railing and fondled the crusted salt of their ankles. Billy Bones was not shy.

"Don't matter what you've heard," he said after the introductions. "Any thing Billy Bones McChesney's done gone and done, ain't nobody else couldn't do the same if he had a mind to.

His sailboat was modest, he told them, but she slid sweet on the water. Long keeled, easy to steer on off shore passages, ideal for the big hop to the Caribbean, just the kind of boat a man and his wife would pick for a round the world cruise. And like many other couples they'd gotten as far as the Caribbean and this was at far as they went. In their case, not all that rare he had heard, his wife had jumped ship on their first landfall.

"She kind of went crazy when we raised Jost van Dyke," he told them, "and she had her duffel packed by the time we docked in St. Thomas. Took the first plane home."

He paused and looked thoughtful. "Offshore sailing is hard on women," he said, "some women."

At first he had stayed behind, out of pride. He had thrown a drunk, let the boat go to hell, and just lay around sick for weeks.

"Then I met a girl in a bar one night," he told them, looking deep into his glass where only the bottom was wet.

"Changed all that," said Billy Bones. "Gave me a different outlook." He stared expectantly at the bottom of his glass. Dave waved to the waitress.

"Thanks," he said, when the waitress put down a full glass and picked up the empties. He smiled at her. She smiled back.

"To this day," he continued, "I don't know who got the idea first.

He looked at them vacantly for a moment, as if still trying to remember. "But I needed money to pay the docking fee. She needed a place to sleep." Dave and Frank drew in their chairs a little closer. "That was it!" he smacked his open hand on the table. They jumped. "All of a sudden I'm in a new business. The bunk rental business." Dave and Frank pushed back, and looked at each other. Slowly Dave began to grin.

"Yep," said Billy Bones, "Rent out my bunks. So much a night, or so much a week."

Now Frank was grinning. He thought he had gotten the joke.

"Turns out there's a market for that kind of business in Charlotte Amalie. Nights-and-weeks works best. Lot of 'em don't last long down here, 'specially the real young ones." By now Dave's grin was big. "Sleeps eight, not counting the captain's cabin. That's mine." Dave stopped grinning.

Billy Bones kept on talking. He had turned to look out over the water where the docks below extended into the harbor. "Works real good. Most of them work nights, bar tending, waitressing. Sometimes I lose count and I think the ones that work days double up with the ones working nights. May be gypping me out of rent. I don't care."

"We got rules," he said, looking up to see Dave and Frank raising eyebrows at each other. "No men visitors. No guests at all after midnight. Keep your own place clean. That kind of thing. Make good money now," he said. "I get to eat, I drink, I pay the docking fee. Plus some."

"That some is what we want to hear about," said Dave, so low that Frank could barely hear.

"Has its drawbacks," said Billy Bones. He stared down into his newly emptied glass. Dave waved again. The waitress came over with a full glass. "Thanks. Problem is I can't never go sailing no more when I take a notion to." Dave and Frank slumped.

"Course, I don't take a notion very often these days."

"Magine not," said Dave. "These days."

"But," said Billy Bones. Dave and Frank straightened up. "It has got its advantages. Some real humdinger advantages." The two men drew their chairs closer. Frank looked quickly over his shoulder to make sure no one else was listening.

"Them women end up with a lot of time on their hands."

"Yeah?" said Dave, hanging right over the table, his chest hairs wet from Billy Bones's glass.

"They get bored."

"Yeah, I 'magine!" said Frank.

"Always trying to think of something different."

"Oh, yes," said Dave.

"Sometimes they get real competitive."

"No kidding," said Dave.

"You know, like each one was trying to do it better than the other one. And of course they have no place else to go for it."

"You're right about that!" said Dave.

"What a man!" snorted Frank.

"Showing off, you know what I mean?"

"I can just imagine." said Dave.

"I can't even imagine," said Frank.

"No," said Dave, "don't make me imagine. Tell it to me."

"Sometimes, like I said. They try to outdo one another, but ..."

He leaned back like there was a big gesture coming up. Dave and Frank were elbows on the table, tense as greyhounds. "... sometimes they team up and you can't believe what they do ..."

"No, no, no," Dave's eyelids dropped in ecstasy.

"Who would have thought it," said Billy Bones McChesney. He tipped forward so fast they scattered. "Those young women can cook!"

"Cook?" asked Dave.

"Cook?" said Frank.

"Yeah. One of them is like part Eye-talian. Turns out she brought her own stuff that you mix into Eye-talian food. Mother sends her mahtso, what do you call it? Mozzarella cheese. Another one is Armenian, or something. You ever have stuffed grape leaves?"

"Grape leaves?" said Frank.

"Yeah, but best of all, is when they all get together and make baklava. Takes 'em all day, sometimes. Little thin dough like you can see right through it. Honey. Walnuts. Melts in your mouth, man. Melts in your mouth."

"In your mouth, huh?"

"You better believe it. Since I rented out my bunks, I put on thirty pounds!"

"Magine you did," said Dave.

Outside the bar Frank counted his change and put it back in his pocket. The two men climbed down the companionway-like steps and walked up the dock toward the hotel. At the top of "A" dock they turned back to look at the marina, where the boats rolled gently to the heave and swell of the bay.

"What do you think, Frank?" laughed Dave, "is he gettin' it or what?"

Frank turned slowly to look at Dave. His companion's face was tipped with sunset's lingering orange. Dave's grin was still there. It was a foolish grin, a porch dog grin.

"Piss off," said Franklin Contalesi, and walked away.

THE ST. THOMAS HILTON—EPILOGUE

Billy dropped his chin into his cupped hands and stared at the two men on the dock below. He watched them separate and go off to their rooms.

He sighed long and deep, tipped back in his chair, hooked his heels up on the rail and looked off over the harbor into the setting sun.

"'S one's on me," the waitress said. She set down a full glass, cold and wet, with a white head spilling slowly over one side. She sat down in one of the chairs the men had left, turned it away from the rail and tipped back, resting one foot on a rung. Billy Bones McChesney nodded, and continued to look out over the water.

"Don't understand, do they?" she said.

"Guess not," he said to the great climbing reds and oranges of the sunset.

"They think you got eight women, you're sleeping with some of them, right?"

"Guess so," said Billy Bones.

"Didn't get the part about not being able to sail either, huh?"

"Nope."

"Real characters, weren't they? 'Specially the hairy one."

Billy Bones didn't answer.

"That red head was cute. 'Magine he'll be blistered this time tomorrow.

Then they were both quiet for a minute. He spoke.

"You know a boat tied up is a sorrowful thing."

"Yeah, I've heard," she laughed, a quick, short, low pitched laugh.

"A crew tied up is an unhappy crew."

"I've heard that, too."

He took a sip and thought a moment.

"Rent-a-bunk people ain't crew," he said finally. He thought awhile longer.

"You get to know crew … sailing," he said. "The good parts."

She looked at him.

"The good things about people," he said. "And how they come through for you in the bad times."

Another silence.

"You know, heavy weather. High winds. Bad seas."

She looked down at her hands. She spread her fingers so she could see the nails.

"Still," he said, "if you have to be tied up, a boat full of women's better'n a boat full of men."

"Sure."

"Yeah," he said. "They get along better. Try to get along with you."

She laughed again.

"Not much privacy on a boat," he said. "And all of 'em so young," he added. He dropped his feet from the rail and leaned forward to look at the boats swaying slowly in their slips. Their riggings tinkled faintly in the gathering dark. Some of the taller masts close to the bar clanked sharply as they rolled to the swells.

"So young. Young and fine looking. And me so old. More like having children around."

She reached over and rubbed her hand across the top of his head. His hair was thinning and there was a bald spot on top gone brown in the sun.

"Oh, you're not so old."

He looked around at her. Her hair had lost the color that blonde women lose in the sun. It was white with faint touches of yellow, and cut short. She had the skin that white women get in the tropics, dark brown with the soft leathern look of fabric, before the first sprays and cracks appear.

"Let's say old enough to know any woman rents my bunks ain't after my body."

"Listen at you!" She jabbed him lightly on the shoulder.

Behind her they heard a rumpus of talking and stumbling on the companionway. She picked up his empties and walked to the bar.

"Wait for me tonight?" She asked.

"I'll wait."

*   *   *   *

When she came out of the building the stars were spread across the whole sky. Where he waited in the darkness the sounds from the bar were lost to the steel drums from the harbor's party raft floating free in the harbor. They walked in silence out onto "A" dock. Slowly at first so her eyes could adjust to the dark, and her feet to the rise and fall of the wooden floats. At the slip of the "Painted Lady" he took hold of the piling and put his weight on a line to swing her bow into the dock. The waitress climbed aboard. Billy Bones followed. They ducked under shirts and shorts hanging from the rigging.

The hatch was open to the tropical breeze. They climbed down in silence. Below decks it was warm with the damp and closeness of female bodies. In the faint light from the companionway they could distinguish a few forms on narrow bunks, turned face to the hull. Some bunks were empty. Books, dishes and makeup lay about the galley table. Sandals and thongs were scattered over the floor. The door of the head swung open. Billy Bones closed it softly. One of the bodies rolled toward them a little and mumbled "... message for you ..." then rolled away.

Billy picked up a white piece of paper lying on the icebox and tucked it into a pigeon hole over the chart table.

He opened the door with the bronze plaque that said "Captain." She went in ahead of him. He closed the door softly. There was just room for the two of them to stand, touching, on the steeply sloped floorboards.

"You didn't tell them I came back, did you?"

"Nah," he said. "Spoil the story."

STICK MAN

Walking down the alley suited him.

It was OK for the lead musician to come by car. After all, the club would have a kid standing by to park his car.

The bass player was new, but he was local which meant somebody would probably drop him off. The patrons waiting in line would see the cars drive up and they would know they were tonight's show.

That kind of living was not for him. He would find the alley entrance and go in through the kitchen. Man, I'm an artist, he'd told the lead, ain't no goddamn exhibitionist, man. The lead had bought it, and he had got to go in the back.

The alley was warm and damp in the summer evening, with bricks rounded and uneven under foot. They would go on at nine thirty. Still plenty of time. A strong sour smell of old mayonnaise in the soft air and a faint rich smell of green and breathy sighs from the canal water that coiled and uncoiled blackly and silently to his left.

Sure enough the paying guests were lined up waiting to get in. Little girl in blue jeans and frilly pink shirtfront checking reservations on her clipboard. Looked up at him heaving back on the kitchen door beside her, probably figured not-her-door-not-her-problem. Inside the cook eyed him too, and went back to cleaning shrimp. Walked slowly past the long butcher block, opened the swinging door with the porthole and was surprised to see the lights up in the dining room.

Bartender was wiping glasses. Looked up, too, but let him be.

The heavy set man in shirtsleeves and yellow tie with black spots, leaning backwards on the bar, elbows behind him. Either the bouncer or the owner. Probably the owner. A younger guy stood by the front door, also heavy set, with a sport jacket, looked red or crimson from here. That would be the bouncer. Talking to the same girl in jeans, her backside just visible from where he had stopped between kitchen and the first table. Yep, from here it looks like the bouncer. The owner watched him, the bouncer kept talking to the waitress or hostess, whatever she was.

He walked down between the tables, letting his fingers trail along the table tops, feeling the marble-ized surface cold and slightly tacky to his hand. He imagined the wet puddles, the soggy napkins, and the sweet smell of liquor a few hours from now, and drifted on down to the one step platform up front just barely wide enough for the bass fiddle leaning in the shadow against the far wall, and his set of double bass drums, a snare, two toms, cymbals and a high hat.

Stepped up on the platform. There were three mikes. His and the bass's were already set. The lead would adjust his own for the first number. Checked the pouches draped across his "throne" and hanging down on either side. Yeah, four pairs of drumsticks. He was set. Walked back to the bar and dropped his hands on the damp, deeply varnished surface closest to the kitchen door. Barkeep looked at him, looked over at the owner and raised his eyebrows. The owner turned to the drummer and smiled. The drummer nodded back, then said to the barman, "Whiskey, neat."

The drummer's name was Calahan Causey. His name was spelled Caw-sey, it was pronounced Coo-sey. Most people called him Calahan. The lead man called him Cal.

An hour later they were flying. The place was in their hands.

The bass player was adequate. He was a pickup, and he could play their music. The lead was the best sax man Cal had ever worked with. He started off with two fast and flashy numbers that caught the patrons right off and he never let them go.

From where he sat Cal had more stage light in his eyes than he liked but not so much that he couldn't see the crowd. The room had an overall blue light feel and the rising smoke swayed slowly around below the big Casablanca fans.

The up front tables were mostly foursomes, knees tight together, tabletops so small their drinks were all bunched up in front of them. Not too many prissy drinks. This was a Collins and Manhattans crowd, maybe a few rum-and-cokes and some martinis, but mostly gins and bourbons and scotches, he guessed.

A conservative crowd. The waitresses were in jeans and tuxedo shirts, and one waiter dressed the same way. The patrons were mostly women in light dresses and men in slacks, shirts and ties. One foursome off to his right was more dressed up. The men in dark suits, the women in cling dresses with thin necklaces over wide, deep necklines.

The lead played wake-you-from-the-dead wailin' hurtin' notes in the second set and tossed off riffs that took away your childhood and left you drowndin' somewhere. The crowd was caught up, dead quiet and left the refill-pushing waitresses pantin' and fretful way too far behind.

This man was good, but hey, somebody here needed to push some liquor.

Next song the lead laid back and when the bass took his solo it was easy and you could hear the whole entire room let go. Some drinks started changing hands. The lead kept looking around and hummin' out over the crowd. Ever so often he'd draw his saxophone up to his lips and kind of run along on top of the melody. Then the bass came down and the sax man took the melody line up and up and brought it down just long enough to run it through one more reminiscin' then tossed it off to Cal.

Cal had been easin' by with the bass player, and just middlin' along with the lead. Now he laid into them sticks. He hit a long fast staccato run that he knew would drill them in their seats. Then he took the melody rhythm and improv'd the whole story again till you felt he'd played all the ups and the downs just like it'd come out the mouth of the old man's horn.

He felt the moment risin'. He knew those mammas and daddies out there had never seen anything like him. His hands by now would be gold in the blur and there would be nothing they could see of his fingers. And the ends of his sticks would be faint silver discs, and nobody would believe a man could move anything this fast. And he was just startin'.

He was playing his life. He was sayin' his piece. He was moving. He was flying. Beside him the bass player was silent and still. The lead turned his head slowly from side to side, looking over the crowd as if unaware of the whirling, soaring, pounding phenomenon behind him. He slowly slung his saxophone onto its stand and stepped lightly down from the platform. He walked between the crowded tables, up to the bar where the barman had a scotch and soda ready for him, took a sip, lighted a cigarette, looked around the house, spoke a few low words to the owner, then turned and leaned back against the counter, cigarette in one hand and drink in the other and watched his drummer drum.

The man was flyin'. Flyin'. Flyin'. They could all see that. Probably no more than half even realized the lead had come down off the platform. They watched the drummer play, and their watching was almost as good as their listening. He was in the zone. Wasn't nobody else there but him, and the things he was doin' ain't never been written down.

He went and he went and he went. He was playing the twin bass babies like the best of the rest played their toms. His toms were like snares. His snare was like heaven. He switched from two basses to one, and you never even saw his high hat move till you all of a sudden knew where your underbeat come from. Sounds you didn't hear with your ear but you got with your whole body all over. He was in the zone. He was in the clouds. He was out of touch with this world. He was leaving them behind. He was taking them along.

The lead took a last draw on his cigarette, turned long enough to crush it out on the counter, took a last sip from his glass and slowly worked through the tables back to the tiny stage in the lights, slowly picked up his saxophone while the man at the drums behind him beat out a thousand explosions, a million megamoks, and battle sounds to launch an army into space. Then the lead blew a soft sweet screaming melody back into the room, called the memory of it in from all its shattered fragments where it had been broken and splintered and ripped up and scattered, called it all in high, fast and lonesome. Called it all in and pulled it all back into him.

In the alley cafe. Here in the dark by the black canal waters. Back where Calahan Causey came back down to earth, landing soft as a candlefly, bringing home his backstop beat, doin' his improv's, now softly with love. Come back and come back, and come back.

Late night in the Alley Cafe. Hot night. Door's open to the alley and the snick, snick, snick of the canal water flowing 'longside. Whole room full of jazz. Whole room full of listeners, listenin' and lovin'.

All of 'em been to heav'n. One of 'em ... dragged back down to earth.

SUGARBOY

"Anybody have a problem with body piercing?" he asked, in a voice he hoped sounded not too loud, not too nervous, not too timid.

The man in charge raised his eyebrows. Someone from behind one of the stands called out, "Long as you can hold a pose."

There was a general rustle of paper and a scraping of easels as the student artists went about settling down. They pulled perceptibly closer in a half circle around him, some messing with brushes and ink bottles, some muddling over pencils, and others fishing their fingers around in blue utility boxes. One young woman, hair tied back in a bun and wearing baggy slacks without creases, set out some very deliberate and business-like pastel chalks, arranged upright in a box like soldiers stiffening into full dress for inspection, all in order by color families.

The head guy said to him quietly, "Start off with a series of six five-minute poses, then go on to one long pose." The man lifted a beat up old chair onto the platform for him and began smoothing the wrinkles out of a clover green cloth he had pulled over it.

Now was the time to get on with it. He pulled off his sneakers and socks, standing on first one leg and then the other, and dropped them softly to the floor just behind the platform. He pulled off his stretch top and turned sideways to the head man's easel, figuring his back muscles would show up nicely in the overhead light. Last he unbuckled his belt and, bending toward them so they would all be looking at his shoulders, pulled off his khaki pants and briefs, knowing that in a second or two they would start looking at his chain.

Released now, after being held against his body heat, the gold chain fell softly and comfortably against his inner thighs. It was a light weight gold chain with tiny links. It went right through his scrotum and bumped gently from side to side between his legs as he turned and stepped up onto the boards.

There came a sudden quiet into the room, about the time he had felt the feathery links falling down against his skin as the chain uncoiled and as the weight of it caught lightly and pulled at him. Abruptly there was a sound of easels being moved again, followed by a general shifting of body weight and a loosening and a shuffling of drawing tools.

The head guy suggested a standing pose. He leaned forward and caught the overhead beam with both hands and brought his left heel up in a kind of Achilles-at-the-Battle pose. It was a position easy to hold. Afterwards there was a fast kaleidoscope of half sitting, half reclining poses, then the break before the long pose.

He had brought along an old bathrobe that belonged to someone in his family, he didn't know whom, because no one in his family ever wore it when he was around. He put on the bathrobe and cinched it around his waist then walked around in front of the straggled half circle of easels, some turned left, some turned right, some where people were still working, a few abandoned for a cup of coffee in the front room. People said "hi," or said "good poses." One said "good body." Others just nodded and stepped aside so he could look at what they had done.

An amazing amount of work had been done with the short poses, especially by the people working in charcoal. On the other hand, some students working with pencil had barely sketched out his general body shape. One woman had drawn only his head and shoulders. The mouth was missing but already the eyes had begun to look out of the paper, and the forehead and hair were definitely him.

He relaxed after the break and was content to let the head guy sort of direct him into a lounging pose, a kind of a Bacchus pose, only not so abandoned, more like a self-conscious artist's pose. One leg was tucked under. Twenty minutes would probably be pushing it. That leg would be dead when he took a break. It would tingle and burn like hell till the circulation returned, but all the rest of him would be OK. This pose would show his scrotal chain to the easels that stood just to his right of center. He wondered what they would do with it.

Again the noise of shuffling and scraping on a large scale as most of the students changed their positions completely, dragging easels, stools, papers and drawing tools across the room till they found their best angles for the long pose, which would be the main pose for the day.

At the first break in this pose, after the head guy and another man helped him mark his position with masking tape, he tried to straighten up and his dead leg about gave way underneath him. When the leg could finally support him the pain was almost more than he could handle. The head guy, who had stood close by to help him up, told him in a low voice next time to flex his leg muscles a little bit now and again. It would be all right as long as he pretty much got back to the same pose.

By this time the break was over. There was a strong coffee smell on the breaths of the people who passed close to him going back to their easels. There were charcoal smears on some faces, and pastel marks on others' aprons and jeans and in between their fingers.

During the second break of the long pose, after the artists had logged forty minutes on this position, his legs were functional, thanks to the head guy's advice. He took advantage of his condition to walk around and see what they had done with him. There were all varieties of media on the easels along the two sides, some ink washes, some chalks, some graphites. Up front in the flatter views all the artists had gone with Pitt, colored pencils on charcoal paper. Some were doing only values—lights, darks and greys—blocking in the shadows over the angles of his body and the muscle masses.

One, a young woman with a flowered scarf tied at the chin, must have been a details person. She had gotten his head very accurately and then gone straight down the front of him and was now roughing in the chair and drape background, making the shadows fall away from the light in a way that looked right to him. She had been particularly scrupulous, he saw, about the anatomy of his penis and, below in the half shadow, the slight twin bulges of his scrotum. Even this early in her work he could tell that she was going to pick up the specular highlights glinting off his chain.

"I'm Mara," she said, offering her hand. "What's your name?"

"David-Mark," he said. "With a dash."

"Well, David-Mark-With-a-Dash," she said, "what do you think?"

She had drawn his member sort of chunky, resting partially lifted and pointing outward on the bulge of his scrotal sac, the chain possessing an nearly independent existence in the partial shadow below.

"I thought I sort of hung down straighter."

"You don't," she said, with a flush and a dimple. Turning away, she picked up a Pitt.

IN THE YARD

In the last three or four days the trees in the woods have leafed out so
quietly and so fully that several of my neighbors' houses have disappeared.

Even the bushes next door that I had given up for dead, the ones with spindly
swept up branches that remind me of crepe myrtle or wisteria but are neither,
have sprouted tiny green buds.

So fast have leaves opened, up to six inches in length and four in width,
on the larger trees that I almost believe if I had stood quietly myself
and long enough, in time measured not in hours but in minutes, I could have
seen them grow.

I've read it is so with bamboo. Maybe we had some of the mountain and rain
conditions of innermost China this spring.

ON UNDERSTANDING
OLD MEN

Gone moments linger past their sight,
A cornered kiss, an eye,
An unplanned, whispered sigh.

As sun-warmed pebbles touch invite,
These call and call again,
Old lovers and old men.

They are loyal, in ways other people cannot appreciate, to old causes. And faithful, beyond imagining, to old loves. To moments that passed too quickly to be grasped yet linger now gracefully in their thoughts. Gifts long since given and often without thought are cherished and fondled in their minds like stones so polished by the gemnist that they glow beyond their physical capacity.

They are grateful, old men, for the memories bestowed upon them by the careless, generous hand, the indolent flick of the wrist, the impulsive kiss, the moment's hug, the fleeting notice, the meeting eye, the wink, the light caress, the impermanence of it in all of creation. No skittering sands, no flowing waters, no waning loam remembers, but they do. As marble warmed by the sun invites the touch of testing fingers, so do these memories call and call again to these old lovers and old men.

SPHERICAL
ABERRATIONS

Chapter 1—Prelude to the Presidency

If you are burning logs in a fireplace and you stick your hand way down deep into the flames, and if you leave your hand in there for a long time, is it possible to withdraw your hand without a mark on it? With no blisters, no burned flesh, not even soot from the smoke?

If you fill a bucket with molasses and you reach into it so far that you can touch the very bottom of the bucket and press your palm down on the concentric ridges of the metal welded across the part that keeps the molasses from running out, if your hand is all the way in so that the surface of the gummy molasses comes nearly up to your elbow, if you then draw out your hand is it at all possible that not the least little bit of molasses will stick to your skin, maybe at least to the hairs of the back of your hand or your arm?

My answer is, I think you can. The first time I traveled in Eastern Europe, behind what was then the Iron Curtain, I felt like there was a film around me and I was walking around the streets inside my own personal bubble. When I first realized it was when I noticed the voices of other people were not as loud as they should have been. They were not reaching me. They were too weak to pierce the thin film of transparent soap, or something like it, that surrounded me everywhere. I could see out, but nothing came in.

Of course nothing went out, either, because I had nothing to say. Not in Russian, not in Czech, not in Polish, and not in Hungarian.

The earliest manifestation of this particular neurosis (maybe it is a psychosis—I forgot the difference, being a first year drop out from Catholic U.'s doctoral program in clinical psychology, my downfall being physiological psychology) dates from a chance encounter with Dwight David Eisenhower when he was president.

I worked in New York City, on the fifth floor of what was then known city wide as IBM World Headquarters. IBM was in its glory days, leading the world in computational and electrical engineering adventurism and was a welcome economic power all by itself, especially in the Soviet Union where IBM's founder, Thomas J. Watson, had served as ambassador.

On that particularly sunny day, I had a desk only five floors below the hallowed sanctum of IBM's then president, also known as Thomas J. Watson, but referred to as "Junior" by the elevator operators, one of whom was my uncle. We heard the sirens and the crowds. I looked out the window, which we had opened so we could hear better and Ike's open convertible limousine passed right beneath me. I have a recollection, grown more vivid with the passing years, of his bald head, pink and glowing beneath me in the sunlight.

It occurred to me that if I had an apple, or particularly a grapefruit, Ike's head would have made an easy, or if not exactly then at least considerable, target. I resolved at that moment that when I became president I would have a closed limousine with a Plexiglas top to protect me from the elements and, if necessary, from the voters, my fellow Americans. Shortly after that Ike took delivery of a hybrid limo which had my top but was also convertible.

The idea of an inside/outside convertible made sense for the presidency of that day, because Eisenhower and his successor were the third and fourth, respectively, in a line of presidential extroverts who liked nothing better than being out among the people, who thrived on personal contact and who drew strength and, more importantly, energy from waving and handshaking and working the crowds.

As it happened, the bubble top limousine was wasted on Dwight D. Eisenhower—watch that name; I was one of the few people in the world at that time and even today to know he was not born Dwight D. but in fact was born David Dwight. The bubble top was wasted on Ike because everybody liked Ike, just like the slogan said, even the Democrats. This came as a surprise to the Democratic party leadership, all except Lyndon Johnson. The party notables had once again followed their communal death wish and nominated an introverted, anti-social intellectual in Adlai Stevenson, having apparently failed to learn any thing at all from their dismal experience with Woodrow Wilson.

Fortunately sanity prevailed when the Republican Party fell into the same hole and put up Nixon over whom the Democrats triumphed with every young person's dream in the Senator from Massachusetts and his star quality wife and there really were, for the briefest of times, goals and promises we have now abandoned and almost forgotten, a certain glamour in Washington and an aura of the possible in our time, for all the world.

By diving into that atmophere I also joined the Washington workforce, prepared to pit my brand of idealism against the best of them. Fresh out of college I showed up at the naval base in Dahlgren, Virginia, only a few miles and across the Potomac from the White House. After all, hadn't my commander-in-chief served in the U. S. Navy? Could I do any less than work for the same organization as the man in charge of PT-109?

Of course my father and two of my uncles had served in the Navy as well. World War II caused three other uncles to don Army uniforms and the Korean War invited the fourth and youngest of the physically fit. The uncle whom I most admired was an army career man, having gotten a boost from the ROTC. Unfortunately for him he was taken into Army Reserves and never made regular army till just before his retirement, where they made the switch to cushion his retirement but saw no need to promote him above Colonel.

In a way that particular uncle came within handshaking distance of greatness. His daughter, my cousin, became a psychologist, and was a consultant to the Oklahoma prison system at the time Timothy McVeigh decided to blow the whole U.S. government to kingdom come and achieved modest, if incomplete, success.

I had only been on the job a month or so, hard at work for the Navy, when my boss's boss was summoned to the Pentagon. This was to be a technical conference where we would discuss the computer-supported targeting system for the Polaris submarines and he felt he needed me if the questions got too technical.

I didn't mind going, for several reasons. First, the Navy provided us with a car and driver. I had never had a car and driver combination before. Second, we were getting closer to the White House. True, we were going to the Pentagon, which is across the river from the White House, but it was that much closer and I knew it would be just a matter of time till I would be working there. Third, and those who have relied over the years on patrolling nuclear submarines to keep them safe can relax because I was absolutely confident that I could handle any technical question the Pentagon should happen to raise at that meeting.

Confident because, first of all I wasn't working on the Polaris missle part of the Polaris submarine. Polaris missiles were the submarine's offensive armament.

I was working on the defensive armament, the nuclear and conventional missiles that the submarine would use to defend itself if attacked at close range.

If any of the brass should ask a question about our Polaris weapons I could honestly say I was "detailed" (in military jargon) to the defensive weapons systems. If pressed I could then add that I wasn't "cleared" for Polaris. After only a few days on the Navy base I had caught on quickly that nothing shut down a conversation faster than your admitting you were not cleared for whatever was about to be brought up. If those officers and their enlisted subordinates believed in anything with all their collective might it was in the sacred doctrine of "need to know." If you didn't have need to know not only did you get shut out but even those around you, however urgent their business might be, got shut down right with you. Nothing, absolutely nothing, stopped a conversation more dramatically. Yes, I had arrived. This was high theater.

Beyond the dodge-the-Polaris missile I had another fallback. There was always the possibility they might ask a question about our defensive missile capability, whose name was Subroc, the label of a ship-to-ship weapon, as opposed to Polaris which was ship-to-shore. If they should ask anything about the capability of this miniature nuclear tipped device, my ready answer was another room-clearer. I wasn't cleared for that either. What I was working on at that time was in fact a computer program that would translate computer shorthand, called assembly language, into the bits and bytes of computer circuitry.

In those days, when a new computer came out, especially the scientific ones, all the programming had to be done, in effect, in numbers. Usually these were numbers to the base 8, in the case of this computer, not even our own familiar base ten that we had learned in grade school. Our computers were, in a certain way, unable to operate with a number greater than 8. That's right: one, two, three, four, five, six, seven and eight!

In a way the work that I was doing had already made me nostalgic for the first computer they showed us on the base, which had been hexadecimal, in other words base 16. That's right. The NORC, which stood for Naval Ordnance Research Calculator, could count one, two, ..., you get the idea, all the way up to 16.

I was engaged at that time in a project whose aim was to allow the programmers to write words like ADD for add, SUB for subtract and STO for store, instead of 10, 20 and something like 80, respectively, which really didn't tell you a lot when you were trying to find errors in your missile targeting equations. Of course ADD, SUB and STO weren't all that great either, but the days of sitting down with a mouse at the keyboard of your own personal computer and making an Excel spreadsheet jump through three dimensional hoops of kinematic ballistic equations were decades in the future.

So, with the national defense system at stake and all these ballistic weapons delivery systems under threat of attack by our cold war enemies, was it likely that someone in the room was going to say, "By the way, how's that octal-to-shorthand English translation system of yours coming?" I didn't think so and I was right. The reason it was not brought up had nothing to do with defense contractor project management, competent or otherwise. It had everything to do with level of abstraction, and who had the gift for which, but more about that later.

In any case I enjoyed the free ride to the Pentagon. It was a chance to get away from my desk and to collect eight dollars or so per diem. What was probably most exciting to a young man fresh out of college was being served a coke or coffee, or whatever you wished, by a young man about my age, wearing a navy uniform. That was the most exalted culinary service I experienced on my way to the White House until a meeting one day with a civilian in the DIA, a little known military intelligence outfit every bit as diligently supplied with "operatives" and missions as its civilian counterpart, the CIA. On that particular day the civil servant I called upon had a man in uniform to open his door. sign visitors in and escort them to his desk. The uniform wearer was a full bird colonel.

Eventually I had my own man to bring in coffee and see to the comfort of guests visiting me in my office but that was much later and I had to share him with a cabinet rank department head. I did get to work in the White House, but I never became president. Hold on. That is getting ahead of my story.

Chapter 2—View From the Top

Those days in the Kennedy years were indeed heady days. Anything was possible, but you needed connections. The Kennedys had Old Boston connections and Old Boston money. They didn't have me, and as far as they knew they didn't need me, so I set out to make myself needed.

First came the abortive doctorate in clinical psychology, to be followed over the years by similar aborted academic careers including an almost doctorate in mathematics and a very near miss in Computer Information Technology. In the latter case the very title should have warned me off. "Computer Information" is an oxymoron, as is "Information Technology." Together the three words make some kind of a three dimensional oxymoron, but it's no worse than psychophysics, and somebody in the rarified atmosphere of university degree program creation must have to do something with his time, at least once in a while. I have records of attendance at some 10 or 12 universities and colleges, in most of which I was enrolled for a degree. About number four or five was the University of Illinois where I received a master's in mathematics and where I wrote my first article ever for a scholarly journal.

TO A CHILD OF DIVORCE

Who rejoiced at night with each school "A"
　　And strained to know the teacher's mind?

Who knew your tutors' names
　　And matched each with a year?

What became of how you knew them?
　　How strong the shell you must have built.

In your remembering do they linger
　　Or have you breathed them into shadows and old dust?

A PRESIDENTIAL WAR

I would be chief among my people
    And I know how to climb there
        Or how to let myself be pushed.

And when I reach our nation's peak
    I'll not be any smarter but
        I'll have about me doers.

I'll find an enemy off stage
    Whose cries need not be real.

I'll have won if whom I've called
    Will send for me his son.

LEARNING

When it was my job to learn, I learned
    By studying
And all who didn't learn that way
    Were dim or party people.

Now some I'm told will learn by hearing
    Others need to see.
Some can only learn by doing
    By engaging in their craft.

All right, if I am paid to teach I'll do it
    Each one's way
And if you pay me to I'll even
    Try and figure which is whose.

I don't know if the theorist's right,
    Who pays is my authority
Reserving while I can the right to pragmatize
    The student that I love.

That's teaching, but what shall I do with
    The rest of my life?
There are experts on whom to kiss
    And whom to bed

But none pays me and I am adrift.

URSULA

Was a sprite, a German speaking, Swiss accented sprite
    In brown close cut hair,
        With pointed ears and a way of searching your eyes.

She made you think of impossible things
    And told you marvelous made up things
    In closest confidence.

And when she laughed
    It was a skipping way
    That danced all around you
    And up and back the length of a railway car.

And when she died
    It would be unconventionally;
    She'd have left her finance heroically

… It would be a fiance, she would have
    Given her heart, but not taken his ring …

She would have left him safe in camp
    And paddled a dark lake in the rain

On a trip to ski at the bottom of the world.

IRELYN

No one has my name, I hope none ever will
I set a second grade class on fire
    When I came late in the year.
I never saw what the others saw or
    Wore what the others wore.
My brother, one year younger, was beautiful
    Too, like me.

It is hard now to believe how beautiful was my
    Skin and how gold my hair
My skin shocked my teenage admirers,
    That anything so perfect could be blemished,
We had no skin doctors then.

They told me that the right kind of exercise,
    In private, would keep my skin cleared up,
But they weren't authority and their advice
    Often enough put me crosswise to it,
So I don't know.

Let's say I did what authority expected
    And let myself be groped with tentative
Encouragement into a safe marriage
    And now I've lost myself in the majority
What's become of my special name and my skin?

BETTY GAIL

Undertakers must have daughters
    And I was one of two.
I would be brown eyed and brown haired
    And medium sized as benefited a girl
    Named Betty
But it was the Gail that made me special.

When I was little a mortuary or funeral parlor
    Was called a funeral home
And lucky for me it was, because I lived there.

I went to movies on Saturday and the
    Wealthiest Baptist church on Sunday
And I always wore dresses and liked looking sweet

But I didn't like
    Being expected to know more about
Death than anyone else.

WOODY

For Woodrow, you know,
    Nobody names a child that anymore.
Now Cornrow they might, but I'd better
    Watch what I say.

When I was a child there were two drinking
    Fountains in the Courthouse,
One marked Colored, the other marked White.

I was glad I wasn't colored, they had to
    Buy their movie tickets in the alley
And go up the back steps.

But what bladder control they had.
    There wasn't a bathroom in all of Princeton
They could go to except maybe the courthouse
    If there was one marked colored,
Maybe in the basement.

But Lord did they have fun, or that's
    What it looked like. They'd stand or
Sit in groups around their grocery

In Bootsville, and what they wore
Was colorful.
    Us we stayed indoors except when
We were going somewhere.

I guess that's why hanging around
    Looked good to me.

And we'd go visit Aunt Sally and sit
    On her porch and talk. Every colored
Person that was grown up we called
    Aunt or Uncle.
We thought it was respect.
    Now we're told it's degradation.
I don't know and I guess I'll never.

PHYLLIS

Me and my sisters were blond and skinny,
    They called us white-haired which wasn't
So. We had long thin faces which I later
    Came to think was our old English
Blood. We had long toes and feet that were
    White on top and pink underneath.
I guess we never tanned, but we burned
    Easy and oh, yes, our hair was thin and
Curled when it got damp, which was mostly
    All summer so we'd look stringy except
At church on Sunday, including Sunday
    Night prayer meeting.

We lived next door because we were kin.
    You always did that.
We may not have done it later though,
    Because my sisters and I may have
Been too wild. I don't know. We had
    A good start.

I'm supposed to tell you what didn't
    Happen. So you'll know about us.

We appeared at a time that must have been
       Spring because the water ran on both
Sides of the road and we helped make dams
       Out of gravel and weeks later it dried up
But you could still see grey humps here
       And there where I remembered we'd piled
A lot to brace the pieces of board that we used
       To push the water back.

I'm supposed to tell you that we didn't
       Invite the boys to play doctor and do experiments
That involved moving strategic garments
       Around our patients. Well, I've told you.

Did I also tell you that my sisters and
       I had thin pinkish nostrils that were always
Running and that one day the boy
       Next door fell out of the apple tree and
Hit on his stomach, crosswise of
       The playpen and had the breath knocked out
Of him? Well, I just did that.

And one other thing. He had a rabbit in a
       Cage under that same apple tree and we poked
Grass in it through the wire and one day
       He gave me a box turtle that he found, but
I gave it back. What would I want
       Something like that for?

KENTUCKY WONDERS

Of a summer's night I'd sit out on the porch
　　Where the morning glory vines
Made black patterns
　　On the sky

I'd shell peas
　　Or snap beans
You didn't need to see what you were about
　　When you did them things

I'd take a lap full of Kentucky Wonders
　　And prop a dishpan between my legs
And drop the ends and stringers in a sack
　　Where you could hear it in the dark

Clement'd walk up from his place
　　And let the children sit by him in the swing
Till they got sleepy
　　And we'd talk or listen to the kids

Clement swung real easy back and forth
    He was solid built
And Lord
    Can't I still hear that old swing creak

I'd touch the beans
    Where they swelled up in their skins
And I'd think how them big muscles of his'd feel
    If once you got your arms around him

GUADELOUPE

Dark brown,

And pink turning red,

They lie on the sand,

Tourist and native son.

She thrills to being naked in the sun,

He is indifferent.

She is territorial about his body

He is concerned about her purse.

Together they are happy,

She in her way,

He in his.

DEAR LORETTA

B.J.'s nomination to be Assistant Secretary of the Navy takes me back thirty years, to when I served as Special Assistant to the Public Printer. The position was awarded to me more as a result of a serendipitous confluence of events than for, as in B.J.'s case, any special merit of my own.

The Government Printing Office (GPO), as every civics student knows, is one of those organizations such as the Library of Congress and the Government Accounting Office which bear the same relationship to Congress that the executive agencies (Department of Defense, etc.) bear to the President. Consequently the Public Printer, his deputy, and his assistants are all nominated by the President and confirmed by the Senate.

My job title contained the qualifying word "special" before the word "assistant" so my position did not strictly speaking require the formality of the nomination-confirmation process. This was probably just as well because I was a Democrat in the Nixon-Ford era. The Congress had at least heard of me because the Public Printer mentioned my work in testimony before the Committee on Appropriations. His comments had been duly entered into the public record, "Hearings Before Subcommittees of the Committee on Appropriations, House of Representatives, Ninety-Fourth Congress, First Session, Part 1," page 224. I have a copy of the report to this day and will pass it to my grandchildren.

You may think I make too much of this microsecond of glory in the public record, but if you look closely at the citation you will notice that my name is prefixed by a most significant qualifier. The Public Printer refers to me as a "gentleman." Even today I feel pride when I re-read page 224. What will my grandchildren think of their patriarch, a gentleman forever among congressmen?

In those days the matter of my being anything like a gentleman was subordinate to the minutia of the daily train commute from Washington Grove to Union Station, just across from the GPO on Capitol Hill, and carrying out whatever tasks the Public Printer set me. Now, years later, the commute and the work have dwindled in importance. What remains instead is a brilliant memory of the trappings of office and all the curiousnesses that went with it.

The silliest part of being a high ranking official lasted about a minute. I saw an organization chart of the GPO shortly after they took me on. You have to understand that the GPO not only drew its sustenance from the printed word in the same way all the other government agencies did but its very existence depended on how well it produced the printed word and all other forms of documentation. The Public Printer came from the printing firm R. H. Donnelly. The Deputy had come up from the ranks with ink beneath his fingernails. To them the printing of texts and their associated graphics were among man's finest accomplishments. To them an organization chart was not only a thing of beauty but the embodiment on paper of a social reality in a form that only a true mystic could appreciate.

There on the chart was I, just three heartbeats away from department head. From the box representing the Public Printer there was a line to his deputy's box and a line to the two Assistants, just like the Secretary of the Navy has, and a line to me. Three heartbeats, then me. Wow!

What did it mean to be Special Assistant to the Public Printer? I was installed in an office in the Public Printer's own suite, next door to the Assistant Public Printer for Administration, who in turn was next to the Deputy whose office adjoined the Public Printer's. The other Assistant, known as the Superintendent of Documents, was located with his own staff in another building.

The first thing I was told when they showed me my new office was that Percy would bring me coffee. And he did. Of all the people I met at GPO, Percy was the one who most deserved to be called "gentleman."

I was not a coffee drinker but I quickly grew accustomed to Percy's popping in every morning within minutes of my arrival, coffee hot in a cup with a real matching saucer—I never saw a coffee mug in the Public Printer's suite—accompanied by sugar and real cream. So impressed was I by this ceremony that I went out of my way to invite people, anybody, into my office just to watch their reactions when Percy appeared with cups and saucers all around. I had no visitors' area with conversational seating and a coffee table like the Public Printer had in his office. My visitors had to set their china on my big desk rather than burn their hands or spill something on their suits. It made for a tighter group than you would expect in a room that size, but there was no furniture other than the desk and a few chairs so we huddled together rather like trespassers in a vacant ware-house.

The only scenario I can remember that brought together a more ridiculous assortment of government officials in a coffee ceremony occurred in my consult-ing days when I called on an army general at the Defense Intelligence Agency. The man who served as the general's secretary, the underling who signed us in and brought us coffee in the general's office, who appeared to be the general's entire administrative staff, was a full colonel!

Being Special Assistant also meant that I was to attend immediately on the Public Printer himself whenever he had a question about or wanted to wrestle with the possibilities of computer technology, because that was my field. When I answered a summons to his private conference room one day I was amazed to find him polishing his own shoes. Embarrassed, he admitted the habit was a holdover from his military days. To me it was awe inspiring. The stars in Wash-ington politics always dressed impeccably—I had been several times summoned to the White House offices of President Nixon's assistants—but I must have assumed they had emerged fully formed from Buddha's, or in this case Nixon's, head. It never occurred to me before then to ponder the logistics of life on center stage and to speculate why their shoes always looked as if they had just come from a haberdashery. My own shoes would never have passed muster. That may be the reason this particular tour of duty in the rarified atmosphere of Capitol Hill marked the apogee of my political career.

There was a downside to having to answer the Public Printer's questions. Tom was gregarious by nature, which is probably a good thing for a political appoin-tee. He thought nothing of calling out to me two or three tables away in the exec-utive dining room to ask my opinion on a matter that had come up at his own table. His tablemates were invariably his deputy, the two assistant public printers and the comptroller, plus whatever guests might be on hand. Since the GPO was subordinate to both exalted houses of Congress neither Senator nor Representa-tive ever dined with us to my recollection, but their staffers often visited. Fortu-nately for me this was before the days of near universal computer literacy and I never got a technical question I couldn't handle. Even more luckily, if the ques-tion had to do with the impact of technology on the work force—the GPO being perhaps the only department that used an inverted hiring list as an instrument of social policy—I could always defer the manpower issues to any of the various heads of the GPO's printing units, all of whom viewed the conversion from hot type to electronic printing with a skepticism bordering on paranoia.

Truth be told I did not really enjoy the emoluments of the Public Printer's executive dining room. When I had first arrived at the GPO I had been allowed to eat in the employee cafeteria which, to someone of my southern upbringing, was a marvelous place. The aforementioned inverted list employees hailed almost entirely from Washington DC's impoverished Northeast and were mostly transplanted southerners like myself. The cuisine featured what was coming to be called soul food. Best of all you could see the choices as you went along the counter and select what appealed most to your stomach. Plus the price was right.

In the executive dining room, on the other hand, you did not get to see the food before you made your selection. Instead they gave you a menu, elegantly printed at the GPO of course, and you had no choice but to rely on your imagination.

There were other disadvantages. You did not get to pay for your food until the end of the month. This was not an insurmountable problem, but you needed to plan ahead in order to have enough cash in your pocket, or make an excuse or borrow, equally embarrassing. Neither could you simply eat and run, no matter how urgently involved you might be in a project. First of all it took quite a while for the waiters to deliver your food. No matter how simple your order they would not serve you before they served the Public Printer if he was in the room. While you were waiting you had to think of something non-controversial to talk about to whoever happened to be at your table. Then you weren't likely to jump up when you were finished eating. You could not just walk out on the people at the head table unless you could think of something that was both suitably breezy and credibly urgent to call out as you excused yourself.

The only reliably enjoyable, absolutely no downside, aspect of the entire Public Printer's entourage experience, after all these years, the one bright light whose radiance subsumes and renders insignificant all the other accoutrements of the job is attributable solely to Percy's stewardship. That was the matter of the GPO's private cars. For some reason that no one ever explained to me the GPO's chauffeurs all reported to Percy. The Nixon administration had strictly avoided the appearance of wastefulness, which meant that the GPO's cars were not limousines. Mostly they were Fords or Chevrolets, I think, all black. But more importantly they were private. If you needed to go somewhere you let Percy know. He told you when your driver was ready and at what door you would find him, then off you went. Just you and the driver. You sat in the back seat because the driver held the door open for you. And he took you anywhere. It did not matter whether it was the short hop across town to the Office of Management and Budget next door to the White House or all the way up to Carderock, Maryland, the U. S. Navy's David Taylor Model Basin, an hour's drive or more even in the lightest traffic. Percy's drivers were not talkers. They were always polite. The ride was restful and it was quiet.

Something there is in me that does not like an institution, however fascinating its traditions, however eccentric and memorable its members, and I did not tarry long in my real capacity as Special Assistant to the Public Printer or in my fantasy position as (almost) Assistant Public Printer. I do not miss the Government Printing Office. I have already forgotten how to find the staff offices where I acted as the GPO's emissary on Capitol Hill. Maybe I miss having the Public Printer try his ideas on me and maybe a little bit the verbal fencing with his other advisors, but mostly I miss Percy. I miss the surprise of his coffee and I miss the gentility of the chauffeured rides.

Best wishes to you and B. J. The best I can hope for is that I made a contribution and didn't know it. My wish is that B. J. will make a contribution and know it.

THE OUPWR

As a rule the Outer Upper Peekskill Writin' Riders were loud and unruly. They were so loud and unruly that all the other commuters from Upstate New York, would usually concede them the entire front section of the first car of the train. Five days a week they extolled, sulked and argued into Manhattan, alternately regaling and appalling one another with literary flights of fancy and cynical witticisms, blithely ignoring the glares and snores of the other passengers.

On this particular morning, poet-in-waiting Larry "Hang the metaphors" McDoubtably had elbowed his way to the first row. According to OUPWR tradition your turn to read was determined by your seating order however ungentlemanly the means you might have been used to gain your seat.

As a poet Larry had little love for meter or rhyme. He was highly mistrustful of structure as well, which was understandable. In the city he worked as Chief Maintenance Engineer for the Borough of Manhattan and dealt primarily with angled pipes and compulsively non-rectilinear streets in the Lower East Side. What he read in a voice magnified by years of yelling at construction crews sounded like this:

I'll not,

Whatever you will,

I may,

Depending on my mood,

Join you for dinner,

At your club,

I don't like your friends.

Mumbles and snorts from those awake enough to be listening indicated that he was, please, to repeat the reading, and he was happy to oblige, using an even louder voice the second time around. Groans and coarse mutterings could be heard from the back of the car where non-OUPWR stragglers who couldn't find seats elsewhere on the train were trying to get some rest before tackling The Big Apple.

There was an immediate buzz among the assembled OUPWR. Bellanegra Rockaway-Cantrell suggested what was needed was a more balanced perspective and recommended substituting "your mood" for "my mood." Thomas Thornberry Thwaitewhistle, the only cleric in the club and the lone black, contributed his usual observation that it was enough for Belle to identify the lack of balance and leave it up to the newly enlightened author to fix his own work.

Tiredly, "Barking" Jimmy Biggs waved a hand and said, "It's the brevity. Too short a poem to develop a complex notion like the interplay of self and non-self."

According to the group's rules, diligently enforced by the Big Three founding pencil-men, it was alright to skewer whoever was reading his works but it was wrong to criticize a fellow commentator. For that reason and only that reason Catherine Cassowary Columberry bit her tongue on the wittiest response ever, to wit "Biggs, you're a horse's ass," and offered instead "No, it's not."

Antoine Bernau Mynott, one of the celebrated Big Three, waved a dismissive rolled-up New York Times. "Remember the rule, no non-constructive redundancies."

Catherine turned her face to the window where dawn was just now lightening the grey morning and covered her nose with her hand, the middle finger of which would have seemed unusually prominent to any of her fellow OUPWR members if they had been looking, which they weren't.

No other comments forthcoming, McDoubtably, with visible reluctance, sat down.

Next up was his seatmate, Maureen Wheatstone Parboil. Known to her inti-
mates as "Bulldog" Parboil, Maureen elbowed her way around McDoubtably's
ample frame, and onto the seat behind him where she put a foot between the
wary occupant's hip and his armrest and raised herself up so that she could prop
her backside against McDoubtably's seat back and turn toward the others seated
behind him. Her voice was high-pitched and carried dramatically over the rum-
ble and rattle of the rail cars.

"I left off last time," she began. Her voice had an aggrieved edge; the
OUPWR's who-sits-first-reads-first rule usually meant that the smaller and
weaker members got to read last, if at all, which in turn meant they read infre-
quently and if, as in Maureen's case, they were working on a particularly long or
intricate story, everyone tended to lose track of the story line, sometimes not only
the listeners but even the author herself. Maureen's face showed some reddish
spots, lingering evidence of the sacrifices she had had to make today to gain the
number two spot. McDoubtably could be seen from time to time rubbing his
shin as if Maureen had aimed today for possibly the first position. Maureen's
voice did not have an accusatory tone exactly, but here and there some people
twisted uncomfortably in their big semi-recliner seats.

"As I was saying," she went on, "where I left off last time, my heroine June
Camden-Compton, had decided to hell with TV, and gone out instead for an
evening's air." She lifted her head to glare at the skeptics. "Yes," she insisted,
"there is evening air in Manhattan ... and clear, too, in case you have forgotten."
She sniffed defensively, lifted her manuscript and began to read.

"So it happened that a man and woman entered a deserted park from opposite
gates ..."

She interrupted her reading to wave an admonitory hand. "This is Greenwich
Village, remember."

There was a general show of resigned nodding, not so much because everyone
remembered as because they all were wearied at being reminded. Some times an
author can be too insistent on anchoring his story in a place and time. All the
OUPWR members hated anything that might interfere with a good plot or
might short circuit the audience's imagination.

"The woman," she went on, "was wrestling with her mind and her
emotions ..." (here Camden-Compton raised her eyes and swept her audience in
an intimidating manner) "... opening them up to the charm of the place and the
moment, whatever might come. The man walking towards her was desperately
trying for perhaps the twentieth time to overlay some startlingly forceful phrase
from Robert Burns over a particularly vexsome legal subclause in a union con-

tract he was negotiating. Neither had been successful. Both had turned to this small park, more a parklet than a park, hoping to find something ... anything."

With that Maureen stopped reading and began to climb down from her perch. She had changed to her patent "so there" kind of look by way of showcasing her moral superiority over the vexations of petty position in reading groups as well as her immunity to such criticisms and improvements as might be wished upon her. Sadly she was unsuccessful, on two counts. First the train lurched so violently that her face immediately morphed from challenge through shock and into stress while the voices of OUPWR commentators erupted all around her.

"One at a time!" shouted a Big Three member and she banged with a teaspoon on a metal pot that she carried in her oversize purse for just such situations as this.

The reader waiting in third position frantically unrolled his damp manuscript and checked one last time for grammatical errors. He grabbed the seatback ahead of him and pulled his trembling body to its feet.

ISABELLE

I admired my grandfather, Oscar Boyd. He was my idea of what a real man should be. If he had any faults they were not part of my time with him, so I can truthfully say I never saw them. The year between my freshman and sophomore years at college I was not popular enough with my own father to be welcome in my parent's house so my grandparents took me in.

The work was farming. It was hard work and I was not good at it. No matter, my grandfather kept me busy and I would like to believe he was satisfied. I was glad to be in his company and pleased to be sharing his life. To my surprise, though we usually worked ten miles or more out in the country and we carried our lunch with us, my grandfather always needed to go into town during the afternoon.

Sometimes he would tell me where we were going. Sometimes he wouldn't, but we always ended up at the same place, my Aunt Isabelle's house. My grandfather wanted coffee, but it was more than that. He wanted rest and a break. There was always coffee ready. I imagine Aunt Isabelle expected him, but maybe she would have made coffee anyway. In any case my grandfather looked forward to being at my aunt's house. I think he would have been disappointed if she had been away from home those afternoons.

I don't remember any particular conversations. I believe there may have been questions about the farm work and maybe a fair share of silence, but most of all I believe my grandfather was happy there. I believe he was comfortable in Aunt Isabelle's house. It was a rest for him from the hard work that was his chosen way of life. At the time it puzzled me why we went there and not to his own house, but now I am older and I realize that home would not have been a break. It would have only been a change in work. A change from one kind of work to another.

This is not to say that my grandfather had an unhappy home life. On the contrary, his marriage was a happy one, by and large. My grandparents had married young. I think my grandmother was only 16 years old when they first married and I believe they celebrated their 67th anniversary together. Their life together had included a renewal of their wedding vows on their 65th anniversary, so going by Aunt Isabelle's was not in any way avoiding going home. I think it was just a way of savoring guesthood.

My grandfather was not a travelling man. In their early married years he had played professional baseball with a St. Louis Cardinals farm team all over southern Illinois and that was as far as he ever got from home till after the second World War when he went to New York City to visit his two sons who had mustered out of the Navy.

Going home, for him, in the middle of the day would have meant re-shouldering the burdens of being bread winner and most responsible adult in his own house. Instead, at Aunt Isabelle's house, he could be the guest, the honored guest whose daughter would refill his cup, and the beloved elder whose word was never challenged, whose opinion when asked was always cherished.

Every man should have such a daughter, in whose house he is always welcome, whose occasional errands he is free to do and whose chores he might, if there is time, offer to perform but whose small jobs he might just as freely defer without cost in fealty or affection.

She gave him loyalty. She was a good daughter. He paid her the highest compliment a country man could give his daughter. He called her "sister."

ATTIC

After their mother had died and left them, the family slowly abandoned the house, one member at a time, and lived their remaining years somewhere else. In time they all died and the house was left without heirs.

I bought the house at auction. I bought it because of a rat-chewed pile of papers I found in the attic.

The family's letters had been stacked there. The rats had left behind only fragments of paragraphs and torn half pages.

Piecing together the scattered words was worth the cost of a hundred such houses.

PRINCETON

I will call this town Princeton, and the county Caldwell. To know Princeton as I knew it then you must learn that the county courthouse sits in the middle of town where Main Street makes a slight plateau running east and west. The courthouse does not interrupt Main Street, but it does block Jefferson Street running north and south.

The courthouse is the only building in town that is made of marble. There is something very 1920's about the courthouse. It looks as if it had sprung full grown with no architectural precedents in the neighborhood.

By contrast the stores along Main Street have grown in an evolutionary way, the wide board floors of many of them gradually giving way to the parqueted and tiled floors of later years. The storefronts tend to be ornate with little carvings here and there on the wood embellishments painted to look like carved stone. The drugstore near the town movie boasts chairs of iron and its hard round glass tables are completely undercoated with long-forgotten chewing gum.

You must walk this town with me and know that there is a creek that runs northwest to southeast through the town, crossing Main Street a couple of blocks east of the courthouse. Though the stream is forced through culverts as it runs from street to street, in many places it is still a free running stream—at least in spring and fall—and the houses which front on the stream have long narrow bridges leading across the water and onto the street.

Looking at the creek as a child would look, walking along the stony bottom of the creek and exploring the town from below street level, you will see that the masonry of the brick walls has given way here and there. The walls have bulged and broken, their large blocks now lying in the stream bed. There is a particular place where the stream once crossed a road and here the masonry looks much fresher. This is a spot where only comparatively recently the street was filled in and a culvert placed underneath.

If you walked with someone who knew the town and loved its history you would come to see that it was at one time a white town with black borders. To the north and west of the town proper lived the middle class blacks in an area called Bootsville. The southeast side of the town was for the lower class blacks who lived in shacks. This was in a time when there was no such word as "black" and the residents of Princeton, black and white alike, used the words "niggers" or "colored people."

Properly speaking, the inhabitants of Bootsville were colored people and the inhabitants of Black Bottom, for that's what the southeast portion was called, were niggers. If you had gone past the eighth grade you would use the word "Negro," but a high school education was rare in those days, especially if you hadn't been brought up in town. Two of my grandparents went to country schools and did not go beyond eighth grade.

Black Bottom is gone now. Urban renewal, though the term was not used in those days, was a plank in my great uncle's campaign for mayor. Whatever he might have called his proposal back then, translated it meant "Black Bottom must go."

Though Bootsville still remains, Black Bottom has been filled in. That same creek flowed through Black Bottom and made a small waterfall just behind the stores on the lower east side of Main Street. The storefronts were all at street level, but behind them the ground fell away one or two stories to the bottom of the creek bed. Their multi-storey basements are no longer visible. Black Bottom is a concrete-based, filling-station-decorated, farm-implement-dealership-abutted and professional-building-surfaced modern monument to 1960's urban renewal.

I am not the sociologist to tell you where the people of Black Bottom have gone. I will be an optimist and assume that they have improved their lot and moved on to Bootsville or even into the white parts of the city, because that did happen ... some.

Princeton lies in that part of the South which gets very hot in the summer, but because of its elevation Princeton is never muggy ... much. Breathless sometimes, but not debilitating. Princeton lies in that part of the South, too, that in the winter gets very cold. The winter cycle is harsh but it seldom snows. When snow does fall there is almost immediately a warming thaw that loosens the snow and turns it to slush. Then comes a good solid freeze. The result is a sheet of ice over all the roads and yards that is difficult for young people to drive on and impossible for old people to walk on.

Frequently there is a misting rain in very cold weather and, for a day or two thereafter, all the bushes and trees are coated with a thick transparent ice cover. It catches the reflections of all colors, from houses and sky, and from people's faces. The ice cover sparkles in such a way that every growing thing might have been planted just to decorate a winter fantasy set.

Princeton is a town of porches. Houses built before the 1950's enjoyed at least two porches, a wide and formal front porch and a modest utilitarian back porch. Except for those houses that sat right on the street, if you visited a neighbor in the daytime, you went around to the back door because that is where you would find the housewife. Only salesmen went to the front door.

The housewives of Princeton are an institution, even today. Many of them are the wives of farmers who have retired and moved wife and household into town. Faced with unaccustomed inactivity, the farm husbands die relatively soon after retirement. The wives, whose labors are not so very different from before, tend to live on and on—the consolation of their children, and the joy and amusement of their grandchildren.

Farm people moving to town are unaccustomed to the smaller houses of city people and invariably choose large, rambling structures for their retirement. This gives the farm-broke housewives tremendous responsibilities in upkeep, but it does give the grandchildren plenty of room to romp and it gives Princeton a hometown look in a dowdy but lighthearted, tree-shaded, sort of way.

THE REVOLVER

Funny thing about war. If you were a Kentucky boy growing up in the forties, war was something that happened far away. Your family saved string and tin foil.

My paternal grandfather had three sons in service. Two of them were in the army and one, my dad, was in the navy. My father's father saved up two balls of string, bigger than grapefruits, maybe one for each of his army boys. He also saved a ball of tinfoil, the size of an orange, that was really heavy. That one must have been for my dad.

When your mother sent you to the grocery store you carried rationing stamps for sugar and, if your family could afford it, rationing stamps for meat. Eating meat was kind of like saving string because you saved the fat after you cooked pork, I remember that. I don't know what you did with the fat after the war, but during the war it sat in a tin bucket on the back of the stove.

My uncle Charles Lee—being southerners we used both given names—was kept over in Italy till a couple of years after the end of the war. The day he came home from service he was carrying a suitcase. It was a real suitcase, not just a duffel bag like my dad brought back.

Charles Lee hefted his suitcase up onto the bed in the front room and we all crowded around to see what he was going to pull out of it. There were clothes on top, then a holster with a service revolver in it. He took it out so all of us could admire the shiny steel. I had never been up close to a hand gun. The only ones I had ever seen were in cowboy movies.

Underneath the holster was a flag all folded up. I don't remember what nationality it was. Maybe it was a United States flag. Maybe it was a souvenir flag from Italy. I don't think it was a swastika flag. I would have remembered that because whenever that flag appeared on the movie screen they always played ugly music and the announcer spoke in dreadful tones. My great aunt took a picture magazine. I think it was "Life," and in those years the Nazi flag only appeared in scenes about bad things that happened overseas.

The flag that came out of the suitcase had to have been a good flag. Uncle Charles Lee handed this flag to his son. Now for sure I was interested. If something came out of the suitcase for his oldest son, maybe there would be something for his oldest nephew, me. There wasn't.

Uncle Charles Lee had named his oldest son Charles Smith. The Charles part was for himself and the Smith part was his wife's family name. I was never particularly close to Charles Smith. He was a couple of years younger than me. After his dad came back from the war they moved out into the country to a farm owned by Charles Lee's wife's family. Her name was Margaret Fern.

Margaret Fern was an only child. Back then when we said the words "only child" in our family we put a pitying tone in our voice because it was a sad thing not to have any brothers or sisters. Margaret Fern was the closest thing in our family to a professional woman. She worked in the ten cent store and that seemed an exalted calling to all of us nephews and nieces.

Margaret Fern's eyes were more staring than ours and her chin receded which gave her a particularly intimidating look. Consequently we were especially careful of our manners any time my sister and I had to wait at the dime store of an afternoon till Mother came by for us.

Margaret Fern and the dime store were directly involved in, and indirectly responsible for, the singly most humiliating experience of my childhood. My sister Marilyn and I were dutifully waiting for Mother, wandering around the store looking at things one afternoon when someone, a stock boy maybe or a customer, bumped into me and I tried to get out of his way. I swung around, lost my balance and caught myself by grabbing two solid vertical protuberances which happened to be the critical components of a horizontal display of women's brassieres.

Somehow Mother heard about this incident even before she arrived at the store. My mother was, if anything, even more easily embarrassed than I by the ups and downs of everyday life. She came into the store redder in the face then than I'd ever seen her and hustled my sister and me outside without speaking to any other adult on the premises. That just wasn't done in Princeton, Kentucky.

Aunt Margaret Fern was a country woman. Tact was not one of her virtues. She had a direct way of handling everything. In those days all the Skees family ate Sunday dinner with my grandparents. That meant she and Charles Lee and their two boys were there at the big table, just like my dad's family were. For weeks after the dime store experience, she'd walk in the front door, catch sight of me and laugh out loud. There was a coarseness about the way she laughed, or so I imagined. I prayed every day that she'd forget about the brassieres. Eventually my prayers were answered.

One of us changed, or maybe both of us. By the time I was a parent myself I had come to respect her as one of the wisest and most considerate women of my mother's generation. But in those early days I didn't feel that way at all.

Aunt Margaret Fern's husband, Uncle Charles Lee, was a laborer, just as my father was. Unlike my dad, Charles Lee worked two jobs. He did carpentry work for the Illinois Central Railroad, and later was in the construction crew on the massive Alben W. Barkley Dam project that backed up the Cumberland River. At the same time he worked the carpentry trade he was also farming. He planted, he tilled, he cut and he cured. West Kentucky farmers will tell you that tobacco is the most backbreaking work there is. That and he ran dairy cows, too.

I think life was hard on their whole family. Once, in the years when we were still having Sunday dinner at Granddaddy's house, I heard Uncle Charles Lee tell somebody that it was too bad, because his son Charles Smith was a'countin' on going fishing. A few seconds later, through the window of the room that served my grandparents as both bedroom and living room, I saw Charles Smith stumbling down the driveway, tears running down his cheeks.

At the time it amazed me that anyone could care that much about fishing, especially a teenager.

Charles Lee and Margaret Fern wanted both their boys to go to college. One boy became a chemist, one an engineer. Charles Smith's job took him all over the world. He married a woman in England and they settled in the States, not far from Memphis.

After Charles Lee retired and long after Aunt Margaret Fern left the dime store, the two of them moved to town. Charles Lee continued to grow things. His backyard garden was a showpiece in the neighborhood. When I would visit he loved to tell me about his corn, his pole beans and his tomatoes. Aunt Margaret Fern got some kind of cancer. My uncle traveled down to the hospital in Memphis every week to be with her. It was about a five hour trip each way. He usually stayed overnight, sometimes two or three days.

Back home you would find him fretting. He had his railroad pension and there were railroad hospitals all around like the one where Margaret Fern was, down in Memphis. But he couldn't get it off his mind. He kept worrying about how he was going to pay all the bills. How could he look after her, just the two of them, and close on seventy years old?

Two days before she was to be released from the hospital he shot himself in the head. The gun he used was the old service revolver from World War II. When they settled his affairs they gave the gun to his son, Charles Smith. I remembered the day Charles Lee opened his Army suitcase. I remembered how Charles Smith had first gotten the flag, now he had the gun. The last souvenir of the war.

We lingered after the funeral at the home of another uncle, one that had been too young to go to war. Their only sister was there. They worried about Charles Lee's soul. At first they were relieved. They were glad he had planned ahead and bought his own gravesite. They were glad that was in the public section of the city cemetery. It would have been sacrilegious to bury him in the consecrated earth of the Catholic section, what with his being a suicide and all.

Objections welled up inside me. Hadn't Graham Greene already discussed this situation with Major Scobie's death? Hadn't any one ever mentioned this? Hadn't Charles Lee always led a good life? Hadn't we always thought he was a good man? How could one last desperate act erase all of that? My aunt and uncle—his brother and sister—would not be convinced. I don't believe they ever heard of Graham Greene.

I hope they have changed their minds, but it would be a hard thing for them to do. Their father, my grandfather, came from Central Kentucky where Welsh Catholics settled in the late 1790's and early 1800's. Theirs was a harsh, demanding view of God's law, combining the discipline of too much rhetoric with a habit of blind acceptance and more than a little superstition.

And what became of the old service revolver they turned over to Charles Smith after the funeral? A couple of years after his dad's funeral Charles Smith went outdoors and shot himself through the head, just like his father did.

I've lost contact with my cousin's wife. Some of the family say she moved back to England. I don't think so. They fought battles over there, and I think she wanted to get away from war. And the guns. And the killing.

A NOTION OF OLIVES

In Arles in the midst of Provence, where the autumn sun is generous and one dusty tourist is all too much like any other, it is only the arrangement of the arms and legs that distinguishes the native French youngster from the American I was noticing as I sat at a tiny table outdoors on paving stones laid by Caesar's engineers and rolled a sturdy wineglass against my lower lip in the afternoon sun reflected off what was left of the nearly pre-Christian coliseum.

French teens at a cafe table, I remember thinking, lean into one another, shoulders touching, elbows scrunched in, foreheads scant inches apart, as if after exchanging three- and four-cheek kisses blown past their ears there is nothing left to do but dive immediately into conspiratorial laughter, with much quick looking to right and to left. American teens, on the other hand, I thought, swinging my eyes about the open space that was neither courtyard nor street but simply a paved area like a cicular plaza completely surrounding the ancient walls, sit not with their shoulders but with their legs. American youngsters are all hips and sprawls, feet thrust out not below the table but beyond so that their owners must call loudly back and forth to one another to keep themselves bound into the same conversation.

Beyond that there is no difference. Many of the Americans have the same dark hair and eyes, the Gallic nose and the abbreviated stature of the French youngster, expansion going immediately to the hip and chest in the female, if somewhat more belatedly, but measured only in months, by those nurtured on the American side of the Atlantic.

If you think I was attending closely to the young people about me on this plaza on this warm and dusty afternoon where all about me was shades of yellow and tending to the reddish browns without intermediate orange colors you were right, but in my defense I could say that it was necessary to avoid falling asleep and risk having my bicycle stolen.

Cafe waiters all over France have a southern Mediterranean way of drifting off after bringing out a medium glass of red. The gay, noisome ways of the local and visiting youngsters about me would have soon dragged in the familiar and not unwelcome mix of melancholy loneliness and nostalgia for missed opportunities that I usually feel in such surroundings had I not been joined by someone about my age in a once-white shirt, opened at the chest, smelling in that French way of impartial bathing and wearing that inexplicable two days' growth of beard.

"Hope you don't mind," he said in what, to my amazement, was a mid-western American English. Seeing that he had brought a nearly full glass with him, I answered not at all, okay, or something to that effect. I was reluctant to come fully awake just yet. I raised my eyes in his general direction but looked past him at a table of three American teens. One of the boys had tipped back his chair and I wondered if the twisted wire legs would support him. They did.

"Seeing those kids make me think," he said, wiping one hand circularly over his other wrist, "about me when I was a kid. I'm from American, you know."

I nodded, as if surprised, without taking my eyes off the kids.

SOUTHERN GIRL

You are a southern girl and you are in a light dress that wrinkles, sitting in the porch swing, with rumples of the skirt puffing through the slats, looking out at the dust rising on the road, and moving your bare feet, hardened but still sensitive, back and forth across the boards of the porch, feeling out their roughness and tracing the cracks between them.

You are thinking distractedly of two book reviews you have due, but you dislike mental work so you are waiting till you have the pencil in your hand at the kitchen table to decide what you will say.

The dust on the road is more interesting to you. A car has just passed. Another is sure to come. You are between boy friends, and there are warm feelings of anticipation just below the surface of your skin, as your thoughts go from possibility to possibility. At this point in life no one breaks up without a pretty good guess about whom she's going with next, and you can do better than guess. In fact, if your interest hadn't long since strayed, you'd not be changing. Still, things with the new boy are not so far along that something new and better might not come along. That is why you watch the road.

STUD

Some boys are not meant to be studs. The year I discovered girls I was struck down with rheumatic fever, which I've always taken to be retribution for my wickedness. It was also an opportunity for everyone around me and all of their friends and people their friends had heard about, to grow in sanctity. As I sank they rose, which is an example of the social version of physics' Second Law of Thermodynamics.

THANKSGIVING
VALEDICTORY

That year we sailed to the Bahamas from Fort Lauderdale and made landfall at Nassau with a minimum of destruction and loss of life. After clearing in we crossed the Yellow Bank in water so clear we could see the coral heads and starfish that swept beneath our hull. We dropped anchor at the northern end of Eleuthera, at Spanish Wells, a refuge and an enclave of whites who had fled the United States after one of our wars, I don't remember which, maybe the Revolutionary, maybe the Civil—it doesn't matter.

Shunning black society, they had intermarried and were inbred. I know something about inbreeding. I danced once with a girl from an inbred country town in Kentucky and I can still feel the touch of six fingers in my hand.

This time in Eleuthera, when we dinghied ashore looking for adventure, we found the locals suspicious in their houses, watching with unwelcome eyes from behind their sun-washed shutters. We adults were the sole patrons of the only bar in town, and the bartender served us grudgingly.

Outside a commotion of powerful motors showed us what the young people of Spanish Wells do for recreation. Two boys were racing. One had the shore to himself, tearing down Front Street on a motorbike, roaring along the docks and scaring the chickens. He checked himself at the far end with his heel and spun the bike around for the thundering flight back again. His opponent was only a few feet away from him, but on the water. This kid drove an open cockpit speedboat the length of the harbor, matching the biker mile for mile, his broad wake spreading across the placid water, bouncing moored vessels around like cornstalks in a cattle stampede. At both ends of the harbor he spun his boat so fast that he crossed his wakes before they caught him. When he throttled ahead his bow came up in his face. No way he could see where he was going. I was glad we were anchored out of harm's way around the bend and not sorry, when my beer was finished, to leave the town to itself and the sociologists.

The British have a way of leaving topsy turvey traditions in the countries they abandon. This was holiday season. The Bahamas are low lying islands, hardly more than sand-covered coral mounds rising above shallow banks that are themselves the tops of flattened undersea mountains. Any visible evidence of celebration could be shared with watchers from all the neighboring towns, but such was not the British legacy. Bahamians celebrate with noise. We ill-advisedly leapt at the opportunity to tie up free to a dock further down the island chain in a place cut out of coral rock, called Governor's Cut. How wonderful we thought, to actually be secure from the weather and snug alongside a stable landmass where we were within, not dinghying distance but, merely walking distance of an actual ice cream counter.

Foolish dreamers. That night we got no sleep at all. Junkanoo is an all night celebration that, in the absence of trained musicians, consists of troupes of small children who should have been in bed, running up and down the sandy streets rattling cans filled with rocks.

Next morning, bleary eyed and shaken, we presented ourselves and our teenagers at the dockside stand for some real ice cream. On Eleuthera as it turns out, all milk-based dishes are made from powdered milk and they taste like it. The milk produced by the Bahama Islands' large dairy herds on Andros island is delivered daily to better paying markets in the States.

Marsh Harbor, we decided, would be the right place for us and the kids to celebrate Thanksgiving, Carol being determined to serve a genuine Thanksgiving turkey dinner with all the trimmings aboard *Carioca*. Marsh Harbor is a fishing resort—a concept that to me is an oxymoron, but I will not pursue that issue here—owned by the Saudis who, regardless of how you feel about their politics, cannot fail to be admired. For their money.

At Thanksgiving time we were the only boat in the harbor, the sports fishermen having gone home to give thanks for, presumably, not having to be out fishing. The harbor master was very gracious, I think because we were the only people he had to talk to, television reception not being all that great ninety miles from the Nassau transmitter. He allowed us to borrow the resort's guest vehicle, a golf cart.

Carol Ann set off bravely at the controls of the golf cart, taking along one of the girls to help carry back all their goodies. There was even going to be a cake if she could find a bakery. By her side on the seat was her weapon of choice for bagging the best turkey, the one bird that would be exactly right for us. She took the only weapon that really mattered—a ruler.

An oven aboard a cruising sailboat is an afterthought, something no self respecting maritime architects would ever expect you to use. Consequently they make it as small as possible and tuck it away in the most inaccessible spot in the galley. Baking or roasting in a four foot by four foot galley is such an intense and intimate experience that the memory of it tends to linger with you about twenty-five years. That's how long we've resisted a repeat performance.

I will spare you the details except to say that, on a boat, if you hold off teenagers long enough they will eat anything. Frozen vegetables thaw extremely well on a vessel at sea and we were assured by both members of the scavenging expedition that the cake had not been dropped more than once on its top.

A closing word about crew, of whom I have made an exhausting study. On this trip we took the aforementioned teenagers, four of them I believe, and Danny who was an infant at the time. The teenagers rotated Danny duty—with exquisite sullenness. I say exquisite because I now realize after all these years that sullenness is not an innate quality of teenager-dom. Rather it is a weapon they employ for protection against the terrifying enthusiasms of wild eyed adults who tend to spring upon them out of the bushes and recommend things, such as work for instance, that may do them actual bodily injury, like building muscles or waking up.

This holiday trip we betook ourselves and our crew to a delayed Junkanoo celebration in Nassau, the logisitics of which—what with anchoring way, way out, and dinghying into town in the dark, having no transport at our disposal at any time that would hold all of us in one trip—I will also spare you. Once again the teenagers were rotating Danny duty and all were equally unhappy, including Danny.

What with the noise and the distractions of the street lights, the fireworks, the competing bands, the soldiers and quasi-soldiers in various uniforms and the citizens in various costumes that all seemed to feature varying amounts of straw appearing from within or without random body parts I must have lost track of my niece Tracy. Sometime long after midnight or one AM she appeared with a handsome young man she was understandably attracted to. In addition to having movie star features and being about her height he had one of those remarkable skin tones that would have allowed him to pass for white in a white community or for black in the Bahamas. Altogether a fine choice.

She announced he was going to walk her "back to the boat." Considering that he would have had to walk on water to pull it off and disinclined to attempt to work out, in my current state of desperation, any of the alternative logistics, I nixed the whole idea. I told him, "Tracy is with us." She gave me a look. He went off into the crowd. We never saw him again.

Tracy to this day reminds me that I ruined her life that night. I don't know how you go about ruining somebody's life, or if I did. After high school she became a beautician and married a local policeman, a parentless bachelor about ten years her senior, to whom she gave a bulletproof vest on their anniversary. She now has two boys in college. She and Robert are divorced. He remarried within a few months. She is the head youth minister in their church.

There is a moral here somewhere. I think it goes something like this, "Use a smaller ruler, or get a bigger boat."

COME MY LOVE, LET
US GO TO TOWN

Mary Frances Cunningham was a woman with a proper sense of time. She knew when there were bushels enough of ripe tomatoes to can. She knew how long salted meat would keep in the smokehouse. She knew when persimmons could be baked into a pie without puckering your mouth and she knew when June apples could be picked and eaten with salt and not give you the runs. She knew when her pains came close enough and when to send for the midwife and she knew when her daughters' pains were close enough and she delivered her own grandchildren when the midwives couldn't come because the mud was deep and the roads were slow. When Mary Frances said the time had come to move to town, her husband Hershell Ray lowered his head and said "All right."

After dinner he walked out to the stable and stood for a long time looking at the Belgians he boarded for Old Man White down the road. Hershell Ray had a skinny neck, deep red brown, like old rust, and a big adam's apple that jerked up and down like a bobber on a fishing line at times of extreme agitation, like now, out by the stable.

"Your father is slowing down," he had heard Mary Frances say to the children. "He's put out less than twenty acres of corn this year. Doesn't use the tractor any more. Just follows that old mule Feisty and that rastus plow round the kitchen garden. Only one milk cow left now. What's a man like him to do all day?"

Sure Hershell Ray hadn't used the tractor this year. His son Bob had driven the tractor over to his place in the spring and told his dad if you wouldn't put out so much corn this year you could use Old Man White's Belgians for plowing. Those horses need the exercise. They'll do fine for twenty acres of corn.

When it came to his garden though, Hershell was partial to old Feisty and the rastus plow. No tractor could plow as straight or as deep, besides you couldn't get a big tractor into the kitchen garden and he'd have had to pay anybody else to come in with a mule. And he had owned Feisty for almost thirty years. When he would come into the barn she would lunge stiff legged toward the stall door, and thrust out her head, lean and rangy as ever, but greying around the eyes and ears. She was a model animal. He could even skip a day feeding or watering her and she'd never raise a fuss. Not like those Belgians. Seven feet tall at the withers, but you really had to baby them. They had to be fed just so much or they would overeat, watered just so much or they would sicken, and you had to rest them every so many furrows. Old Feisty you could plow all morning, let her stand in the shade while you ate lunch, hitch her up again and go all evening.

Hershell Ray Cunningham stood in the afternoon sun thinking about the Belgians. Fine looking draft horses. Matched pair. Old Man White claimed he'd have them in the county fair next fall. If so, Hershell would like to be there to see them. He'd grown partial to the Belgians. He had to stretch up to rub their noses. Old Bob and Old Will, he'd been calling them, after his eldest sons. Seemed sometimes like he knew these Belgians better than he knew his own children.

Looking back on it he felt his woman had been after him all summer. He shouldn't be climbing around on the barn worrying about the roof, she had said. Why wouldn't he call one of the boys to help him load the beef cattle? Come out the middle of the morning to see how he did, suckering tobacco. Hard work, yes, and hot, but he'd taken his ice water out with him into the fields every day every summer since they had first electrified and got a Frigidaire that made ice. Must be she had been studying about moving into town for a long time. Couldn't get her to go a' fishing all summer long.

Well, moving to town mightn't be so bad. Old Man Sethridge had moved to town right about the time the mayor had the hitch rack torn down. Guess Old Man Sethridge's woman had gotten on to him, too.

Hershell expected he'd have his hands full fixing up for his own woman. Maybe he and Mary Frances would look for a house close to the Sethridges. Old Man Sethridge had been a good farmer. Have to find out where they had bought. Maybe Bob or Will would know.

Hershell Ray and Mary Frances Cunningham found a place, little white frame two bedroom house on the corner of Jefferson and McCandress. Three blocks from the courthouse and three blocks over a low hill from Bootsville—Niggertown they'd called it in their courting days. Two bedrooms was all they needed. A bedroom for themselves and a guest room for when the children came. Mary Frances asked her husband to build her a sun room off the dining room where she could put her sewing machine and where she could have her african violets

Don't know what she sees in them little purple flowers, he told all his children, seems like she cares more about them than she does about me and Scooter. Scooter was his hunting dog that there was no room for in town, so after the first week Scooter got left with Will and Bessie.

The dining room was small, half the size of their dining room on the farm. But we'll eat at the kitchen table, just the two of us, she said. A metal table, enamel finish, cold to the touch of a morning, even when the weather was warm. There toward the end, back on the farm, she reminded him, you and I taken to closing off the dining room and eating off the wash stand. That had been her idea, to save on heat and what with the children all gone, why go to all the trouble to set a big table?

Two bedrooms plus a rollaway bed in the new sunroom for when the children came. All the children did come the first Thanksgiving in the new house. They overflowed the dining room and had a card table set up in the sunroom for the grandchildren. The mothers hollered at them out in the backyard to go find something to do and stay out of the street. Back on the farm the kids had never lacked for something to do. No cars ever drove past their farm. Anybody came your way in a car was coming to see you, and you could generally see their dust coming a mile away.

Maybe he had built the sunroom too small. The foldaway bed took up a lot of the space, and after Mary Frances visited her old farm friends who had moved to town ahead of her she lost interest in sewing with her treadle machine. Said Miz Marshall's electric sewing machine made more sense. He offered to buy her a new one, a White's or a Singer's, maybe, like her old one, only electric. But she said no it was a shame to throw out a perfectly good sewing machine so they left the machine where it was up against the white wainscoting, under six african violets with doilies.

Houses in town run small, she had told him when they first went looking. They had given away pickup trucks full of furniture and things in boxes to the children, and still they were crowded up inside the walls of their new home. The big divan wouldn't fit in the living room, so they gave it to Bob's wife and used the love seat instead. Some of the overstuffed chairs had to go, and his old reading lamp. There wasn't room enough on the floor. One good thing, he could get up on the coldest mornings and walk barefoot to the kitchen, they had piled up rugs two and three deep over the hardwood floors in every room. Some were big rugs, others small, almost all of them she had hooked by hand while the children did their homework on the big dining room table, first by coal oil lantern, then after REA, by a hundred watt bare bulb hanging from the ceiling.

Somehow town didn't seem as cold as a farm in the winter. Mary Frances gave away their feather blankets. The old feather bed they had bought for their honeymoon had a headboard two and a half feet too tall to stand upright in their new front bedroom, and she had given it away to Bob and Frannie. She had kept the dresser that matched. "You can't find marble top dressers anywhere anymore," she had said. She gave up the feather blankets but she kept the blankets she had quilted on the frame that had been suspended so many years from the ceiling in their parlor. "We never used that old parlor," she told him, but he had remembered her and the girls lowering the half finished quilts from the ceiling and inviting other women over for the evening, while the men sat out on the porch and smoked.

He wasn't allowed to smoke in the new house and nobody ever came to sit on the porch though they had kept back three porch chairs and a porch swing. He had instead found Old Man Sethridge in a group of other ex-farmers down town on the Courthouse lawn, sitting on benches, chewing and spitting in the sun. He took up whittling, like some of the others. There were grins and nods in the mornings when he joined them, all the men glad to get out of their houses.

Old men, all of them, loose skin burned dark by years in the sun. Hunched over whittling, clean coveralls now too large and baggy for their thinning bodies, chins swinging aside now and again to spit.

Skinny old ladies walked by in twos and threes, going shopping up the street. Big-knuckled hands locked on clasp purses—'widder women' whose husbands had passed away, leaving them to clean house alone and cook alone and deal with making beds alone and dusting alone and seeing to the stove in winter alone. Keeping house all alone, just like they had done it on the farm. Old skinny women who enjoyed each other's company and never ran out of things to talk about, and walked past the silent men who looked up and nodded. Some of the women they recognized from days of farming and church suppers and county fairs.

In the second summer after moving to town Hershell Ray Cunningham got up from his place by the Courthouse steps, put in his pocket a hickory mule he was carving for his grandson, Tommy Dean, spit out his tobacco into the stone urn that held sand and cigarette butts, said "Gentlemen" to the men he had helped plow as they had helped him, men he had swapped knives with and traded horses with, men he had hunted with as boys, old men he had chivarreed as young men, men he had bought land from and sold land to, men whose hay he had cut, and calves he had helped wean, men he had wrestled with under the oaks on the banks of his own father's fishing creek, men who had won blue ribbons against him at county fairs, men whose sisters he had courted, men whose mothers had baked him blackberry pies when he'd come to spend the night and go a' dancing by wagon, men whose hard spined mules he had ridden in the heat of summer out into pasture ponds warm as fresh milk. Told them all good bye, walked north and west toward the corner house that he had continued to call the new place, tottered backward before he had quite gotten out of sight, suffered a stroke and died right there on the street.

In a few days, after the funeral attended by old friends and their wives, and by all Hershell Ray Cunningham's children and grandchildren and his one surviving sister, from which they had taken his body back to the country church and the graveyard where his parents were buried and their second child April Ann, and after Mary Frances had given away all his old clothes to the Baptist church in Bootsville, and the boys had divided up the tools and knives, and the shotgun she had let him keep in town, and while she was at it gave away some more of the furniture she had had to walk around to get from room to room, including his old overstuffed chair, and had taken the new reading lamp over to a spot near her rocker and the radio at the window from where she could watch for the postman and the delivery boy, and had stopped delivery on the seed catalogs that still came to the house, and after she set out new cuttings of african violets and gotten her son Will to put insulating tape around the door to the spare bedroom that it seemed they never used and had arranged her work routine so that she could see out the front windows and the side windows to the streets from wherever she was in the house, Mary Frances Cunningham took to going to town, walking past the old men sitting in the courthouse sun, and nodding primly, and making small purchases in modest packages that she could carry with one hand, sometimes twice a day, and always found another skinny old woman like herself to put on a bonnet and join her, and after she had a telephone put in she called at least one child or grandchild every day, she was very happy.

FAITH OF THEIR MOTHERS

A Novelette

Chapter 1

Return To Sender

For Her second coming, being a black Korean had its drawbacks, as Li Cho confessed to Her heavenly father, but only in Her private prayers, the ones where She wrestled with despair and fought the temptations of Her flesh.

By Her friends and followers She was called Jesus Christ Herself, and Li was no stranger to disadvantage. Her mother was black, possessed of the most velvety coal black skin it had been Her privilege to see in all Her short life. Even now, at a time when She allowed himself few pleasures of the body, She loved to remember the touch of Her mother's skin, rich and deep to the touch, and the way the light, all kinds of light caressed her skin and fired it here and there with the inner glimmers of a thousand faceted diamonds the color of nighttime's silkened inside. Her mother had been blackest black before the West Coast discovered the luxuriousness of deep royal black. Her mother's disadvantage came from getting born and being beautiful in a town where beauty belonged to the whites and power, through wealth, to the Orientals.

Her father's disadvantage came from being Korean poor in a town where Oriental rich meant Japanese first, Chinese second and Korean last, then being among the most destitute of Koreans. Customarily Koreans in towns other than San Francisco found other Koreans who helped them get started in business and helped them to work hard, and helped them to become affluent. Upon arrival in the States Mr. Cho had experienced no difficulty in connecting up with the local hard working, upwardly mobile Korean citizens, but Kim Cho's particular disadvantage derived in part from a distinct but uncharacteristic disinclination for hard work. His life was further disadvantaged by an early infatuation with an especially lovely woman whose eyes and teeth and nails and palms flashed white out of an opiate of darkness so complete that only the boldest most sumptuous delicious highlights of the moon could reveal her nighttime form, a woman the smell of whose skin bestowed upon him an ecstasy too intense for his modest years to accommodate without doing serious damage to his soul.

From these improbable beginnings it may have been supposed that Li Cho, with Her dark skin too light to share in the glory of her mother's and Her slant eyes too round to belong to her father, might have missed the message from God that She was His only son returned to earth except for certain extremely significant signs that Li observed shortly after She was old enough to study religion. First, there was the matter of Her virgin birth. She emerged into womanhood relatively untutored in the mechanics of procreation, confident in the assurances of her mother that Kim Cho had never really touched her.

Second, there was the testimony of her very own grandmother, who, upon first meeting her granddaughter, looked squarely down at the child then about eight years old, and emphatically pronounced her true name in the hearing of all present, "Jesus Christ!"

Whatever the physical relationship between Her parents it was clear to all that they truly loved Her, and they early showed their love by taking the most profound care to guarantee the success of Her education and removing all secular and familial distractions that might have interfered with Her learning and depositing Her, wide eyed and not a little uneasy, into the solicitudes, ministrations, devotions and aspirations of the Sisters of St. Euphrasia's as a promising, by dint of being as yet unformed, young boarder.

All the tender females attending St. Euphrasia's were encouraged in piety and personal devotion, those who were boarding being among the most consistently exemplary. Li Cho was enthusiastically reminded that the most devout of God's children made profitable use of their free time through such pursuits as exploring the writings of the commentators, and She, being a boarder unburdened by over-frequent parental visits, had an unusual amount of free time for a young lady, and was particularly and irresistibly drawn to reading about and meditating on the parallel years of Her first coming, and the doings of the young Jesus in the temple and in His earthly father's carpenter shop.

Youthful, tentative experiments had convinced Her quite soon of two things. First, regardless of the radiance She felt about Her, most of those in whose company she dwelt, adult or child, religious or secular alike, were insensitive to, or deliberately chose to ignore, Her true nature. Whether charmed or intimidated by the earthly vision she offered of mahogany skin with, in certain lights, its ebony-violet accents, delicate features with high cheekbones and large, liquid brown eyes with their dramatic slant, packaged in the year-round First Communion uniform of good St. Euphrasia's, the effect was the same. They were unable to see beyond Her material presence to the glorious golden soul with its powerful demanding throb that She alone could not ignore.

The second thing She knew, through long and tearful solitary praying in the shadows of the remotest pews in the Common Chapel, was that, due to the state of the world and the many demi-miraculous accomplishments of Mammon himself, when it came time She would have to go out and repeat, oh dread of dreads, Her earlier public ministry. It need not have been this way if mankind had heeded Her message the first time. But they hadn't and, greatest of the prophets as assured by the scriptures She already was, She would just have to do it again. But not until time. She could not wait to enter into adulthood as She had before. But She would wait and study, and be ready.

Meanwhile She looked about Her for disciples, as She had the first time. Quiet, and gifted, even as a small child, with a steady rich voice and able to speak whole chapters with Her vulpine eyes, She never lacked for followers. Some, especially among the "day trippers" were enchanted with Her and often brought Her treasures from home, like compacts into which She looked searchingly for absent signs of vanity, and cookies which She blessed, to their intense excitement, charging them to tell no one. Few were able to bear the weight of such charges as She commissioned them over the years, so that She had almost no friends that actually stayed with Her from year to year.

One only, a skinny anemic girl, with pink toes, translucent skin and long straight yellow streaked hair that fell beneath her waist and caught at her knees when they crawled up under the nuns' big desks to tell secrets, this one only stayed with Her from year to year. This first grader who remained loyal to Li Cho through adolescence and into young womanhood, was in fact the first to conceive the idea of beginning a missionary ministry in some backward state, like in the South, Kentucky, for example, where actually her parents were from, and where she had summered and experienced more of the world perhaps than she was immediately prepared to share unreservedly with Li Cho. Here they would go, and she would find a place and arrange for them to survive, and Li Cho could begin Her ministry. This girl, this young woman, with insatiable energy and countless enthusiasms and possessed of resourcefulnesses Li Cho had never exhausted, this young woman, who was christened Alouette Lueva Settlesquire, Li Cho renamed—one day before graduation while packing twelve years of boarding school notes, holy cards, skirts, shoes and bracelets—Pauline.

Besides Pauline there were, for Her, in the auditorium on graduation day several nuns of St. Euphrasia's, who had emerged uncertainly from retirement and among whom Her catechism teachers were most prominent, bringing Her to rare stinging tears in the aisle, and two others, Her mother and Her father whom She did not fail to recognize, from their casual attendance at occasional vacations and by dint of their material contribution to Her education through the upbringing they had purchased for Her out of their own reserves for which She would prayed She would be properly grateful.

Chapter 2

She Smiled, She Smiled, She Smiled So Sweet

Some women mother easy. Some mother hard. For Nellie Alice Gepner mothering was the most worrisome, exhaust-some, up-all-night-foreversome, suffocate-some, lose-yourself-and-drown-and-never-come-up-some experience ever visited on mortal soul. And with the last one grown up and gone off and grandchildren in school and rightly some one else's worry—though young parents today are foolish and neglectful—and sitting at last on her solitary front porch, looking eagerly ahead to a hymnally-betokened twilight of golden contemplation—maybe she would go away to a church meeting, like some had been heard to do—she felt her mothering years loom up behind her like a bottomland thicket that eye could not penetrate nor sickle cleave.

No light shone through that thicket from her past, seemed like. As if her mothering had been all there was to her life and nothing earlier had ever happened. As if there had been no girlhood for her, no barefoot years in the dust below the catalpa trees. No years of crocheting or needlepoint for herself, no laying up for her hope chest, no play parties, no dress up, no cutting out from catalogs, no riding hogs, no mean streak cussedness and blame the boys for it. Such of that as she might remember were, if old fashioned, probably tales from her own mother's childhood, or, if framed in modern clothes and heard to modern tunes, something fleeting glimpsed from the window at her own children who at least had had real, palpable childhoods, that she might only envy.

For her there had been no youthful times that she could remember. No sleep overs, no visiting, no potlucks, no Sunday School meetings, no dating, no hay rides, no sisters baking cookies, no strangers come to the door a-begging or a-selling. No younger, shorter days.

Particularly there had been no twelve year old hot summer, the hottest ever heard of, when she and Henry went down to the hog pond. There had been no commotion over at the tobacco barn, old peeling red barn, with slat sides open vertical to air the strong damp leaves of burley. There had been no disappearance, no Night Riders, no moon shine, no brother come home from the war mean and crazy. Nothing had ever come out of Black Bottom or Bootsville, and by God she had learned everything she knew from the women in her own family, all respectable, all white, all god fearing Christian ladies.

In a way she was glad of the thicket that grew up in her mind, the brush and brackle she had no hope of ever cutting through or will to penetrate. Glad of it.

And that was the way it s'posed to be, looking into the sunset. The sunset coming. Just like the hymn book says. She was going to have a sunset, going home to Beulah Land.

But sometimes late of an evening, the sun taken too long to set, the quiet more than it ought to be, no cars passing, a fly maybe settling, no wasp sailing by, its long keel dragging in its own breeze, honeysuckle faint out by the fence, smell getting stronger warming up, sometimes like that seemed like maybe she *had* had a childhood. Maybe some things had happened. Wished her mama was still living and they'd set, of an evening, the dishes done and the supper covered against the flies, preserved soft and sweet memories on sticky glass stands, times when she would hear her mother take the dipper and scrape it against the bucket, take a drink, fling the leavings in the garden, gently pull the screen door to, bring a sack of green beans out to snap and they would sit, and Nellie Alice would ask her. Ask her when talk was slow, and the bustle of getting settled and light talking was over, and your eyes wandered out to the road and looked over the fields across there, where maybe a deer or two came out anxious, hungry and watchful, belly high in the corn.

This evening one car slowed up approaching her place. It's a wonder, she thought, they're going to stop. The car turned in, coming slowly over the bump at the ditch where her grass covered the driveway with its own faint twin depressions where occasional tires left memories.

The car had State Police markings, and there was a straightness about the grey uniformed driver, the way he had of sitting right up at the wheel, and there was a formality, too, about the passenger side man in a brown business suit. The windows were rolled down. The ride hadn't been too dusty, this time of year, must be.

She sat silently on her front porch, her swing come to a halt. She saw the two men get out, nodded gravely in response to the driver-trooper's wave, turned her speculations on the passenger. She watched as the two men stepped considerately around her marigold beds and planted their footsteps responsibly in the centers of the nearly overgrown flagstones leading up from the grassy ruts where their car's wheels rested.

The neat, official look of the trooper's uniform, the way he carried his hat in his left hand, leaving his right free and near his gun, the way his passenger hung back a little, the angle of view she had on them from up four steps on the porch, and the small wooden porch itself, with no railing was almost identical to the way it was when as a young mother she had sat over the body of a young man she had never met, a young man whose friends or murderers out of respect or fear or daring, had thrown his corpse onto her front porch some time during the night and left it for her to find next morning. To find, to go white with horror, to run to the phone and dial her husband's emergency number with hands shaking so badly she could barely force the fingers to turn the rotary full around, then, still trembling, gone back to the porch to sit in the only bright light she could find in the early morning shadows of the deep hollow where their trailer stood, and wait for the state trooper, her own newly commissioned husband, and the medical examiner. Sit and wait, her and the corpse in this lonely god-forsaken part of this hill country where your neighbors' secretive ways, living bleak and peculiar in their own solitary, remote hollows, included leaving a corpse for you to find in the morning, so frightened you sat out in the early morning sunshine in your nightdress with a pullover, sat with a dead stranger, ears straining for your babies who might wake up at any moment. Babies you had been too screaming inside your own head to think about checking on scurrying out of your own dark rooms to get into the light, the only light around, and right beside a stranger's dead body.

And now it was another day, and someone else's husband was the state trooper in his grey trim uniform with the wide brimmed hat and the tight pants and a civilian in tow walking up to her porch. He set a foot on her lowest step, the loose one, felt the give to the boards and hiked his leg up to rest his boot on the second step, the solid step. One more step and he would be on her porch, but his mother must have raised him right. He didn't presume to her front porch, not till invited.

"Hi-dee," he said. She nodded again, solemn. Looked from the trooper to the civilian. Light weight brown suit, red and black striped tie. He looked back at her. Not from around here. His mother would have taught him more polite.

"I'm Private Barnes, ma'am," he said, "I was here last fall?" The question meant did she remember. Not likely she would forget.

"I remember ye." She held her chin steady. Don't offer too much encouragement to the Law. You don't remind them they're servants of the people, they start acting uppity.

"This is Detective Hansacker, Ma'am. From Frankfort."

"From Frankfort?" She meant what was so special about his credentials, but the civilian mistook her.

"The state capital, ma'am," said the civilian, in a reedy impatient voice.

The state trooper, who had understood her question, said quickly, "He's our best man, Miz Gepner, we only bring him out from Frankfort when we need special help."

She was silent for a minute, watching the civilian to see if he had caught on yet. What was so special about him? Couldn't talk respectful to a lady. She smoothed the wrinkles of the dress fabric across her knees. He had caught on that he had blundered, but hadn't caught on to how, and foolishly he leapt ahead, hoping to overcome the link between woman and trooper, to somehow take charge.

"Ma'am, it's about that problem last fall," he said. Another mistake. He had used an official sounding tone, the kind you would use down at the jail if they had brought you in, not the way you'd speak to a woman on her own front porch. She wished she could meet his mother. See what kind of a woman had raised him. How she could have gone wrong. Probably one of those hippie hyper women, let your children do as they please.

"What's over is past history," she said, setting her jaw.

"Ma'am," the trooper came in. Save his friend, she thought. "The State doesn't look at it that way. May have been a crime committed. 'T may *be* some guilty party needs apprehendin'."

"Waste of time and taxpayers' money," she said, jaw muscles flexing. "Ought to let people rest in peace."

"We'd have to go out there anyway," he continued in a respectful tone, "but it being your daddy's place, well, yours now, we'd rather you went with us. If you could spare us the time, Ma'am." He looked straight into her eyes, standing half on her steps and half in her yard, just below her eye level. Looked straight at her face, avoiding looking at her work, avoiding let on he knew she had nothing more to do than to snap beans, and widowed with grown children, no one to look after but herself, and from the grass grown up in her driveway ruts, no body come recently and no car in the driveway to take her some where. No, she was free to go, but he was raised right and didn't throw it up to her by looking at her work.

"I'll take you out there," she said. "Don't want strangers tramping around the place, tearing up my daddy's farm and leaving all the gates open." She looked down at her lap, the brown paper bag with its curled and wrinkled collar turned under, and the beans half finished. "Have to set this aside. A pore old woman. Think they'd leave a body alone."

She gathered up her apron full of hulls held by a fistful of fabric, set the paper sack in the pan, on top of the good beans and stood up. The trooper instinctively reached out to take something. "I can manage just fine, young man. You wait right here. I'm going to have to call my daughter. She'll have a fit if she calls and I ain't to home."

She heard her voice dropping into country talk and wondered at it. Must be all that remembering about the home place, she thought.

They put her in the front seat. The trooper made such a fuss about the seat belt till she put it on just to please him. Front seat. Made her feel like somebody's grandmother. Only person you ever put in the front seat was the elderly or the infirm, and she wasn't either one. When her husband was alive the men always sat up front and the women took the back seat. Women could visit and there would be children to look after back there. You sat in the back. If you weren't elderly or couldn't hardly get around.

And why would they come around bothering a poor widow woman, anyway? Any decent people were welcome to go out to her home place any time. Nephews and grandboys used to go out there squirrel hunting and bird hunting all the time. They'd stop by if they shot any thing and tell her about it. If their mamas cooked up squirrel they might send her some over by the children. She liked it when the little ones came by. Kept cookies for them. They'd visit long enough to be polite. No TV to watch, and no youngsters their age to visit, they didn't much stay long. Only ones that'd stay were the girls. About twelve or thirteen they'd start to come over. Wanting time to be out of their mama's house and on their own for a spell, she'd guess. They'd go through her things. Finger her quilts, hold her bonnets up to the mirror or her brooches to the light, draw her hair pins out between the strands of their pigtails and look daydreamy at her walls ...

Chapter 3

Bible Camp

Nellie Alice Gepner rested her arms across the gate of the wooden paddock fence that marked the edge of the clearing and watched the men walk on into the broad grassy area surrounded by the burned and crumbled relics of the little one-room cabins that once made up the real property improvements of Blue Springs Bethany Bible Camp.

The clearing was knee-to-waist high in tasseled grass, Queen Anne's Lace and tall red clover. Up close to the cabins she could see the tall broad-leaved poke weed and she thought of pork chops and poke salut.

What did these men expect to find, wading through the weeds like swimmers in troopers' uniforms and suits? Those cabins still standing were mostly grey-streaked whitewash white with warped and sagging palings. White wash and nails was what they needed. No telling what they were like inside, where the men were looking now, curious as little puppies, tails in the air all aquiver.

Last time she was inside the cabins there had been mattresses on the cots. They would smell of mold now, the bed frames would be rusted, from windows broken open, cabin roofs leaking. She saw the suited man jump back all of a sudden. Something small had leapt out of a building, and by the waving of the grass she could follow its frantic passage to the woods.

The trooper came outside and spoke to the suited man then led him off to one of the burned out cabins. A few round headed, blackened palings marked the edges of a pile of ashes and debris, fixed somehow to the stubs of what was left of the framing.

The trooper nudged at the soft charcoal rubble with the stiff toe of his official state boot. What did they hope to find?

The nearest cabin was some distance away from where she was leaning, chin buried in her arms. A warm breeze swept the hem of her dress and cooled the backs of her knees. It lifted the tight curls of her short hair and brought a quick thrill to the back of her neck, then the sun's warmth came through, and felt all soft and welcome behind her.

The nearest cabin was the first of a row that led away from where she lingered and joined another row of cabins at right angles, together making the shape of a letter L. That's all the cabins there were. Each of those standing had a simple pitched roof, a window on each of two sides, and a tiny front porch where bible campers could say good night without going inside.

To her right, and opposite the first row of cabins was a larger building, long, with thin, rectangular windows like a church that couldn't afford arches, and a wide front porch. That was the meeting house for when it was too rainy to gather outside, and where the Bible Camp people had eaten their meals, and where the children had taken their naps with all the windows opened on hot suffocating days. In back was the kitchen where Vangie Mae had worked the summer Nellie Alice met Miz Jesus.

Chapter 4

Rock of Ages

Vangie Mae was the daughter of Aunt Sally, back in a time that Nellie Alice missed now very much, a time when all the older black women you lived around were "Aunt" somebody, and their husbands were "Uncle" somebody else, and all older white cousins were Uncle and Aunt to little children. Nellie Alice never knew whether Aunt Sally could read, but of a Sunday afternoon in a summer when she and Vangie Mae were teenagers, and Nellie Alice was courting age and Vangie Mae had been working in people's houses for a while, if you went by Aunt Sally's you'd see her sitting in her porch swing and fanning with a magazine. Vangie Mae's name had Evangeline in it, and that came from the magazines that maybe got read to Aunt Sally or maybe she read herself, but Nellie Alice had never seen her do anything with a magazine but fan it.

People Aunt Sally worked for gave her magazines. What could you do, really, for a woman who could make a lemon meringue pie so sweet you didn't know it had a lemon in it, and a meringue so pretty and so light the angels must have brought it down in their own two hands?

On Sunday afternoons Aunt Sally didn't give you anything to eat, even though you got hungry feelings just being around her. She was big and she was solid. She wore print dresses filled gloriously by breasts resting heavy over her stomach, and she about filled the swing so that only the littlest kids could sit by her, taking turns. And she was always glad to see Nellie Alice.

Sunday mornings, Sunday nights and Wednesday nights Aunt Sally went to church. She sang in the choir, which meant she was up front in the church behind the preacher, but when Aunt Sally took Nellie Alice to Blue Springs Bethany Baptist Church Nellie Alice was made to sit in the pews with Vangie Mae. Really she couldn't tell the difference between the choir in Bethany Baptist and the congregation, because everybody sang and everybody knew the words, and Nellie Alice, who could play the piano, saw the notes on the page and they weren't singing those notes. They were singing a whole lot more notes than there were printed in the book, and they were holding notes that weren't marked hold, and hitting the beat where it wasn't marked and doing it all wrong according to the book, and it was all so fine and happy and big time, and she could see the sweat rolling down Aunt Sally's face from back in her own pew and it was so grand and so glorious, it must been that black Baptists got to heaven different from how white people got there because her own church was nowhere near as much fun and she wished her own mother would never ever make her go to her mother's church again.

And everybody was so nice to her. The preacher would say some time in the service, which went on and on so happily and was mostly singing, "Now let us sisters and brothers, sing a special hymn for a favorite loved one and let some brother speak out or let some sister speak out, let your voice be hear, and tell us all, tell us all, what hymn to the Lord you choose, brother, tell us what hymn-ah sister, what hymn-ah you pick for the glory of the Lord on this day-uh and let us sing that hymn to the Lord on this blessed day, this blessed day, this blessed day of the Lord's." And all around people would be saying "Amen," "Amen, Brother," "Praise the Lord," and "Hallelujah, Brother."

Then the preacher would look at her and Nellie Alice's heart would pound and her throat would close up, and he would say, "Why, Miss Rawlings," for she was still a Rawlings in those days, "Miss Nellie Alice Rawlings, would you tell us what special hymn you want our brothers and sisters to raise their voices and sing to the Lord on this glorious Sunday, this day of the Lord?"

And Nellie Alice would be so happy to be selected and so confused and so afraid, because Bethany Baptist's hymnal was different from hers and she would have liked to ask for "The Old Rugged Cross" which was her grandfather's favorite, but she had never heard Bethany Baptist sing it, and her head would be dizzy and she would barely squeak out her own very personal favorite, "Amazing Grace," and the preacher would grin big with the look that said to her she had picked the easiest singing song of all and no challenge to his congregation, and they would all sing it, even the littlest children from out of their daddy's arms and the music was so strong, and it had such a way of swelling as the voices would slide up all the scale notes heading for the fourths and fifths it was like a gully washer going to lift her up on it and take her clear to heaven.

That was the way Aunt Sally was, always seeing after her, and always doing for her, and there was no way she knew of to pay her back, but when she was grown and set up housekeeping she tried whenever she could to hire Vangie Mae to help out in the kitchen. But Vangie Mae was not like her mother. She didn't appreciate what you did for her. She was thin and drawed up tight where Aunt Sally was loving fat and loose and easy. And, the summer Nellie Alice let Miz Jesus and her people take over the old Bible Camp, Vangie Mae left her without a kiss my foot nor nothing and went off to cook for the Miz Jesus church.

Chapter 5

Wuz Standin' At Her Side

The shame of it all was that it was Vangie Mae was the one introduced Nellie Alice to Miz Jesus. Three summers ago. Or was it four? She straightened up from the gate where she had been leaning, turned her back on the men drifting lazily across the field from the ghost of one cabin to the bones of another. Her own children thought it had been the medicine. Only thing she knew was she was not afraid of them, had never been afraid of them, and after she talked to Miz Jesus, she had gotten used to them and had begun to look forward to their visits and then her children and her doctors had come around meddling and they'd never till yet come back.

Her children grown and gone, and only the grandchildren come over now and then. No one but herself to do after and fix for. She had gone to cooking in little pint sized saucepans. Took her three days to eat a fried chicken. Mess of beans would last her a week. Didn't care for no TV. Doctors had all this medicine they wanted her to take. All a body could do to keep up with it, what time of day you were supposed to take what. It was all a chore just keeping everything straight. All those little bottles looked the same to her except what color the caps were, and she wasn't always sure she got the right colored cap on the right bottle afterwards. Then her company started coming.

Two little girls. Both black. They might have been twins. They were standing by the door, just inside, right there by the dish cabinet when she turned around. Startled her at first. She hadn't seen them come in. One had on a pink pinafore, the other was in shorts and a little tee-shirt with a blue teddy bear stitched onto it. The one in the dress had black patent leather shoes with a single strap and little white socks with ruffled turndown tops, and the one in shorts was bare footed. They were both solemn looking at first. She thought it might have been the smell of chicken frying had drawn them in and she asked if they wanted something to eat. They shook their heads, then grinned real big, but neither of them said a word. By the time she had finished eating they were gone.

Over time she got used to their comings and goings. Sometimes she would find them in the living room. Once they were both barefooted and wearing coveralls, sitting up on the back of her sofa and swinging their feet, looking at her and grinning.

Sometimes they would stay for hours and she forgot about them till they were gone. Sometimes they would come and stare and not smile at all. Sometimes they would follow her from room to room. Other times she would have to go back to the room she had just come from to see why they had stayed behind.

At meal times she always asked them to eat, and they would sometimes come and stand around the table, but they never would eat with her.

Sometimes if she was very busy she would hardly notice their being there, for hours at a time. Then she would find them right where they had last been. Always they would be polite, and always they would mind and get out of her way, if she needed to get where they were, but mostly they stayed in places like corners and beside doorways and around furniture where they were in nobody's way.

Sometimes she could not get them to look at her even when she spoke directly to them and she thought at those times that maybe they had been naughty in the house where they lived and were ashamed.

At different times when her daughters had been over she had pointed them out and each time whichever daughter it was had taken on and raised such a fuss, making out like she couldn't see the little black girls, so that after a while she stopped mentioning them. That was about when her daughters started nagging her then about if she was taking her medicine, and took to getting into her medicine cabinet and making a big show of counting out her pills and writing things down till she wished her daughters would just go home and stay, because the truth of the matter was, the two little girls were a comfort to her and her own daughters had taken to meddling. And after the uproar of her own daughters died down and they forgot all about it the way young people do, with their short memories, she was fine. She was doing fine, even up till when the angel came to church.

Maybe it wasn't an angel but it *was* a person in a white gown and it floated, and it was up there during service, but it was a little higher than everybody else, and everybody pretended not to notice, and nobody said anything, even after church, when they stood around in the heat and sunlight and stood in their Sunday dresses, the sweat running down, and fanning their Montgomery's Funeral Home fans. And she wasn't about to bring it up. If they didn't want to let on there was somebody floating around up there above the preacher she would go along with it, too. But the person had looked at her, and had had long hair, but she didn't know if it was a woman person or a man person or what.

But there was a man came to her house. That's why she told Vangie Mae, and why Vangie May took her to see the Jesus lady.

She had come home from church, it was not the same day she saw the person floating, and she had sat down tired and out of breath to take off her hat and clean off her powder and rouge. Hers was a sit down dresser with a covered bench and a deep, broad mirror that went right down between drawers in rounded arm-like stacks. Her daughters hated this dresser, called it old fashioned and Art Dee-Coe. Some of her things they wanted to get their hands on, like her marble top table stand in the hall, the one with the carved black oak pedestal, but this dresser they despised. She had always told them she felt like a lady sitting down to put on her makeup but they never paid her no never mind about it. Well she would show them. She would leave it to one of the grandbabies. It would serve them right.

She didn't know what got into her daughters sometimes, they were so contrary. Her boys, now they always went along with her, always saw after her when they were around, carried for her and ran errands and drove her places and did all they could till they had to go home, and she would find twenty dollars or something stuffed in her purse later on. But her daughters got bossy as they got older, so she didn't tell them about the man. And she didn't tell her sons either. Him being a black man they'd want to take out after him and run him off. But she needed to tell somebody, so she told Vangie Mae. There was good black people and bad black people, though she didn't herself know any bad black people. But Vangie Mae was a good black woman, even if she did take on airs. Vangie Mae would know who he was, or know what to do about him.

After all, it wasn't like he come around after dark or done anything scary. That first time Nellie Alice saw him he was standing in the dark corner of her bedroom, there where the light shines through the window at you of a morning and you can't see past it till the sun is way up. He wore unionalls like he worked for the railroad and he wiped his head with a red handkerchief the way railroad men do, and he looked at her kindly hard, harder than the little girls ever did. So she asked him if he'd come looking for the two little girls, but he never answered her, just stood there looking at her. She'd felt her eyes on her when she turned around to clean off her face some more, so she just spoke right up and asked him to leave, and he had left.

What bothered her about it later was that he didn't just go out of the room the way the little girls would, following her. It was just one minute he was there and the next minute when she looked over that way he wasn't there. Nothing there but a pair of her husband's old boots she had kept around for working in the garden. She took them up and put them by the kitchen door, aiming to fling them down in the gully where she threw all her other trash next time she went outdoors.

But they were still there a couple of days later when he come back. He stayed for awhile and watched her sweep up the kitchen, then he left. It really hadn't bothered her that the girls never spoke to her, but it made her uncomfortable to have a man hanging around the house, not knowing what he might be up to, so she told Vangie Mae that afternoon.

They'd already been going rounds, she and Vangie Mae over Vangie Mae's wanting to go off and cook out at the bible camp. Nellie Alice felt as long as they had known each other that Vangie Mae owed it to her to help out here at her place, and after all who was going to help her out any more with the cooking and the cleaning.

And Vangie Mae had looked right at her and said "Miz Nellie, what you getting all fired up about? Ain't nobody lives here but you. I cook you a good meal, I come back two days later and you still ain't ate it all up yet."

Nellie Alice had wanted to say something but Vangie Mae had gone on.

"I clean your house one week. I come back the next week, everything's in the same place I left it. Lord knows, half the time nothing here to do but dust, and you can do your own dusting. Nothing wrong with your hands."

Nellie Alice had felt the blood rush to her eyes and opened her mouth to get back at Vangie Mae, then thought no she wouldn't. So she just flat out told Vangie Mae about the man in the coveralls, more out of spite than anything else. That was why she needed somebody to come around. No telling who might just be coming in here any time of day or night and what could she do about it, a poor widder woman living all by herself?

Vangie Mae looked at her right up close, that skinny, pinchy way she had, not like her mother at all, and asked her who that man was.

Well, Nellie Alice didn't know. That's why she was telling Vangie Mae. Didn't she, after all, live over in Bootsville, and didn't she know everybody that lived there?

"Miz Nellie, I don't live on both sides of town!" Because the other side of town, whose name Nellie Alice had never heard spoken in front of a black person, they knew who lived there and it wasn't Vangie Mae's people. Even Vangie Mae, who went to the cafes and rode around in cars with what some said was a wild bunch, as far as Nellie Alice knew, didn't never go over to Black Bottom. Maybe more than upstanding blacks it was trash whites that went there. There was liquor there, in a dry county, and knives and razor blades, Nellie Alice had always heard, and women she didn't even know names for, but names in the Bible that her mother had called Jezebels and let it go at that.

So Nellie Alice had to tell her about the two little girls, and it went on from that to the angel or whoever it was that floated, and that's when Vangie Mae said she would ruther Miz Nellie went to see the Jesus lady and the sooner the better.

Chapter 6

Trans American

For the newly christened "Pauline" Settlesquire the problems of transporting Jesus Christ Herself across the continental United States, from San Francisco to an unimaginably obscure spot in west central Kentucky began before the first day, with the first idea, and grew daily more aggravating and besetting till her trembling imagination began to yield to the mounting horror of it all.

A miracle or two somewhere along the way would have been useful. Li Cho, however, balked at miracle making, except in extreme emergencies. This attitude made it particularly burdensome for Pauline, causing her to pray hard and often and frantically to keep her discipleship strong.

Li Cho balked at first against the idea of leaving San Francisco. She was at home there, but Pauline felt in her heart there was too little room in the daily pattern of San Franciscan lives to welcome such an overwhelming change as a follower of Li Cho, Christ Herself, must practice. Pauline worked hard at convincing Li Cho to transfer to Kentucky where the days were long and distractions light and the people thought often and motivationally about the hereafter.

Then there was the matter of the cost of train tickets. Li Cho's parents, who had been minimally supportive but emotionally distant throughout their daughter's school years, had withdrawn even their grudging financial assistance after Li Cho's Transfiguration, and in the last few weeks their daughter had earned Her lodging by going, sandalled and draped in white, up to strangers on Market Street and asking for money in the name of Her Father. At a distance Li Cho's divinely based asking was indistinguishable from the other panhandlers begging and the time passed harmlessly, which to Pauline meant that the two of them stayed out of jail and avoided being kidnapped or attacked, because she was always close to Li Cho, suffering the humiliations for her Lord who was insensitive to them.

It was Pauline's greatest concern that, left to Herself, Li Cho would go on begging and consoling by way of aphorisms until the moment of either the Second Coming or else another crucifixion, because it seemed Her lack of success and dearth of followers had caused Li Cho to suspect that another crucifixion had to occur as part of the Second Coming package and might, to Pauline's intense concern, in fact be required to precede it.

So, on a Monday morning, while Li Cho knelt praying on her pallet facing the open window with the cool fog of the Golden Gate and the sounds of office-bound traffic rising from three stories below, Pauline pulled on her treasured white angora sweater, the one she had not yet been told to donate to their common store, fastened at her waist the pink ballerina skirt which had likewise escaped the Lord's crusade against vanity and personal possessions, drew up the long wool socks that Li Cho allowed so that Pauline could comply with the sandal wearing code, and quietly went to their mutual chest of drawers and begin packing the rest of her clothes and Li Cho's other white robe and sandals into the only suitcase she had been allowed to retain from those she had possessed in high school so that they could move with some marginal convenience from one rented place to another, and carried it out into the hall and sat on it where she knew Li Cho would find her when She eventually experienced hunger. Hunger always came later upon Li Cho than most people.

Chapter 7

Entrained and Encumbered

Pauline was a thin, nervous, worrisome young woman, with pointed elbows and tiny ankles below flaring muscled calves and knees coarse and callused from praying long tedious hours with Jesus Christ Herself and cleaning up behind Her.

It was bad enough that she had had to go off looking for Li Cho at bedtime only to find Her waiting serenely for a strenuously objecting porter to make Her a bed. Bad enough she had to bring Li Cho back to their stiff upright seats in the day coach, with its stuffy iron smell, mercifully free of smoke, but then as soon as she closed her eyes Li Cho wandered off to proselytize and Pauline found Her in, of all places, the men's smoker, visible through the open door sitting Indian fashion on a plastic covered 1920's lounge chair, listening with brows knit and long graceful fingers pressed vertically together below her chin, to some heavy set young man in a brown leather jacket who seemed to have discharged from service after some encounter with a grenade in the Southeast Asian conflict.

Pauline listened to the part about seeing his buddy's arm blown off and about lying in the mud crying for hours, and not being able to sleep for days, because every time he closed his eyes he saw his friend's face when the grenade exploded.

Pauline braced herself in the doorway against the swaying of the rail car and tugged at her collar and sweater trying to get Li Cho's attention and get them both out of the men's lounge. But Li Cho seemed unaware of her presence and unwilling to notice Pauline's agitation.

"Your friend will live," Li Cho said quietly, just above the noise of the rails. There was a sour smoke and metal smell about the room, and Pauline could feel the dirt rising from the grey linoleumed floor with its flattened butts and scattered specks of ashes. There was a floor model ashtray in heavy grey enameled steel with a chrome rim, and a hopeless mound of crumpled cigarette ends, both filtered and raw. The filters were almost all stained brown in their centers, and Pauline wondered how long it would take it to get the smell out of Li Cho's habit.

"He died," the young man said sullenly.

Li Cho's eyes, normally slanted in her mystical inner looking way, widened, not in alarm as some people imagined, but in sympathy. The man in the leather jacket looked up at her in the silence.

"He will live," said Li Cho, eyes large and copper brown, "with My father in heaven." She reached a long fingered hand over to the man and squeezed his shoulder lightly, then with the other she touched the tips of her tapered finger-nails to his cheek. The young man half rose from his chair, leaning toward Li Cho.

"Let us pray to My father," said Li Cho. She unfolded her legs from under-neath her, where the dust from her feet had already dirtied the whole bottom part of her long dress, Pauline noticed, and knelt down gracefully in the men's lounge, looking out the wide window with its rounded edges toward the lights flashing past in the darkness. She prayed silently. The young man looked up tensely at Pauline's reflection in the mirror, rose awkwardly from the chair, supporting himself with both arms, and bulkily shouldered past her into the passageway. Pauline watched him sway along the passageway and turn the corner. A second later came the loud rush of the wheels and the interclacking of the rail cars' plat-forms that meant he had opened the door to the next car, and a second after that the sound died as the door closed behind him. Li Cho remained kneeling on the hem of her robe, on the dirt of innumerable cross country passages.

After a while another man brushed past Pauline, gave a puzzled look to the kneeling Li Cho and turned back to Pauline, pointing at the inner door marked "toilet." Pauline shrugged. The man pulled open the door and locked himself inside. Pauline quickly bent over Li Cho and lifted with both hands at Li's right elbow. "You need your sleep," she said.

The next day was less bad. She managed to get Li Cho washed up in the tiny women's toilet that had no outer lounge area. She brushed off the dirt from Li Cho's robe the best she could and managed to get Li's hair pulled back into something graceful. So winning was the effect that several of the families in their coach stopped by to offer them shares of breakfast from their own brown paper bags and lunch boxes. Pauline tucked away everything given to Li Cho as soon as Jesus Christ Herself had blessed it and the donors had gone back grinning to their seats. It would be enough to see them through the evening meal, she thought, and tomorrow we will be in Kentucky.

Louisville was the best they could do. Cairo, Illinois, would have been closer to their destination, but Pauline had worried about whether they could get trans-portation out of so small a town, and, though she hesitated to mention it to Li Cho, she thought there was less chance to begging money for either food or bus tickets. She need not have worried.

Louisville, when they arrived, was in holiday spirits. This was the day of the annual race between the Belle of Louisville and the Delta Queen, two antique riverboats, and the whole downtown area was decorated with signs and bunting and there were splashes of confetti on the main streets, as if a parade had recently passed by.

Unencumbered by the suitcases Pauline carried, Li Cho walked down among the crowds at the river's edge and, fresh and exotic in her long white dress and straight black hair with her almond eyes, she had soon filled her graceful hands and inside pockets with donations more than sufficient for a bus ride to south central Kentucky. They were headed for the vicinity of Pennyrile, not far from Hopkinsville. The bus let them out where two roads crossed, a federal highway and a county road. There was corn standing bright and green on all sides, some high and some short, all smelling of vigor and sunlight and dust and tassels and cornworms.

A farmer in a pickup truck with as much red dirt in the cab as in the bed with all the pitchforks and sickles ("You can't go fur in them sandals") had stopped going the opposite way, made a U-turn and driven them back into town. There was a revival meeting sign over the main street of Beulah Springs, outside the courthouse. The farmer, in unionalls without a shirt, and red wherever the sun had seen him, let them off in front of Ruby's Sunrise Cafe ("You'll get a good meal there"), made another U-turn, lifted his hand slightly in a wave, and drove off talking to himself, Pauline thought.

They stopped for a moment at the screen door where the smells of chicken frying and turnip greens and corn bread billowed through the mesh at them. It was like Pauline remembered.

"Well look at you. You them new deaconess ladies! Come right on in here!" The screen door swung open toward them. They had to step back out of its way. A large woman held open the door with one hand while in the other, tucked back against her wrist, she gripped a dishcloth. "You need to get you something to eat before the meetin' starts!"

Her voice was big to match her size. Tiny eyes, big rounded cheeks, a deep rich brownish skin, with more reddish highlights than Li Cho's which, even with the dust of travel, still glowed a velvety black under its copper accents.

She set them down to a family style round table with a blue checked oil cloth cover that was almost immediately anchored by two tall sweating glasses of iced tea that had lemon wedges floating among the ice shavings. There was indeed fried chicken. There was also cornbread and there was real creamery butter, with the dairy's monogram pressed right into the top of it. There were mashed potatoes with chicken gravy and the kind of turnip greens that came with a bottle of vinegar and home grown hot peppers choking its tall narrow neck.

The matron's eyes had widened when Li Cho blessed their food and she had stood proprietarily over them while they ate, talking about the revival meeting and who all had come and how far away they had come from. Her fervent hope was that it would run long enough on this first night that she would be able to get over there for some of the preaching.

Because they were having preachers come from all over, from she didn't know where all. And she didn't know who all was going to preach. And where had Li Cho and Pauline come from?

"San Francisco? Well lord-a-mercy! All the way from San Francisco."

She watched them eating hungrily. Li Cho had always had a laborer's appetite and seeing after the both of them had kept Pauline thin and starved for fuel. Pauline had a way of anticipating Li Cho's needs and invariably passed the dish or drink before it was called for. Li Cho ate European style, fork always in the left hand, knife in the right. The matron was fascinated with the way She lifted Her food to Her mouth on the back of Her fork.

Pauline ate more conventionally, switching off between knife and fork so she always lifted her fork with her right hand, but she had a way of taking bites in furtive little snatches, like a smaller dog in constant fear of having what little was her own snatched away from her before she was done with it. Even her iced tea and milk she took in tiny nervous gulps, while Li Cho sipped slimly at her glass, lips softly feathered against the surface.

Pauline had been close with their money on the long train trip and they had not eaten well. They had depended mostly on what little food she had packed for them. In the first excitement of dedicating herself to Li Cho after school she had looked forward to seeing Li Cho work miracles with food, but the intense embarrassment of their first encounter unassisted in the real world of restaurants had been more than Pauline could assimilate. She was not prepared to try again.

Li Cho had led the way serenely into an Italian restaurant that had smelled especially good after strenuous hours of preaching during which they had been barely sustained by watered down Gatorade in athlete's bottles. They had eaten well. Pauline had relaxed and enjoyed half the bottle of red wine Li Cho had requested and blessed for them. When they had risen to leave, Pauline trying to look as serene as Li Cho, but instead feeling quivery and slack jawed—partially attributable to the wine—their waiter had come hurrying over with their check. Pauline had been fervently hoping the miracle had already happened, but there were numbers on the check, and a sum much larger than Pauline's calculations had attained. She turned her eyes, perhaps too wildly, to Li Cho.

Jesus Christ Herself had smiled tenderly upon the man and said, "Give thanks that We have shared your hospitality this night." The waiter did not give thanks.

Pauline had spent many painful minutes negotiating with the waiter and then again with the manager, while Li Cho had stood tall and remote from them, alone and iconic in the hallway. Ultimately they were allowed to leave after Pauline had surrendered all the money she could find on herself and in her pocketbook. She had come at that moment to understand finally what Li Cho had meant by repeating the saying from Her First Coming, that Her kingdom was not of this earth. Indeed she was sure from that moment that Li Cho's kingdom was of a different world, and powerfully aware that it might be Her own job to safeguard Li Cho in the pathways of this one, until Her purpose was fulfilled.

Now, in Beulah Springs, with the apple pie almost gone and their glasses refilled with iced tea and time for the tab to be totalled up and paid, Pauline became more and more nervous. She could feel the perspiration beginning to form again under her arms and where her legs crossed, and a bead began to run down inside her blouse lightly tickling the skin till it blended, soaked and spread into the coarse elastic of her last and only brassiere. The pie had been good, as good surely as she had remembered, maybe even better. In this life maybe it was not even possible to make a piecrust that light, so light she could blow the flakes off her fork in the routine process of everyday inhaling and exhaling. The pie had been good, but it was not worth, surely not worth, the anxiousness that now began to gnaw at her insides, crawling tightly up from her stomach, through her chest, headed for her throat.

Tillie Louise, as the proprietress had called herself, walked quickly and heavily back to their table after replacing the iced tea pitcher. She looked right into Pauline's eyes and said "Some preacher folks wait till first collections to pay for their dinners."

Pauline's pinched face could not hide her relief. Li Cho, if She had been of this world, might even have heard her sigh, so loud it was in this wood floored room, with its wooden straight cane bottom chairs, wood screen door and ghosting fans overhead, this room of round tables with sticky checkered oilcloth covers. "Don't you worry none. You going to do just fine, Honey."

Jesus Christ Herself had smiled tenderly upon the Tillie Louise and said, "Give thanks that We have shared your hospitality this night." Tillie Louise straightened up and smiled broadly and maternally at both of them.

"I 'spect you going on out the Revival?" asked Tillie Louise.

"Yes, ma'am," said Pauline.

"No need you carryin' them bags," Tillie Louise nodded toward the corner to the right of the door as they'd come in. There were all the worn bags Pauline had managed to carry, each tied carefully round and through the handle with string.

"Let me send 'em over't the Brotherhood Hall. Won't be no trouble ..." Then, "The Brotherhood Hall? Lord 'a mercy, child, that's where the choir sleepin'. You sure as the world don't think they gonna sleep where them rowdy preacher men be sleepin'? Lord a' mercy. Lord a' mercy." And she laughed, and looked at them, and laughed and tears rolled down her cheeks.

"Lord 'a mercy," she said again, bending over to gather up plates and silverware, turning her head from side to side. "*Lord* 'a mercy. Lord 'a *mercy*." Then she walked over behind the counter to the sink, threw back her head and laughed falsetto. "Hoo, hoo, *hoooo!*"

Li Cho watched calmly, Her expression even, Her eyes serene.

Chapter 8

Tents and Folded Chairs

It was supposed to be a two mile walk from where Tillie Louise administered to them in Ruby's Sunrise Cafe to the site of the Revival, but they had scarcely gotten out of town when they began to hear the singing and the clapping from the big revival tent. Across the open fields they could see the glow of the tent lights long before they could make out the tent itself in the darkness.

Up closer it was like a big Barnum and Bailey tent except not so tall and not so wide, but there were several main poles holding up the entire middle seam, running from up in the front where the platform was all the way to the very back where all the seats were full and men in brown suits stood by the shorter side poles to find upfront seats for the latecomers. The side flaps were up to let in the cooler nighttime breezes and the two women could see everything going on inside as if it were a lighted theater show, and they could feel the heat from all the bodies flooding out onto the crushed brown straw of the field and warming their ankles and calves as they walked up in their sandals, Pauline stepping carefully so as to avoid spearing her skin on the stubble, Li Cho gliding gracefully and heedlessly as if Her feet were immune to the thrusts and jabs of stobs and dried grasses or if they knew their own way in the dark among the stubble.

One of the brown suited men, big and mustached, with bright white teeth in the spilling tent light, would have directed them into two of the empty chairs up front, folding chairs that said "Mason's Funeral Home" on their backs in uneven white stenciled letters, but Li Cho walked in understated solemn majesty straight up to the platform in front, Pauline trailing unenthusiastically along behind her.

978-0-595-42137-4
0-595-42137-7